# ODDS OF DECEPTION

Thomas Puck

Copyright © 2025 Mill Pond Ventures, LLC

All rights reserved.

ISBN: 9798990809734

Cover art by @padrondesign.

To Megan, my love.

# CHAPTER ONE

"To see the dead walking means your path is cursed."

It was an old proverb that a squadmate had often repeated. Max didn't know its origin but it flared to life in his head when he saw the woman who looked like his sister.

It wasn't Lulu. He knew that. She was dead almost fifteen years, but the woman who was wheeled past him in the hallway was almost an exact replica of her. It unnerved him and he tried not to stare, continuing down the hospital corridor.

Unlike most people, Max liked hospitals. He didn't like the smell, or rather the lack of smell, but he appreciated the orderliness. It wasn't that he sought out opportunities to visit, but when he did, the efficiency and organization that existed on every floor comforted him. The color-coded markings and clear directions contributed to a sense of well-being.

His friend Philip had come in for hip surgery a couple of days earlier, but complications with his recovery had transformed an overnight visit into several days and counting, so Max had delayed the start of a new job so he could spend another day looking out for the old man, who had no family in the area. Like many of his friends, they had forged a lasting friendship through many long nights of poker. It wasn't the same camaraderie as he'd had in the Special Forces, but it was more of a bond than he had with most people in town.

It had been a good day for Philip, so it seemed like he would be headed home the next day, and Max had agreed to sneak in some fast food to celebrate. Visiting hours on Sundays extended to midnight, so Max had returned at eleven thirty with burgers and fries from In-N-Out and that was when he had seen her. He didn't mention it to Philip while they ate.

It was a little past midnight as he made his way out of the hospital. He'd been in the building often enough to know that the one flaw in the visitor mapping was that it took everyone out through the main entrance. Max, on the other hand, knew that the quickest way to the taxi stand was through the emergency room waiting area, so he'd detoured from the directed route.

The automatic door swung inward, and he could see the exit at the end of the hall, but as he began walking, not five paces in, a hand shot out from behind a curtain, attempting to grab his arm, accompanied by a pleading whisper.

"Hey!"

Instinctively, he twisted before the fingers took hold, turning in surprise to see the panicked face of his sister. He froze. It wasn't his sister, but it was the woman he'd seen earlier. She was distraught, but despite this state, or perhaps because of it, he couldn't shake the similarities.

"Hey," she repeated in a light voice that had a slight southern tinge, "I need help."

Max met her eyes and immediately gaged her intentions as true. She had none of the telltale signs of drug abuse that would have sent him in the other direction. Outwardly, she didn't seem injured, but the patient wristband and her location behind the curtain indicated she was here for something. Her slim figure stood at five and a half feet tall. She dressed modestly, but her clothes were unworn—another sign that she wasn't part of the ever-expanding underbelly of Las Vegas that Max detested. She had dirty-blonde hair that was pulled into a ponytail but, at this moment, appeared slightly unkempt. More than anything, her steel-blue eyes made him pause. They had a troubled yet determined look that made him want to help. The eyes were his sister's eyes. They brought painful memories of an unfinished life.

"Please," she whispered, stepping back and waving for him to enter.

His first impulse was to turn away. This wasn't Lulu, but he couldn't ignore her pleading eyes. He took a breath and stepped into the area behind the curtain.

"Thank you," she said, grabbing his arm, and this time he allowed her. "I need to get out of here. Can you please help me? I'll pay you."

"Hang on." He raised his hands in part to maintain separation and in part to slow her down. "Let's start with names. I'm Max."

"Staci." She looked down briefly and then back, immediately continuing, "Look, I'm sorry, but I don't have time. I've got a thousand dollars, if you can get me out of here in the next five minutes." She pulled a wad of cash out of a purse that had been on the bed behind her, offering it to him. "Promise to get me out and take it now."

Max raised his hands even higher and almost turned to leave. That much cash was usually a bad sign.

"Look, Staci. I don't know who you are, but I don't want your money. What's going on?"

Tears welled in her eyes. "I need to get out of here."

Max took a deep breath. He believed her but needed more. He reached a hand to her shoulder. "OK, I hear you. Can you tell me why you're here and why you need to leave?"

"I was in a stupid accident, but I'm fine. Really." She wiped away a tear, but the fear in her eyes remained. "People are going to be looking for me. Bad people. And if I'm still here when they get here, they'll kill me."

"Nobody's going to kill you—" he started, but she cut him off, grabbing both arms.

"Max, I'm telling you, they will kill me. Maybe not today, but I won't last the week."

"Who's going to kill you?"

She stared at him with his sister's eyes and spoke in a whisper. "Do you know Geno Abruzzi?"

He nodded. Everyone in Las Vegas had heard of the mob leader.

"I was running from him. That's how I ended up here, and I know he'll be sending men after me. Do I need to say more?" She spoke quickly but with an accepting calm that seemed to overcome the earlier panic. "So can you please stop asking questions and help me?"

As with so many decisions in his life, Max allowed his gut instinct to answer.

"I'll help, but why can't you simply walk out?"

"Did you see the cop?" she asked incredulously.

"What cop?"

Not waiting for an answer, Max pulled the curtain aside and looked toward the entrance, quickly pulling his head back as he saw a cop sitting in a chair down the hall between them and the exit.

"What's he doing here?"

"My accident . . . I ran into a cop car, but there's more than that. Can you get me out of here?"

Sounds of commotion came from the hallway, and Max peeked out to see a gurney being pushed through the main entrance, which was lit up by the flashing red lights of an ambulance. Nurses and doctors were waiting to help guide the new patient to an area across the hall from where Max watched. The EMT pushed the gurney alongside a waiting bed, and the well-practiced team transferred the patient to the bed while the EMT recapped what they had already done.

Thirty seconds later, the ER squad had taken over, and Max watched as the EMT pushed his gurney into the empty bay next to Staci's bed and then took off his hat and windbreaker and tossed them on top before he crossed back down the hall toward the bathroom.

"Stay here," Max whispered and walked out into the hall without waiting for her response. With the staff busy attending the new arrival, nobody paid any attention as he stepped into the bay with gurney and calmly pulled the curtain around to enclose the area. Down the hall, the officer was still slumped in his chair, staring at his phone and apparently uninterested in the commotion.

He put the EMT's jacket on and pulled the hat down low on his head before reaching over to open the back end of Staci's area. She leapt across the gap without waiting for him to ask and was already climbing onto the gurney when he stopped her.

"Hey, we're going past the guard. I can't wheel you out in the open."

"Then what are we doing?" she asked.

Max looked from the gurney to the empty bed, trying to form a plan.

"Curl in a ball," he said, grabbing a pillow and pulling the sheets off the bed.

"What is the plan?"

"I'm going to hide you in some laundry," Max said. "It may sound stupid, but as long as it seems natural for a moment, that's all we need. I can't have it look like a person."

"How's this?" she said, and Max turned to see her folded forward so that her body was completely flat against extended legs.

"Perfect," he answered as he placed the pillow beyond her head and lumped the sheets haphazardly to conceal her body. "Try not to move."

He slid the curtain away and pushed the gurney out into the hallway. The exit was at the other end of the hall, through a set of extra wide doors that led to the ambulance parking area. Above the doors, a row of lights glowed red. He kept eyes forward and tried to act casual as they neared the sitting police officer. Holding his breath, he thought they were in the clear.

"Hey," the officer called as he moved past. "Hang on a sec."

Max stopped the gurney. He didn't want to fight a cop, and he'd been in enough tricky situations to know that confidence would solve eighty percent of challenges.

"What's up?" He managed a smile, looking directly at the officer.

"That guy." He nodded across to the recent arrival. "What's his story?"

"Hell if I know," Max answered calmly. "Anonymous call. Nobody on the scene. Did you hear it on your radio?"

The cop appraised him coolly but didn't answer.

"I think he'll live though." Max continued his lie. "What are you doing here anyway? You guarding someone?"

"Babysitting is more like it." The man sounded annoyed. "Some floozy ran into our car. No ID. I've got to wait here till she's released, then I'll bring her back to the station to find out who she is. Waste of time, if you ask me."

"Good luck with that." Max wanted to move on. "I'm headed back out. Have a good night."

"Same." The cop looked back down at his phone, and Max rolled the gurney down the hall and out of the building.

Outside, the red lights of the ambulance continued to pulse, and Max pushed the front of the gurney into the open back, but before he could move around to release the wheels, another body moved in from the side to help. It was the other ambulance driver.

"Where you been, Nat?" the EMT said as the wheels folded up and Max pushed the gurney into the ambulance.

As soon as his hands were free, Max grabbed the other man's arm and guided him into the back of the ambulance.

"Nat will be OK," he growled. "Right now, I need you to stay calm and get into the back, and no one gets hurt."

He could feel the other man tense up. "Where's—"

"I just fucking told you." He glared at the man. "Nat will be OK. Now get into the vehicle."

As he spoke, he pushed the EMT inside the vehicle and closed the doors behind them, locking them for good measure. Staci was now moving under the sheets, which threw the man off guard even more.

"What the hell?" He began to turn, but Max grabbed his opposite shoulder and spun him into a position where he could pin the man's hands behind his back.

"You see any tape?" he asked Staci, who had vacated the gurney, allowing him to position the EMT in her place. Thankfully, he wasn't getting much resistance.

"Here." She passed him a roll of white tape.

"Perfect." Max pulled the man's arms together behind his back and wrapped them several times with the surgical tape. He grabbed a towel and had the man bite down before he wrapped the tape around his head, holding the gag in place.

"Can you breathe?" he asked. When the man nodded, he tossed the remains of the roll to Staci.

"Wrap his feet together."

Outside, he heard a commotion, followed by banging on the door.

"Hey, open up in there."

It sounded like the cop, but Max was in no mood to find out.

"The feet," he repeated to Staci, not waiting for a response. He moved up to the driver's seat and found the keys in the ignition.

In a moment, the ambulance was running, and as the banging intensified on the back door, he threw the engine into drive and slammed on the gas, tires screeching as he sped out of the emergency entrance. A left took them to the exit and then a right onto Maryland Street. Staci let out a scream, and he heard her fall down.

"You alright?" he called back.

"Fine," Staci responded. "Keep going."

Looking at the controls, he spotted the switch for the lights and turned them off. The street headed north toward downtown, but he knew he would need to ditch the ambulance sooner than that. It would be too easy to find them. He glanced in the rearview mirror and saw no sign of pursuit, but it was only a matter of time.

Moments later, Staci moved into the seat beside him.

"Thank you," she said.

"His feet tied?"

"Yes, but I don't think he's comfortable."

"That's fine. We won't be here long."

He turned right into a residential area and cruised for a minute before finding what he needed.

He drove for another block and pulled into a spot on the street.

"We're getting out here." He told her, looking back to see the EMT staring back at him but still sufficiently bound.

He stepped into the back and unwound the gag.

"Sorry, dude. Needed to borrow the truck. We're leaving now."

"Let me go," the man pleaded as Max closed the door and walked around to meet Staci on the sidewalk.

"We aren't done yet," he said. "They'll be looking for this box, and we need to get farther away from here."

"Do you have a car?" Staci asked as she caught up to him.

"I will in a moment," he answered.

* * *

Twenty minutes later, Staci sat opposite him in a booth at Lou's Diner, one of Max's favorite haunts outside of downtown. He'd hot-wired an old 1990s Econoline van that he'd spotted on the street. It wasn't the greatest ride, but it allowed them to get far clear of the ambulance, and they'd subsequently ditched it at a Pep Boys tire shop a few blocks away. The owner would find it easily, and Max had stuffed a few hundred dollars in the visor, hoping they would feel it ample compensation.

"So," he began after the waitress served the coffee, "that was all a bit of fun, but do you want to explain what we're involved with?"

She shook her head. "Trust me. You don't want to know."

"Try me."

"I saw something I shouldn't have." She looked out the window before turning back to him, her face stern. "I saw people I shouldn't have. It was an accident. I was in the wrong place at the wrong time. So I ran for my life. At the end, I tried to stop a cop car but ended up getting hit. I'm probably lucky I did because they took me away from the scene, but I have no doubt there were men coming to get me. So thank you again. If those men found me, I'd be dead."

Max finished a sip of coffee and put his mug down. He thought about his sister. Her story was different, but she had also fallen in with the wrong people in Las Vegas. For her, it had been drugs, which had eventually taken her life. Situations do not make a person, he reminded himself; it's how we react that defines us. Staci was pushing back, and she needed help.

"No offense, but why are you hanging out with gangsters?"

"I told you. It was an accident." The girl was indignant. "And in case you weren't aware, this town is pretty mobbed up."

"And how do you know they won't still find you?"

"For one thing, I'm not saying anything about what I saw. Besides, there's a lot of girls in this town, and they didn't get a good look at me." She smiled. "How would they know?"

"Maybe they'll start with surveillance footage?" Max offered, seeing the confidence drain from the woman's face. "Look, you can keep your secrets, but I don't think this is over. If they want to identify you, they only have to get to the hospital's security feed."

"Shit." She reached into her purse and pulled out the same roll of money she had earlier. "I'll pay you if you can get the tapes."

Max shook his head and smirked, pointing to the money. "Why do you keep trying to pay me? And what's with the cash? Why are you carrying so much? You a dealer?"

Staci pushed the money back into her purse. "Hardly. It's not even mine."

She made an effort to look at the menu, but when Max said

nothing, she put it back down in a huff.

"I have friends who are dancers, OK? They collect a lot of tip money but don't have bank accounts, so I'm like their banker. You OK with that?"

"For a fee, I bet."

"Everyone's got to live." She straightened her back. "I'm a lot cheaper than their other options. But that won't matter if I'm dead, and I will be if they get that video. Will you help me?"

"I'm already involved, Staci," he answered calmly. "And my face is also on the footage. I'll see what I can do about it."

"Thank you." Her eyes brightened. "And I don't expect somethin' for nothin'. I know what you said, but let's be fair. I can pay you."

Max shrugged. "I'll be fine. What about you? Do you need a place to stay?"

A playful fire lit in her eyes, and she cocked her head. "Why, Max, are you inviting me to your home?"

"I want to keep you safe." He hadn't told her about her likeness to his sister. She was quite attractive and probably used to the attention, but he could never look at her that way.

"I'll be fine," she answered but held her hand out between them. "Give me your phone."

Knowing what she would do, Max checked it was unlocked and handed her his phone, watching as she typed her information into his contacts. As she handed it back to him, her own phone rang from inside her purse. She pulled it out and hung it up then started typing.

"I put my info in, Staci Johnson, and you just called me, so I have your number too. Is there a last name, or should I call you Max Hero?" She looked up from her screen expectantly.

"Kline," he answered, putting his own phone away.

"Max Kline," she repeated, smiling. "That has a nice ring to it. What do you do when you aren't saving the day, Mr. Kline?"

"I do project work. Changes a lot. How about yourself? I don't imagine that dancer banking is a full-time job."

"No, that's a side hustle, but I'm in finance. I'm an accountant."

"Sounds like fun."

The waitress came by for their order.

"You want anything?" Max asked. "My treat."

"No, thank you. I'm not hungry. It's been a long night already."

Max ordered a burger and fries, and the waitress sped away after refilling his coffee.

"I think mine's just begun," he mumbled to himself.

Staci slid out of the booth. "What's that?" she asked.

"Nothing. Go get some rest, and I'll let you know when I figure out the security footage."

* * *

It was two in the morning by the time he got home, but he'd already started a chat with Carolyn on his Signal app in the taxi from the diner. Once inside the apartment, he turned his screen on and started a video chat, knowing Carolyn would pick up immediately.

"What have you gotten yourself into now?" she asked without even greeting him once her face materialized on the screen. She obviously was typing on a different screen, her eyes focusing to one side. The dark birthmark on her jaw stood out against her coffee-colored skin and stressed her distinct jawline.

"Good to see you too," he laughed in response.

Carolyn turned to the screen. "Sorry, Max. I've got a lot going on, and now I'm trying to hack into a hospital in Las Vegas because my old friend got himself in trouble again."

He noticed she didn't use the term boyfriend, but he didn't comment.

"Anyway, I've seen this type of system before. It will take me a few rounds, but I can get in. You want to tell me why you're worried about security footage?"

"I helped someone get away from some bad people, but they're resourceful enough to get to the video. If they do, she won't have long to live."

"She?" Carolyn mused. "Have you fallen for another damsel in distress?"

"You know I've only got one love, C." Max was somewhat irritated by the teasing. "I'm not the one who called things off."

"Yeah, well, you don't make things easy, Max. Take this, for example. I haven't heard from you in months, and now you need me to break a few laws."

"You asked me not to call unless it was important."

"And you do everything I ask?" She looked back at the camera with a spark in her eyes. "Anyway, how've you been, other than getting yourself in trouble?"

"Been good. Cards haven't been coming my way, but I've got a new consulting gig starting tomorrow."

"What's the job?"

"Chinese company purchased a small-time casino here. I'm to work with their team as translator and to help them with due diligence."

"Sounds riveting."

"It pays." He smiled at her and was pleased to see her return the grin on his screen. "How about you?"

"Tinkering with a few pet projects."

"So I assume you turned down that offer?" Max asked, knowing the answer.

"Yeah. No interest in working for a big corporation. Not right now anyway."

"If you have too much time on your hands, it's a good time of year to visit Las Vegas."

Carolyn shook her head, but her face brightened as she remained focused on her other screen.

"Oh, I've got plenty to keep me busy," she answered. "But I'm not saying no."

"Well, I guess that's a win." Max relaxed a little in his chair.

Carolyn looked into the screen, pausing in thought before she spoke.

"You look tired, Max. Why don't you get some sleep? I'll work on this and check in with you in the morning."

"That is not a bad plan." Max saw she was already back at work but wanted to look into her face once again.

"Hey, C?"

"Yeah?" She finished a few keystrokes and turned back to look at the screen.

"Thank you," he said, meaning it deeply. "I really appreciate you."

Her expression brightened once again, and that meant more than anything she could say.

"Of course, Max. Now go get some sleep." She ended the call without waiting for his response.

# CHAPTER TWO

Max wasn't entirely certain how Haoyun Casino had located him, but they had made him a generous offer, and after Max slow-played his response, they had sweetened it such that it had been hard to say no.

Haoyun had an extensive gambling empire in mainland China, and they were looking for a foothold in the American market. They'd wanted Max's help in their acquisition of the Desert Jewel, a midsize casino that operated on the outskirts of Las Vegas. Max would serve ostensibly as a translator, but his actual role was as an adviser to the negotiations. His value was both in his skills honed in years as a hostage negotiator and in his knowledge of the local market.

The Desert Jewel appeared to be bleeding cash, but Haoyun and much of the Vegas world believed this was less operational and more a result of poor or corrupt management. They had already identified a number of accounting irregularities during their audit, but the Jewel still had remarkable potential. Most prominent—a high-speed rail was in the works to connect Los Angeles with Las Vegas, and the Jewel would be almost on top of the first Las Vegas station.

There were other issues, to be sure, including the expected decline in revenues during construction, but Haoyun was optimistic about the future. Meanwhile, the Jewel promised they would resolve the accounting irregularities, and Max hoped this was true. While the terms allowed for extensions as necessary, he knew from experience that these contracts were best if things wrapped up quickly.

Located off Interstate 15 on the principal thoroughfare from Los Angeles to Las Vegas, the Desert Jewel had always been both a first stop and a last stop for millions of avid gamblers every year. While it lacked the grandeur of the strip or bustle of the downtown core of casinos, its player-friendly table odds and relatively inexpensive rooms maintained a steady flow of clientele that had made it a darling of the independent casino scene for over sixty years.

Although the ownership group had rejected many corporate suitors, the word on the street was that they had finally agreed to sell because of an increasing need for capital improvement.

For his part, Max was skeptical of the financial irregularities that had been uncovered. The Desert Jewel casino enjoyed an excellent reputation, but it was also known as a mob hangout and a repository for dirty money. That was the second part of his role. While Max knew little about double entry bookkeeping, he had a decent handle on common sense and the broad brushstrokes of business in America. The Haoyun team needed an American to provide a perspective that went beyond translation and to filter out the inevitable bullshit from the mob-connected owners group, Tri-Star Enterprises.

He had woken early for his workout, as was his routine, and saw that Carolyn must have been up all night, as her email was time-stamped only twenty minutes before he opened it. She had told him she still needed to work on it, but for the time being, she'd successfully hidden the access point to the video files and assured Max there was no need to take further action until she could get back at it after some rest. She did note that she thought someone had tried to hack in unsuccessfully ahead of her. It wasn't a problem, she said, but it was curious.

As his Town Car pulled into the Desert Jewel, Max wondered exactly what Staci had seen.

One of the casino managers greeted him and escorted him up the elevator to one of the high-roller suites where the Haoyun team had set up headquarters. The manager politely indicated the door and then left Max in the hallway, apparently not wanting to interfere with the Chinese group at all.

When the door opened, Max was surprised to see Wei Zhang standing in the doorway and extending his hand, which Max shook as he stepped in. Max had met Wei over a video call during his contract negotiation, but he had not expected the Haoyun CEO to be present today, and he certainly did not expect him to answer the door.

"Welcome, Max." The older man greeted him in Chinese and gestured inside, closing the door behind him. "As you can see, the team is already hard at work."

Max looked over a large living room transformed into an office—an acquisition war room, in a sense. Someone had pushed all the couches to the perimeter of the room. Six desks, each with a computer and two monitors, were arranged front to back in the center. Three larger desks, each with similar computer setups, were positioned facing inward at the far end of the room, near the windows, which undoubtedly had a beautiful view of Las Vegas.

Ling Wu sat at one desk, her suit jacket off but otherwise in formal business attire, her jet-black hair pulled into a ponytail. The Desert Jewel acquisition had been her brainchild from the start, and except for Wei Zhang, she was definitely in charge. To her right sat Jun Chen, who was the head bean counter and, from what Max had gleaned, the biggest skeptic of the deal. In theory, the two of them worked together, but they approached the acquisition from opposing perspectives. Looking at the two of them and recalling earlier conversations, Max suddenly thought he understood Wei Zhang's presence.

He nodded as he looked around the room.

"Quiet the setup," he responded in Chinese, turning back to Wei. "Where do I sit, and how can I help?"

"I am sure you will have many opportunities, Max, but I'll leave that to Ling. Your Chinese is quite good."

"You are too kind," Max replied politely and then switched to English. "Seriously, what do I do?"

Wei smiled and offered a slight head bow, continuing in Chinese. "Be patient, but Ling will guide you. I'm only here as a pretty face to smooth over these final discussions."

"Understood." Max returned the head bow to the CEO and turned to find a seat, but to his surprise, Ling Wu was standing a few feet away. She offered her own polite head bow, and Max did the same before she extended her hand, which he shook delicately.

"Nice to meet you in person, Ling," he said.

"And I you." She offered her business card with two hands. Max accepted but felt awkward that he did not have one in return.

"Sorry, I don't carry any cards," he said sheepishly.

"Not to worry." Ling responded in English that had an Australian twang to it. "Come with me. We've got a few things to discuss before we meet with the Desert Jewel team."

Ling turned without waiting for his reply and strode into one of the side rooms. Max followed with a courtesy nod to Wei as he left.

The room held a couch, two chairs, and a coffee table supporting two bound paper packets. Ling took one chair, grabbing a packet and indicating that Max should take the other. He left the couch empty and took the other chair, along with his copy of the paperwork.

"We've got one day to bring you up to speed," she began. "In your hands, you have a summary of our business model, along with a list of the Desert Jewel's accounting issues. It is quite a long list, I'm afraid, but we want you to have this as background when you're listening."

"Makes sense to me," Max answered politely.

There was an edge to Ling's voice. "I'm not looking for your opinion. And I definitely don't want to hear it during our negotiations with Tri-Star." She raised an eyebrow as she met his eyes.

Max nodded his ascent.

"Wei Zhang seems to think you can add value, and I'm willing to listen to you in private," she continued, "but you do not represent Haoyun Casino. I do."

"Yes, ma'am," Max answered. "I have no problem with that."

"I didn't think so." Ling's voice softened slightly. "I've seen your résumé. You seem to know how to follow orders."

Max nodded again.

"As you may be aware, the casino has been tied up with organized crime for as long as it has been in operation. We've known this and expected to find some irregularities." Ling was very casual now. "Frankly, we don't care. The legitimate business makes money, and we think we can do better. We know they've hidden things in the books. The question will be how well they covered their tracks. We aren't looking for any skeletons but want to make sure we don't inherit the sins of the previous owners."

"Aren't you buying their financial history though?" Max had been wanting to ask the question since they hired him.

"Yes and no," Ling answered calmly. "If they inflate the cost of cheese to increase profits at another company they own, that looks bad on the books, but it is an operating expense. We'll be more concerned when things affect the balance sheet. But our team has experience in this. We'll ask the right questions."

"Understood, but can I ask you something?"

"Go ahead."

"Your English is excellent, and I've had conversations with Wei Zhang in English as well. I appreciate the job, but why do you need me?" The question was not entirely genuine. Max knew his value as a negotiator and wanted her to admit it.

Ling stood, answering him in Chinese. "I think you understand this game more than you let on, Mr. Kline. Many of us speak English, but sometimes we benefit from a buffer between ourselves and our adversary."

She'd avoided acknowledging his talent, and Max did not respond, but he found "adversary," or its Chinese equivalent, an interesting word choice.

"In your case," Ling continued to speak her native tongue, "we also value your people-reading skills. You were not a random choice, as I hope your paycheck shows."

She nodded and crossed to the door, pausing at the opening.

"I expect you'll have some interesting insight, and we'll meet in private after each meeting. For now, study up. I'll send others in to further brief you."

Max began to reply, but Ling had already turned and left the room, so he settled back and waited.

CHAPTER THREE

The desert sun was never forgiving, even at eight in the morning, and Staci was glad she'd been able to fix her air conditioning. The car had been a sweatbox the previous week, but everything was running well now. She pulled into her usual parking spot.

Although unassigned, everyone generally parked in the same spot, and because Staci typically arrived early, she usually got her preferred space. The vanity mirror's small size always frustrated her, but she flipped down the visor for a quick face check and reapplied her crimson lipstick. There was nothing special about the day, but she always liked to look good, and after the previous night, she didn't want anything to seem out of order.

Inside, she waved her badge over the key fob to get through the first level of security and then offered her phone and purse to the guard as she walked through the metal detector.

"Good morning, Bobby." She always tried to be friendly. So many people pushed through as if the guards were antagonistic—which they weren't. They were only doing their job.

"Hey, Staci," Bobby replied, reflecting her smile. "Gonna be another hot one."

"Not in here, at least!"

"No, ma'am."

Her purse came through the X-ray scanner as it did every morning, and she picked it up, turning to walk down the hall toward the accounting department.

"You have a good day," she called over her shoulder, hearing the standard reply.

One more swipe of her pass and she entered the large open space where she had worked for the past three years. It was always at least a quarter full—with the casino open all day and night, their department needed to stay active as well. While it wasn't as active as the cashier's booth, it was staffed round the clock nonetheless. At this time, it was still on the lighter side, but the room would be over half-full in little more than an hour.

Staci said hello to the few people she passed and took her seat in the cubical that was her home away from home, turning on the computer and straightening her desk as she waited for it to initialize. She took a deep breath and tried to calm herself down.

"Business as usual," she told herself, thinking back on the previous night. Talk about bad fucking luck. She had not intended to see what she had seen and had no desire to remember it. She had to stay calm and hope no one identified her. Getting out of the hospital had been such a godsend. Maybe He was looking out for her. She shook her head as she thought of where her life was in contrast to her arrival in Las Vegas three years ago, a doe-eyed graduate from Ohio. "Vegas will take your soul," the old saying went. She could attest to that.

"Hey, Staci." A male voice broke her reverie. "Pam wants to see you."

She looked up to see Jerry's familiar face, highlighted by throwback square glasses that gave him the look of a 1950s tech worker. His tousled, somewhat short black hair contributed to the look, even though he wore casual business attire with a floral button-down shirt, open one button too many.

"And good morning to you too, Jerry," she responded, raising her eyes in mock criticism of his manners. "Nice shirt."

"Sorry," he corrected himself and might have even blushed. "Good morning, Staci. Pam would like to see you."

"Is it hot? Or can I get a coffee first?"

"She didn't seem bothered. I think you've got time."

"Cool. Thanks. How're you doing?"

"Tired. I'm at the end of a double. Ready to go home and crash."

"I hear you," she laughed. "I just got here and feel the same way."

Jerry tapped her cubical as he continued down the row. "Coolio, no rush, but don't forget. I'll see you next time."

"Thanks, Jer." Staci stood as he left and went to the kitchen, where she waited for the machine to make her a large caramel latte. It came out piping hot, as always, and she grabbed an ice cube from the freezer and dropped it in her mug, taking a seat at the empty table to give it a chance to cool down. She wanted to enjoy a sip or two before confronting her least-favorite shift boss.

A couple of coworkers came through while she waited, and she exchanged the usual canned pleasantries but did not engage beyond the superficial greeting. After a few minutes, her coffee was cool enough to drink, but she waited until she had finished half before she left the break room and went around the outer edge of the room to her supervisor's office.

She tapped lightly on the open door and entered. "Good morning, Pam. Are you looking for me?"

"I was. What took you so long?" Pam sat tucked behind a large mahogany desk, her obese body crammed into the already large chair. She had thinning blonde hair that always looked a bit oily, and her face was a constant scowl.

"Sorry. Jerry had to find me in the kitchen," she lied, taking the empty seat opposite her boss. "I was getting my coffee, and I enjoyed that first sip."

Pam actually smiled for a second.

"I know how you feel," she said as her scowl returned. "Anyway, the Chinese have been digging through the books and want a report on last year's food and beverage P&L."

"Isn't that in the financials already?" Staci felt her face flush.

"They want more." The older lady turned to her computer, fat fingers typing away with almost inhuman dexterity. "I've sent you a formal request with data access for twenty-four hours. If you need more time, let me know, but I want a complete report as soon as possible."

Staci wanted to throw up. Pam knew that the books were off, but was there more to it? For years, Staci had helped Tri-Star skim profits under Pam's supervision. The books were so obfuscated that they had done little to adjust them before handing them to Haoyun. What Pam didn't know was that Staci had hidden an extra skim. Were they now suspicious of her? She quickly dismissed the thought. If Pam knew, she'd probably have fired her already or, worse, had her arrested.

She moved to the edge of her seat.

"Can someone handle my daily runs?"

"Yes." Pam was still looking at her computer screen. "We'll

handle the routine. You focus on this report."

An eerie calm passed through Staci's body. She couldn't understand why, but it was almost like a moment of acceptance. Shit was going to happen, and she could do nothing about it. Might as well relax.

"I'm on it, Pam." She stood up. "You need anything else?"

The fat fingers stopped clicking for a moment, and Pam looked up at her dismissively.

"Nothing except that fucking report."

Staci moved to the door but stopped when Pam called out.

"Staci?"

"Yes?"

"You do realize we'll all make a nice little bonus if this sale goes through, right?"

"That's what I hear."

"Make sure that report is spotless." Pam turned back to her computer. "And say hi to your boy for me."

Staci nodded but knew her boss was not looking. Her mind raced—how much did they know? And if it wasn't already obvious, how much could she keep hidden?

CHAPTER FOUR

"The title is solid and one hundred percent owned by the Desert Jewel Corporation." Ling was pacing at the end of the long conference table, speaking in Chinese as she had been for the past two hours. "So the asset is good, and the operating business is marginally profitable despite everything we've reviewed."

It was ten thirty. Max had arrived at the high-roller suite-turned-war room as the group sat down and had taken his spot at the far end of the table. He really didn't need all the financial details to do his job correctly, but Ling had welcomed his presence.

For over two hours, she had been summarizing the accounting difficulties they had uncovered, many of which they would not dispute when they met with the selling group. Tri-Star had been skimming profits, but that only understated the value of ongoing operations. After identifying the issues, Ling had dismissed them as something that would simply require additional monitoring in the future. Similarly, the payroll numbers did not align with tax filings, and the Haoyun team had discovered several employees who either did not exist or had been dead for several years. Here, again, Ling had pointed it out and then moved it to a list of actionable items after the deal closed.

Ling had noted that they did not want to appear to have completely missed these details, so she made a point of elaborating on the abuse of comps and perks that were blatantly obvious among the ownership group and a small army of associates. They would bring these up at the negotiations, she said. It was important to show that they had done their due diligence, but eventually they would either let this slide or request some minor adjustment.

Here again, the excesses reduced profitability, so they had inadvertently helped lower the acquisition price. Ling explained that they wanted to point out the problems but did not want too much focus on the issue.

Now, she shifted from the financials to review the selling group itself. She reminded everyone that Tri-Star was composed mostly of known members of the Marchetti crime family, who were the ones indulging in the excessive perks. That fact alone would make things awkward at the negotiating table, and she meant to use that to her advantage. She took a moment to look around the table with a warning that everyone should be careful to avoid insulting their adversaries.

Last, she highlighted the potential issues with the regulators, which included the IRS, the US Treasury, and the Nevada Gaming Commission. Investigating agencies received all formal concerns raised against the selling group, and this information could be used against them during license renewal applications. That said, they were fairly deep into the transaction and so far had the support of all the agencies involved.

Following several questions and a review of the issues, Ling dismissed the group. Max started to leave, but she caught his eye.

"Max, could you stay for a moment?"

He waited as the accounting team shuffled past him and then moved to the front of the room, where Ling now stood behind Wei Zhang and Jun Chen, the company's chief financial officer, who both remained seated. Max nodded to them as he approached then faced Ling.

"Seems like you've done your homework." He spoke in English, knowing that all three were fluent. "I'm not sure what help I'll be."

"The deal is too good." Ling sat down next to Wei and motioned for Max to sit across the table so that he faced them. "We expected to find more trouble when they opened the books, but it's all acceptable. We found four large write-offs in the past three years, but even if they were completely false, they are not ongoing issues.

Another problem is a significant relationship with Genoa Imports, which serves the catering arm, but nothing that is a major red flag for the casino. It looks like bad business and maybe some bad bookkeeping, but otherwise the casino is solid."

"So there is nothing left to discuss." Jun seemed irritated. He was a small man, but his high-pitched voice somehow still maintained an air of calm. "This will be a great asset for Haoyun."

"I'm not so sure." Ling continued, "I think there is something we are missing."

"Nonsense." Jun spoke in Chinese, standing as he did. "If I may have a moment of your time, Wei. This discussion is going nowhere."

Wei looked from Jun to Ling and then stood, offering a polite nod to Ling as he followed Jun out the door.

"Your country is very political," Ling began after the door closed. "We'll be meeting your mayor tonight, and from what we are told, he is very supportive of our deal."

"If it helps the high-speed rail, he'll be behind it." Max repeated the sentiment of most of the town. The mayor had been pursuing the rail since before his days as a councilmember.

"That is a phrase we've heard before." Ling sat up slightly. "Why? How does our purchase of the Jewel help his pet project?"

Max nodded. "The mayor wants a vibrant city. Maybe he sees you as fresh blood to invigorate the southern end of town. If I can be completely honest, I think he also sees you as a pipeline to Asia and hopes you'll bring in more visitors from that area of the world, though God knows we already have quite a few."

"Yes, there is that." Ling allowed a slight nod. "I still feel like we don't have the full picture. I'd like you to help me understand why they are selling."

Max raised an eyebrow and looked from Ling to the closed door before responding.

"I'm a negotiator. I can help figure out the pain points and execute a good deal, but I'm not an investigator. I'm sure you have people who can dig deeper."

"You have certain skills," Ling responded.

"Hang on." A chill ran up his neck. Not an alarm but a warning sign, and he put his hands on the table, pausing to gather his thoughts. He did not want to insult her.

Before he could continue, Ling interrupted, leaning forward.

"You misunderstand me, Mr. Kline. I'm simply asking that you finely tune your perceptive skills when we sit down with the selling group. I'm sure you will identify things we do not see. They are selling an asset that appears to have been doing very well for them. While we welcome this opportunity . . ." She paused, apparently searching for a word. "I think your expression would be 'eyes wide open.' Is that correct? I'd like to know more about Tri-Star's motivation."

Max relaxed his shoulders slightly and removed his hands from the table.

"Okay," he said. "I can watch for clues about what's driving them, but usually I'm better at the price negotiation."

"Aren't the two connected?" she asked.

"I guess they are."

"As you know," Ling started. "The principal argument against the purchase is the construction of the high-speed rail over the next three years, but our team is projecting only minimal impact, and the rail project will compensate us for any significant drop in occupancy."

Max had heard all of this before. After many years of political wrangling, the high-speed rail was finally under construction, linking Los Angeles to Las Vegas. The Desert Jewel, for better or worse, was located by the freeway, which was also the public right-of-way that the rail was using to enter Las Vegas. The construction work would be a major interruption to traffic flows all over the southern half of Las Vegas.

"We know that business will be more difficult in the short term," Ling continued. "But it still doesn't fully justify the sale. There must be a reason we haven't seen."

"I'll watch for any indications," Max replied.

"It might require a bit more than that," Ling added. "But from my understanding—"

She stopped speaking when Max glared at her with his head half cocked.

"Mr. Kline." She returned his stare. "There is much we don't know, but such is business. I would appreciate any help you can provide in this matter—above and beyond your negotiation skills. Perhaps we should revise your contract to compensate you for this. We still have many questions."

"I hear you, and maybe it's in the financials." Max ignored the implied offer. It wasn't clear what she wanted, but he suspected it might not be to his liking. "I feel like the ones who will find your answers left the room a while ago."

"Our bookkeepers are good." Ling rose, signaling that the meeting was over. "If there is something in the numbers, they will find it.

"But it might be something beyond the numbers," Ling added as she pushed in her chair. "Keep your eyes open, Mr. Kline. We'll expect you to be alert at the meeting this afternoon."

As she left the room, Max sat uncomfortably at the empty conference table. What was she expecting him to do? She had certainly suggested more than he had signed up for.

* * *

It was noon when Max left the suite. The Haoyun team had ordered a large buffet for lunch, but Max politely declined. Over the last day and a half, he had been up to his eyeballs in the acquisition details and needed a break and some fresh air, especially after the last interaction with management. Beyond that, it was one of his personal rules to maintain some distance from his work. When he'd first started consulting, he'd become too tied up with his clients and either ended up upset with results or disappointed when the other side did not return his camaraderie. He'd eventually decided it was best to maintain an arm's-length relationship with his clients.

He took the elevator to the pool deck, happy for once that he didn't have to walk through the casino floor gauntlet. The Haoyun team had provided him with a guest room to use throughout the negotiations, and his key card allowed him guest access, which he used to shortcut across a relatively full pool deck to The Taco Stand, where he had eaten many times before. Its literal name fit the need for fast recognition by the weekend guests but, he had to admit, it was also one of the best taco stands in town.

The Desert Jewel was not a regular haunt for him—its poker tables offered lower stakes and a less professional crowd than he preferred. Lower-level gamers often populated them, looking to take advantage of amateur players who arrived weekly, thinking they could emulate the various poker shows they'd seen on TV. It wasn't Max's style. He could win here, but the stakes didn't offer enough reward. Even so, the Jewel occasionally hosted a tournament worth playing and, when they did, Max would frequent The Taco Stand.

The service area was meant to look like a simple food truck, but as with everything in Vegas, Max knew there was much larger infrastructure supporting it on the back end. Rather than standing in line, he took a seat at the elevated "players deck," flashing his player's card and handing the maître d' a twenty on his way past.

Fifteen minutes later, he was finishing his first of three chicken tacos when a familiar voice sounded behind him.

"Hey, Max!" A hand brushed his shoulder, and his friend Ben Carpenter moved into view, pulling out the other chair at the small table and taking a seat. "How have you been?"

Max finished swallowing and wiped his mouth before laughing. "Hey, Ben, make yourself at home," he offered sarcastically. Ben was a detective with the Las Vegas Police Department, a fellow veteran of the Middle East, and also an excellent poker player.

When Max first entered the Las Vegas poker scene, he had immediately connected with Ben, and though they'd each found different niches, they still saw each other fairly frequently on the circuit. He was probably Max's best poker friend, but the thing about most poker friends was that they were all a mile wide and an inch deep. When the end of the night came, everyone was still most concerned about their own stack. Max had always felt that Ben was more than that, though one never really knew.

"Seriously, how're you doing?" Ben asked. He was in plain clothes, but the badge at his hip indicated he was on duty. Several years older than Max, his head was bald but accented by a close-cropped gray beard that contrasted his light-chocolate skin. His gently wrinkled face and light-blue eyes appeared to show concern as he looked at Max.

"Top of the world." Max put on a false grin.

"Your luck improve at all?"

There was no hiding losses in Vegas. The casinos certainly knew, but within the poker community, everyone watched each other, and everyone knew about Max's current losing streak.

"Can't lose if you don't play."

He liked Ben, but there was more to this conversation than a social call.

"So what are you up to? How can I help?" he offered, looking to get some insight into the visit.

"I hear Philip Marsh is doing OK."

*There it is*, Max thought to himself. *Ben's looking into the thing at the hospital.*

"Sure is," he responded, not wanting to be evasive. "Saw him Monday night. I think he'll be released soon."

"That's good to hear. He's a good man when he's not taking my money." Philip had long been the senior member of a group that played monthly at the Wynn. As with any such group, the regulars drifted in and out, but Philip and a small cadre of uber-regulars, like Ben and Max, had been steady attendees for several years.

"What time were you there?"

Max took another bite of his taco before answering. He knew where Ben was going but didn't want to let on. Just like at the tables, the dance involved both hiding your hole cards and trying to guess your opponent's.

"I brought him a burger," he chuckled, deciding he should at least start with the truth. "Right near the end of visiting hours. You should have seen his grin as he chowed down."

"That's great." Ben did not act like he was hearing anything he didn't already know. "You see anything odd at the hospital?"

Max stopped mid-bite and looked questioningly at his friend.

"Like what?"

"We had a suspect there around midnight, and she escaped in an ambulance."

Max shook his head.

"Didn't see anything like that. How'd she get the ambulance?" Max could play the game, if that was what Ben wanted.

"You see, that's just it, Max," Ben continued. "Someone helped her. Are you sure you didn't see anything?"

"Sorry. No."

"You're going to think this is funny, but based on the descriptions, I'm probably looking for your doppelgänger." The detective looked around as if to make sure they were not overheard. "I know it wouldn't have been you, but the description of this guy sounds like a dead ringer, so if you saw anybody, it would be super helpful."

Max wiped his mouth again, shaking his head.

"Sorry, Ben. I wish I could help, but I didn't see anyone. Certainly not my twin!"

"OK, thought I'd ask."

Ben looked at him with the eyes of a detective, possibly hoping he'd crack. For a long moment, they just let the unspoken truth circulate between them. Was it a warning? Max wasn't sure, but he knew Ben was smart enough to know he was on the right track. He wouldn't have come otherwise, but he didn't have any real evidence.

"I assume they have surveillance footage?" Max pushed his luck, trying to see what his friend might reveal. "I'd love to see this guy if he's as good-looking as you say."

"Ha." Ben pushed back his chair and stood. "Not yet. We've got a technical issue, but we'll have it soon enough. I'll be sure to let you know."

There was a knowing edge to his last comment that made Max

shake his head again, but he managed a smile as he reached out to grasp the man's hand.

"Good to see you, Ben. I'm tied up this week but will probably see you at the Wynn over the weekend."

"OK, Max." The detective turned back to the casino entrance.

The last taco sat on his plate, but Max had lost his appetite.

* * *

The second floor wasn't accessible by the public elevator banks, so the Haoyun team had to travel down to the casino floor and traverse the massive gaming room to get to the security elevators. Around them, throngs of guests filled the tables and slots, eager for the thrill of gambling and careless of the inevitable losses.

Las Vegas was an incredible machine, built in an area that nobody wanted, an oasis designed to take all the savings from its visitors while leaving them thrilled at the opportunity.

Max loved the town for its insidiousness. He wasn't part of the system that was Las Vegas, but he respected it. People loved a chance at glory, even with poor odds—that wasn't his game. The group passed the poker room, and Max scanned the crowd, seeing a couple of small-time pros who spent their time fleecing amateurs at low-stakes tables. That also wasn't his game.

At the far end of the floor were the security elevators, where a smiling man in a light-gray suit welcomed them and led them past security and around the metal detectors. The man clearly knew Wei Zhang and Ling Wu, and he led them to an open elevator then stood to one side as the rest of the team filed in, introducing himself as they passed.

When it was his turn, Max shook hands and immediately appreciated the firm grip in response.

"Max Kline," he said, looking the man in the eyes.

"Mike Sullivan, welcome to the Desert Jewel." He hesitated for a second, hanging on to Max's hand as if to keep him out of the elevator. "So you're the local talent?"

"I'm a translator," Max replied curtly, releasing the man's hand. He entered the elevator and Mike followed, allowing the door to close. The large car comfortably accommodated all nine passengers.

The Haoyun team comprised Wei, Ling, Jun, three accountants, another translator, and himself. He was uncertain of the accountants' specific talents, but he was confident that Ling had vetted each of them. Not that it would matter to him. He was there to observe and of course translate when needed.

It was a quick ride to the second floor, where the doors opened to a professional lobby, which was nice but unpretentious and staffed by two receptionists wearing the same uniform as the front desk staff.

They were escorted down the hall and into a large windowless meeting room. In the middle of the room was a horseshoe table, its open side facing an oversized television screen. Comfortable-looking chairs lined the outside of the table. Max was initially surprised by the lack of windows, but he found the room elegantly adorned. The wallpaper had an abstract motif in navy and burgundy—Art Deco, but not so much that it forced itself on the viewer. Gold leaf crown molding surrounded the top of the extra-tall walls. When he thought about it, he doubted there was a good view from this floor, so they were probably better off without windows.

As if on cue, another door opened on the opposite side of the room, and Max got his first look at the opposing side. Six men entered the room, and the stereotype could not have been more obvious or accurate. He felt like he'd stepped onto the set of a 1970s gangster movie. Even if he hadn't been aware of the selling group's history, it would have been hard to have any other feeling. They all wore gray suits in various tones, from almost black to light ash, several of them with vests. But despite their outward appearance, their arrival came with a very positive vibe. They crossed the room quickly with hands extended and smiles on their faces, bypassing a more traditional introduction and catching the Haoyun team somewhat off guard, though Wei Zhang quickly followed suit, pocketing the business cards he had planned to exchange.

Max stayed in the back, inwardly acknowledging their opponents for scoring the first point.

For most, this was not their first meeting. The selling group had welcomed the Haoyun team on their arrival the previous Saturday with cocktails in the lobby, though Max had been unable to join them. There was another, larger party planned for later, which he would attend.

Among the group, Geno Abruzzi was easily recognizable not only for his size but by the way the others deferred to him. He was at least six feet six and probably weighed over 250 pounds. Dressed in a dark chalk-stripe suit, he looked like a professional football player on his way into the stadium, except for his hair, which was gray and thinning. From the neck down though, he could have been twenty years old—trim and solid, despite his size. Max was impressed and noted the man's agility. He wasn't lumbering like some larger men.

As the two groups met at the open end of the table, Geno and Wei shook hands at the center, allowing the others to greet each other in what became a round robin of handshakes and pleasantries.

For his part, Max smiled and introduced himself as an interpreter. The others acknowledged him, but all seemed eager to talk to the Haoyun management team and glossed over introductions until one gentleman engaged a little more.

"You from around here, Max?" He introduced himself as Eddie

Difusco, vice president of operations for Tri-Star. Max guessed he was in his thirties, and his light-gray suit did little to hide a well-built frame.

"Not originally, but I live here now."

"No shit? That's great. Whereabouts?"

"Winchester." Max was a little surprised at the man's interest.

"Know it well." Eddie nodded. "Near the golf courses?"

"No, I'm over by the Omelet House."

"No shit!" The man's eyes lit up, but Max couldn't shake a falseness in the conversation. "Geno, this guy lives by your favorite spot."

Geno had been in an expanded conversation with Wei, Ling, and Jun, but turned at the mention of his name. He swiveled his head back to the group and said something before he turned and stepped toward Max.

"What's that, Eddie?" His voice was deep but still had a sharpness.

"This guy's a local. Lives by the Omelet House."

"Oh-ho," Geno cooed. "Best Grand Slam breakfast in Vegas! I love that place." He covered the short distance to stand between them, and putting his left hand on Eddie's shoulder, he extended the other to Max, who took it firmly, rewarded by an equally powerful grip.

For a brief moment, Geno looked him up and down before releasing his hand.

"I used to live over that way. Great part of town." He smiled. "What are you doing here?"

"I'm an interpreter."

Geno nodded for a moment, again eying Max.

"Interpreter, huh?" He turned to Eddie. "Who would have thought a guy could earn a living by talking, eh?"

"Yeah. Go figure, right?"

Geno still had a hand on Eddie's shoulder, and he now put his other hand on Max's left shoulder. The grip was as strong as the handshake.

"Well, I'm glad to have you here." He then dipped closer and lowered his voice. "Might be nice to have someone help us understand these guys."

Max ignored the implication, responding out loud.

"I'm happy to help. That's what interpreters do."

"Yeah, well, we often need help with some things." The big man was obviously going somewhere Max didn't want to go.

"I can translate Chinese and Farsi, if you want me to send you my rate sheet."

"Is that all you do?" Geno continued to smile, but his tone

sharpened, and his eyes bored into Max, waiting for his response.

Max returned the stare, internally telling himself to let it go. Without looking, he could sense that Eddie was also awaiting his response.

After a moment too long, he forced a smile. "I play cards too." He nodded. "You're right. Hard to earn a living by talking."

"Nice!" Eddie patted Max's shoulder jovially. "Don't tell us you're a card counter!"

"Oh no." Geno's face lightened. "We don't like those guys."

"Not me," Max said. "Poker."

"Where do you play?" Eddie asked.

Before Max could answer, he felt a pull on his elbow and turned to see Ling with what looked like a forced smile.

"Gentlemen," she spoke softly, addressing Geno, "I'm sorry to interrupt, but if it is OK with you, we'd like to begin."

"Of course." Geno's voice returned to its gregarious volume. "Let's do this."

The mafia boss did not wait to end the previous conversation. He stepped between Max and Ling, putting an unwelcome arm around her shoulders as he guided her around the table.

"Nice to meet you, Max." Eddie spoke in a low voice from the side, slapping Max's shoulder once again. "Geno doesn't waste words. He meant what he said."

Max turned and offered his hand, which Eddie took.

"Nice to meet you as well, Eddie."

The two men parted and took seats on opposite sides of the table.

Max scanned the men from Tri-Star, assuming most of them were members of the Marchetti family, and he imagined Staci trying to get away from this group. She wouldn't stand a chance by herself.

# CHAPTER FIVE

Staci pushed back from her desk and rubbed one side of her face. She glanced up at the clock on the wall but already knew the time. It was a little after five in the afternoon, and she only had an hour before she had to meet Eddie.

Around her, the office moved at increased activity. Though there were shifts all day and night, the largest number worked standard hours, and the office always picked up as that group worked to finish their tasks to close out their day.

For her part, Staci was nowhere near complete and would definitely need to come in early tomorrow. The report itself was easy. She knew what the files were supposed to say, but the difficulty was providing the supporting documents. Of course, she had access to all the back data, but organizing it was a nightmare—one she was partially responsible for making.

In her time in the casino's accounting department, she had learned three things. The first was that it was all about the front-page numbers. It wasn't uncommon for a supervisor to ask her to bury an expense under a highly profitable line item. She'd often stretched her imagination to make things line up as her bosses instructed. The second thing she'd learned was that when the front page looked good, most people never looked any deeper—even, to her surprise, the auditors. But it was the third thing that was frustrating her today. Probably most important, Staci had learned that in case someone looked beyond the front page, it was best to obfuscate the data such that anyone looking would grow frustrated and quit long before uncovering the actual details.

Apparently, Haoyun wanted to see the background data, and they'd already pointed out many of the questionable tricks that Staci had been instructed to implement the previous year. Now, she had the task of unraveling the convoluted ball of twine she had created, but she had to do so in a way that would continue to hide or at least gloss over the irregularities that had caused such a shitstorm.

She still remembered the day two years prior when she had been called into a conference room with Pam and a quite handsome, well-built man who turned out to be Eddie Difusco, one of the casino bosses. Staci had been under no delusions. Even if she hadn't seen his face in the paper, everyone knew Eddie was a member of the

Marchetti family. Back then, it had been exciting.

"Nice to meet you, Staci." Eddie had stood and taken her hand between both of his own. "Seems like a waste to have something as beautiful as you hidden down here in accounting. How do you like working here at the Desert Jewel?"

He was tall, maybe six feet three, and had very trim taper-cut black hair. His shoulders were broad, and even through his blue suit, she could see he had the biceps of a bodybuilder.

"It's work." She smiled back and nodded to Pam. "But I enjoy the team."

Eddie sat down next to Pam and Staci sat opposite them.

"Pam speaks highly of you."

"I do my best."

"Well, you're doing great. But I need to ask a favor of you. You remember in school when the teacher would add a question at the end of a test and call it extra credit?" He rolled his index finger, as if that helped explain his question.

"Of course." Staci had known where he was going, and if she was being honest, she'd felt a rush of excitement at the prospect.

"Well, this thing I'm asking, it will be extra credit too. You prepared the food and beverage P&L, right?"

"Yes, sir," she answered.

"It looks pretty good."

"I think it is our best year ever." She had spent weeks preparing it, and she knew the division well. "Revenues are higher, and margins reached a new peak. The catering section is off the charts."

"Yeah, that's why we're talking." Eddie leaned on his elbows and looked at her with a glint in his eyes. "We think maybe you missed some expenses."

That line was the beginning of a long road for Staci. She knew exactly what he was asking, and if he'd asked a year earlier, she might have refused, but Vegas wore on people. Her bills were high, and she'd yet to see the glamor that had first attracted her to Vegas. And the man asking was an absolute hunk. She'd agreed to help.

Now, with the acquisition pending, the list of irregularities she was addressing was only a little over half finished, and she had a pit in her stomach knowing she was covering lies with lies.

On the plus side, her life had improved dramatically over the past two years. Besides the bonus pay she now received regularly, she and Eddie had hit it off, and if there was one thing she wanted to take with her when she left Vegas, he would be it. In person, he really wasn't a bad guy, like the media portrayed.

She clicked on the corner of the folder to close it. She'd done enough for one day and needed a break. It had been a few days since she'd seen Eddie, and she was excited to see him. Monday night had been a disaster, and something she couldn't share, but she could only hope it was over. The irony was glaring. It was Eddie's boss who was looking for her, so she couldn't tell him or enlist his help—at least not now. If someone caught her, he could intervene, but she didn't want to test his loyalty, even though she knew he returned her love.

Max was helping, and he seemed genuine about getting the surveillance footage, so she held on to that hope even though past experiences had hurt her. She had little choice. Getting them herself was impossible, and if they identified her, it would probably be over—unless Eddie helped.

She pulled up her email and sent a quick message to Pam requesting another twenty-four hours of access to the data files. She knew it would be approved. Pam trusted her. Staci had squeezed a few indiscretions past the old spinster, but she'd never been caught. The real question was—could she fool the Chinese?

## CHAPTER SIX

The top floor of the Desert Jewel, in typical Las Vegas fashion, held a sprawling indoor-outdoor bar-restaurant called Wildfire. When Max was told the selling group was hosting an informal event that evening, he had assumed it would be on the restaurant side, so he was a little taken aback when the hostess led him toward a roped-off area in the corner of the outdoor patio with a view north to the strip. He smiled and shook his head when he was still too far off to be seen.

The Haoyun contingent, he knew, would look awkwardly out of place. He could see Geno and his men already enjoying themselves, and he had to admit that maybe this was the right move. It would certainly put the Chinese on unstable footing, at least for the night.

"Hey, Winchester!" Geno called out as the hostess opened the velvet-rope gate. He sat in a large cushioned chair, surrounded by several of his men in similar seats. An assortment of bottles, mixers, and a large bucket of ice filled the table between them. "You're the first to arrive from your side. Let me make you a cocktail. What do you like?"

Max glanced quickly at the bottles, but there were too many.

"Whatever you're making," he answered, stepping into the circle and greeting the men, some of whom he had spent the afternoon with. Each of them stood to shake his hand, except Geno, who was busy making a cocktail. Two of the men did not reseat themselves and moved off to another area where more men gathered with several women.

"Try this on for size." Geno passed him a large lowball glass filled to the rim.

"I used to be a vodka guy," he explained, raising his own glass in cheers. "But Eddie got me hooked on these things—Tequila and soda. Ranch water, it's called."

Max nodded and raised his glass in return salute. He took a long sip and then raised the glass slightly again.

"This is delicious. Thank you."

"Glad you like it." The big man reclined in his chair with the obvious ease of a boss. "So what'd you think of today? Your side happy so far?"

Max finished his second sip and raised his eyebrows. "I'm just a translator."

Geno's face lost all levity. "Cut the crap, Winchester."

Turning to the other two seated men, he motioned for them to move. "Give us a moment, will you, boys?"

The men stood up without comment and moved to the area where the others had gone moments earlier. Max couldn't help but think he'd rather be there as well.

"You know who I am?" Geno asked, but it was more of a statement than a question.

Max nodded, putting his drink on the table.

"Good. I know who you are too." Geno reclined in the soft chair, arms wide on the armrests. "I know you served our country. Thank you. And I know you've been playing cards for a number of years here. By all accounts, you're pretty good, which means you're probably good at reading people." He paused but maintained a fierce stare. "That leads me to believe your translation skills are probably secondary to your negotiating skills. I mean, come on, we're all talking in English."

Max saw no reason to protest, but he wouldn't outright acknowledge the accuracy of Geno's assessment.

"There are nuances in the language that don't exactly translate. After the meeting, I bring the team up to speed on the things I heard."

"So I ask again, is your side happy?"

While there was no reason he needed to answer, Max felt like perhaps he was still at the negotiating table, so a minor concession here might loosen the way in the future.

"I think things are headed in the right direction," he replied, picking up his drink once again and sitting back, though his chair was not the same size as his host's. "The price seems fair . . . if the numbers play out. We're still waiting on the food and beverage report."

He'd said nothing new.

"There aren't any problems with the books, Max." Geno looked at him with a face void of emotion. "I meant what I said, you know. We could use a guy like you."

Max knew exactly what the implication was, but he ignored it, turning to look at the growing crowd standing by the balcony.

"You stocking the pond tonight?"

It was a common Vegas expression for the practice of paying women to join a party. Sometimes they served as eye candy; sometimes they received payment for doing a lot more.

"Most of them are plus-ones for my guys," Geno responded with a mischievous grin. "But I'd be lying if I said I didn't bring in a few to make sure everyone was havin' a good time.

"Give it some thought." The big man returned to his own agenda, pushing forward in his chair. "Why not earn with us?"

Before Max could respond, Geno looked up toward the entrance and raised his glass.

"Yo, Eddie, get over here!"

Max turned to see Eddie coming through the rope gate. He waved to someone in the standing area but came directly to their table. Geno stood up, and the two large men shook hands then embraced, Geno patting his cheek as they separated. Eddie then turned to Max, who had also risen. They shook hands, and then Eddie pulled him in for a much briefer hug, his hard body confirming to Max that the man was strong.

"Good to see you, Max," he said with little sincerity. He moved to the other side of the table and took a seat next to Geno, who had already sat back down. "How did it go for your side today?"

"All good." Max resumed his seat. "Geno already asked."

Eddie looked at Geno for a few seconds then back to Max.

"If he's hitting you up to work for us, forget about it. Maybe sometime later, but we know it can't happen now." He started to make himself a drink under the now disapproving eye of his boss.

"I love this guy," Eddie continued, inclining his head toward Geno. "But he still thinks everyone wants to work with us. And that may be true, but some guys need a little time to warm up to it."

"Why do I keep you on?" Geno directed his gaze at Eddie while pointing toward Max with the hand that still held his drink. "This guy would fit right in. Give him a chance."

Eddie shook his head, raising his newly made cocktail in a toast.

"Like I said, I love you, Geno, but let's give Max some room. Salud."

Everyone raised their glass and took a sip.

Max felt obligated to respond. "I'm flattered but not interested. Appreciate the invitation tonight though. This is a sweet setup."

"Yeah." Geno appeared put off. He offered Max a faint smile and stood up. "Stick around. You might find we're more alike than you think. Anyway, you guys enjoy yourselves. I've got to welcome our guest of honor."

Max turned to see Wei Zhang and Ling Wu approaching the private area. Geno stepped toward them, and Max could hear bits of the large man's overly honeyed welcome as he draped his arms around them.

"Ignore him." Eddie's voice pulled him back to the conversation. "He's a good guy but thinks too highly of himself. That said, we should vacate. This is Geno's area, so he'll expect us gone when he returns. Fill up your drink, and I'll introduce you to some of the guys."

* * *

True to form, the party had done nothing but grow as Max enjoyed a few ranch waters, and Eddie introduced him to others from the Tri-

Star group. For the most part, nobody wanted to talk about the transaction—except for the occasional questions into Haoyun's strategy, which he easily evaded. What was a little more surprising was how few of the Haoyun team were in attendance. Apart from himself, Wei Zhang, and Ling Wu, Max had only seen one other from the team of over twenty-five. Even Jun Chen was absent, no doubt still in their suite, poring over the numbers and preparing the next salvo in the negotiations.

Max, for his part, was enjoying the company. While he knew these men probably all had dark secrets, he found them incredibly welcoming and full of life. When he'd accepted the invitation, his plan was to make an appearance and then leave after a couple of drinks, but he'd quickly changed his mind. He'd met so many from the opposing side that he barely remembered names except for Eddie and a couple of others who seemed to stick by his side. At one point, he wondered if they'd been tasked with watching him, but they were such good company that he decided he didn't care.

Though he had yet to meet one female who worked with the Tri-Star retinue, the party was filled with attractive women. Even for a Vegas resident, the amount of eye candy amazed Max, though he wisely limited his interactions with the hired talent to polite conversation. There were also several good-looking women who were not paid talent. Most of these women were with the men from

Tri-Star, but that didn't stop Max from enjoying their company.

Jeanine was one such woman, whom Eddie had introduced before another of the Desert Jewel contingent pulled him away. She was relatively tall, almost six feet, with a slender body wrapped in a very short, tight-fitting dress. Her blue eyes and tanned face were accented by dyed blonde hair that had a streak of red above her left ear, and he found himself mildly attracted.

"It's all about getting eyes on the prize," she said, explaining how she sold high-end jewelry. "Get them when they're flush with cash, and the sparkles are like magnets."

She was a manager at one of the jewelry stores at the Desert Jewel, and Max had asked about business. The industry built around keeping players' money in Las Vegas always amazed him.

"Do they haggle?" he asked.

"Not usually. Some try, but we don't play that game. Sometimes I'll mark up another item on the fly and then tell them they can have the pair at a discount, but I'm always getting full retail one way or the other."

"Amazing," Max mused, genuinely impressed by her bearing, but before he could continue, a face in his peripheral vision startled him. He had to pause and took a sip of his drink, casually turning back toward the entrance to confirm his sighting.

Sure enough, he spotted Staci waiting to be let in, dressed to the nines in white jeans and a pink halter top, both of which accented her tanned and tight abs. Her hair was down but pulled back behind her left ear. As if she felt his gaze, she looked up at him and a slight panic flared in her eyes before she turned to speak to the bouncer, who was holding the velvet rope open for her. Max watched as she crossed to the bar without looking back.

"See someone you know?" Jeanine asked, pulling Max back to the conversation.

"Sorry." He turned back, upset with himself for being obvious. "No . . . yes. Someone I hadn't expected to see."

"So what about you, Max? How do you fit in here?"

"I'm not sure I do," he answered. "I'm working with Haoyun."

"Oh my God." Her expression changed from friendly to curious. "You guys are buying the place. Aren't you the other side here?"

Max laughed to himself. In theory, this party was all about the acquisition, but some guests were not even aware.

"I'm not sure we're completely on the other side," he responded. "And I wouldn't put myself in the group doing the buying. Haoyun is making the acquisition. I'm the hired help. I'm a translator."

"Oh, how cool." She pulled back slightly and seemed to look him up and down in a new light, flaring her eyes. "Can you introduce me to the new owners?"

"I'd be happy to." Max was only half paying attention to the conversation. He'd monitored Staci and now saw her standing alone at one end of the bar. "I need another drink. What can I get you?"

"Kir Royale, please." She smiled. "Thank you."

Max excused himself and moved through the crowd, making eye contact with Staci as he approached the bar. She smiled and glanced at the empty space next to her, which he took as an invitation to join, but he did not immediately greet her. He put his glass on the bar and called the barman over to place his order. Only then did he turn to Staci, making an effort to introduce himself in case he was being watched.

"Hey, I'm Max," he said with a smile, pretending he was meeting her for the first time. He extended a hand, which she took gingerly.

"Staci," she said, following quickly in a lower tone with, "What the hell are you doing here?"

"Believe it or not, this is work," he answered. "You?"

"It's complicated."

"Seems you live a complicated life." He made a point of looking at her outfit with a grin. "You dress up nice. Not the same woman I had breakfast with."

"Shhh." Panic flared again in Staci's ice-blue eyes. "Don't fucking talk about it, especially not here."

Max felt the back of his neck tingle. Something, or someone, had her spooked.

"I'm sorry. I didn't mean to." He stopped himself and switched his approach. "Look, how can I help?"

"Did you get rid of the footage?"

"Not yet, but I'm working on it. What else do you need?"

"Nothing." Staci looked up into the night before turning a saddened gaze back at him. "I wish I could make this whole week just go away."

"I'm sorry."

"Don't be. You've been great, and thank you again."

Max couldn't help but feel bad for her, but this wasn't the time to find out more.

"Where're you from?" he asked, changing the subject.

"Louisville."

"I thought I heard a bit of a Southern twang."

"In Louisville, you need to be careful when you say that." Her eyes lit up in mischief. "Half the crowd are good ol' boys who want to claim the South, but the other half say we were a Union state."

"And what do you think?" He smiled, happy to see her mood improving.

"Why, Mr. Max!" She put the fingers of one hand on his forearm and emphasized her accent. "I do believe I just love playing the Southern belle."

"So long as he knows you're *my* Southern belle." A familiar voice interrupted, and Max looked up to see Eddie standing beside them with a grin, looking at Staci.

"Hey, hon." She stood and wrapped him in a warm hug.

"You look great, babe." Eddie returned the hug then planted a kiss on her lips, lingering a moment longer than was comfortable.

"I see you've met Staci." Eddie ended the kiss and looked over the top of her head to lock eyes with Max. "You having a good time?"

"I am, thanks."

Staci released her man and sat back down.

"How do you two know each other?" she asked innocently.

"Max is actually on the team that's buying the Jewel." Eddie clamped a hand on Max's shoulder. "But we still like him."

Staci looked back at Max with eyes slightly wider.

"It looks like I might work for you some day."

Max shook his head. "No, ma'am. I'm helping with the deal, but I'm not part of ownership. Are you part of Tri-Star?"

"Ah, no." She wagged a finger. "Like you, I'm part of the workforce, not ownership. But you may have seen some of my work. I'm in accounting here at the Desert Jewel."

"Yeah, well, right now, you're my beautiful date," Eddie interrupted. "Sorry, Max, I need to grab her. Want to introduce her to the mayor."

Max couldn't help but notice Staci flinch as Eddie finished. She slid slightly back into her chair, and Max's instinct told him she needed help, but he knew better than to act on it.

"The mayor's here?" he asked Eddie.

"Yeah, Geno and him are pretty tight. He spent some time welcoming your employers. I think it went well." Eddie nodded toward Geno's area, where Max could see Wei and Ling standing next to an older Hispanic man whose black hair was heavily streaked with gray.

"Mayor Rodriguez has really helped this town," Eddie continued. "Oh, hey." He hit Max on the shoulder. "But you know that. You're a local too."

"Yeah," Max answered, ignoring the hit. "I know Rodriguez."

In truth, he knew little about Rodriguez, except that most of the city believed he was in bed with the casinos, which meant he was in bed with organized crime. He was midway through his second term, and Max couldn't really think of anything he'd done to improve the place. He'd been a councilman from the Paradise district prior to his run as mayor, and he'd made his name supporting the Sphere, which was now a growing Vegas landmark.

His big push as a candidate and as mayor was the high-speed rail project connecting Las Vegas to Los Angeles. It was a controversial issue, because while everyone seemed to agree on the concept, many pushed back on the cost and financial burden to the city. Rodriguez had fought hard for its survival and continued to get very mixed press.

"Come on, Max." Eddie had already pulled Staci up and under his arm, steering her toward Geno's area, but he paused to wait. "Join us. He's a good guy but hard to catch, so this might be your only chance to meet him."

"Let's do it." Max picked up his new cocktails, holding the Kir Royale in the air. "I've got to drop this off and I'll be right there."

* * *

"What happens in Vegas stays in Vegas," Johnny laughed as he tapped his shot glass to the one in front of Max. The party was still in full force even though they were deep into the night. The two of them finished their Tequilas.

"That's such a piece of shit," he continued, "They should say, 'What happens in Vegas is always under surveillance!' The eye in the sky knows everything."

While traditionally the "eye in the sky" referred to the ceiling cameras in the casinos, Johnny had spent the last fifteen minutes explaining to Max how there were so many cameras in the city that he didn't think anyone got away with anything in Vegas that those in charge didn't allow to happen. And by that, he meant the mob.

"Check it out." Johnny leaned closer even as he motioned to the waitress for another cocktail. "The other day, some chick was in a place she shouldn't be, right? She thinks she got away from us, but she didn't."

He pulled back for a second, looking around, and Max thought he might be deciding if he should continue. Max stayed silent, not wanting to appear eager, but he left a curious expression on his face that seemed to draw the man back.

"The thing is, she went to a hospital but got away before we could find out who she was. Again, seems like she's gone, right? Wrong," Johnny continued loudly, twisting his lips and extending the word. "We have a guy who's going to get us the surveillance tapes from the hospital. Like I said, there's no getting away from the eye in the sky!"

Max laughed and shook his head.

"Sounds like you're right, but why would you care so much? She steal from you?"

"No, man." Johnny shook his head. "And that's not really your business, is it?" He straightened in his chair.

"Whatever, dude." Max definitely did not want the conversation to end, but he did not want to sound curious either. "I couldn't care less. I hope you find her."

"Oh, we'll find her." Johnny quickly dispelled his caution. "Eddie's not one to let things go away. We should have the tapes by tomorrow, and we'll tie up the other loose ends. The whole incident will be put to bed before the weekend."

"Eddie seems like a great guy," Max pressed for more. His mind was racing—he had less time than he thought.

"Did I hear my name?" Eddie's loud voice penetrated the house music around them as he pulled back the remaining chair and sat down to join them. He was holding Staci's hand, and he pulled her to stand behind him, his hand raised to ear level, holding hers.

"Hey, Eddie." Max raised his glass then nodded to Staci as well. "Staci. You guys having fun?"

"I was telling Max here that you're a good man to work for." Johnny offered with a smile, but the look he gave Max was a clear signal that he didn't want to reveal what they had talked about. "Staci, please." He gestured to his seat as he rose. "Have my seat. I gotta hit the head."

Staci sat down after he left.

"Max, you've got quite the charm. I think the mayor liked you," Eddie began.

Max laughed. "What's not to like?"

"And shy too?" Eddie raised an eyebrow and looked at Staci. "You were there. Tell me Max didn't cozy up real nice?"

Staci smiled and nodded slowly. "He had Rodriguez cooing."

Max put his hands up in mock defense. "Hey, I simply asked about the high-speed rail."

"Yeah, the high-speed rail that happens to be the mayor's pet project and possibly his ticket to another term," Eddie continued.

"And a project that will tie up traffic and negatively impact the Jewel's business for a couple of years," Max countered. "You know as much as I that the city's tax breaks are one of the main reasons that Haoyun is at the table. The mayor might have enjoyed talking about it, but I wanted to make sure he understands our position."

"He knows where his bread is buttered."

"What does that mean?"

Eddie looked surprised at the question, but his face quickly returned to a smile.

"I'm saying the mayor will do what's right for Las Vegas."

"Well, I think it's fair that Haoyun protect its interests. They are in this for the long run but are buying this thing on the eve of the rail project, which will be disruptive, to say the least."

"Geno has his assurances." Eddie's face became more serious. "It is in everyone's interest that this deal closes. You can trust Geno with that."

Max nodded. "Then tonight was a good night." He raised his seltzer water in toast, and the other two joined him.

## CHAPTER SEVEN

When Max got back from his morning run, he had three messages on his phone, each from a different woman but only one that he'd been expecting. He'd spoken to Carolyn the night before, so hopefully she had some good news, but he had no idea why Ling Wu would call this early—it was barely seven. And Staci had been a random connection the previous night. He wondered why she would be contacting him again.

Before responding to anyone, he started the coffeemaker and finished a glass of water. The air conditioning felt good. It was already in the sixties outside, and he'd pushed himself fairly hard on the run in an effort to sweat out the previous night's toxins. He put his earbuds in, tapping the number for Ling Wu as he pulled a pair of hard-boiled eggs out of the fridge.

"Max?" Ling answered on the first ring.

"Hi, Ling, did you need me?" he asked.

"Yes, I think we do." She paused for a moment, and Max waited. "Wei and I had an interesting conversation with the mayor last night."

"Go on."

"At first, he was very welcoming and encouraged our bid, emphasizing the tax breaks that the Jewel would receive during the high-speed rail construction. It was all very positive."

"That's great."

"Yes. He told us that everyone would be happy once the rail was in place. Plenty of money to be made by all, he said. Then he said something curious. He pulled us to one side and told us he would handle the district attorney. We shouldn't be concerned."

"What's going on with the DA?" Max asked reflexively.

"We had the same question," Ling continued. "Apparently, she's investigating a drug connection. Mayor Rodriguez assured us it was going nowhere, but we need to know more. It might give us leverage."

"I suppose we can't just call the DA."

"I don't think that would be wise." Ling's tone lowered. "But I'd like someone to delve a little deeper—possibly dig up a little dirt on Tri-Star?"

The phone went silent for a few heartbeats.

"Max?"

"I guess that's a good idea."

"So?" Ling answered crisply. "I'm thinking that your role here could expand."

"Hmm." Max was noncommittal.

"Look, Max. We value you at the table, but I've done my homework and know you can do more."

He sighed to himself. "That's not what you hired me for."

"I'll double your contract. I need you to look deeper into this."

"I'd really prefer not to."

"Max, this is important." Her tone hardened and he could sense borderline anger beneath the surface. "This transaction could fall through if we can't be certain of the value. I'll triple the contract. We need to know what's going on behind the scenes."

Max had been happy with the double, but tripling his contract was a significant boost and way more than he could have expected for *any* service. And he genuinely felt like they needed him.

"OK," he said. "Two conditions. First, you pay the first two-thirds up front."

"No problem."

"Second, I have full autonomy on this part of my job and a corporate credit card."

"Agreed. And I already have a card in your name. I'll see you at the office at nine."

"See you then," Max answered, but the line was already dead.

*Fuck*, he thought to himself. He should have seen this coming. Ling had obviously planned to use him in this manner. So much for the cushy job as a negotiator.

His stomach growled, so he ate the eggs and poured himself a coffee before looking back at his phone. Carolyn had sent him a text. "Call me," it read with a heart emoji at the end, so he had to assume it was good news.

He tapped her number and waited as it rang. She picked up after three rings.

"Sorry, I was in the middle of a string." Her silky voice sounded like she'd just woken up, but Max knew she'd probably been working all night. "I've got your footage secure, but I can't fully delete it."

"Thank you, and good morning," Max replied. "So what does that mean?"

"It means you're going to have to do some of your G.I. Joe shit."

Max thought he could hear a smile as she spoke.

"Great," he answered, looking at his watch. "What's the deal?"

"The hospital has two main servers. The first is right next to security, and that's where they would typically get the video. I've cleared the footage there, but they have a backup server, and the security feed writes to a read-only chip I can't clear."

"And where's that?"

"It's in an electrical room on the second floor. Not where I'd put it, but that's definitely the location."

A vibration indicated a text message, and he looked down at his screen, putting the phone on speaker as he looked at the map Carolyn had sent him.

"I can get you in the room, but you'll need to pull the chip."

"OK, I'm on it. Any live monitoring?"

"Not that I'm aware of. This is pretty low-tech. How are you doing?"

"Better than when I spoke to you last." He had called her on his way home the night before. "Seven miles and some push-ups help clear the head."

"Good to hear. When do you think you'll go in? I'll be your overwatch."

"Probably an hour. Does that work for you? I've got to get back to the Jewel by ten."

"Yeah, I can do it." Her voice held a hint of excitement. "Ping me five minutes before you go in. I'll need a few to set up."

"OK, C. Thank you. I'll talk to you soon."

* * *

Cold showers were a stable in Max's routine. He discovered them during his time in the Middle East and couldn't think of a better transition from workout to work. Over the years, he'd tempered the experience so that it wasn't pure cold, though sometimes at the end he would cut the hot water entirely. It was invigorating, and he felt completely refreshed despite the prior night's activity.

The conversation with Ling lingered in his mind as he shaved and got dressed. The pay was great, but he couldn't shake an annoyance that maybe she'd planned to use him for something like this all along. Whatever her source, word must be circulating, and that was not the line of business he wanted attached to his name. He'd do this job, but from now on he'd have to make it clear that translation and negotiation were the only services offered.

He was buttoning his shirt when his phone vibrated on the counter. He stepped closer and saw Staci's name on the caller ID.

One call was odd enough, but the fact that she was calling again raised his level of concern. He tapped the phone then put her on speaker.

"Good morning, Staci," he said as he resumed buttoning.

"Max, I need to see you." Her voice cracked as if she had been sobbing. "It's fucking serious."

He instinctively looked at his watch, knowing he already had a full morning.

"Are you OK?"

"No. Yes. I'm fine, but those bastards . . ." She took in an audible breath and Max thought he could hear crying.

"Staci," he spoke in a soothing voice, hoping it might calm her, "where are you now?"

"I'm outside Lou's."

"Lou's?"

"Yeah, I needed to get away—to find you." She inhaled and let out a slow breath before continuing. "And when you didn't answer, I told the taxi to take me here. I figured it must be close to where you live."

"It is." He looked at his watch again. "I'll be there in ten minutes. You're going to be fine, Staci."

He could hear her breathing, but she didn't respond.

"Staci, you are going to be OK," he repeated.

"Please come," she said softly, and he heard another sob as the line went dead.

* * *

Eight and a half minutes later, Max got out of a cab outside Lou's. He went in, waving hello to his favorite waitress, Sally, but he didn't see Staci anywhere. Stepping back outside, he pulled out his phone to call her, when he heard his name and turned in time to catch her as she wrapped her arms around him in a tight hug. He returned the hug, rubbing her back in a conciliatory way for a long moment.

Eventually, she loosened her grip, and he reached to turn her face up to look at him. Her eyes were red from crying, as were her nostrils. As if realizing where she was for the first time, she took a step back, lowered her head, and then flipped her hair back, wiping her eyes with a tissue she had in her left hand. A Walgreens bag hung from her right. She wore the same outfit as the night before, and despite her obvious tears, Max admitted she still looked pretty good.

"Went to the drugstore for tissues." She held out the Walgreens bag and tissue. "When the waterworks start, I have a hard time stopping them."

"Let's go inside," Max suggested, raising one arm toward the door, which he held open for her.

Inside, a hostess seated them, and Max thanked her. As she left, she gave him a look with a raised eyebrow that Staci couldn't see. All the staff knew him well.

He ignored the hostess and reached across the table to take

Staci's hand—not in a romantic way, but she obviously needed a friend.

"What's going on?"

Staci leaned back without removing her hand from his.

"Oh God. Have you seen the news?" she asked.

"No."

"Remember the other night?" She pulled her hand away to take out her phone and typed on it.

"Yeah?"

She turned her phone toward him. On the screen, she showed him a building engulfed in flames. It was a newsreel, and he took the phone and watched as emergency responders ran around. The caption at the bottom read: "At least 12 confirmed dead in Wild Horse Club inferno."

"That's where I was," Staci said while Max watched. "I was in there on Monday night. Those girls were my friends." She seemed past tears but was still in pain. "I'm the reason they died."

"What do you mean?" Max did not get the connection.

"Coffee?" Sally stood next to them with two mugs, a carafe of coffee, and that broad smile Max knew well.

"Uh, yes. Please," he said.

Staci nodded.

"Anything to eat?"

Max looked at Staci, and both declined politely. As quickly as she'd appeared, Sally moved off to another table to top-up some coffees.

"I told you I'd seen something." Staci wasted no time continuing as soon as they were alone. "Well, I was in the Wild Horse, banking for my girls. There's a back office that nobody uses, so it's always been free for me to set up shop while the girls come through. Never a problem, and I keep the door locked. Anyway, I was in there packing up when I heard male voices and someone trying a key in the lock, so I grabbed my shit and hid in the closet. Barely got in there before two men came in. You want to know who I saw?"

"I'm not sure, do I?" Max answered, even though he knew it was a rhetorical question.

"Geno and fucking Mayor Rodriguez. That's who. And a whole pile of Molly."

It was Max's turn to push back in the booth as a shiver ran down his spine. In the nineties, it was known as Ecstasy—a pill or powder that sent users into a euphoric state, and a popular club drug in Vegas. It was also one of a cocktail of drugs that had led to his sister's death.

"Are you sure it was Molly?"

Staci looked at him with an unmistakable expression. "Please, I've been around enough to know what Molly looks like."

"What else happened?"

"I didn't hear everything, but I heard enough to know two things. The mayor and Geno are in business together, and if anyone finds out that I know, I'm a dead woman." She hesitated, throwing her hands in the air as tears welled in her already red eyes. "I . . . I didn't think they would take it this far. My girls are dead."

She pushed a tissue into her eyes, attempting to dry them, but her voice cracked. "My sweet girls."

"Are you sure it wasn't an accident?"

Staci's eyes flared in anger.

"Accident, my ass," she hissed through tears. "Nobody got out, Max. This was no accident."

Max sat still. He wanted to hold her—to help her—but he knew she had to absorb this. If she was going to move on, she needed to accept the loss. He waited a few minutes as the shudders and tears began to slow.

"Did anyone see you directly?" he said after she'd settled in.

She shook her head.

"But you said they knew you were there?"

"Yes." Her voice was soft. "I waited till they left. This is after-hours stuff for me, so I was dressed casually and wore a baseball cap I pulled down low over my eyes. Then I waited another five minutes before heading for the door myself, but as soon as I turned down the hall, I heard Geno's voice behind me.

"'Told you I heard something,' he said, his voice is unmistakable. So I ran without looking back. For some reason, the bouncer wasn't at the door, so I was on the street with nobody to stop me. I wouldn't say it was crowded, but enough people were on the sidewalk that I thought I could disappear. I was a block and a half away when I heard someone call out, 'Over there, the ball cap!' And I knew I had to run. I sprinted for the corner, and that's when I spotted a police car coming from the left. I threw up my arms and jumped into the street, but he didn't see me immediately and slammed the brakes at the last second. My hands were on his hood, and my momentum sent me tumbling over the other side. Thankfully, there weren't any other cars. He didn't really hit me, but he thought he had."

"Did you tell him what had happened?"

"Hell no!" Staci's eyes flared, indignant. "But I told him a strange man was chasing me, so he stood over me, scanning the street. 'Which one?' he asked. I peered over the hood but didn't see Geno or anyone I knew, so I shook my head and cried."

Max allowed himself a smile. "The girl card," he said almost to himself.

Staci let out a short laugh and smiled back.

"Yeah, I played the girl card. He called in on his radio then told them he was taking me to a hospital. I knew I wasn't hurt but needed to get outta there, so I acted a little sore and allowed him to help me up and into the back of the squad car."

"OK, so you're still in the clear," he summarized. "If I get the surveillance footage, they can't identify you."

"Are you paying attention?" Staci stared back at him with a mix of anger and confusion. "Everything's fucking changed. If these fuckers are going to slaughter twenty people, do you think they will stop there? They know me there. Fuck, I *know* Geno, Max. I'm Eddie's fucking girlfriend. They'll put two and two together."

"Did anyone see you go in?" Max had to admit she was probably right, but he'd long ago learned not to assume that everyone else saw things through the same lens.

Staci paused before answering. "Actually, no. Well, Jerry in the kitchen, but otherwise just the girls."

"That's a positive." He glanced at his phone and saw it was almost 8:45 a.m. "Here's what I know. We have to solve this one piece at a time, and we have to remain calm."

He knew he was taking an unnecessary risk but was drawn to help her. Maybe if he'd been there for his sister, she wouldn't be dead. Either way, he could help Staci. He reached over to take her hand again. "You hear me?"

She nodded.

"I have to go. I'm going to handle the video this morning. You go to work. Do everything you normally do, understand?"

Again, she nodded.

"Do you think Eddie can help?"

"No fuckin' way. He can't know."

"OK. We'll handle this together. People are trained to expect what they know. If you stay the same girl who's been dating Eddie, they have no reason to connect you to the other night. Step one: I get rid of the footage. Step two: We'll confirm no one saw you. The most important thing is to stay calm. Nobody wins in a panic. We'll get through this." He dropped her hand and slipped out of the booth.

He threw a twenty-dollar bill on the table and reached over to put his hand on her shoulder. When she looked up, he nodded and repeated, "We'll get through this."

## CHAPTER EIGHT

The cab pulled into the visitors' parking section of the Sunshine Hospital & Medical Center. Max thanked the driver and handed her two hundred-dollar bills.

"Do you mind hanging around for the ride home?" he asked.

The driver looked at the cash then back to Max with a semi-questioning look.

"As long as you're not doing anything illegal."

In Vegas, large tips were not unusual, but at nine o'clock on a Wednesday morning in front of a hospital, his request must have seemed odd.

"I don't like waiting." He avoided the question. "If you give me your cell number, I'll text you on my way out. I shouldn't be too long. I have a meeting to get to by ten."

"OK."

She pushed the bills into her pocket, and they exchanged numbers. Max sent her a quick test, which she acknowledged.

"Thank you," he said again, knowing the driver could easily leave after he went inside. It was important to reinforce the contract. "I really appreciate this."

"All good," she replied, tipping a hand to her forehead. "I could use a quick nap while I wait."

Max got out and closed the door, immediately hit by the dry heat that was already settling in on the day. He tapped his phone to redial Carolyn, who picked up immediately.

"You there?" Her voice was a welcome sound in his earbud. He had one in his right ear so he could still hear everything around him.

"Outside."

"OK. Check in, then turn right to elevator two." She spoke softly but had an air of control. Max knew she'd done her homework on this problem. He was more than happy to follow her lead.

"Roger that," he said as the doors slid open and he entered the pure hospital air.

The lobby was busy, and the seating was more than half filled, but he was fortunate that no one was waiting at the check-in counter. He walked right up and provided the name of a patient that Carolyn had given him on their last call.

Moments later, he was stepping out of the stainless steel elevator on the second floor.

"Left out of the elevator," Carolyn instructed.

The floors were all color-coded, and his visitor pass matched the floor, so he strode confidently past the hefty security guard, who nodded from his desk in the hallway. Carolyn guided him through two sets of double doors and two additional turns before he found himself in Wing F and located the target electrical room.

He slowed his pace as he walked past but didn't stop and continued to the corner, where a bay window with a couple of chairs looked out toward the strip.

"Key card at the door," he spoke quietly, knowing his highly sensitive mic would pick it up.

"I know." Carolyn was unfazed. "I've got your location. When you approach the door, I'll trigger it."

He sat for a moment longer then slid on his transparent nitrile gloves and glanced back down the hall, which looked relatively normal. A pair of orderlies wheeled a bed past his position, and several others bustled about doing their jobs.

When things seemed to quiet down, Max rose and walked slowly down the hall. He was not ten feet from the door when he spotted the same security guard he'd seen earlier approaching in the opposite direction. The man was even larger when standing, well over six feet, and while he'd appeared overweight when seated, he carried his mass well. Max looked back to the door, and seeing the keypad glow transition from red to green, he quickly signaled Carolyn.

"Abort," he whispered.

"What's up?" Carolyn responded almost immediately, and the keypad quickly switched back to red. Max checked his pace and watched as the security guard waved his own pass at the door and entered when the light turned green. Thankfully, he didn't show any sign he'd noticed the light changing color earlier.

"Security arrived ahead of me," Max reported as he continued to walk down the hall, finding another group of chairs so he could sit down and still see the door.

Max could hear the tapping of her keyboard over the open mic. After a moment, Carolyn's voice returned. "My fault," she said.

"What's up?"

"I scrambled the video today so there would be no record of you, but I miskeyed the loop from yesterday's footage, so they must have seen a scrambled feed. The front desk alerted security, so they are correcting it."

"OK. What next?"

"Give me a sec, Max. Sorry."

After a long four minutes, Carolyn spoke again.

"OK. We're good. I let him reset the video, but as it went live, I swapped in a feed from yesterday. They'll catch on after a while, but we should have time to do what you need to do and leave before it's noticed. Hopefully, I can switch it back and nobody will be the wiser."

"That was close."

"Sorry."

"Don't be. I appreciate all you're doing."

As they spoke, the security guard exited the server room and walked back toward the main elevator. As he passed Max at the hallway intersection, he gave him a polite nod before turning left through the double doors.

Max waited for another five minutes, watching the hallway traffic. Nothing seemed out of place. He looked down at the gloves on his hands and wondered if anyone thought them unusual, but the hospital was good cover.

"OK. You ready for round two?" he asked.

"Let's do it." She sounded excited. "The door will be open when you arrive."

"Here we go." Max got up and returned to the server room. In the hallway ahead of him were a pair of orderlies, but the only person facing him was a middle-aged lady walking with an IV stand. He could see the keypad glow green as he approached, and he paused to look causal then he twisted the handle and pushed the door open. Inside, the automatic lights lit up in sterile white as he entered and the door closed behind him.

Racks of servers filled the room's walls, and a desk with a full computer setup and four monitors displaying the hospital's name and logo sat against the left wall. On the opposite wall was another door, but with no key-card access pad. The room was even cooler than the rest of the hospital and oddly smelled even more sterile.

"Do I need to log in?" Max asked, eyeing the computer.

"No. Go into the second room," Carolyn directed.

In three strides, Max had the second door open, and again automatic white lights sprang to life. This space was tighter. It was narrow, almost a hallway, and lined on both sides with racks of servers. The ones on the right wall seemed to be larger and had more lights, but apart from that, it was a mass of black cabinets to Max.

"OK, the right wall is storage. You are looking for NAS-3. They should be labeled."

Max stepped farther in and scanned the wall. Sure enough, along the bottom, spaced a little farther apart than the others, were four boxes labeled NAS 1-4.

"Got it."

"Open the top. The screws are on the sides at the corners, but you only have to loosen them for the top to come off."

Carolyn had reviewed this with him earlier, so he was already at work using the small screwdriver he'd brought with him. The top was off in no time, revealing the expected jumble of circuit boards, fans, and wires.

"There is a row of eight black boxes about the size of a paperback . . . Shit." Carolyn's calm broke. "You've got to hurry. Remove the third one."

"What's wrong?"

"Security is returning. Get the drive. I'm jamming the door."

"Third from which direction?"

"Fuck. Give me a sec."

Max could hear her typing, but he also heard a bump at the outer door. He reached in and pulled two drives out, the third one in from each side.

"I think I've got it," he reported, not waiting for a response. He left the drive cover on the floor and moved back to the first room, closing the door behind him and putting a hard drive in each of his back pockets.

"Confirming it's offline, so you have the right drive . . . and something else."

Max could see the door shaking.

"Release the door," he instructed, stepping to the side that would be blocked when the door swung in.

"Done."

A click confirmed her work, and the door almost instantly swung in.

"Hey, I'm in. Disregard previous." The squawk of a two-way handheld chirped as the guard reported his progress. He was still on the other side of the open door.

"Roger that," came the staticky reply. "Thanks, Dan."

The guard entered and moved to the computer, allowing the door to close behind him, but with his back to Max, he was not alerted. He leaned over the computer, put his radio down, and typed on the keyboard.

Max quickly ran through his options. He could easily get out of the room, but not without alerting the guard, and he was too far from the exit. That meant he'd need to incapacitate the guard, but he didn't want to hurt the guy either—at least not permanently.

On the other side of the guard, the four screens came to life, and he must have seen what he wanted because he tapped another key and then stood up, turning to look at the door to the server room.

Max pulled one of the hard drives out of his right back pocket and palmed it, taking a quiet step closer.

The guard slowly turned the handle to the server room and pushed the door open wide, his hand immediately dropping to the gun at his waist.

"What the fuck?" the guard said, staring for a moment at the floor of the server room before he started to spin back into the room.

As his head came around, Max closed the final two feet between them and slammed the hard drive against the man's forehead, knocking him backward onto the computer desk. The guard fell hard, but the desk supported him, while the keyboard, mouse, and walkie-talkie bounced off, clattering to the floor. Max had hoped that would be all that was needed, but the man's eyes, still scrunched in pain, stared back at him with a brightness that told Max the fight was not over. He followed up with a quick jab to the man's right eye, but that was to distract him. He didn't want to go toe to toe with this guy, but he needed to keep him away from the still-holstered pistol.

Instinct taking over, he dropped the hard drive and quickly bent to grab the big man's left foot, twisting it aggressively, which forced the guard to flip over and crash to the floor. Max was on top of his back in an instant. He clutched the man's left arm, but before he could get it into a pinned position, the man's strength returned, and he yanked it away. Max's only opening was to go for the throat, and he only barely got his right arm around the man's thick neck as the guard flipped himself over, landing on top of Max and arching his back so his shoulders pressed hard against Max's chest.

The move had put Max on the defensive and he was vulnerable. It would be a battle of wills as to who could last longer. Max pulled hard with his right arm, now locked in place with his left hand, anchoring the grip. He tucked his head as low as he could, but the guard reached it with one hand, grabbing some of Max's hair and pulling even as he dropped his weight on Max's lower body then lifted himself on his toes and did it again.

Max withstood the blows, but his own head was spinning from lack of air. He knew it was only a diaphragm spasm, but that knowledge did not help. He gritted his teeth and continued to pull.

The big man raised himself to his toes again and for a third time dropped his weight on Max, this time almost breaking the hold, but Max re-gripped with his left hand and continued to pull, finally feeling some of the fight leaving his opponent. The hand in his hair slackened and let go, and the man's weight no longer moved on top of him. Max counted slowly to ten before releasing the hold. After that struggle, he didn't want to risk the man recovering quickly.

He rolled the limp body off to one side, pausing on all fours and breathing heavily to bring oxygen back to his system.

"Max?" Carolyn said faintly, but it wasn't in his ear. "Max? Talk to me."

He looked around and saw the tiny earpiece on the floor close to his left hand. He needed a couple more breaths to steady himself before he retrieved and reinserted it.

"I'm OK," he said, still breathing heavily. "Had a discussion with the guard. I won."

"Max?"

"He'll be fine, but he will have one hell of a bump on his forehead."

"You should get out of there."

"I know." He picked up the hard drive and returned it to his pocket, checking that the other was also still there. Bending over the guard, he unfastened the safety strap, and removed the unused pistol, tucking the gun into the back of one of the computer racks.

"Am I clear to leave?"

"Looks good," Carolyn reported. "Head out."

In the hallway, he casually removed his gloves and tossed them in a bin on his way to the elevator.

* * *

Max's body was sore, but he had accomplished his goal, and felt a modicum of relief as he passed through the automatic doors into the large breezeway. The surveillance footage was out of the picture. Staci was safe, but he felt only a moment of calm before his mood dimmed when he locked eyes with another visitor coming in through the second set of doors.

"Hey, Max!" Johnny called out, louder than he needed to.

The breezeway was deep, maybe thirty feet between the inner

and outer doors, and the two men met in the middle, shaking hands and stepping to the side.

"Hi, Johnny." Max put on a smile.

"What are you doing here?"

"I was dropping in on an old friend," Max lied. "Turns out he's already gone."

Johnny's face dropped, and he put a hand on Max's shoulder. "I'm sorry to hear that."

"No." Max's smile broadened and he genuinely laughed. "No, he's fine. . . . They sent him home yesterday."

"Oh, man!" Johnny slapped Max's back, returning the laugh. "What are you doin' to me this early? I thought you meant gone as in no longer alive."

"Yeah. He's fine, but I wasted a half hour of my morning." Max wanted to leave but did not want to appear in a rush. "How about you? What are you doing here? Everything alright?"

"Yeah. Fine," Johnny replied then made a point of looking both ways even though the breezeway was empty except for them. "I'm checkin' in on that thing I told you about last night."

Max put a puzzled look on his face and pretended not to remember.

"You know, that girl from the other night and the tapes."

"Oh yeah. The eye in the sky."

Johnny poked a finger on Max's chest. "Bingo."

"Alright, I've got to get back to the Jewel. Still working out the details." Max clapped a hand on Johnny's shoulder and then shifted toward the outer door. He could see his cab pulling up.

"Hey, dude." Johnny's hand caught Max's elbow lightly before he got past. "Are you alright?"

"Sure. Why do you ask?"

"I don't know. You seem sort of out of it."

Max politely pulled his arm away and shook his head.

"Hungover, maybe." He put on a smile. "That was a good party. Better than my usual haunts."

Johnny returned the grin. "Get used to it. Eddie likes you."

Inside the hospital, an alarm sounded, drawing both men's attention. At the inner door, a light flashed red, and Max could see more lights down the hallway.

"What the fuck?" Johnny groaned, still looking inside.

"Something's wrong," Max offered, knowing exactly what was wrong.

The two watched as a pair of security guards ran past the inner doors, which opened and closed automatically. Others in the hall were pulling to the sides as the alarm continued its pulsating, siren-like wail.

"Hey, dude. I'm not sticking around. You want a lift?" Max offered, turning once more toward the exit.

Johnny looked back at him with a questioning glare.

"Nah. I'm gonna stay here and do what I was gonna do."

"OK." Max couldn't help but feel like the tone had shifted. "I'll see you around."

"Yeah." Johnny answered over his shoulder. "You be good."

# CHAPTER NINE

For the second time in an hour, Max handed his cab driver two hundred-dollar bills as he exited her cab at the Desert Jewel.

"Thanks, hun. Have a great day," he offered, receiving only a perfunctory reply as the cab peeled off into the Las Vegas morning traffic.

He didn't really care, but two things in Vegas always amazed him. First, how easy it was to get what you wanted by spending a little money. Second, and very much connected to the first, was how matter-of-factly everyone treated big tips. Anywhere else, a two-hundred-dollar tip for a twenty-dollar ride would have provoked thanks and maybe even some enthusiasm. Here, it was just another tip—higher than most, but expected. Move on to the next job.

Still standing outside, he rolled his head slowly in a full circle in both directions, enjoying the slight cracks and pops that helped relieve tension. Next, he turned his torso left and right, allowing his bruised core to stretch. He would be sore later, and every little stretch now and throughout the day would help improve the healing process. He wanted to stretch more, but it was too hot on the porte-cochère, and he was already almost an hour late.

Upstairs, now in the cool casino air, Max walked toward the makeshift conference room, aware that he could not hide his late entrance. He quietly eased the door open and slipped into a seat at the near end of the conference table, catching a few welcoming nods, though he knew none of them would approve of his late arrival. In truth, he didn't either. Being punctual was one of his defining traits. There were several reasons, but principally it showed respect for others and encouraged trust. In his past career, it could mean the difference between life and death.

Wei Zhang had been speaking, and when he finished, he turned to look directly at Max with an expression that appeared similar to the acknowledged disappointment of a father when his son came home after curfew.

"Mr. Kline, thank you for joining us." He did not smile, but Max guessed that would be the last he heard of it. "We were discussing a pair of stories in the news this morning. Have you seen?"

"The fire?" Max asked. "Yes. Very sad."

"Tragic," Wei replied. "And not great for us either. The Wild

Horse is another Tri-Star property, and the papers are up in arms about the mafia connection."

"That's good for us, no?" Max asked. "Puts them on a weaker footing."

"You might think that." Wei's voice was strained. "Except our friend the mayor has come out railing against the tragedy and backing an unsubstantiated story that the fire was set by undocumented immigrants.

"On the surface, this has no effect on our transaction, but it's a short step from 'undocumented alien' to 'foreigner' in general. We've already seen a couple of bloggers who've made the leap and are posting against our takeover."

"I don't see the issue." Max leaned forward. "We have the blessing of the regulators."

"Open your eyes." Ling's tone was dismissive. "As with almost everything, it is always about the politics. Whatever existed yesterday is now gone. We're starting from scratch, and there will be more scrutiny of Haoyun and the deal.

"It's curious," Ling added immediately. "Given the Marchetti family history, we did not expect that we would be the ones under the microscope."

"Do we have any skeletons in the closet?" Max asked, following the obvious implication.

"Not in the least," Wei answered. "Haoyun has an impeccable reputation both here and at home."

"That's not really what I asked," Max could not help but say, holding up a hand to prevent his employer from responding. "But I get it. We're clean. So where do we go from here?"

"I think that's why we hired you, Mr. Kline," Jun spoke for the first time. "What is the most painless path to closure?"

"Isn't it obvious?" Max was sincere, but as he looked around at blank faces, he continued, "Jump on board. Issue a statement agreeing with the mayor. As a new business in Las Vegas, we are against crime, and illegal immigration is a crime, right?"

"Isn't the mayor a democrat?" Jun asked. "Why is he anti-immigrant?"

"He'd flip on his mother if he thought there was an edge. Immigration is like that. Both sides will play off it depending on the wind, and right now it seems like the wind is blowing anti-immigration."

"Won't that ring hollow coming from us?" Ling asked.

"Not in the least. People look at headlines and rarely think things through. You make a show of support for the mayor, and you'll not only push away the anti-foreigner sentiment, but you'll be winning points with Rodriguez."

"It makes me wonder who Rodriguez really has in his pocket,"

Wei added quietly.

All eyes turned to Max, but he did not immediately respond, allowing the ideas to rattle through his head.

He straightened in his chair. "I assume you are referring to Geno." He crafted his reply to deflect the implication and refocus the room on the true enemy. "And there is definitely more to their relationship than campaign funding."

He couldn't reveal what Staci had seen connecting the mayor to the Marchetti family and he hoped it wouldn't affect the deal.

"Yes." Ling smiled. "We have reason to believe that they have deeper ties, but we have nothing concrete. Your advice on this issue is sound."

Max acknowledged with a nod, and others did the same. Only Jun Chen seemed unimpressed; he showed little reaction, his eyes downcast and his lips pursed in what looked like disapproval.

"Good." Wei returned to his seat and put his elbows on the table, interlocking his fingers and surveying the group. "Politics aside, we're pretty much there. James has reviewed the latest reports from Tri-Star on the discrepancies in the Jewel's books, and while we still don't believe they are accurate, we don't see them as a major impediment to either our purchase or to ongoing operations.

"James?" He looked over at his lead accountant. "The floor is yours."

Wei unceremoniously pushed his chair over to Ling's side so that the table had an uninterrupted view of the large TV at that end of the room. The screen sprang to life with a mirror view of James's laptop and a very complicated financial spreadsheet.

For his part, Max ignored the slides and instead watched the table to see who was interested in the presentation. He had no suspicions, but in a deal this size, it was smart practice to watch your own team as much as the opponent's. He still heard bits of the report, but most of it was noise.

# CHAPTER TEN

Not twenty-four hours later, little had changed despite hours of presentations and discussions about the details of the merger. They had meetings well into the previous night, and the day's sessions had started promptly at eight.

While he acknowledged it was appropriate for him to take part, Max had questioned the value of rehashing numbers that would not truly have a significant impact on the future business. The current speaker had at least captured Max's attention with two points in his report. First, he'd mentioned the large increase in the Desert Jewel's catering business, which prepared and delivered vast amounts of specialty food to the other casinos. The overall size of the business had tripled in the last two years, though curiously, profitability had remained close to break-even.

The Jewel's accountant team had prepared a detailed profit-and-loss analysis, but James had identified several potential problems with the report. At the end, he'd concluded that Haoyun could run a much more profitable operation if they eliminated many of the bookkeeping shenanigans. The other option, he had suggested, was to shutter the catering business, but when that surfaced, Jun was quick to interject without room for discussion that the catering division would continue after the acquisition.

The second thing that interested Max was that James had uncovered a minor embezzlement case within the Jewel's accounting department. He had relayed his data to the Tri-Star team, and they had told him they would handle it before the ownership transfer. To James, this was another minor issue, but Max thought about Staci, wondering if she could help. He made a mental note to ask her what she knew.

The meeting ended at twelve thirty, and the group headed to the main room, where another large buffet of Chinese food was waiting for them.

Max was filling a plate when he felt a tap on his elbow, and Ling was at his side.

"Come sit with us." She nodded toward Wei's office, and Max could see him already seated at the small round table within.

Moments later, he allowed the door to close behind him and put his plate on the table. To his right sat Ling, with a similarly full plate in front of her, and to his left sat Wei, with only a cup of water in his hands.

"Why were you late, yesterday?" Wei asked, eschewing any formality.

"Something came up," he answered honestly. "I had to take care of it."

Wei nodded but said nothing.

Max looked from one to the other. "It won't happen again," he offered.

Ling put her chopsticks on her plate purposefully and turned back to Max, holding her left hand in front of her mouth for a moment before speaking.

"We are paying you very well. I respect that you have other interests, but Haoyun must be your only focus right now. This is too important for distractions."

Max nodded his agreement, but it wasn't enough.

"Please tell us you understand," Ling demanded.

For a moment, Max considered walking away from the entire transaction. He liked the work but was a free agent and not some feudal vassal. But he wasn't a quitter either. *Check your ego*, he told himself.

"I understand the importance," he said slowly and deliberately.

"Good." Wei rose, leaving his water on the table as he left the room.

Ling watched him leave then turned back to Max.

"Have you found anything?"

"On Tri-Star? No, nothing yet. Any contact with the DA?"

"No." Ling shook her head. "And we've made inquiries. Whatever the DA is working on, it is not public."

"Odd." Max was genuinely curious.

"What do you know about Genoa Imports?" Ling asked abruptly. Max shrugged.

"Nothing. I assume you are about to tell me why I'll care."

"Genoa Imports is a distribution company owned and controlled by the Rodriguez family, as in Mayor Rodriguez. They supply the bulk of the specialty food products to the catering arm of the Desert Jewel, which serves a good number of the casinos on the strip.

"Genoa's business with the Jewel has grown significantly in the last year," Ling continued. "As you heard this morning, the food and beverage division experienced a spike in volume, and Genoa supplies most of the product. But profitability has been stagnant. The Jewel has seen no benefit from the increased activity."

"So are they skimming? Or is it a kickback?" Max guessed.

"They are skimming everywhere." Ling sounded disgusted. "But it's most likely a kickback. Have you heard of the American Construction Corporation?"

"No. Why?"

"They're building the Las Vegas section of the high-speed rail. Or, they will be. The deal hasn't been signed, but they are close. Some of the news outlets have run a few stories questioning their experience."

"It's a big project. But around here, they must know someone."

"Exactly. How does a construction company with no history on major projects get awarded a two-billion-dollar contract?" Ling did not wait for a response. "I'll explain. Do you know how Tri-Star plans to use the money from the sale of the Desert Jewel?"

Max shrugged, putting a piece of kung pao chicken in his mouth.

"The American Construction Corporation is a Delaware corporation fully owned and controlled by the Marchetti family," Ling continued through pursed lips. "You won't be able to trace that, but it's true. The Marchettis are using the money from the sale of the Jewel to finance the ACC. They are literally planning to start digging in a few months, and unless this deal closes, they don't have the money for shovels."

"So why are we paying a premium?" Max asked before thinking, immediately wishing he hadn't.

"We are fine with the price," Ling bristled. "We were discussing Genoa Imports."

Max could sense there was something more that she wasn't saying.

"You don't like the price." He gambled. "Do you, Ling?"

She put her chopsticks down and straightened in her chair.

"My opinion is not part of this discussion." She spoke with icy calm. "I wanted you to have some context. Rodriguez and the Marchettis are definitely tied at the hip, and that's where we need your . . . expertise."

Max said nothing but tilted his head slightly as if to offer her an opening to explain.

"Haoyun Casino has a long history in the gambling business, but we are at a disadvantage here. It is not, as you say, our turf. We'd like to gain some leverage while we're here, and Rodriguez seems to be the one at the center of it all."

"I understand." A warning light flicked on in the back of his mind. He was crossing into a gray area and would have to be careful. "Sounds like I need to know more about Genoa Imports."

"It would be a good place to start." Ling picked up her chopsticks and took a bite. When she finished chewing, she reached to the desk behind her and picked up a stack of papers, handing them to Max.

"This is what we have so far. Public records and their financial history with respect to the Jewel."

"Thank you." Max finally put his finger on what had been bothering him. "Wei doesn't know about this, does he?"

"Don't make more of this than there is," Ling answered without looking up from her plate. "Wei is completely in charge."

"Sure, but you think he's making a mistake and you're hoping I can help prove it."

"Mr. Kline." She met his eyes with an unblinking stare. "You know nothing of Haoyun Casino. Please do your job, as we have discussed."

Max couldn't stop a smile from appearing. "Damn it, Ling," he said. "I think I like your style."

Ling gave him a slight nod as she resumed eating. "I shouldn't hold you any longer. I know you have work to do."

Max looked down regretfully at his almost full plate, knowing he was dismissed. He pushed his chair back and rose, returning the nod to Ling.

"Thank you. I'll let you know what I find."

"Things are moving quickly, Max." Ling was almost apologetic. "We need to know what we don't know, and I don't have time for . . ." She paused as if searching for a word. "I don't have time for traditional due diligence."

"Got it."

Outside the office, Max headed toward the food service, carrying his forsaken meal. He dropped his plate on a tray of used dishes, hating the waste.

As he did, Wei appeared on his right side, leaning in to whisper, "The food isn't any good anyway. Try The Taco Stand by the pool."

Max returned a smile, wondering if the old man would approve of Ling's work.

"Will do."

* * *

After a quick elevator ride, Max once again sat at the players deck by The Taco Stand. Part of him didn't like that he was following Wei's suggestion, but good food was good food, and he was still hungry. The conversation with Ling had been uncomfortable and a surprise. He had to remind himself again that this was a payday, and when you took someone's money, you played by their rules. You didn't have to like it.

At the entrance, he caught a familiar face and saw Ben Carpenter wave, clearly indicating to the hostess that he would join Max. He wore a Hawaiian shirt and slacks and could have passed for an islander, though his tight physique might be slightly off from the stereotype.

"I'd say we have to stop meeting like this," Ben began as he nestled into the chair opposite him, "but I was looking for you, so this really isn't a coincidence."

One thing about Ben—he was a straight shooter, at least with Max. The two had a bond beyond the poker table, having both served in the Middle East. Ben had been deployed with the Army Rangers right after 9/11, first in Afghanistan and later in Iraq.

"So you've come to apologize?" Max bluffed.

"Apologize?"

"By now you've got the surveillance footage." He pressed his bet. "So I assume you're going to tell me you've cleared my name and are sorry to have implied that it could have been me."

Ben didn't respond but looked Max in the eyes and stroked his mustache, mouth firmly closed.

When he spoke, he seemed to change the subject.

"How's Phil doing? Did he go home?" He lowered his hand to his beard.

"Yeah, he checked out yesterday," Max offered. "I assume he's doing well."

"So you weren't at the hospital this morning, were you?" Ben's eyes were piercing.

"Why do you ask, Ben?" Max grinned. "I actually was there. Totally forgot that he'd checked out. Stupid because it made me late for work too. What's going on?"

Answer the question and ask a question. That was his playbook. They had trained him well as a negotiator. If you only answered questions, you were always on defense, and the opponent had control, but give a straightforward answer and return with your own question, then you were fighting back. It was like tennis—put the ball back in the opponent's court. Keep *them* on defense.

"I honestly hope you don't know," Ben answered as he pushed back and crossed his legs.

A waitress arrived with Max's tacos. She asked Ben if he wanted anything, and he ordered a root beer.

"Put it on my tab," Max told the waitress as she spun away.

"I know you aren't an investigator," Ben began again when they were alone. "But do you know one of the key tenants to an investigation?"

"Tell me." Max picked up the first of his tacos and took a bite.

"We learn early on that there is no such thing as coincidence." Ben spoke slowly with the slight twang that made him sound like an Old West lawman. "Now, granted, at some point we may determine a thing exists that might rule out one thing or another, but most of the time, in an investigation, there is no such thing as fucking coincidence."

Max finished the first taco but couldn't help but feel his anger rising. He wasn't really angry at Ben. The man was doing his job, but this was the second lunch in under an hour that was getting ruined.

And he had no choice but to keep playing the game.

"You're not telling me what's going on."

"OK. Let's pretend you don't know that someone broke into the hospital security room this morning and removed the surveillance footage for the past week." Ben uncrossed his legs and leaned his elbows on the table. "Whoever it was took out a security officer and managed to jam the live feed while all this was happening."

"And?" He left the question hanging for what became an uncomfortable silence before he gave in. "Wait, you think this was me?" Max put on his best puzzled look. "Ben—Officer Carpenter—I was in the hospital for maybe ten minutes. I made a mistake about Phil. That's it."

As an alibi, he thought he should bring up the meeting with Johnny when the alarm sounded, but that would tie him to a known criminal, so he left that part out.

The waitress interrupted again to deliver Ben's soda.

"Two events have occurred at the hospital in the last four days that are highly irregular, and you've confirmed you were there when both events occurred." Ben took a sip through the straw, which seemed to disappear behind his thick mustache. "No coincidences."

Max allowed his friend's words to sit as he finished his second taco.

"I get it, Ben," he finally answered. "It doesn't look great, and if I were in your shoes, I'd be asking the same questions. Unfortunately, I don't know anything about it."

"If you're in trouble, I might be able to help," Ben offered, changing tone.

Max was tiring of the game. Ben was nothing if not thorough. This wasn't over, but he had other things to do, so it was his turn to throw a changeup.

"You know anything about Genoa Imports?" he asked.

"Why do you ask?" A note of recognition, followed by a quizzical stare.

"Doing some recon for my employers. Genoa is a large vendor to the Jewel. Intel op only."

They didn't talk about their shared past much, but they'd occasionally slip into military lingo. It was never intentional but it was comfortable. They both held on to a love of country and dedication to the military establishment.

"I know enough to suggest you should probably leave that one alone." Ben had finished his root beer and pushed the glass to the center of the table. "Genoa is a Rodriguez property, and the Marchettis will protect him. Don't get yourself in trouble."

"Look, this is business. We want this transaction to close, but we need to make sure the ongoing operations are secure."

Ben's eyes narrowed. "You do whatever you have to do, but I'm warning you to be extremely careful with Genoa Imports. They are on my radar too, and I wouldn't want you getting caught up in something you don't understand."

Max nodded. "Fair enough. We done here?"

"Yeah. We're done, but you remember what I've said. I will find out what happened at the hospital, and I can't help you if it turns out you're involved."

Max nodded again, standing up.

"And stay clear of the Marchetti family," Ben warned as he rose from the table. "I don't want to see you in a body bag."

Max left cash on the table, and the two men departed the courtyard together.

"Thanks for the soda." Ben's tone had softened. "And you call me if you need anything."

"Will do." They shook hands, and Max turned away.

"I mean it, Max," the detective called after him. "Call me."

Max lifted his hand to acknowledge his friend but didn't turn back. He liked Ben and knew the offer was genuine, but the guy had suggested he was a suspect. Right or wrong, he didn't need to get too close.

# CHAPTER ELEVEN

As he weaved through the slot machines to the casino exit, Max thought about the situation as it now stood. Haoyun was close to closing the purchase of the Desert Jewel, but they wanted dirt on the mayor. Ironically, Max already had dirt on the mayor, but that would require turning over Staci, and that was a nonstarter.

On the other side of the equation was the Marchetti crime family. If he was being truthful with himself, there was something about Eddie that he liked, but he couldn't shake the reality that the man was a convicted felon. The family was also likely responsible for the deaths at the Wild Horse and were searching for Staci and, by extension, him. That simple connection could blow up the whole deal. What was it he had told Staci? One step at a time.

He laughed internally. A little over a week ago, his world was fairly simple. He'd been on a bad losing streak, but cards were cards.

Now, things had become complicated. Shaking his head to clear his thoughts, he pushed through one of the ten glass doors and made his way to the taxi stand, which was annoyingly thirty yards down the sidewalk.

"Yo, Max!" a voice called from the other direction, and he turned to see Eddie leaning against the trunk of a black sedan that Max recognized immediately as a BMW 7 Series. "You need a ride?"

Max raised a hand in greeting, but he was tired and did not want to engage.

"No, thanks. Headed home."

"Aw, come on!" An unfamiliar voice spoke in his left ear, and he found one of Eddie's men standing beside him. Vinny was his name. Max had met him at the first meeting with Tri-Star.

The mobster put his arm around Max's shoulders, steering him toward his boss.

For a moment, Max contemplated taking the man down—something he knew he could do in a heartbeat—but he decided to let things play out and allowed himself to be guided.

"My man," Eddie said slowly when Max arrived in front of him. They shook hands, and Eddie pulled him in for a perfunctory hug. "How are you?"

"I'm doing well. Thanks." There was no reason not to be polite. "How about you?"

"Another day in paradise." Eddie motioned to the surrounding air. "Negotiations seem to be going well, eh? You'll own this place in no time."

"Not me," Max reminded him, "but things seem to be on the right track."

"One way or the other, it's a payday for us all."

"I'm all for that." Max continued the banter. "Good to see you, Eddie. I'm going to go grab a cab."

He started to turn, but Eddie stopped him with a hand on his shoulder, and Max couldn't help but notice that Vinny was still behind him.

"Not yet," Eddie said. Then, as if recognizing that Max did not report to him, he changed tack. "Sorry, if you really have to go, it's OK, but I want to show you something. Maybe something that will help the transaction." He lifted his hand and motioned above him, indicating the Desert Jewel.

"Go on." Max hated how Eddie, Geno, and the others always talked in ambiguities.

"Not here." Eddie started toward the driver's side without confirming that Max would join. "Jump in. Just you and me. Vinny has some things to do inside."

"Yeah." Vinny backed up a step before turning toward the casino. "Nice seeing you, Max."

When Max turned back to Eddie, he was standing in the open driver's door.

"You coming? It won't take long."

Max let out a sigh. He would not be getting any rest this afternoon. But getting closer to Eddie couldn't hurt, and maybe he'd find out a little more about the mayor. He put on a smile and moved to get in on the passenger's side.

The black bucket seat was warm from the sun but incredibly comfortable. He made a couple of minor adjustments and buckled in. The whole interior was top of the line, and when the engine purred to life, Max could not help but admire the car. He hadn't owned a vehicle since before his service, and he was intentional about it, but being in a car like this made him rethink the decision. His rentals were never this nice.

They pulled out of the Desert Jewel and onto the street, where Eddie quickly went through three gears before needing to stop at the next intersection.

"Where we headed?" Max asked.

"Uptown." Eddie kept his eyes forward. "I've got something for you."

The light changed, and Eddie was quick off the line, only to coast into another light a block away.

"Look, we think we found someone embezzling at the Jewel."

The car sat at the light, and Eddie turned to look at Max. "I can get you details, but that will help, right?"

"I don't know." Max knew Haoyun had already uncovered this, but he played along. "I guess so."

"You guess so?" Eddie's voice had a tinge of anger. "I'm going out on a limb for you here. I'm waiting for a report, but when it's ready, I should have a name and evidence of one of our employees who stole from us."

"OK, thank you." Max did not want Eddie mad. "That would be great. I'll pass this on to Haoyun."

"It's on the down-low for now though, OK?" Eddie was driving again, but still he turned to glance at Max for confirmation. "Slow down the transaction until it comes up, but they can't officially know you're hearing this from me."

Max nodded.

"I understand. Thanks, Eddie."

"I got another thing to talk about." Eddie pulled onto the highway, headed north.

"Shoot."

"Ha. Funny choice of words." Eddie seemed to have relaxed. "Geno made you an offer the other night. Look, I'm as loyal to Geno as anyone, but it doesn't have to go down that way. We know what you can do. What you've done. I mean . . . your service to our country. I want you to know there are other avenues."

"Other avenues?" Max mirrored, wondering again how these men knew so much about him.

"Yeah. You don't have to be official. I could use a man on the side."

There it was—exactly what Max did not want. He started to respond, but Eddie interrupted him.

"I can set you up in a legitimate job, anything you want. And no one would know what you did for me. You'd be needed once, maybe twice a year, tops. Forget about Geno's offer. This would be super part-time for you."

"Sorry, Eddie. I'm happy doing what I do."

"I thought you might say that." Eddie did not seem deterred. "That's OK. It's an open offer and not one I make lightly. There are other benefits too. Most importantly, you'd be under my protection."

Max hated this position. No way he was going to work for this guy, but offending him risked his best chance of digging deeper into Genoa Imports.

"Do you think I need protection?" he asked lightheartedly.

"No, man. Not protection in that sense. I mean serious 'don't fuck with this guy' protection." Eddie's voice was serious too. "That means something anywhere, but in *this* town it's huge."

"I'll give it some thought," Max offered.

"You do that." Eddie had an air about his speech as if he knew better. "You never know when you're going to need protection."

They turned off the highway near downtown. In Las Vegas, the original downtown area had long been the slightly dilapidated younger cousin to the massive casinos on the strip, but the area had improved since the turn of the century, especially after the Downtown Project of 2012.

Max had expected them to stop at one of the casinos, but they continued to drive deeper into the suburbs of East Las Vegas.

"Where are we going?" Max finally asked again after several minutes of quiet driving.

"You'll see, we're just going for a drive, but I had a thought a moment ago. There was a big to-do at the hospital the other morning. You were there, right?"

"Yeah." Max knew he couldn't deny it. "I was standing there with Johnny when the alarm sounded. Kinda nuts."

"I don't know if he told you, but we've been doing a little private investigation, and he was supposed to get some surveillance video from the hospital."

"No offense, Eddie, but this sounds like something I don't want to be involved with."

The big man turned to look at Max, which was a little disturbing, as they were still moving down the street.

After several seconds, Eddie looked forward again.

"Yeah, you're probably right. You don't want to get involved, but listen to this story. Monday night, we had a friend at the hospital, but she got away before we could talk to her. Somebody helped her slip by a police guard and left with her and an EMT. We thought the footage would help us clear things up."

They reached a stop sign, and Eddie turned back to look at Max. "But somebody got there ahead of us and took the tapes, but here's the deal." He held up a finger, half pointing it at Max. "We got the EMT on duty that night."

"OK," Max responded casually, but inside his senses immediately became more alert. "What of it?"

Eddie looked at him with an innocent expression that seemed intentionally false.

"I think you should meet him," he offered. "Johnny saw you at the hospital, so maybe you mighta seen the same guy? You know, compare notes? You good with that?"

While Eddie's voice maintained its friendly tone, the threat was unmistakable. Max's mind raced to find a way out, but nothing came to mind. Adrenaline pulsed unbidden in his veins. He needed to be ready to fight if push came to shove. For now, he had no choice but to play along.

"I doubt I have much to offer, but it can't hurt. Right?"

* * *

Five minutes later, they pulled into a large apartment complex consisting of two-story buildings that sprawled out from the entrance on both sides of a main drive. Typical of many older apartment complexes in Las Vegas, they were all external walk-ups with stairs on both ends and catwalks across the upper stories. Max guessed they built the complex in the seventies or early eighties.

Eddie cruised almost to the end of the main road before jerking to the right, down a smaller street that led to another row of buildings. He slid into an available parking spot and turned to Max as he put the car in park.

"You remember what I said, OK?" His demeanor had shifted and his voice was almost a growl.

Max had been handling bullies for the past twenty years, but it never stopped getting under his skin. At least now he recognized the feeling and could divert from the more aggressive response that was second nature. He played dumb.

"Sorry?"

"You work for me and—" Eddie clamped his mouth shut and looked down, slapping his hand on the wheel. After a moment, he looked up. "Sorry, you work *with* me, and no one will ever fuck with you."

"They don't fuck with me now."

Eddie laughed.

"Yeah, that's probably true, but you have to earn it. What I'm offering won't take any effort at all, at least not that anyone sees. You take care of things behind the scenes—it stays between you and me. And to the rest of this town, you're a guy they know they can't touch."

"I'll think about it." Max wanted to avoid any commitment, and his mind was still racing about what the EMT would do when he walked in the room. "So you've got this guy holed up here? Isn't that kidnapping?"

Again, Eddie laughed.

"Nah. He can come and go as he pleases. Our guys keep him company when he's off work."

Max raised a questioning eyebrow.

"We're helping keep an eye on his dogs too." Eddie opened his door, adding, "Everyone's got a soft spot for something."

Outside, Max joined Eddie on the curb, and the car beeped twice as Eddie put his keys in his pocket and they walked along the sidewalk that led to the center of the building.

As they passed through an open breezeway to the other side of the building, Eddie turned to the left and went about halfway down, where he stopped and knocked on the door of a ground-level apartment. Almost immediately, they could hear high-pitched barking in response.

Max took in a deep breath, rolling his fingers on both hands behind his back to loosen them up. If the EMT recognized him, he was probably in for a fight, and it always helped to prep the body. When Eddie was facing away, he loosened his shoulders as well. Unless the guys inside were fully armed, he could probably manage the situation.

The door opened, and the sound of barking intensified. One of Eddie's men stood in the doorway. Max had met him at the rooftop party, but he could not remember the name. He nodded without saying anything and stepped aside, opening the door wider.

Eddie entered, and Max followed, scanning the area for the EMT, but no one else was there. Ahead of them, a hall led to the back of the house, and to the right was another small room. To the left, on the other side of a short pony wall, was a living room with a couch, two chairs, and a coffee table that was strewn with chip bags and soda cans. A cooking show played on the TV on the far wall, but the volume was low. The dogs continued to bark from the interior and Max thought he glimpsed one jumping at a gate down the hall.

"Yo, Johnny!" Eddie called out and, as if on cue, Johnny appeared in the hallway, stepping over the gate that Max had seen, a plate of nachos in one hand. He wore casual clothing but sported a dark-blue blazer.

"Eddie!" he replied, putting the plate down on a credenza in the hall. "I thought you were coming later."

The two men exchanged a hug. Johnny then offered his hand to Max, who accepted it and was surprised when Johnny pulled him into a hug as well. Max returned the hug as gracefully as he could, noticing the shoulder holster under Johnny's jacket.

"Good to see you, Max," Johnny said before turning to Eddie. "Our boy isn't back from work."

Max tried not to change his expression, but he relaxed slightly.

Eddie shook his head. "Johnny, I fucking told you I was coming with Max."

"I know, Eddie, but the guy's still got to work. Otherwise, we draw attention."

Max stepped toward the TV and pretended to be interested in the show. Behind him, the two men continued to bicker, but his mind was processing the conversation. Eddie planned to take him here, so they were obviously suspicious about the hospital, but why had Eddie made his offer on the drive here? If he was trying to identify him, the offer made little sense, unless he was also offering amnesty. Maybe this was effectively a blackmail situation: "Work for me, or Geno learns what you did."

A hand rested on his shoulder.

"We'll come back another time," Eddie said, already moving toward the door.

"No problem," he said, following his ride. "Do you mind dropping me at the Wynn?"

Eddie turned in the doorway, his large frame blocking most of the sunlight.

"I can drop you at home."

"The Wynn is great," Max responded. He had a rule against giving out his home address, and he could check out the poker room. If there was a good game, a few hours at the table would be a great diversion.

"Building B, Room 204?" Eddie asked, but it was not a question. It was the building and room number of Max's apartment. It was also a message: "I know where you live."

Max nodded but for a moment was speechless. Finally, he let out a laugh.

"OK, I guess I should have known that." He met Eddie's gaze, and the big man raised an eyebrow as if to say, "You see, not so dumb."

Max lifted his hands to either side in surrender. "I'd still like to go to the Wynn though."

Eddie moved out of the door, calling over his shoulder. "You got it, maestro. And you should give some thought to my offer. It's good to have protection."

CHAPTER TWELVE

The whine of the air-conditioning fan was a constant distraction. It wasn't that it was blowing too hard, but behind the airflow Staci could hear a faint squeal and wondered if she was the only one who heard it. For probably the tenth time that afternoon, she tried to dismiss it, shaking her head slightly and rubbing her ears.

Her desk was a mess of paperwork, but on her computer screen was the final draft of her summary report. It had taken longer than she had expected to complete, but she was fairly sure she'd answered all of Haoyun's questions without revealing the accounting irregularities that had allowed her bosses to strip value out of the casino.

In truth, her accounting hid more than that. She had learned much in her time in Vegas and had put some money aside for herself too. It had been one of the scariest things she had ever done, and for six months she had been in constant terror of being uncovered, but the acquisition of the Desert Jewel had been a lifesaver. Her boss had given her the responsibility of covering up past indiscretions, which meant she had carte blanche to slide her own transactions under the rug with the rest.

She hit return and moved her mouse over to the spellcheck box one last time. As she clicked through the results—mostly proper names she could override—she started to question herself. Would Haoyun accept the report? She knew Pam would accept it. That ornery bitch rarely looked past the cover of anything. Inhaling deeply, she let out a breath. *No sense wondering*, she thought to herself as she attached the Excel file to her email along with the written report and clicked send.

"You finish that report?" Jerry's voice startled her, and her left hand inadvertently knocked a small stack of papers to the floor.

"Jesus, Jerry," she scolded him, immediately reaching to pick up her mess.

He squatted outside her cubical and picked up the few that had spilled out, handing them back as he stood up.

"Sorry, Staci. I know Pam's been hot and heavy about getting that report to Haoyun. She told me to see if I could help."

"I literally hit send a second ago."

"Oh, cool. Hey, what are you going to do with the money?"

Staci froze, feeling a rush of blood to her face. How could he know about the money she had stolen? She made an effort to restack her papers while she thought of her response.

"We're all getting a bonus when this goes through," Jerry continued. "I'm going to put it toward an apartment, depending on how much it is."

The blood left her face.

"I'm not sure, Jer. I guess I'll wait to see how big it is."

She couldn't care less about the bonus. After the deal's completion, her theft would be permanently concealed, and she could plan to move on—hopefully somewhere with Eddie.

"Yeah. Close the deal already. Right?" Jerry was still leaning on the wall of her cubicle.

"I hear that." She collected the other papers that had taken over her desk, stacking them on top of the first pile. "Hey, Jer, I've been so consumed by this report that I've got to catch up on some things. I'll stop by later to see you."

"O-kay." He extended the word in jest, adding, "I know when I'm not wanted."

Tapping her wall twice, he turned and strode toward his own cubicle, not fifty feet away.

Staci hadn't been lying. She had an inbox loaded with unopened emails on top of a to-do list that was a page long. After collecting the papers, she considered tossing them, but old habits wouldn't allow her that comfort. There was, of course, a slight chance that someone might ask questions about the report, so she wrapped a large rubber band around the stack and tucked it into her already packed filing cabinet.

Turning back to her computer, she scanned her emails to make sure nothing was pressing. Most of them were things she needed to process but that could wait one more day. She answered a couple of simple inquiries from vendors and was about to return to her to-do list when she saw two emails arrive almost simultaneously. Both were replies to her report: one from her boss, and one from Eddie.

She immediately opened Eddie's but was disappointed to see it only read, "Great work."

Eddie wasn't really on the financial side of the business, but as vice president of operations for Tri-Star Enterprises, he was being copied on everything related to the acquisition. She'd enjoyed seeing his name more frequently in her inbox, and every once in a while he'd include an emoji or a subtle hint of their relationship in his comments. This week, something had changed. Maybe it was the intensity of the final negotiation, but all of his notes had been cold and impersonal. Even the other night when they'd been together, he'd seemed more distant.

The whine of the air conditioner returned, and she shook her head to clear it as she opened the second email.

"Finally," Pam's email read. "I've forwarded this to Haoyun. Hope it resolves any issues."

Classic. Pam clearly hadn't bothered to read the report before sending it on. Not for the first time, Staci wondered how Pam could have reached her position. The woman was lazy and drunk half the time.

Another email from Pam appeared in her inbox and she clicked on it immediately, then regretted doing so. "My office," it read simply.

* * *

Ten minutes later, Staci knocked on the half-open door as she entered Pam's office.

"Hey, Pam." She smiled. "You wanted to see me?"

Inside, her boss sat behind her desk, eyes focused on her computer screen as she typed away at the keyboard. She held one hand out, pointing to another chair where Staci should sit, but her eyes never left the computer, and she offered no words of welcome. Staci sat down and waited. Her boss was very task-oriented, and this was not uncommon. Everyone in the office knew Pam preferred to work on one thing to completion before starting another.

"This acquisition sure has changed the office, right?" Pam added a purposeful concluding tap to her keyboard as she turned from it to meet Staci's eye. "We've gone from repetitive filings to special reports and analyses, and they keep asking for more."

Staci wasn't sure if she should respond, so she nodded slightly.

"I wonder if we'll ever get back to the good ol' days," Pam continued. "Once Haoyun takes over, will we be doing more of this shit or less?"

"Who knows?" Staci offered weakly. "It's harder work though. I'm OK as things were."

"Yeah, I was too." Pam moved her legs to one side and leaned her right elbow on her desk. "Apparently, we aren't the only ones. So I'll get right to it. You've been a great help on the catering books. Have you noticed anything unusual?"

Staci felt a chill down her spine, but she answered coolly.

"You mean, apart from the work I've done at Eddie's request?"

Although they both knew Staci had been forging the catering books for the past two years, neither of them actually spoke openly of what was being done. It was always "that work" or "Eddie's jobs."

"Yeah." Pam lifted her eyes in recognition. "I mean something else. Have you seen anything besides the work for Eddie?"

"Nope," she lied, putting a questioning look on her face.

"Because that last report you made—not the one you just sent but the one before—Haoyun's team returned it with several questions, so I did a deeper dive myself, and while I know most of it is, as you say,

Eddie's business, I think there is someone else taking a slice."

What was previously a slight chill now turned into a full-on freeze at the back of Staci's head.

"Where?" she asked, hoping she sounded surprised.

"The numbers in our exotics ballooned for two quarters last year. It's not a huge sector, so it wouldn't have stood out except to the pencil pushers at Haoyun. You know that thing you do for Eddie? It looks like a much smaller version happened in exotics for a short time."

"Do you want me to review?"

"No, I've got Jerry digging into it. I wanted to double-check to make sure it wasn't something you knew about." She turned back to her computer.

"Well, it might be." Staci wanted to stay noncommittal, but maybe she could still cover her trail. "These jobs have become more and more convoluted, and I've touched up multiple areas. Maybe you're right. It could have been an Eddie job."

Pam raised an eyebrow, spinning back to face her.

"Oh, really?"

"Yeah. Sure." Staci wasn't sure if her boss was taking the bait or not. "Do you want me to talk with Jerry?"

The look on Pam's face moved from curious to puzzled.

"No, I spoke with Eddie yesterday, and he assured me that his 'business' had no impact on exotics. Frankly, I'm a little surprised you don't have a better handle on this. You're an excellent accountant, Staci. It's not like you to be uncertain."

"Well, it feels like I've been working two jobs for the past week—my regular job and then all these reports."

"Hopefully there's a payday at the end." Pam turned back to her computer and began typing, adding, "For us all."

Staci sat in her chair for a moment before she realized the conversation was over.

"Thanks, Pam." She stood up and moved toward the door. "Here's hoping."

In fact, she was losing hope.

"Try to get some rest." Pam's voice followed her out the door. "No more special reports today."

## CHAPTER THIRTEEN

Everyone on the Haoyun team had been provided with comped rooms to operate. As a Vegas resident, Max didn't need the room to sleep, but it came in handy for a bit of quiet work. He'd spent the last hour skimming through the Internet on Genoa Imports and the stack of relevant financials that the accounting group had delivered before he'd returned from lunch.

Genoa Imports was thriving. Its business with the Desert Jewel alone had increased from several million a year to almost fifty million on an annual run rate. In the past two years, Max counted eleven different stories celebrating the Desert Jewel for winning a concession at a new Las Vegas property, most of them among the larger casinos. Cross-referencing the stories with the financials, every new concession corresponded with a significant boost to business with Genoa Imports. Several of the stories connected the two businesses, but with both companies privately held, there was little detail on the financial end, and perhaps more surprisingly, none of the stories addressed the Rodriguez family ownership, though a few suggested mob ties.

Interestingly, he'd found that Genoa had two distribution centers —one at the main McCarran International Airport, and a second at the Henderson Executive Airport to the south of town. The main airport was completely logical, but Max was puzzled by the second location. Surely no major freight would come in through the much smaller executive field. He dug around further and none of the other major distributors had facilities there. It struck him as odd that a company like Genoa, tiny compared to the global networks, would have the two facilities.

He opened a new tab, plotted the distance to the Henderson location, and found it was 4.6 miles from the Desert Jewel. It was only two thirty, so he had plenty of time for a run.

He'd expected to need exercise, so he'd brought a workout bag, but as he got dressed, he wished he'd brought his CamelBak. It was going to be hotter than hell on the streets, but he could carry a water bottle. He'd seen worse, for sure.

Thirty minutes later, he approached the building he'd seen online. GENOA IMPORTS ran along the upper-right corner in large white letters. The parking lot in front was less than half-full, and Max didn't stop but slowed his pace considerably. On the far side, he saw a few employees standing outside an open door, taking a smoke break, and he decided to use the opportunity.

"Hey, guys," he said as he transitioned to a walk and approached them, holding out his empty water bottle and putting a pained expression on his face. "Fucking hot in this town. Do you have a place I can fill my water?"

The three men looked at each other and said nothing until one of them, a tall and skinny man in his twenties, answered, "Yeah." He took a pull on the very butt end of his cigarette then put it out against the wall and flicked it away, blowing out a cloud of smoke. "Come with me."

Max followed him inside, where he had to pause briefly to let his eyes adjust to the much darker interior. Directly in front of him was a storage rack that rose twenty feet and was full of plastic wrapped pallets extending far to his left. Through the gaps, Max could see a more expansive area on the other side where someone was loading a truck with a forklift. Beyond that, he could see through the half-open hangar doors to the airstrip. Above them, the racks yielded to open space up to the exposed rafters of the two-story roof.

"Over here." The man called his attention to the right where he stood at a door that was open to an even darker area. "Light's out, but there's a sink in the storeroom on the other side. The light works in there. Switch is on the left."

"Thanks." Max walked into the darkened room. There was enough light to see the next door, which he pushed open. The light switch for that room was on the wall, as suggested. Bright white industrial lights flared to life, causing him to pause once again as his eyes adjusted. Unlike the outer area, a low ceiling enclosed the room, and the air felt cooler. It was about twenty feet deep and ran to his left for about fifty feet to two large doors. Along both walls were more storage racks full of boxes and shrink-wrapped items.

To his right, an industrial stainless steel sink stuck out from the wall with a large gooseneck faucet. He stepped over and turned the water on. His host had not followed him, so while the water ran, he put his bottle on the counter and walked down between the storage racks.

What he saw was impressive. Even with his limited culinary skills, Max knew they were almost all high-end items. Although many boxes only had random numbers for labels, Max saw others open or clearly labeled with items like Beluga caviar, black truffles, white truffles, and squid-ink pasta. He looked closer at the caviar, knowing it was likely the most expensive item on the rack, but the boxes remained sealed, and he realized there would be nothing inside to help him.

Toward the end of the row were large bottles of olive oil and balsamic vinegar, wrapped into packs of two or four together. It reminded him of Costco except he knew the price point was significantly different. Then something strange caught Max's eye—two large gas canisters tucked to one side after the racks ended.

He glanced back down the room and saw the water still running, but nobody had joined him, so he moved over to inspect the canisters, which were almost his height and about two feet in diameter. They were identical, with what seemed like standard warning labels on all sides. Max looked to find something that identified the gas. He could see a white label on the back side but couldn't get his head around to read it, so he slid his phone between the two containers and took a couple of pictures.

He heard the creak of the door, so he quickly pocketed his phone and moved to the opposite row to examine a pallet of fine chocolate. He turned slowly to give no indication that he was doing anything wrong.

"What are you doing?" The tall worker stood in the door.

"Water was hot. I'm letting it cool," Max answered, stepping quickly up the aisle. "This place is amazing. Are you guys chefs?"

The man shook his head but seemed to lose his patience.

"No, man. We sell stuff to chefs. Now fill yourself up. I got things to do, and you're really not supposed to be here."

"Got it. Sorry."

Max filled his bottle and shut off the water, making an effort to move quickly around the man and back toward the exit. When he stepped back into the main area, he glanced to his right but was immediately told to keep moving, so he complied, unable to see anything else.

The area outside was now vacant, the other two presumably returning to work as well. Max turned to thank the man, but the door was pulled shut without another word. He took a long swig from his bottle. The cool water was delicious and much needed. Behind him, the roar of an engine filled the air as an executive jet prepared to take off. He tried to watch, but the surrounding buildings blocked his view.

Wiping his brow with his forearm, he turned to the hot street and headed back the way he came.

* * *

If anything, the short stop had reinvigorated Max, and he pushed himself on the run back to the Jewel. The sun continued to beat down on him, but he found a steady pace that put him into a Zen-like state —his feet moved on their own, and he allowed himself to think about the events of the preceding week.

Haoyun was an impressive operation, and Max doubted they would have proceeded this far in the transaction without a thorough understanding of the Desert Jewel, the Marchetti crime family, and their holding company, Tri-Star Enterprises. They clearly thought they were on the better end of the deal despite the high price, but there were always two sides to any negotiation. Max had seen comparison charts that put the price at least twenty percent above what most considered the market value for an aged institution like the Jewel. In a normal world, Haoyun was overpaying, but that ignored the significant potential for business if the high-speed rail succeeded. Either Haoyun had outsmarted everyone, or they were taking a significant gamble— one that might never pay off.

The high-speed rail line was the most obvious unknown. In theory, it could be hugely beneficial to the Jewel, but that assumed it was a success, and in the meantime it would create huge congestion for the property. Both Tri-Star and Haoyun estimates predicted a decline in revenue during the planned three years of construction, which would begin at the end of the year. They did not expect the rail to be fully completed for another five years, as construction started at both termini, planning to connect the lines in the desert, mirroring the transcontinental railroad of 150 years prior. Once the line was operational, Haoyun's numbers suggested a significant uptick in revenue, and they were even modeling a buildout to increase their room numbers.

The only reasonable explanation for the sale of the property was that Tri-Star did not share the same upbeat model. Or they questioned the completion of the rail entirely, and given the status of the California high-speed rail, which had languished in uncompleted status for more than a decade, that may not be the wrong side of the wager.

A horn tooted twice, snapping Max out of his thoughts, and he turned to see an extended black Mercedes with tinted windows pulling over on the opposite side of the road. A cloud of dust followed it as it pulled into the breakdown lane then spun around the open road and headed toward him. They were on Las Vegas Boulevard, and this far south, the road ran through a fairly undeveloped strip of town.

Max backed away from the road, and the car, now headed in the same direction, pulled into the breakdown lane next to him. Another dust cloud followed, and Max covered his mouth and turned his head away. When the sand passed, he turned back to see the car parked in the near lane, and he watched the darkened rear window come down.

"You're gonna kill yourself in this heat," a familiar voice called out. "Come inside."

It was Abruzzi.

"Hi, Geno," Max replied between breaths. "Trying to stay in shape."

The opposite door opened, and Eddie stepped out. He nodded but didn't say anything.

"Get in, Max," Geno insisted, opening his door. "We need to talk."

Max looked across the car at Eddie, who raised his eyebrows, nodded, and threw his hands up as if unable to refuse his boss's command. He stood there, knowing he couldn't decline, but wanting to take his time, he finished his water before climbing in.

It was a standard limo setup, and Geno had moved to the opposite seat, with his back now to the driver. Max sat facing forward, and Eddie climbed back in, sitting next to him.

Max was a little self-conscious of his sweaty body, but Geno tossed him a hand towel, responding to his unspoken thoughts.

"Don't worry about the seats. It's a fleet car. I'll get another tonight. Besides, leather seats will clean up nice. Fuggedaboutit."

Max almost laughed. He knew Geno was born and raised on Staten Island, but to hear such a classic stereotypical phrase was surreal.

"What are you doin' down this way?" Geno asked.

"Out for a run," Max replied. "Fewer traffic lights in this direction."

"True. Although why you want to be outside running in hundred degree heat, I'll never understand."

"I'm used to it."

"That's what I hear." Geno straightened in his seat and seemed to make an effort of looking at something out the window. He had the back of his index finger on the glass, and it seemed to direct his gaze, but the conversation within the car continued. "Marine Raider. Three tours in the Middle East. Retired in 2017. Since then, you've been kickin' around this town, right?"

Max did not like the way this was progressing.

"Yes, sir," he answered coolly.

"Been making a living at the poker tables," Geno continued. "But your luck hasn't been so good of late."

It wasn't a question, but Max replied, "Correct."

"Now, you've got a nice payday advising a few foreign nationals." Geno continued to look away.

"With all due respect, it's a friendly deal. I'm an interpreter."

Suddenly, Geno slapped the car seat with his left hand, turning his head to look directly at Max, his eyes burning with anger.

"Enough bullshit." His voice was impassioned, but an instant later, he took a deep breath and then continued in a calm voice. "Look, Max. I like you. Eddie likes you. And we know you can speak a few languages, but let's drop the facade that you are merely an interpreter."

Max returned the man's stare and offered a gentle nod.

"2014, assigned as special operations negotiator. February 2015, deployed to Beirut for Operation Close Home. May 2015, Fallujah,

Operation Red Star . . . Do I need to continue?"

Max squirmed. His role was not a secret, but Geno had rattled off his first two covert operations as a negotiator. As with most of his operations, both were classified as Special Access Programs (SAPs), a level of secrecy far above anything Geno should have access to.

"No," he answered. "You've made your point. But why am I here?"

Geno laughed. "You're here because we like you."

He tapped the glass behind him and called to the driver. "Take us back to the Jewel."

"How can I help?" Max changed his line of questioning.

"This deal is very important to us." Geno smiled. "We'd like to make sure this goes smoothly, and beyond that, Eddie thinks you'd fit in with us. We can help with those poker losses."

Max had been losing a lot, but he also had a lot in reserve. He was not in financial trouble, but he'd let the town think what they'd want. He also had no interest in working for a crime family, but it couldn't hurt to leave the conversation open. It might help with the negotiations.

"Look." He glanced at Eddie before returning to Geno. "Haoyun has hired me. Until the deal closes, I can't change sides. I appreciate the interest though, and maybe we can talk when things are done."

Geno looked out the window again.

"When things are done, we may not need you," he said solemnly, and the car was silent.

For the first time, Max considered the fact that he was riding, unarmed, with the boss of one of the city's biggest crime families. If the stories were true, many had sat where he was now and had never returned.

"What are you doing tomorrow night?" Eddie spoke for the first time, breaking the silence. "I'm going out for steak with the boys. You want to join us?"

Max wasn't sure he did, but he liked Eddie.

"What time?"

"I'll pick you up here at seven."

The car came to a stop at the Desert Jewel valet, and the doorman opened the door next to Max.

He shrugged, looking back at Eddie.

"OK, I'll see you then."

"That's two, you know," Geno spoke, once again turning back from the window.

"Sorry?" Max asked.

"That's twice you've turned me down." Geno sat forward, putting his hands together as if in prayer and pointing them at Max. "You only get three strikes."

Max met his glare and dipped his head slightly in respect.

"I understand."

And he did. Not only that, but his respect for Geno had skyrocketed. If he had access to SAP data, then he was far more than a local gangster.

He got out and headed inside for a shower.

* * *

When the door closed, Eddie immediately turned to his boss.

"I don't think he's coming over," he said.

"We'll see." Geno tapped the glass behind him. "Mikey, head back to Henderson."

"We've got other problems." Eddie finally started the conversation he'd been dreading since he heard the news.

"What's that?"

"Somebody intercepted the security footage at the hospital."

"What?"

"Johnny went down there this morning to pick it up, but somebody was there ahead of him. Took out a guard. Footage from Monday night is gone."

"What the fuck? What about the video from today? Did they see who did this?"

"Nope. Someone scrambled today's feed. Hacked from outside."

The car started moving, but Geno sat motionless, staring off into space, apparently digesting the information.

"This doesn't make sense." The large man shifted his weight, now looking directly at Eddie. "Some broad sees something she shouldn't. How is it that she gets away from us, escapes a police watch at the hospital, and now we're talking about a full-on hack of the security system and some thug taking out a guard? Who's protecting her? You know, the Ghost tried to hack it, but he couldn't get in. This is a pro."

Eddie was at an equal loss to explain. He'd been thinking about it since Monday night's escape and had no valid ideas.

"I reached out to Vinchenzo but haven't heard back," he said. Vinchenzo was a captain in the Napoli family, who ran a lot of the off-strip areas on the east side of town, including the hospital.

"Nah." Geno threw up a hand in dismissal. "The Napoli wouldn't pull something like this, not on their own turf."

"We've still got the EMT."

"He better provide some answers. There's too much riding on this to risk something coming up. I told Rodriguez that I handled it."

"I'm on it, boss." Eddie hesitated and decided not to share the last bit. The fact that Johnny had seen Max at the hospital was certainly suspicious, but he liked the guy. Geno would not look for proof. He'd take him out, and Eddie didn't want anything to interfere with the deal closing.

"Good. You follow up on that. I've got the Ghost involved too. He'll chase down the video."

Eddie felt a rush of heat come to his body at the second mention of the name. The Ghost was what the movies called a "cleaner." He was also the key to Geno's rise in power over the past twenty years. Nobody knew who he was, but it was well known that the Ghost handled things when Geno needed them "taken care of."

Geno switched topics. "And what about this other thing? The girl stealing from us?"

"I'm on that too." The warm sweat that was already building increased as the subject came up. "We don't know for sure that she took it. But, Geno, I've told you I'm good for it if she did."

"That's not the point, and you know it."

Eddie had heard this before. In Geno's view, everything was black and white. Either you were trusted or you were an enemy . . . and enemies often died. It was no use arguing the point.

"She's a good girl, Geno."

Across from him, the big man held up a hand for silence.

"I've asked you to handle it, Ed. You do what should be done."

The car was silent for the rest of the ride. Geno stared out the window and Eddie looked down at his hand. He knew what Geno was asking, but he wasn't sure he wanted to listen. He'd wait to see if they uncovered evidence of her guilt, and he prayed she'd covered her tracks. Staci had been the best thing that had happened to him in many years. He didn't want to lose her.

# CHAPTER FOURTEEN

As the waiter delivered a tray of sambuca, Max had to admit that Eddie and his crew had really grown on him. As promised, Eddie had picked him up a little after seven. Mickey and Paul then joined them at the High Times Steakhouse. Eddie introduced them to Max as associates unconnected to the Desert Jewel. Despite that caveat, Max had met Mickey at the rooftop party a couple of days earlier. Both men were good-natured, and the dinner had resulted in a lot of laughs, though Max did not feel like he had gotten any further in his investigation.

"Where's Johnny tonight?" Mickey asked, raising his glass. "He loves this shit."

All four men raised their glasses in a silent toast before taking a sip, avoiding the floating coffee beans.

"He's taking care of that thing from the other night," Eddie responded then took a second swig, downing the entire glass.

"I thought that was handled."

"Yeah, it was, then it wasn't. Geno took care of the whole place, which is a cryin' shame. Those girls aren't talking no more, but they didn't need to die. Anyway, we're still working on IDing the one who ran away," Eddie answered, putting his empty glass down and shaking his head.

"We were supposed to have surveillance footage from the hospital." He turned and looked at Max before continuing, "But somebody got there ahead of Johnny."

He took a sip of water.

"They got the video," Eddie continued, turning back to the table, "but we've got the EMT."

"What does that mean?" Paul asked.

"It means we've got someone who can positively ID the girl from the hospital." Eddie had a hand up, signaling the waiter for more sambuca.

"But you still have to find her."

As soon as Paul spoke, Max could see he regretted it, and a quick glance at Eddie confirmed the reason—his face was turning red, and it was obvious he was holding his temper back.

"Yeah. You could say that, Paulie," Eddie said through gritted teeth. "But we might also find the guy who helped her. We got a shot to make good here. I don't want this goin' back to the Ghost."

Paul looked down, and Mickey shook his head, muttering, "Aw, fuck."

Max looked from the two men back to Eddie.

"What's the Ghost?" he asked.

Mickey cut in, "Not what—who."

Eddie moved his angry stare from Paul to Mickey before turning to Max, his face softening.

"The Ghost is a guy who works directly for Geno. He solves problems."

Max thought he understood, but it was worth pressing.

"Solves problems?" he asked, using a classic mirroring technique used in negotiation.

"When the shit really hits the fan, Geno will call in the Ghost to make things right. Things start to happen. If people are in his way . . . let's just say they don't stay that way. He makes problems and people disappear."

"OK, I'm not sure I want to know any more."

"You definitely don't. It's crazy shit that doesn't need to happen, like that fire. That was the Ghost's work. But, I'll give him this— people fear him and everyone thinks twice before crossing Geno."

The next tray of sambuca arrived, but Max left his on the table next to his first, which was still half-full. He'd had a few glasses of wine, but he was technically in enemy territory, so he wanted to keep his wits about him. He wasn't about to risk revealing any of his side's strategy, but if the night continued as it was, perhaps his new friends might.

* * *

A few hours later, Max sat on a well-cushioned black couch, watching Eddie get another lap dance from a beautiful half-naked young woman. They had gone from the steakhouse to a bar and from the bar to the Crazy Kettle strip club. Mickey and Paul had wanted to head home from the bar, but Eddie had insisted they visit the Kettle before calling it a night.

Max hated strip clubs. Not that he didn't enjoy the beautiful naked women—he did. And he knew they made a pretty penny dancing, so in that respect he didn't have any high-minded qualms about exploitation. It was a fair deal all around. Still, when he was younger, he'd always preferred what he called hunting in the wild rather than in a reserve. It was his favorite way to explain that he would rather be out bird-dogging women in the bar scene with a chance of taking one home instead of spending exorbitant amounts on women he had no chance of sleeping with.

"You sure you don't want a dance?" Eddie had to yell over the house music. His current girl was bent over him with her bare breasts rubbing up his shirt. He had his arms open, and he gestured with a wad of twenties in his left hand. "Pick anyone. Tonight's on me."

"I'm good, thanks." Max raised his soda water in gratitude. He'd let Eddie buy him a dance earlier, but one was enough.

"Suit yourself."

Mickey and Paul had been there for the first dance as well and then peeled off, earning some sarcastic remarks from Eddie, now very drunk. Max had stayed, hoping they would move back to a bar where he could try to get a little more intel about Genoa and Tri-Star.

The club was not as large as many in Las Vegas. It had one main stage that stuck out from the back wall and had three poles where various women danced. Booths and dancing areas surrounded the stage on three sides, filled with groups of adoring men. To the back and slightly raised was the VIP area where Max and Eddie now sat alone except for the entertainment. The area could hold another group, maybe two, but at the moment no one else had paid to enter.

"Be right back." Max pushed himself off the couch and moved to the restroom.

He took care of business and washed his hands, looking at his own face in the mirror. What was he doing? Partying in a strip club with a known criminal. He never would have predicted this, but he reminded himself he wasn't one of them.

When he returned to the VIP area, he saw that another group of men had joined them, occupying a collection of chairs behind Eddie. There were six of them, and most already had girls dancing for them, while another was busy placing an order with the waitress.

"Eddie, I think I'm gonna head out soon," Max called over.

As he did, Eddie's chair jolted forward, knocking his girl off him, and she fell to the floor. Behind him, two of the men were playfully wrestling, and before Eddie could even react, their chair knocked his again, sliding into the girl on the floor, who let out a yelp.

"What the fuck?" Eddie practically flew out of his chair, spinning to confront the two men. He paused to lean down and helped the girl up. She seemed shaken but fine. He handed her a bunch of twenties before turning back to his unintended assailants.

"Show some fucking manners," he bellowed at the two men, pulling his shoulders back in a "come fuck with me" posture. Eddie might have been drunk, but he was still a large man.

Max took a step closer, raising his hand to try to defuse things.

"Hey, guys, we're all here to have fun. I'm sure it was an accident."

The two wrestlers had untangled and now stood up on the other side of the chair. They were not as large as Eddie but were pretty well built.

"Hey, bub," the first one said with a smile. "You shouldn't have been there. Accidents can happen."

Behind them, the other four now stood up, pushing their girls aside. To Max's eye, none of them held a fighter's pose, but he had been in enough fights to know they were very close to one. He put a hand on Eddie's shoulder to restrain him. It was unlikely the others would back down, but maybe they could simply walk away.

"We don't need this shit, Eddie," he said, turning to the two wrestlers. "And you don't need this either."

The second wrestler looked at Max with disdain.

"Yeah, Eddie, you don't need this," he parroted in a whining voice. "Why don't you run home to Mama?"

As he finished his sentence, he lifted his foot and shoved the chair in front of him forward, sending it into Eddie's shins and forcing him to kneel into the seat.

There was no stopping what was coming now, so Max shifted from appeaser to warrior at the flash of a synapse. He quickly surveyed the area. Six against two wasn't great odds, so he would want as much open space as possible, and he found it in an area at the entrance to the VIP section.

As Eddie regained his feet, Max moved around him to where the area opened up. Eddie instantly expanded the space by sliding the chair that had struck him off to the right, eliminating any obstacle between the two groups.

"You want to do this one on one, like men?" Eddie growled, motioning to the others. "Or do you want your little girlfriends involved?"

"Fuck that," one man in the back cursed.

No one waited for further discussion. Eddie dove into his assailant, but Max had no time to watch, as he immediately faced off against two of the men. The first had charged at him, and he easily used the man's momentum to send him flying into the railing that separated them from the main floor.

The second man paused briefly, raising his hands like a street fighter as he looked past Max at the crumpled body on the floor. It was all the time Max needed, as he planted his left hand on the railing, spun his legs into his opponent, and knocked him onto his back. Before the man could recover, Max was at his side, and he delivered two crisp blows to the man's eye, the second of which slammed the man's head into the floor and knocked him unconscious.

Max stood up but, before he could turn, a body hit him hard from the right, throwing him into the railing. The man held on, following him to the rail, but now Max had the upper hand. Both of his arms were above his assailant, and he put his fists together and hammered down at the vulnerable collarbone, hearing a scream of pain simultaneous to feeling the bone break.

The man released his hold, and Max pushed him to the side, focusing on the remaining combatants. Eddie seemed to have beaten his first opponent, now curled against one sofa, but the last two had overpowered him and were now trading kicks as Eddie flailed on the floor, unable to get away.

Max crossed the short distance in less than a heartbeat, and as one man pulled his foot back for another blow, he grabbed it and yanked upward, instantly flipping the man to the floor. The leg was already at an awkward angle, and Max met the man's eyes for a split second, raising an eyebrow in mock apology before he violently twisted the leg farther in the wrong direction. The man's face instantly flared in pain, but Max held for a couple of seconds more before releasing the foot and letting the guy curl up in agony.

"Stop this shit right now," a voice called from behind, and Max turned to see a beefy security guard at the top of the short stairs. "Police are on the way."

Max started to relax but heard movement to his right and turned to see the last assailant charging him. He jumped back, allowing the man to miss, and then stepped in with a shove, hurling the man into the guard, and both men tumbled down the steps into the larger room.

For a moment, Max took in the scene, looking out over the club from his elevated position. The music continued to blare, and surprisingly many in the club were still enjoying dances, oblivious to the chaos that had overtaken the VIP lounge. Only a few of the tables closer to them had witnessed the fight, and Max looked down at shocked faces. Beyond them, he could see other security guards crossing the room.

He turned back to check on Eddie and was glad to see him already rising on his own.

"Can you walk?" he asked.

"I'm fine," Eddie grumbled, but his face was scratched, and he cradled his ribs like they hurt. He spat at one of the men. "Fucking kickers."

There was an emergency exit sign by the bathroom, not twenty yards away, and Max nodded toward it, but as the two men started to move, he heard the all-too-familiar sound of someone slide-racking an automatic weapon—metal on metal, crisp and unmistakable.

Max reacted instantly, throwing Eddie forward and over the last couch while he spun and dove to his left.

A burst of gunfire followed and Max slid behind a chair, but the attack was not directed at him. He looked over to see the original assailant had pushed himself up on one knee, holding a machine pistol, and was firing several bursts into the couch protecting Eddie. There was rage on his face, so much so that he didn't see Max until it was too late. At the last minute, he tried to swing his fire, but Max was already in motion.

In two steps, he closed the distance between them and delivered a right kick to the hand holding the gun, instantly separating it and sending the weapon skidding across the floor. A left knee to the face followed, knocking the man on his back, blood flowing from his nose.

Max knelt closer and delivered a crushing blow to the man's throat. It wasn't lethal, but it would be a while before the man swallowed comfortably.

"Fucker," he wheezed mostly to himself as he rose, looking up to see that Eddie was once again on his feet and did not appear hit.

"You good?" Max asked to be sure.

"Yeah." Despite the fight, Eddie actually had a slight grin.

"Let's go." Max led Eddie to the emergency exit.

He glanced back to see several security guards yelling from below the VIP dais, but the gunfire must have halted their advance. He could see two of them waving something at the men on the floor, and as he pushed the door open, he could already taste pepper spray in the air.

# CHAPTER FIFTEEN

In three years working together, Jerry had always been the nicest of coworkers. He was one of those people who seemed to both fit in and be an outcast at the same time. He dressed like someone confident in his style, throwing off a retro look without going over the top. He seemed to have neither friends nor a social life. Despite confident talk around the office, he rarely joined the others for drinks after work, and if Staci was being honest, she'd been disappointed early on that he had never tried to come on to her—at least not with anything beyond playful office banter. He was five years her senior, but she probably would have taken him up on it back in the day. Now, she had to hope that some of that casual affection and friendship was real.

"Hey, Jer," Staci called as she approached his cubicle. "You've had your head buried in work this week."

It had been two days since her conversation with Pam. At first, she hadn't known how to approach the topic, but after stewing in her thoughts for forty-eight hours, she'd finally come to the conclusion that she had to at least try to deflect potentially damning evidence.

"Uh, hi, Staci." Jerry turned away from his computer, but not before closing three different windows. He looked like he had not slept, with tousled hair and unkempt clothes. There was a smile on his lips, but his eyes were weary behind wide-rim square glasses that sat slightly askew.

"You working on another special project?" She tilted her head toward Pam's office.

Jerry's eyes darted toward the office and back to meet hers. He nodded. "Yeah, you know how fun those can be."

"Need help?" Staci hated to use her womanhood for an advantage, but there was too much at stake for principals. She leaned on the edge of the cubical so that it only blocked half her chest, and she'd worn a low-cut top for this purpose.

His eyes widened, and he nervously looked back at his computer before replying.

"No, uh, I finished it earlier." He moved his mouse, and Staci saw another window close.

"What was it about?" she asked. "I assume another report for the acquisition team?"

"I don't think so, actually." He stood up and shifted his eyes briefly toward the break room before looking at her with concern. "I can't talk about it though. You understand?" His eyes shifted once again to the break room and back.

"OK," she replied, understanding. "Well, let me know if you need help."

"Will do. Excuse me, I've got to hit the restroom." He slid out of the cubicle, leaving her standing by herself.

She considered snooping on his computer but decided against it. She hoped she'd get more from him in private, so she strode casually toward the break room, stopping at one friend's desk along the way for a quick hello.

By the time she reached the break room, Jerry entered right behind her.

"Come to the back," he whispered as he brushed past, heading to the second room.

The break room was actually two rooms. The first was a large open kitchen with a fridge, coffeemaker, and toaster oven. At the back, accessed by a glass door, was a second room with two round tables, each with six chairs. Most employees rarely used the second room because they ate at their desks or, preferring a real lunch break, went out to eat. The only time the tables were full was for some of the lame team meetings that Pam would hold periodically.

Jerry closed the glass door after she entered so that the two of them were alone.

"Holy fuck, Staci," Jerry exclaimed, agitated. "Was it you?"

Staci knew to act surprised. "Was what me?"

He shook his head and sat down at one table, indicating Staci should sit with him.

"Pam tells me she needs me to check up on some 'irregularities,' and I did the work." He glanced toward the door, speaking in a high whisper. "Staci, there have been massive money flows through catering. I had no idea how large. Anyway, it's fairly easy to spot the skim, even though they've covered it well enough for most."

Staci nodded, not wanting to admit what they both knew was true and also encouraging him to continue.

"So I bring this to Pam and she says, 'That's not the problem.' She was almost angry at me for bringing it up. She says, 'Look deeper at the crypto activity in the January books.' So I do, and at first everything looks fine, but Pam asks me to look into the blockchain at the receiving wallet. That's where it gets interesting."

He ran a hand through his hair, took off his glasses, and rubbed his eyes.

"Crypto is a hobby for me, so I know what to look for. While the Marchettis have been taking a weekly skim to their wallet, they send the money to another wallet once a month. From there, it disperses pretty quickly, and that is the beauty of crypto, because all of this is visible on the blockchain. It would take a while to really trace everything, but that's not really important. It always goes to the same wallet from here."

"So why does that matter?" Staci thought she knew where he was going but wanted to play dumb.

"It matters because in January through early March of this year, something changed. We started to split the transactions. The regular transfer remained fairly constant but, hidden behind the regular transaction, a second amount was sent. On the Jewel's books, the extra money was pulled from exotic food and beverage, but the key is that we split the outgoing funds, sending most of the money to the same wallet, but a small portion to a new address. On our books, it looks like one transaction, but for a few months there were two each week."

"So?"

"It looks like a skim within the skim. Another layer of money is moving. It's like someone with knowledge of the first cri—sorry, the first indiscretion embarked on a second indiscretion."

"Are you sure?"

He took a deep breath. "Pretty much. My mind is still spinning."

Staci moved her chair closer and put a hand on his shoulder, thinking this might be an opening.

"Let me help, Jer." She moved her hand closer to his neck and flicked some of his hair playfully with a finger.

Jerry froze and turned his head to look at her hand.

For a moment, Staci wasn't sure what to do.

He chuckled, putting his glasses back on. "I'm on your team, Staci."

"Huh?"

"I'm gay." He widened his eyes with the statement and shrugged to remove her hand.

Staci felt a rush of blood to her face. "I'm sorry."

Jerry immediately held up a hand. "Don't be. You're a great friend. That's why we're talking." He paused. "Look, I know you've done a lot of work on the catering division. And I know you've helped your boyfriend arrange the books for a while now. I didn't know the scale of it, but seriously, Stace, we all know who runs this place."

She slumped in her chair and reached over to grab his hand, this time in genuine friendship.

"Was it that obvious?"

"To me? Yes, but the books look good, and if the Marchettis sanctioned it—no harm, no foul." Again, he paused, staring into her eyes. "But this second skim, that could be a problem. Was that you too?"

Her head tingled, and she thought about confessing to him. It would be so nice to get this off her chest, but something inside told her to stay the course, so she put on her best look of shock.

"What are you saying?" She sat back upright. "Look, I've been loyal to Eddie. And I don't know enough about cryptocurrency to be sending things to different addresses," she lied, spitting out her words.

"OK. Good. Because whoever is responsible is under the gun. The Marchettis are aware, and Pam's got a stick up her ass about it."

"Are you still digging?"

"That's the thing. I delivered my first report, which identified the activity, and less than twenty minutes later, Pam calls me in and tells me she wants to find out who's behind it. Problem is, at this level, it's only an internal investigation, and how the hell am I supposed to look into a crypto account?"

"I'm sorry, Jer." She felt a wave of hope. "Can I help?"

Jerry took in a deep breath and let out a sigh, shaking his head.

"I don't think so, Staci."

Once again, he paused, staring into her eyes, and she felt like he was trying to look into her soul.

"I think I'll paddle through this one alone."

Above them, the hum of the air-conditioning fan kicked in, and Staci wasn't sure if it was the fresh air or her friend's scrutiny that chilled her. She got up from the table.

"OK, you know where I am."

She turned and started to leave when she heard him mutter.

"Do I?"

At the door, she rested a hand on the jamb and looked back, trying to confirm her ears. "What was that?"

Jerry shook his head.

"Nothing. Let's get back to work before Pam writes us up."

# CHAPTER SIXTEEN

Eddie and Max had made it out of the club, and with the confusion following the gunfire behind them, no one pursued. Within a minute, they found a cab and were already blocks away before the police cars zipped past, blue and red lights flashing. Eddie had dropped Max at a corner near his apartment and continued on. Neither of them had said much on the ride, but as Max exited, Eddie had shaken his hand firmly and looked at him with sincerity as he thanked him.

News outlets covered the incident extensively, referring to it as a gunfight, although no one had suffered gunshot wounds. All the local morning news hosts covered the story, interviewing police and firsthand witnesses. Max tuned out most of it, though he was happy to see Ben Carpenter talking to one reporter. His friend downplayed the potential mob connection, explaining that nobody had actually been shot.

Max had other things occupying his time and spent most of his day sitting through more long discussions with the Haoyun acquisition team. He had to admit that he enjoyed learning about the intricacies of the business, but he was tired of the endless spreadsheets, most of which repeated similar themes. The Desert Jewel was a break-even business, mostly because the Marchetti family was using it for their own interests. Some skims were so obvious that it was actually surprising the state auditors had never flagged them. As Ling suggested, there were likely more people working for the Jewel than showed up on the payroll.

By Tuesday morning, the aches and pains of Sunday's fight had finally loosened. He'd slept well, getting almost a full eight hours before his internal alarm clock had woken him at five. He'd gone for a run and spent an hour at the gym before cooling off over breakfast.

Now, as he exited his cab at the very familiar Desert Jewel, the day was once again heating up. Inside, he looked at his watch and decided he didn't have time to visit the Haoyun war room upstairs. Jun Chen had arranged a tour of the catering division, and when Max learned of it the previous day, he'd asked to join. If he were to find out more about Genoa Imports, this would be a good place to look.

Max headed to the plain door on the far side of the casino, identified only by a room number plaque. He waved his access card over the pad and heard the click of the lock before he pushed it open.

On the other side, true to form, Jun Chen and his two aides stood waiting for him in the medium-sized lobby. He'd expected nothing less. The Haoyun team was always punctual. All three were in their usual suits, and the two underlings each held iPads. It was only 8:54 a.m., but Jun's expression clearly implied that he thought Max was late.

"Good morning, Max." Jun offered his hand, and Max shook it and did the same with the other two.

"Morning, gentlemen," Max replied. "Are we waiting for our host?"

"Not really." Jun's falsetto voice was almost a squeak, sounding strained. "She was here, but as you were not, she ran back for her coffee."

Max ignored the implication. He knew enough about Jun to know that the man hated to waste time, but Max was early and had nothing to apologize for.

"Good morning, Max!" a voice called from his right, and he turned to see Maria Gonzales, the curvaceous director of catering operations. She wore a relatively tight-fitting red dress and modest heels, both of which accented her long tan legs. Her black hair had loose waves and hung to one side over her shoulder.

They'd met a couple of times during the transaction, and Max had found her to be as genuine as she was attractive, though he'd also learned she was happily married with seemingly no connection to the Marchetti side of the operation.

"Good morning, Maria." Max offered a smile and nodded as she approached.

She had a coffee in each hand and extended one to Max, which he accepted gratefully.

"Thank you." He widened his eyes in grateful surprise. "This is a bonus."

"My pleasure," she said. "The others declined, but I figured it would be no harm to bring one in case you wanted it."

She turned to Jun. "Are we ready?"

He simply nodded, and Maria started back down the hall she had come from.

"As you know," she began, edging to one side of the hall and turning her head slightly to look at Jun, who was closest to her, "the Desert Jewel catering operation serves not only our casino, restaurants, and clubs, but about sixty percent of the casinos on the strip in one way or another."

It was obviously not Maria's first tour. She had her facts polished and even some humor along the way that Max suspected had been scripted for her, and her presentation was almost perfect. It was an impressive operation and far larger than Max had thought, even though he had seen the numbers many times. He had naively thought they were done when she finished taking them through the industrial kitchens, but then she stopped before a set of large unmarked industrial doors.

Max had been at the back of the group and thought it odd that Jun had drifted back with him, allowing the accountants in front. He was even more surprised when Jun leaned toward him and whispered.

"Now we get to the meat of things," he said.

"So that's the beautiful face of the operation," Maria said, holding a hand out and pointing to the kitchens they had left. "Does anyone want anything before we go downstairs?"

"Beauty can be in the heart, as it is in the face," Jun answered. "The kitchen is impressive, but the distribution center makes this business attractive. We are here to see that."

Both accountants nodded their agreement.

"Let's continue."

Maria led them through the doors and down a large open stairwell. The noise level immediately rose as they entered, and a cleaner, more neutral scent replaced the pleasant aromas of the kitchens. They descended one story to a landing, and as they made the turn, they could see a vast area stretching out ahead of them, bustling with workers. It was at least the size of a football field, two stories high, and alive with activity. There were rows stacked with pallets and boxes, and between them, Max saw carts and forklifts moving things in all directions. At the far end, he noticed trucks of various sizes parked at loading docks. He couldn't help but think it was a much larger version of the operation he had seen at Genoa Imports the previous Friday.

Rather than continue down, Maria took them along a catwalk that extended to the left along what was one wall of the cavernous space. Though still industrial, the floor of the catwalk was a finished wood laminate that matched the stairs and added a level of elegance.

She detailed the daily product flow through the distribution center, the sorting process, and other details that Max found uninteresting.

After crossing the short end of the room, the catwalk ended at the far wall with a narrow staircase to the floor below, and the group descended.

Something had been niggling at the back of Max's mind, and as they arrived at the bottom, it finally occurred to him.

"How did you manage a basement?" he blurted out, unintentionally interrupting one of the accountants.

Maria's eyes brightened, as if she had been waiting for the question.

"Who cares?" the accountant whom he had interrupted countered. "If you don't mind, Maria, I'd like to know about—"

Jun put his arm across the chest of his underling, silencing him immediately. Then he nodded to Maria.

"With apologies, Maria. We would like to hear about the basement."

"No problem." She seemed eager to field the question, addressing the accountant with her response. "As odd as it may sound, Las Vegas has a high water table. It makes underground construction very difficult, if not impossible. Very few of the large casinos have true basements, and I'm sure that's why Max asked."

She turned to Jun.

"We are in a unique location here at the south end of the city. Our casino is on a strip of bedrock running east-west across the city. In places, it's as much as a mile wide, though not as much here. So while a basement like this would be prohibitively expensive on the strip, it was fairly easy to complete at our location. Originally, they planned for a parking garage in the seventies, but partway through construction, the city declined to approve it. Don't ask me why. That was years ago, and I can never explain Las Vegas politics."

Maria flipped her hand in the air, rolling her eyes and, once again, Max had the feeling he was watching a performance.

"Anyway," she continued, "we pivoted. For a long time, it was simply storage until the Jewel began catering in the late nineties. I think you'll all agree it has worked out pretty well. That's also why the southern terminal for the high-speed rail will be across the street. It's the only section of the project that's underground, but by coming in here under the freeway, they saved hundreds of millions of dollars."

"And that project will have no impact on this operation, apart from the traffic delays?" Jun asked, obviously unimpressed by the geology.

"Not in the least." It was another question she was clearly prepared for. "The tunnel runs about one hundred yards to the north and will have no impact on the distribution center."

They walked for a little while along the wall, staying out of the way of bustling workers, as Maria described the operation in more detail. When she finished, the accountants asked several questions, all of which were deftly handled until Jun interrupted.

"Where has the money gone?" he asked in his squeaky but demanding voice.

"I'm sorry?" Maria seemed genuinely put off.

"Your volume has tripled in the last year," Jun stated, "but you aren't making any money."

"It's a competitive business," Maria responded, pushing her hair back over her ear nervously.

To this point, the performance had been perfect, but it was immediately clear to Max that Maria had exhausted her limited knowledge. She was the pretty face to put in front of most tours, but Tri-Star had erred if they thought the tour was perfunctory, and she was now out of her depth.

Jun pressed his line of questioning, and Max stepped slightly away from the group, knowing there wasn't much Maria could offer as far as the actual answers that Haoyun was probing for.

The operation impressed him as he looked around the room. The far end was a hive of activity, loading and unloading trucks, which made him think about the air quality. In most facilities like this, the diesel fumes would permeate everything, but that was clearly not the case. He looked up and saw a massive air-duct system that looked more complicated than anything he'd seen. It must have cost a fortune.

He was wandering back the way they had come when he saw a forklift with unusual cargo. It was gliding steadily across the room with two large gas canisters, not unlike the ones he had seen at Genoa Imports. He pulled out his phone and took a quick picture, making a mental note to dig deeper. After the commotion Sunday night, he'd forgotten to look back at the photo from the warehouse.

The forklift stopped at a pair of industrial doors on the opposite side of the room and seemed to wait there for a good minute before a red light on the wall flashed and the doors opened, allowing a motorized cart to exit and the forklift to continue within.

Max strained to see where it was going but could not see much besides what looked like a long hall. The doors closed behind it, and the red light stopped flashing.

Unable to follow the lift, he watched the cart, which had continued heading toward him, only turning to the left at the last row.

Looking back to the group, he could see they were still deep in conversation, so he strode over to the next aisle. The cart had already stopped about fifty feet in, and he saw the worker unload a few boxes before continuing on.

Knowing he was already on borrowed time, Max picked up his pace and reached the boxes quickly. A chill ran up his neck as he recognized the caviar boxes from Genoa Imports's warehouse, but now he saw that each of the boxes had a blue stripe slashed across the lower right corner.

"Max?" Maria called from the end of the aisle. "What are you looking for?"

"Sorry, Maria." He turned immediately and walked back toward her. "My attention span is like a goldfish. I was a little bored, so I wandered."

"OK. Well, try to stick with us. Personally, I don't care, but I've seen some of the folks down here get pretty territorial." She put a light hand on Max's shoulder when he reached her, guiding him back to the others. "I think they are afraid their precise organizational system might get thrown off."

* * *

The phone rang six times before Carolyn answered. With each ring, Max silently urged her to answer, and when she finally did, he was so elated that he briefly forgot why he was calling.

"Hey, Max!" Her voice had that just-out-of-bed sound, but it was a little after six at night.

"Carolyn," he fumbled, "how are you?"

He could imagine her laughing at him. She always threw him off his game.

"I'm well, Max. Don't tell me . . . There's more footage to destroy?"

"No." He collected himself, wishing she were in the room. "Thank you for that, but that's done. I . . ."

He stopped, realizing he was in fact calling about more of the same.

"What are you up to?" she asked, and he knew she was shaking her head.

"Are you at a computer? Can we Zoom?"

"Sure, send me the link."

He hung up and stepped back to his laptop, where he'd been working prior to the call. With a few clicks, he opened a video meeting and emailed the link to her.

This time, he was confused and even a little upset that she didn't join the call until the timer was almost at five minutes, but when her olive-skinned face filled the screen, he quickly lost all anger and fell into her deep-blue eyes. Her wet hair was silky smooth, and her skin shimmered in the webcam light. Her birthmark always struck him as beautiful despite the reddish hue, and he wondered if all men felt the same.

"You look great," he said.

"Thanks. Had a great workout and was cleaning up when you called." She flashed a smile. "Sorry for the delay."

Max raised an eyebrow with a mischievous grin.

"It's fine, but you didn't have to dress for me."

"Oh, zip it. We're two thousand miles apart. So what's up?" Carolyn was not one to waste time.

"Check this out."

He shared his screen then opened the photo showing the two gas containers.

"See these?"

"Yup."

"I took this photo in a warehouse owned by Genoa Imports."

"What's that?"

"It's a distribution company owned by the mayor's family. They are a major supplier to the Desert Jewel."

"Wait a sec. You're saying that the mayor, who is green-lighting the sale of this casino, which is currently controlled by the Marchetti family, is also a business partner of the casino? Yeah, that sounds legitimate. But why are we looking into this? I thought you said you were a negotiator." There was a hint of anger in her voice.

"I am. Well, I guess I'm doing a little extra work."

He was still sharing his screen, so her face was small, but he could see her shaking her head, and he knew if he made it full screen, he'd see disappointment in her eyes.

"Anyway, Rodriguez owns Genoa, and Genoa is a big part of the Jewel's catering business," he continued, and his mouse clicked the next photo. "Check this out."

On the screen now was a slightly blurry and dark photo of the backside of one canister. Next to a tri-colored warning label and surrounded by other warnings, the label read, "AMINE GAS."

"What's that?"

"That's where you come in." Max stopped sharing his screen, looking intently at his onetime girlfriend. "I'm hoping you can help me figure this out."

"Go on."

"I've been doing some web surfing, and Amine gas is a generic term. It refers to the type of gas, but nobody sells a product labeled simply Amine gas."

"So? What's this, then?" she pressed.

"That's where I need your help. I don't think it's needed in the catering business."

"Was there a shipping label?"

"No idea." He shook his head. "Wasn't there very long."

"OK, I'll do some research. That looks like a serial number at the top of your photo. I might be able to track it down."

"Thanks, C." Max was sincere. "I really appreciate the assist."

"Yeah, let's see if it comes to anything." She paused, raising an eyebrow slightly. "How are you otherwise?"

"I'm good. Thanks."

"No fights?"

He paused, not wanting to lie.

"I'm a typical negotiator." He allowed himself to smile. "You know, nine to five."

Carolyn stared at him through the computer with a gentle nod. "So you weren't involved in the gunfight that's all over the news?"

Max offered a weaker smile, nodding to acknowledge her. "For what it's worth, it wasn't a gunfight. We handled the situation until some hothead pulled a weapon, but nobody was hit."

"Max, you don't have nine lives. Stop this shit."

"Yeah. I know."

"You're OK though?" Her tone softened.

"Yup. Not even a scratch."

She didn't respond but gave him that faraway look she always did when she disapproved.

"Do you want extra credit?" he asked, knowing he was pushing his luck.

"What now?"

"Can you put on your hacker's hat and see what you can find at Genoa Imports or even Tri-Star?"

Carolyn held his gaze through the screen then closed her eyes, taking several deep breaths before she reopened them.

Max knew it was not something she enjoyed doing, and seeing her sadness now, he almost retracted his request.

"Last time, Max," she said slowly, making her disappointment clear. "You've got to stop putting yourself in danger, but that's your decision. You do you, but I've got to do me too. I'll see what I can find, but this is the last time you can ask. Understood?"

He started to reply, but the window closed. Carolyn had hung up. He almost redialed to tell her she didn't need to do it, but he knew he'd already crossed a line.

## CHAPTER SEVENTEEN

At seven o'clock Thursday night, Max was once again back at the Desert Jewel. He'd been on the strip having modest success at the poker tables before he received a text from Ling—they were having dinner with Tri-Star and the mayor, but Jun had not been feeling well, and Ling asked if Max would take his place. He had no choice but to agree.

He now rode the elevator to the top floor of Tower B, dressed in slacks, a gingham button-down, and a lightweight blue blazer. They were meeting at the Ocean, which was one of the town's top-ten seafood venues, its avant-garde sushi fusion serving as a mecca for traveling foodies. To Max, it was overpriced and served portions that were far undersized, but this wasn't a social dinner.

Wei and Ling were waiting for him outside the restaurant when he arrived.

"Mr. Kline." Wei offered a polite bow of the head. "Thank you for joining us tonight."

Max returned the head bow, first to Wei and then to Ling.

"Of course." He smiled at Wei, and then to Ling added, "Thank you for inviting me."

"Jun abhors these things," Ling responded dismissively. "But it's his . . ." She seemed to stumble on her words. "It's his call if he doesn't feel well."

She obviously did not think Jun was feeling unwell.

"You won't need to say much," Wei added, and Max took that to mean, "You should keep your mouth shut tonight."

"We're interested in the mayor's involvement," Wei continued, "but we don't see any threat to the deal. His primary focus is the high-speed rail, and we have been more than cooperative in that regard."

"Have you learned anything more about Tri-Star or Genoa?" Ling asked.

Max shook his head.

"Not really. Eddie offered me some intel on an embezzlement, but I wonder if that's the same one James already identified." He left out the two offers they'd made to hire him.

"OK. Shall we go in?" Wei seemed anxious. It was three minutes past seven, and the reservation was on the hour.

They were seated immediately at a spacious corner table, but it was another twenty minutes before their hosts arrived.

Geno approached the table with arms wide.

"Why am I not surprised?" he said. "You guys are always on time. We got hung up in some traffic, and the mayor refused to call for a police escort."

He turned his wide frame to reveal the mayor behind him and Eddie beyond that.

"Everyone has met, no?" He made a quizzical face then proceeded to shake hands. The three men greeted Wei, Ling, and Max, going around the table in their seating order. Geno insisted on hugs, and Max noticed both Wei and Ling tense up during the interchange. The mayor and Eddie seemed comfortable shaking hands, though when Eddie came to Max, he ducked in for a hug.

"Thanks again, bro," he whispered in Max's ear.

"You guys are getting a good deal," Geno abruptly stated after everyone had sat down. "But let's forget about these things tonight and enjoy a meal together."

"Yes, indeed." Ling tilted her head with a slight acknowledgment. "We are *all* getting good deals, the mayor included."

"Yes." Rodriguez nodded. "With thanks to both of you, we appreciate your accommodation for the construction of the high-speed rail. Its arrival here will be the culmination of many years of hard-fought negotiations. I'm excited for our town and hope this station is a boon for the Jewel."

A waitress filled champagne glasses, and he paused, waiting for the last to be poured, then lifted his glass in a toast.

"To the friends here at this table, to a long and healthy relationship between Haoyun and the city of Las Vegas and . . ."—he turned to Geno with a wink that Max wasn't sure was meant to be seen—"to the continued prosperity of Tri-Star Enterprises as they branch out into other ventures."

"Hear! Hear!" Geno was the first to touch glasses with the mayor, and the table all toasted success. "Well said, Joe. Here's to the Desert Jewel. We will miss being a part of her, but we'll never be far."

Again, the table clinked glasses, and Max wondered if the toasts would go on all night, but that seemed to end it, and things settled down as the server returned, capturing Geno's attention. Even as they talked, a tray of cold seafood arrived at the side of the table, and another server began delivering appetizer plates.

While Max would have preferred something like a pile of crab and a plate of oysters, he looked down at three small but intricate hors d'oeuvres. One was an oyster, but it had a small dollop of what he assumed was caviar along with a pair of flower petals. The other two were equally chic and admittedly tasty but so small that he wanted more.

"I have to say," the mayor said, addressing Max, "I find your role here very interesting."

Eddie had taken the seat next to Max, and the mayor was on the other side of him. With Geno engaging Wei and Ling on the other half of the table, they were left on their own.

Max wiped his mouth, though he didn't really need to. "How so?"

"Haoyun is a foreign entity, which of course we welcome as an investor in our great town," the mayor began, but Max couldn't help but remember the "Local Joe" mayoral campaign in which Rodriguez had rallied the town for local workers and opposed foreign influence. "And yet here you are—one of our locals, albeit a transfer, and you're sitting on their side of the table."

It was not the first time someone had brought this up, and Max acknowledged the fact with a nod before answering.

"I like to think of us sitting at a round table, much like this," he said, gesturing in front of him. "There are no sides, are there, Mr. Mayor? In fact, we are all on the same side."

Rodriguez's smile drooped a little.

"Please, call me Joe," he responded. "And you are correct. We are all on the side of the great city of Las Vegas."

"The guy's got a point, right?" Eddie interrupted. "I think we all want the best for the Jewel, so long as it's good for Las Vegas."

"Absolutely," Max agreed, feeling he needed to defend Haoyun.

"Joe, I know you understand how much the rail's construction will impede the Desert Jewel over the next few years. Haoyun is acting in good faith, moving forward with the acquisition even though the project will hurt business in the short term."

"And increase business in the long term," the mayor added, raising an eyebrow to make sure Max acknowledged him.

"Yes, that is the hope." Max downplayed the future benefit. He turned to Eddie. "What did he mean about 'other ventures' for Tri-Star?"

Eddie looked like he wasn't sure of his answer, glancing across the table at Geno, but the older man was deep in conversation, gesticulating with his hands toward Wei. Eddie looked down and slowly shook his head.

"We've got some things in the works to diversify our current business."

"Diversify?" Max asked.

"He means to say we're getting into the construction business," Geno interrupted, apparently not as deeply distracted as he had appeared. "It's OK, Eddie. It's no longer a secret."

The big man reached for his champagne flute and raised it again.

"Wei, Ling, Max, if you've been wondering why we are selling, Tri-Star needed to divest the casino business so we could be free and clear to sign a contract with the city. We've always had a small construction business, but last year we merged our unit with a larger company, and as of this morning we have agreed to build the Las Vegas component of the high-speed rail terminals."

"Salud!" Eddie chimed in, and the whole table raised their glasses.

Max settled back to read the reactions. Wei and Ling both put on enormous smiles and congratulated Geno. They seemed well practiced in faking surprise.

"That sounds like a big deal," Max said to Eddie in a lowered voice as the table chatter resumed.

"Huge."

"How did you win something like that without much of a track record?" The words were out of his mouth before he even thought them through. This was Las Vegas, and Tri-Star was effectively the mob—of course they won the contract.

"It wasn't easy," Eddie answered, clearly thinking the question was authentic. "Joe has things he wants, and we can help him. But trust me—this is not a handout. We're making a big bet here and are giving up one of our most profitable businesses to do it."

Not the answer Max had been expecting, though he had a hard time thinking the Desert Jewel was their most profitable business. It barely made money, and even if you added back the skim, the juice was barely worth the squeeze.

"You given any more thought to that thing?" Eddie asked quietly, clearly alluding to the job offer.

"Not yet. Too much going on." Max evaded the answer, which would most certainly be no when the time came. "Whatever comes, I have to complete my current contract before making any decisions."

* * *

When the elevator door opened, Max walked purposefully to the door he'd seen on the tour marked "Manager's Lounge." He waved his key card and was relieved to hear the gentle click of the lock releasing. The Desert Jewel had promised them all-access, but Max still didn't trust Tri-Star, and with every new door, he half expected his ID to fail.

He'd stayed through the end of the dinner, which had remained unsatisfying—the entrée portions were barely appetizers. The group had then moved to the bar, but he'd politely excused himself, explaining it had been a long day—and that was not a lie.

After saying his goodbyes, he'd gone to his room, where he managed to catch a few hours of sleep before emerging around two in the morning for his current exploration. He'd followed the same route down to the distribution center, which was still bustling.

Inside, the manager's lounge was nothing more than a small locker room that included a small square table with four chairs and a

TV on the wall that displayed a split four-panel screen showing different security camera views. Every thirty seconds, the views switched to a fresh set of cameras.

Most of the lockers were unlocked, and on his fourth try, he found what he needed. The badge read "Victor Cruz," and Max silently thanked Victor for leaving his jacket, hat, and badge unlocked and available. The extra-large jacket was comfortably loose. He adjusted the hat to his head, pulling it low over his forehead, and clipped the badge at his waist after sliding his own pass card into the slot behind Victor's name. He purposefully left the name flipped inward in case someone actually looked.

Next to the door was a row of clear plastic bins, and all but two held clipboards, presumably for keeping track of the various activities. Max assumed that at least two managers would be on the floor, but with 50,000 square feet, he hoped he would not run into them. He took a clipboard for himself and exited the lounge.

The distribution floor was still alive with activity. Workers in electric carts pulled trolleys laden with various goods from one location to the next, while others pushed hand trucks down the aisles. Above them all, the forced air continued to whir, circulating cool air that smelled like cardboard.

He intentionally started in the opposite direction from his goal, striding down an aisle with purpose, turning once to look down at his clipboard and then up at the racks of boxes. He doubted anyone was watching him, but if they were, he wanted to appear to be doing something.

Twenty minutes later, after various stops on his route and even one incident when he criticized a worker for a loosely stacked collection of boxes, he walked down the aisle he had visited on the tour. Toward the far end, the boxes of caviar still sat in the same location, and he made a snap decision, slipping his pocketknife into his hand, blade already extended.

He made a quick cut along the bottom of one box and then up about an inch at the corner. The knife was back in his pocket within twenty seconds, and he backed away to check that the aisle was still clear. Reaching back to the pallet, he pulled open the flap as gently as he could, allowing his fingers to slide inside, and he immediately felt the cool metal of a caviar tin. It was maybe an inch thick, thin enough to get through his hole, though he wished he'd cut it larger.

The circular tin spun as he tried to get his fingers on it, and he almost gave up, but he forced his fingers deeper, tearing the cardboard more than he'd intended. His forefinger finally found purchase on the other side of the tin, and he forced it out of the carton, immediately pushing it into his pocket. There was a loose wrap of green plastic around the center of the box, so he pulled it down to cover his work. He stepped back, again checking that nobody had observed, and then continued to his ultimate destination.

At the end of the aisle, he turned to his left and crossed the floor toward the area that had piqued his curiosity earlier in the week. The two doors were alone in this wall of the building and unmarked except for the inert caution light on the wall above them. He tried to get his bearings, looking across to the catwalk and trying to imagine where the elevator was in relation to this wall. The north wall, he figured. Silverado Ranch Boulevard, that was where the main entrance was.

Suddenly, a siren beeped, and the light above the doors flared red as they slowly opened inward, doors folding against the interior walls. Max stepped closer but then had to back off as a motorized cart exited, pulling a flatbed piled with boxes neatly stacked in two layers behind it. The operator of the cart nodded as he passed, and Max lifted his clipboard in salute, still trying to maintain the illusion. He watched the sled pass, counting each layer at eight by three boxes, so almost fifty in total. As before, each of them had a blue stripe across the writing on the visible sides. He lifted his clipboard to write forty-eight for no other reason than to appear occupied.

Then the beeping stopped, and the doors started to swing shut. Max glanced casually around and did not see anyone, so he stepped through the doors before they closed.

The lighting in the tunnel was bright, though not as bright as the distribution center, and the air was definitely not as fresh or as cool.

Ahead of him, the lights of a tunnel ran off for maybe twenty yards before they sloped downward, still heading straight north if Max's sense of direction was correct. Max took several steps forward, but there was nothing to see besides the lights on the tunnel wall.

Behind him, the light changed again, and Max turned to see the cart driver had manually pushed the door open, staring at Max.

"You looking for something?" the man called out with the air of a parent who'd caught their child breaking the rules.

"No." The answer was reflexive, and he added a touch of truth. "I was curious where this leads."

The man pushed the door, which clicked against the wall and remained open, then took several steps toward Max.

"This area is off limits," he said, ignoring the question and eyeing Max's outfit. "You of all people should know that."

Max lifted his arms up to both sides, clipboard still in his right hand.

"Yup. I'm definitely in the wrong spot." He shook his head with a smile. "What area is this anyway?"

"It's called none of your business. What's with the questions?" The man reached and immediately grabbed the ID card at his waist, flipping it to peer at the name. "Time to head out, Victor."

Initially unsure, the worker was now quite convinced he was right and had caught "Victor" in the wrong place. He grabbed Max's right arm and pulled him toward the open door. Despite the many countermoves that rushed unbidden through his head, Max allowed himself to be steered out of the tunnel.

Back in the main area, he pushed Max away from the door as it closed for a second time. The man's cart sat half turned into the second aisle, where he'd obviously left it to follow Max.

"Mind your own business," he said over his shoulder as he walked away.

Max started to apologize, but the man was no longer paying attention. He got back on his cart and drove off, leaving Max alone. He was about to head back to the manager's lounge when movement caught his eye to his left, above the floor, and he felt a moment of panic.

On the catwalk overlooking the warehouse, Eddie and Johnny had walked out to the railing. Worse, they looked in his direction, and he felt certain that Eddie had identified him. Then a loud crash echoed through the room from the far side, and both men turned away. Max reached to pull his cap even lower as he turned to walk into the relative safety of the nearest aisle, scanning ahead for a possible exit. In hindsight, the cap and vest were probably enough to throw Eddie off his scent, but he didn't want to stick around to be sure.

About halfway down the aisle, he spotted an emergency exit staircase, but the door had a sign next to it that read, "Emergency Exit

Only—Alarm Will Sound." And he'd much prefer to leave quietly.

He looked around for alternatives, but as he did, he caught a glimpse through the storage racks into the next aisle where the worker who had reprimanded him was returning with another manager. If leaving was in any doubt a moment before, it was no longer a question.

He turned back to the door. While the sign still threatened unwanted attention, Max knew it was not uncommon to disable these alarms in non-public areas. It really didn't matter. He needed to leave, and this door was his best option. He'd find out quickly if it was going to be a loud scramble or a quiet exit, so he crossed directly to the door and pushed it inward, bracing himself for a siren that never came.

A moment later, he was inside the stairwell, and no alarm had sounded. He bounded up the steps, two at a time, spinning at each landing to start the next flight. After four landings, he listened for pursuit but heard nothing, though he continued at the same pace. Two flights later, he was at the ground-level exit door, where he paused to take off the manager's jacket, depositing it in a corner with the clipboard. He kept the hat in case an exterior camera picked him up.

Once again, he pushed open a door, uncertain if an alarm would sound, and for the second time in as many minutes, he was relieved to hear nothing.

Outside, the dry nighttime air hit him, a stark contrast to the climate control he had been in below. He'd emerged at the taxi waiting area, facing north toward Silverado Ranch. Across the road, he could see the Deep Texas BBQ with its chimneys still spewing clouds of smoke. None of the cabbies paid him any mind until he tapped on the glass of the first cab.

The cabbie rolled his window down a few inches and motioned away from himself. "You need to go to the taxi stand."

Max had expected this and already had cash in his hand. He held a pair of twenties inside the window.

"I don't want to walk over there," he grumbled as the man took the bills, and Max heard the doors unlock. He slid inside, and the driver pulled away, turning away from the taxi stand and toward the rear exit.

Max looked back to see a valet throwing his hands up and shouting something, but he couldn't care less. This wasn't the first time someone had broken a rule in Las Vegas.

Across the road, Max caught sight of the BBQ place again. The kitchen seemed at full blast despite the late hour. Vegas nightlife was a machine of its own.

* * *

When he got home, the first thing he did was remove the caviar tin from his pocket to the island counter in his kitchen. Crisp plastic wrapping still sealed the gold tin. Max stared at it for a minute, wondering how much trouble was inside, before he turned to get a beer from the fridge. When that was open, he enjoyed that first long drink that was always so good.

He exchanged the opener for a knife and cut the plastic from the tin. He chuckled to himself, thinking, *The best-case scenario is I'm now a felon.* From what little he knew about caviar, a can this size was easily north of a thousand dollars, and he'd stolen it. Even so, he didn't think the best case was likely. Grabbing a butter knife from the next drawer, he pushed the blade between the two ridges along the edge, twisting to pry open the top. It was definitely well sealed because he failed on the first try but then heard the satisfying vacuum release as the top opened to reveal—caviar.

The tin contained what looked like perfect little fish eggs, tightly packed. He held the bottom and dipped the blade of his knife in the center, pulling the mass to one side to see if anything was underneath, but all he saw was caviar. When he disturbed it, the tight mass of eggs released and seemed more voluminous than the tin, tumbling out and making a nice mess of his counter, but that was all it was—a mess.

Somewhat disappointed, Max took another sip of beer and opened a cabinet to pull out a box of crackers. *If I'm a felon, I might as well enjoy the spoils*, he thought to himself as he slathered a cracker with the roe and took a bite. Probably the most expensive protein he had ever eaten, but it was well worth it. The buttery flavor had a slight hint of ocean, and he almost wished the cracker weren't there as he popped the second half into his mouth and removed another scoop.

Then he paused. The tin did not look as deep on the inside as it should be. He held the tin closer to his face and tapped down with the knife—it definitely was not tapping on the bottom. Immediately, he turned the tin over and scraped the rest of the caviar onto the counter.

Somewhere inside him, his culinary self abhorred the waste, but he ignored it. When he turned the tin back over, he could definitely see that the bottom was only about halfway up. A label surrounded the outer edge of the tin, and he felt it again with his thumb, now noticing a ridge of sorts beneath the label.

In an instant, he'd swapped the butter knife for a sharp one and cut the label along this ridge. When he was done, he twisted and after minimal resistance found himself unscrewing a bottom piece that eventually dropped into his hand, revealing another compartment as packed as the caviar had been but with a different content—small plastic bags filled with white crystals.

Max put the tin down on his counter next to the mess of black caviar, which seemed to accent the illicit white substance. Despite his expectations, it was still a shock to have found drugs. He took in a purposeful breath and pushed himself away from the counter.

He could look the other way on a lot of things, but he hated drugs.

His sister had come to Vegas for a fresh start years back. He had been serving overseas, but they'd always stayed in close contact. She'd chosen Vegas over a college education despite his attempts to convince her otherwise. Then, she'd started partying and they'd slowly drifted apart. He'd never forget the call he'd received from his mother when she'd been found dead. The details had never been fully known, but the coroner had suggested a cocktail of drugs. No foul play, but that was almost worse. There wasn't anyone to blame. When he'd first moved to Las Vegas, he'd tried to ask after her, but it was years on and he'd never found anything.

Looking at the stuffed tin, Max could not help but feel anger rising. If he couldn't avenge Lulu, maybe he could hit back at the machine that helped kill her.

His feelings aside, this was going to change things. He felt certain that Haoyun Casino would bring this to the police, but before or after the deal closed? This was an important transaction for them, and they'd been insistent on speed. For sure they would use it as leverage, but he didn't have enough to bring it to them yet. He still had too many questions. For one, he wasn't completely sure what drug he was looking at, though he guessed it was Molly. That was something he could find out. He took one pouch and tucked it into his wallet.

It was too late for more answers. He left the tin and the caviar on the counter, knowing he could clean it up after a few hours of important sleep. He had to be at the Jewel by ten, and that wouldn't give him much time.

# CHAPTER EIGHTEEN

As the week progressed, Max found himself increasingly sidelined in the Haoyun war room. It was now Friday, and the deal was essentially done, though the Haoyun team was still pursuing the embezzlement claim and locking down the distribution contracts with their major clients—relationships that were key to the ongoing profitability of the Desert Jewel.

Wei Zhang and Ling Wu seemed happy with the progress and had steadily yielded more control to Jun Chen, who had never seemed interested in Max's role. They invited Max to fewer meetings, which suited him fine. Wei Zhang had actually left for New York, though he was expected to return for the closing. Today, the teams were meeting to iron out what minor details remained, and the lawyers would work on closing papers over the weekend. The two sides would meet again on Monday, followed by an expected deal closure the following day.

Geno had already arranged for what promised to be a lavish celebration on Tuesday night at his house in the Southern Highlands.

For his part, Max had used his time digging into Genoa Imports, and though he had failed to find anything new with respect to the mayor's connection, it was not entirely fruitless. Almost by accident, he'd discovered that the Genoa contract was actually with Tri-Star and not the Desert Jewel. The Haoyun team had quickly remedied the situation, and Max had even earned a rare compliment from Jun Chen at the next strategy meeting.

He had been trying to avoid too much contact with Eddie since the unexpected "drive," and while he knew his ultimate answer, he'd been happy to deflect answering the employment offer. Beyond that, he still wanted to avoid a confrontation with the EMT from the hospital, so when Eddie approached him prior to the meeting, his mind immediately went into defensive mode.

"Good to see you, Max!" Eddie extended a large hand and pulled Max into the familiar hug, which Max returned awkwardly. "You been thinkin' about that thing?"

"The fight?" Max lowered his voice. "I've been ignoring the news."

"No, man. The job I told you about."

Max really wished the man would be direct.

"Only thinking, Eddie," he replied casually. "As I said, no

decisions now."

He purposefully left the ultimate answer non-committed.

"How are things with you?" Max continued.

Eddie motioned with his head toward an empty corner.

"Let's move over here, and I'll tell ya."

The two men stepped away from the primary group.

"First, that was no accident. Those guys were connected." He held up an index finger in emphasis. "Out-of-town crew, but they were connected, and I think they were looking for me. Now you know why I want you to take the job."

"Yeah, well, I'm hoping nobody knocks on my door."

"You'll be fine. But listen, bro. I've got more problems."

Max did not respond but raised his eyebrows in interest.

Eddie looked around them nervously before continuing.

"It's fuckin' Staci." Eddie sounded angry.

"Huh?"

"Fuckin' Staci is the one who embezzled," Eddie continued. "It doesn't look great for me, but when I found out, I helped uncover her."

This was new. Max nodded as he processed the news. Staci was a good person, he knew in his core. Embezzlement? Good for her.

"Really?" he muttered, trying to fill the space as he absorbed the news. "I wouldn't have guessed."

"Me neither," Eddie replied with a tone of disgust. "It's a damn shame. And now I got eyes on me."

"So you guys are done?" Max ignored the last comment.

"Absolutely." Eddie was incredulous, scrunching his face in disgust. "She stole from us. Deserves whatever she gets."

He couldn't help but feel a little disappointed in Eddie. He'd seen the two of them together enough to know that they had a strong connection. Was Eddie so shallow that his allegiance to his boss took precedence? The man actually seemed more focused on defending himself than the sanctity of Tri-Star or the Desert Jewel.

"What will happen to her?"

"First, she has to return the money," Eddie answered, raising an index finger. "Then, who knows? She won't be at the Jewel no longer. That's for sure."

Disappointment was turning into disgust. From what Staci had shared, she was in love with this man, and Max had seen Eddie reciprocate. Now, he was tossing her aside like garbage.

"Geno's not happy about it, and he's taking it out on me," Eddie continued, "but I'll survive."

Max stayed silent. He had nothing to add, and it seemed like Eddie wasn't done.

"He's pulled me off the hospital thing. Said the Ghost would take care of things."

Mob politics was not really a topic Max cared about, but he needed to know if someone was on his trail.

"What does he mean when he says the Ghost will take care of things?"

Eddie looked around as if to confirm nobody was within earshot, and he spat on the ground before leaning closer to Max.

"The Ghost is a fucking monster. Doesn't care about anyone or anything except keeping Geno on top. Whenever Geno has a problem, the Ghost is the answer. Look, you know that thing at the hospital? The Ghost was originally handling things. That cathouse fire? That was the Ghost doing his thing. He couldn't care less that those women were innocent. But he came up empty-handed on identifying the girl, so when my boys located the EMT, Geno told me to handle it. That was a first. Me taking over for the Ghost." His shoulders slumped slightly. "But we got nowhere, and now this Staci shit came out. The Ghost is back on the case."

"Sorry, bro," Max said truthfully—he was sorry to have started the conversation.

"I gotta make a move." Eddie's tenor picked up. "Gotta take this back before the Ghost closes things."

Max did not know why he was apparently Eddie's confidant and was at a loss for how to respond. Should he be consoling the guy?

"I don't know, Eddie," he offered, nodding toward the conference room. "Seems like you're in a good position at Tri-Star."

"Yeah, for now. But if I'm no good on the streets, I'll be out faster than you can take out your phone to call 911."

"You want me to see if Haoyun will turn down the heat on Staci's theft?" Max was still concerned about this revelation.

"Nah. What's done is done. She'll be out of the picture soon enough."

Eddie nodded toward the group that was drifting through the door.

"Meeting's about to start," he added as he moved to join them.

Max didn't follow him immediately. He watched as the group filed into the conference room, trying to imagine how Eddie lived with himself.

He pulled out his phone and sent Staci a quick text.

"Need to talk ASAP."

He slid the phone back into his pocket and caught the door as it was closing.

* * *

Max had sat quietly as the meeting droned on until his phone vibrated.

Thankfully, no one in the large group noticed as he slid his phone into his lap to see that he'd received a reply from Staci.

"Can we meet at four? I've got a lot going on at work."

"Go for a smoke at four," he replied after checking his watch. It was 3:40 p.m., which gave him plenty of time.

He excused himself and made a quick trip to his room, where he changed shirt and grabbed a baseball cap. If anyone really wanted to follow him, he couldn't evade the eye in the sky, but it never hurt to throw off a more casual observer.

Back down on the casino floor, he crossed to the side exit that led to the parking lot. He wasn't a smoker, but in his time at the poker tables, he'd often taken breaks with friends who were, so he knew a lot of the locations. At the Jewel, there was a smoking area beyond the taxi lot, facing Silverado Ranch Boulevard, and he'd learned on one of his tours that the finance department was nearby.

As the door closed behind him, he looked across to see the area was empty. He checked his phone—it was a few minutes past four. There might be another smoking area, but based on his knowledge of the layout, this was the closest. He started to type a message to Staci, but a door swung open, and he saw her emerge, cigarette already lit in one hand.

It took him less than thirty seconds to cross the remaining distance.

"Hey." He gave her a brief hug—way less than the exchanges he was now accustomed to with Eddie. "How are you holding up?"

"I'm fine," she answered, looking down, then turned worried eyes to look at him. "No, I'm not fine. I'm in trouble."

Max raised an eyebrow. He already knew she was in trouble, but he was curious to hear how much she would admit.

Staci edged away from the door and motioned Max to come closer. When he complied, she continued in a panicked whisper.

"Oh my God, where do I start?" She shook her head. "The Jewel's books are full of holes. I had been here less than a year when they first asked me to adjust the books."

She raised four fingers with air quotes as she said "adjust."

"The overall business is fine," she added defensively, "but it could be better. I've helped a lot of things fly under the radar. That's how I met Eddie, and I don't want him to get caught."

The obvious love in her voice put a pit in Max's stomach, knowing her boyfriend was preparing to get rid of her. He had to warn her.

Staci grabbed his hand and met his eyes. "The system was so smooth that, last year, I decided to take some for myself. Not huge, but enough. I've been doing it for them for three years, so why not take some for myself? Nobody would miss a little, right?"

"Except for the Haoyun acquisition." Max completed her thought, thinking this would be a good time to fill her in. "I know. That's why I texted you."

"Shit."

"That's what happens when they scrutinize everything," he said. "I don't think it's a deal-breaker though. Can you return the money?"

Staci paused and gave him a look that said she had never considered that option.

"I've put up with too much shit to walk away empty-handed. Eddie can help. Maybe he and I can leave. Start somewhere new."

Max took a deep breath and stepped away, looking out over the parking lot. He saw the BBQ chimneys billowing smoke as they seemed to do at all hours, and something struck him in the back of his mind, but he didn't have time to dwell on it. He had to get Staci out of this situation.

When he turned back, there were tears streaming down her face. She took her last pull off her cigarette and flicked it into a sandpit by the door.

He knew he couldn't tell her that Eddie was betraying her. "Maybe you should think about taking care of yourself for now. Eddie will be there when it's over."

"I love him, Max. We're meant to be together."

He cringed. "The other thing from the hospital, that's not completely done, but I think you're in the clear. That cook you said you saw, he was one of the victims, but it would still be better if you left town."

"I've got to talk to Eddie, but he's been busy all day."

He ran a hand through his hair. "Geno knows about the embezzlement, Staci." He was on thin ice, trying to maintain the confidence of both sides. "I think it's best that you stay away from Eddie for now until the deal closes and things blow over."

Her eyes welled with more tears.

"No," she mumbled to herself, repeating it several times. "No, no, no, no. Things were so great a month ago!" She spoke as if Max were not even there, then she turned to look at him, wiping her eyes with the back of her hand.

"I'm sorry, Max," she said. "You've been great, but you don't know Eddie like I do."

"How about this?" Max knew he had to buy her some time. "Four days. You disappear for four days, and when the deal is closed, I'll either help you stay disappeared or bring you to Eddie. Either way, you call the shots."

"Why four days?"

"The deal closes Monday. At that point, tensions will be lower, and maybe you get your cake and eat it too."

"Where do I go until then?"

Max looked at his watch.

"What time do you get off?"

"Five thirty."

"OK. You're going to leave early at ten after five. Don't tell anyone you're leaving, but come out here as if for a cigarette."

"Why?"

"Enough with the questions, Staci. I think you're in more trouble than you know. I'll be here to meet you, and I'll put you in my apartment for the weekend. Can you trust me on this?"

Staci looked at him with eyes that had given up. She nodded.

"I almost forgot." Max stepped close and reached into his pocket, deftly pulling out the small drug bag and showing it to her in the palm of his hand. "What's this?"

Her eyes bulged slightly, looking at him in surprise.

"That's Molly. Where did you get that?" she asked.

"Doesn't matter." Max shook his head and re-pocketed the bag. "I thought that might be it. Is that the stuff you saw . . . that night?"

Staci nodded, her eyes moving back from surprise to fear.

"Max, what are you doing?"

He rubbed his eyes, wondering the same thing.

"Ten after five," Max repeated, ignoring her. "And don't speak of this to anyone . . . including Eddie."

Again, Staci nodded acquiescence, mumbling weakly, "OK."

Max put a hand on her upper back as she turned to go back inside. He walked with her to the door and reached over to turn her chin so that she was looking at him once again. The tears were gone, but the sadness remained, and it triggered a memory of Lulu.

"We'll get through this, Staci," he spoke softly. "Remember what I told you. We take it one step at a time and don't panic. I'll get you through this."

* * *

As the door closed, Max couldn't help but think of his sister. Maybe if someone had been there to help her, she'd still be around. He also felt sorry for the young woman who had thrust herself into his life a week and a half earlier. He knew she was a good person, but it was more complicated now. Regardless of her innocence with respect to Geno and the mayor, she was an admitted thief. It didn't matter that her victims were criminals. She was far from blameless, and how little she knew of the man she claimed to love. From what he had said, Eddie was done with her without a second thought. Worse, it hadn't been clear, but her life was potentially in danger.

Across the street, the BBQ chimneys continued to erupt in a constant stream of smoke. He stared at them, trying to understand what had struck him as odd moments earlier. The restaurant sat nestled in the corner of a parking lot that served the large mall on that side of the street. Max had looked up its online reputation, which contained some decent reviews but probably not enough to keep the restaurant full.

*So*, he asked himself, *why does it always seem to go full blast?*

He continued to stare at the building and finally understood what had triggered his unconscious feeling that something was out of sorts. There were two sets of chimneys. More than two actually, but what Max thought was odd was that one set, the set that appeared the busiest, was on the opposite side of the building.

On the far left side, three brick chimneys rose out of the building, only one of which was currently in use. Each of these had three vent caps, which Max assumed represented various smoking pits. Then, on the street side of the building, almost to the far right, though not quite, a set of three metal vent pipes rose from the ground. Although the chimneys on the left were clearly part of the building, someone had secured the newer pipes to the building's exterior. Two of them were venting white smoke, while the third seemed to issue clearer but obviously hot exhaust. Thinking back on it, these were the pipes that had struck Max as always in operation.

Wheels turned in Max's head. Looking down to his left, toward the casino entrance, he spotted the fire escape that had been his exit the previous night. He looked from the door across to the BBQ then tried to orient himself to the distribution center. He felt a buzzing in his head. The tunnel in the distribution center had headed north—toward the BBQ. As he put his hand back in his pocket to feel the plastic baggie, he felt like he already knew the answer but needed to check things out.

He looked at the time and saw he had forty minutes to return for Staci. He'd get her secure then make a plan to come back later. This would mandate what he could only think of as black ops, and the prospect of danger thrilled a certain part of him, even as another part knew he shouldn't be taking these risks. It had been a while since he'd been to the storage locker, and with good reason.

## CHAPTER NINETEEN

It had started in a closet. After retiring from the Marine Raiders, Max had transitioned fairly well to the civilian life. He'd set himself up in Vegas and quickly found work as a translator for a few of the casinos. Between the jobs, staying fit, and long nights in the poker rooms, he'd kept fairly busy, which kept his mind off the war, his past, and his losses. But there had always been the occasional afternoon or evening when he was idle and thinking about the skills he no longer needed. In those moments, he'd begun collecting equipment he was fairly sure he'd never use.

After about a year, the closet in his guest room was full, and some of his gear was on and under the bed. By that point, he'd allowed this "hobby" that was once his life to take a legitimate position in his routine, and he'd even returned to the firing range on weekends, which led to his decision to add a couple of guns to the collection.

Eventually, the trove grew too large, and he'd moved everything to a self-storage pod on the outskirts of town. That had been five years ago, and Max would admit to himself, if not to anyone else, that he now had a veritable arsenal of weapons and gear at his disposal should he have need. There had been a few times he'd put it to use, but mostly it was there to help fill a void that had always lingered under the surface after he'd left the service. He still went to the range every few weeks, but even that he kept to himself and was careful to use remote facilities where he would not see anyone he knew. Sunglasses and baseball caps helped with that too.

It was half past midnight as Max jogged down the empty Flamingo Arroyo Trail that bisected the eastern part of Las Vegas. He wore a skintight black long-sleeve shirt and dark shorts along with a baseball cap pulled low. It wasn't the nicest of trails, and there were several areas with homeless encampments, but it ran right past the self-storage location that housed his arsenal.

Earlier, he'd picked up Staci as they had arranged, taken her home to gather an overnight bag, then brought her to his apartment and set her up in his guest room. She complained about the three-story walkup, but the hardest part had been getting her to consent to give up her phone. Eventually, she agreed, and he traded it for a burner phone with instructions to answer whenever it rang. He knew she didn't fully understand the danger she was in, so he repeated his instructions several times. He made simple pasta with pesto and shrimp, and they'd settled in front of the TV to watch a couple of episodes of a streaming series that Staci wanted to see. Max had never heard of it, but he had to admit that it was fairly entertaining.

Staci had headed to bed around eleven thirty, but Max had waited until he was sure she was asleep before slipping out of the apartment.

He slowed to a walk as he approached the footbridge that crossed South Nellis. To his right, he could see the well-lit storage facility, and to his left an access path connected the trail to the sidewalk. He made his way to the street, cautious of finding someone under the bridge, but there was no one around.

Desert Storage was probably twenty years old and typical of most facilities, with orange roll-up doors lining the rows. It was all one story, with a horseshoe building on the outer perimeter surrounding a central rectangular building and vehicle access between the two. Max's unit was on the front end of the horseshoe building, which made his access slightly less secure, as he did not need to key the gates, which sat at the entrances between the two buildings. The flip side of that arrangement was he could access his locker with no record of his own entry.

After leaving the trail, it was only fifty paces before he was in front of his locker, spinning the wheels on his combination. He paused with the lock in his hand to turn back to survey the courtyard and the street beyond. There was no one in sight—not even a car on the street—so he flipped the latch and heaved the door up, slipping quickly inside as he let the door roll back down. As he reached the wall to trigger his lighting system, the room filled with bright white light, and simultaneously he heard his alarm's familiar beep. He keyed his code into the keypad, and when the light switched from red to yellow, he held his thumb to the sensor, which then clicked green. The beeping stopped.

If a stranger opened the locker, they had thirty seconds to disarm the alarm before tear gas filled the room and much of the surrounding area. That was intentionally non-lethal and would hopefully clear the area because Max had carefully wired the entire stash to explode two minutes after any unwanted entry. He would not risk others getting a hold of his arsenal.

The unit he was in, Unit 1A, was actually only a five-by-ten end unit, but Max had also purchased Unit 4A, which was the first ten-by-twenty regular-size locker along the main corridor. The two units shared a wall, and Max had simply knocked out a doorway between the two, creating a large space with easy access. Both gates had redundant security, and he had paid up front for a twenty-year lease, so he felt well secure in his design.

Unit 1A, where he now stood, was more of a marshaling area. It had a small table where he could assemble his gear and a footlocker on one side, while the opposite wall contained racks of tools and non-lethal gear. He paused here to change into a pair of lightweight black combat pants and a pair of trail runners that would keep him nimble. He pulled an ultra-light plate carrier off the rack and left it on the table. The body armor would also hold his weapons, but there was no need to strap it on yet.

With his rudimentary carpentry skills, Max had accidentally undersized the door between his units, so he had to duck slightly as he entered the larger unit, which was also lit by the same sterile white lights. This area held his arsenal and had racks of gear on two sides, one of which blocked the roll-up door for 4A, and three large gun safes on the wall opposite Max. To his right, on the end wall, were a good number of handguns and knives positioned for easy access. These Max considered somewhat harmless compared to the contents of the safes, and they were all he would need for the night's sortie—at least that he hoped. He was risking enough going into the city armed —no way he wanted to bring more-advanced weaponry.

He removed a Heckler & Koch VP9Sk subcompact, and after a quick inspection, he flicked the safety on, chambered a round, and strapped the ankle holster on his right ankle, allowing the pant leg to hang loose to cover it. While he did not plan on needing a firearm, it was always a good precaution. Tonight's work would be more subtle, so he pocketed a length of Kevlar cord and a pair of knives—both of which he would position on his armor for quick access. Last, he opened a small safe that was bolted to the demising wall between his units. He removed a neatly wrapped stack of bills about a half-inch thick. Sometimes all the weapons in the world would not help as much as cash would.

On one shelf, his eye caught a row of tear-gas canisters, and he grabbed a couple on his way back to 1A, tucking them into the body armor along with an extra magazine and the knives.

He donned the armor vest and tightened the various straps before throwing on a black windbreaker that concealed the kit. The whole thing had taken maybe ten minutes, and he rekeyed the alarm and shut off the lights before sliding open the roll-up door, which was once again closed and locked in a matter of seconds.

* * *

He walked four blocks to the spot where he'd arranged to meet the cab. As always, he'd greased the driver in advance. While he never used the same driver twice, he'd only been stiffed once in one of these arrangements, and on that occasion he'd been able to find another quickly.

The ride down to the mall across the street from the Desert Jewel took less than twenty minutes, though the roads remained relatively full. He'd given the driver the address of one of the other restaurants in the mall north of the Jewel and, as agreed, paid him handsomely on the drop-off. He gave the man a pinned location for the pick-up.

The mall itself had an indoor-outdoor element. The larger retail area was closed at this hour, but there were several satellite buildings clustered near the exits that all held restaurants and bars. One even had a rooftop disco that seemed to be in full swing, and this was the spot where Max had been dropped off. The BBQ was a little more remote, set apart from the other buildings in the corner of the parking lot, but close enough to the patio-bar that the lot between them was still filled with cars.

Max walked casually through the rows of vehicles, passing a few twenty-somethings on their way to the nightclub. Ahead of him, the BBQ still billowed smoke, though Max noted that the cluster of chimneys on the far side, the ones that looked built in, were relatively quiet, with only a few wisps of smoke escaping from one chimney.

In contrast, the near cluster of pipes, closer to the entrance, were issuing a steady plume. These were the ones that appeared to run up the outside of the building, and Max made a point of walking past the building to the south edge of the lot as if looking at the view of the Desert Jewel. Between the lot and the casino, traffic continued to flow on Silverado Ranch Boulevard.

Immediately below him, a car drove past on the mall access road, turning right about a hundred yards down. He looked down the side of the building where a chain-link fence separated the lot from the embankment and access road below. He'd seen most of this when searching the location online, but it was good to confirm. Turning back, he headed toward the entrance. As he passed the corner of the building, he confirmed his earlier suspicions when he saw the set of pipes rising through the ground on the outside of the foundation. He paused, briefly wondering at the audacity, but then continued to the doors.

Once inside the restaurant, a hostess greeted him, pointedly checking her watch before giving him a questioning look.

"We stop serving at one," she said. "You've got a few minutes to order if you want, but you'll have to eat quick." She grabbed a menu without waiting for an answer and motioned to a nearby table.

Max followed, looking around at a sparsely filled dining room. To his right were long rows of picnic tables that were probably filled most of the day, and along the far wall was a classic Las Vegas salad bar. Along the left wall were a pair of restrooms and then a set of swinging doors that obviously led to the kitchen. Farther down that wall was an opening that allowed guests to view the cooks at work.

The hostess conveniently sat him at a table with a view of the kitchen doors then mumbled something about a server and walked away. Getting his bearings, Max looked at the interior wall. Somewhere off to his left were the curious vent pipes. The restrooms were the only doors on that end of the wall. His eyes swung past the kitchen entrance, and as he looked through the open window, he could see the brick from the main chimney on the far right.

A server came by, and Max ordered a Diet Coke and brisket platter, sending the man on his way as quickly as he'd arrived. He knew he had little time, so he got up and crossed to the restroom. It didn't seem promising, but it was the closest door to the suspicious vents.

Immediately inside, a counter with three sinks ran along the right wall, and opposite them were three urinals. Typical of many bathrooms, a tiled wall separated this area from the toilets with an opening in the center. Max continued in, observing that all the doors were open. There were three stalls along the right wall, two on the left at the back, and inside the room where the third stall would have been was a door with an "Authorized Personnel Only" sign on it.

With no one else in the bathroom, he tried the door, but as expected, it was locked. On the door, above the handle, was a Yale keypad lock. Max thought about some common key codes, wondering how secure the door would be, when he heard a voice on the other side of the bathroom door, and he quickly crossed to a stall on the opposite side. As he slid the latch into place, the outer door burst open, and the formerly muffled voices entered the area.

"So I'm like, what does that mean?" a loud voice stated. "She stares at me for, like, twenty seconds then bursts into tears. Nice backbone, sweetheart."

"Classic. So now all is well?" a second voice responded, and Max thought it sounded familiar.

"Yeah, it was good last night."

Max carefully lowered his pants, making sure none of his gear was visible, but if anyone looked, he needed to appear to be doing his business.

The two men had come into the bathroom and moved immediately to the locked door.

"Hey, Johnny?" the first voice said.

Through the crack in the door, Max could see the first man nodding toward the stall. He didn't recognize him, but he now knew the second man for sure. He lowered his head and decided he needed to get active, so he pushed, creating an audible splash.

A knock came at the door, but Max kept his head down.

"You OK in there, buddy?" Johnny asked.

Max grunted and pushed again.

"Leave him alone," Johnny spoke to his partner at the door. "He's doing some good work."

Max heard four beeps—all of them the same tone—and a click signaled that the lock had opened. He heard the door swing open.

"We're fine," Johnny said to his partner as they both stepped through the opening and the door swung shut. "He didn't see us, and it sounds like he has bigger problems, if you know what I mean."

Once again, Max was alone, and he heard the lock click shut again. He finished up in the stall, washed his hands, and returned to the table. He needed to give Johnny and his man time to move away before he attempted to follow.

The brisket arrived and was actually nicely cooked, especially at this hour of the night, but he ate only a couple of bites before he got back up to head to the bathroom. He'd given them over ten minutes, and he didn't have much time before the place closed. Before leaving, he pushed cash under his plate to cover the meal and tip, not knowing if he'd be back in time to pay in person.

* * *

Back inside the bathroom, Max contemplated his options. He knew from experience that while keypad locks could be incredibly secure, they were often the opposite when users left the factory codes in place or changed the code to something very simple.

He'd heard the same tone four times, so he needed to figure out which number they'd repeated. A common factory default was four zeros, so he keyed it in, wondering if he could be so lucky. Nothing happened, but then he noticed a green key with a checkmark at the bottom of the pad, almost like the enter key on a keyboard. When he pressed it, he heard the satisfying click when the lock opened.

"Classic" was the only thing that popped into his head.

Pulling open the door, he peered into the semi-dark to see that it lead to a small area and the top of a stairwell. It was decent sized, big enough that two men could walk side by side. Several boxes, mostly toilet supplies, were stacked against the surrounding walls, but there was no other exit. He looked down between the railing and saw brighter light where the stairs ended, three flights down. Industrial noises rose from below.

He reached down to unholster his pistol and tucked it into his body armor, where it was more easily accessible. Not the scenario he would have hoped for—one point of entry, likely limited cover, and an active situation. If need be, he had to be ready to fight his way out, though he still hoped that would not become necessary.

While everything looked well built, he saw the walls of the stairwell were only rough cut, as if not intended to be permanent. He moved slowly so as not to make a noise on the metal stairs, but as he descended, he realized the noise from below would likely cover his movement. When he approached the last flight, the noises became even more pervasive. Over everything, there was a constant whoosh of ventilation, but there were other sounds too. Occasional pops or cracks accented an undertone of industrial work. The lights were bright white and spilled from a wide opening into the base of the stairwell. At the bottom, he edged to the side of the opening to see a large industrial room below him.

Unlike the stairwell, the room had been fully finished and resembled a chemical factory. Another set of stairs descended from his position to the floor below, but it was completely exposed. Immediately below the staircase and extending into the room was a series of large pieces of stainless steel equipment. Each unit had a bank of dials, screens, and buttons, and pipes connected some machines to each other. From their tops, vent pipes ran upward to another bank of machines on the ceiling. This was the source of the whooshing that overwhelmed the room, and Max immediately recognized the same style of industrial filtration apparatus that he had seen inside the distribution center.

Things clicked in his head. This was definitely a cookhouse. During his last tour in the Middle East, he'd been part of several raids on Syrian and Iraqi production of Captagon. This wasn't Captagon, which had no presence in the United States, but the setup was familiar, and ventilation was always key.

Scanning the room, he could only see one technician at work on the machinery, dressed in white with eye goggles and rubber gloves, but off to the left, at the far end of what was a decent-sized room, he could see two others in white talking to Johnny and his partner. Beyond them were several stacks of boxes, one of which was being loaded onto a carrier not dissimilar to the one he had seen in the bowels of the Desert Jewel. Even more curious, in the far wall was a set of double doors that were almost identical to the ones he'd seen in the distribution center below the casino.

He heard a faint sound and moved back into the stairwell. Something was wrong, but he couldn't pinpoint it. The noise of the air filter was so dominant—but he'd heard something. He looked up the stairwell, and something moved above him, then a light flashed, and he quickly pulled back. Someone was coming down the stairs.

Checking the room below, he hoped to find an opening to sneak down the stairs, but Johnny and his partner were headed back toward him. In an instant, he ran through his options and turned to head up the stairs, hoping it was only one or two men. If it came to a fight, the stairwell would limit their movement. With any luck, he could be back in the BBQ before closing.

He lowered his head and took the first flight of stairs two at a time, trying to get as far away from the room below before encountering whoever was descending.

"Hey, watch where you're going." A large man backed against the wall as Max moved past.

There were two more above him, and they stood side by side, blocking his path. Max's cap was still pulled low, and he was eye level with their belts. One of them had his hand on a pistol that was still tucked into his belt but was clearly ready to draw. He slowly raised his eyes to meet theirs, contemplating his plan of attack as he did.

"Move aside," he said, hoping they wouldn't question him.

"I don't think so," the one with the gun responded. "Who are—"

Max's left hand struck the man's genitals like a cobra strike. His right grabbed the barrel of the pistol and yanked it free of his stunned opponent. In the same motion, he spun his body, swinging the heel of the gun into the face of the man below him. Something cracked on impact, and Max let the gun fall onto the stairs as he turned back to throw his right fist into the face of the man he had first struck, knocking him backward onto the stairs and throwing the third man off balance.

Voices called from below, and Max knew he had little time. Forced to one side, the third man had his hand against the wall, but his other hand was reaching behind his back. Max charged up the two steps and lowered his shoulder into the man's side, knocking him against the wall, but he remained standing.

"Motherfucker," the man grunted as he pulled a pistol and tried to bring it around toward Max, but they were too close, and a moment later, Max had his left hand on the gun, forcing it above them as he clamped his right hand on his opponent's neck.

The man's other arm came up under Max's, locking on to his shoulder and using the leverage point to hold off Max's attack. For a few seconds, they wrestled, each fighting to control the pistol. Max knew he would win, but he didn't have the time to see it through. He could hear footsteps on the outer stairs below, so he reversed direction and took a step down the stairs, pulling the pistol and the man's right arm down with him.

He hadn't been aware of it, but the big man had recovered and was below him when he'd turned, and Max used his left hand to propel his victim into the large man, sending both tumbling down the stairs.

Beyond the men, Max looked down to see Johnny at the top of the inner stair, and for a brief second they made eye contact, but he wasn't sure the other man recognized him. He turned and bounded up the stairs two at a time, already on the middle flight, before the first shots rang out.

"Get out of the way!" Johnny growled below as he continued to ascend.

At the top of the stairs, Max looked for something to slow his pursuers, but seeing nothing, he stepped back and fired two shots into the stairwell. He could see movement below but didn't really aim at anything. He only wanted to slow their advance. Then he remembered the tear gas and paused at the door, where he quickly pulled the pin and sent the canister spinning toward the top of the stairs, gas already beginning to spew. That would slow them down.

As he closed the door, he thumbed his phone to tell his driver where to meet him, and knowing he had bought himself a small window of time, he walked casually out of the bathroom and returned to his table. He didn't sit down but pulled the money from under the plate to a more visible location, motioned to the server with a wave, and walked to the entrance.

He was passing through the door when he heard a commotion behind him, but he didn't look. He sprinted to the near corner of the building, out of sight from within. This side of the building ran along the outer perimeter of the parking lot, and a chain-link fence separated it from the access road that was sunken maybe ten feet below the lot. Earlier, he'd seen a gap in the fence about halfway down the building, and he headed straight for it, down the litter-strewn alley. At some point, someone had tried to mend the broken fence with zip ties, but Max drew a knife and made quick work of them, pushing himself through the gap and sliding a few feet down the embankment to the roadside below.

Behind him, he heard someone cursing and coughing, but not at him. So far, they had not located him, so he stayed low and speed walked up the side of the road, heading away from the restaurant and toward his rendezvous. He'd sent the cab to meet him on this road but around the corner, where it wouldn't be seen from the BBQ.

"There!"

He heard a shout from behind him followed by several gunshots. Nothing came close, but the distinct zing of bullet fire activated his senses, and he broke into a run. He knew that whoever was firing was likely dealing with the effects of tear gas and couldn't put a good mark on him, but he wasn't taking any chances. A few more shots rang out, and Max saw one hit the embankment to his right, but in a few strides he'd gotten far enough around the corner to cut off visibility from the BBQ.

Ahead of him, his driver had already parked at the designated stop sign, and Max straightened up upon seeing him, though he maintained a brisk pace. There was no need to panic the driver, even though the man's head was focused on his lap. Max made an effort to look both ways despite the deserted roadway, walked in front of the cab, and got in the back seat on the passenger's side, immediately assaulted by loud dance music.

"Can you turn that down?" he yelled as he closed the door.

"Sorry, boss." The driver turned the music lower as he put his phone into its holder. "Didn't see you. Where are we headed?"

Another shot rang out, and the driver's rear side window exploded, throwing glass all over the seat. The driver did not wait for instruction, slamming his foot on the gas and spinning the car to the right, away from the mall. The wheels screeched and fishtailed, but he soon corrected it and increased his speed as shots continued to fire. Max ducked low, and another bullet struck the rear window, shattering it as well, but the window stayed in place.

It was over as fast as it started. The road led under the freeway, and they were quickly both out of range and out of sight from the BBQ. At the next intersection, the driver gunned through a yellow light then took the next turn at a secondary street and pulled over.

"What the fuck was that?" he yelled, turning to stare at Max in a panicked rage.

He didn't wait for an answer but turned the other way and got out of the car, walking to the back to survey the damage.

Max got out and joined the driver behind the car, his hand held up in a defensive expression.

"I'm really sorry about this," he said calmly, "but I'll take care of it. We need to leave."

He reached to the back of his vest to bring out the cash he'd stowed earlier, but before he could, the man dropped to his knees, hands in prayer.

"No!" he yelled, still panicked. "Take the car. Don't kill me. I have family."

Max shook his head, pulled out the wrapped stack of hundreds, and held it toward the man.

"Nobody's going to die." He used his late-night DJ voice to calm the man. "This is ten K. And if that's not enough, I'll make sure you're whole." He paused, allowing the man to absorb the information. "But we need to get out of here. Those are bad men, and we haven't gone far enough."

The man put his face in his hands.

"What's your name?"

"Roland."

"OK, Roland. We need to move. I'll keep you safe, but we need to move . . . now."

"Fuck." He slowly regained his feet. Taking the money, he looked at it for a moment, rubbing his thumb down the side, then he pushed it into his pocket while tossing the keys to Max. "You drive."

CHAPTER TWENTY


It was four in the morning by the time Max finally arrived home. He'd driven the cab to a side street near the self-storage locker, then sat in the back with Roland for a good twenty minutes to be certain that the man understood the importance of his silence. The cash would cover the damage—Max was pretty sure of that—but Max assured him he would cover anything additional. He gave Roland a contact at an auto-body shop that would take care of everything—no questions asked. Plus, he would pay him another ten thousand in two weeks' time, so long as everything stayed quiet. Max had to repeat a number of times he was sorry that Roland was involved, but he emphasized that his adversaries would have no such care. If this went to the police, the consequences would be far more severe.

When Max was certain Roland understood, he gave him an untraceable pager number, explaining that his current burner phone still had sixty days on the plan, but the pager did not expire.

"Anytime you think something is wrong," he'd explained, "you ping me on the pager, and I'll be in contact within twenty-four hours."

The driver left, and Max had to reverse his routine at the storage locker, putting everything back in place and then retracing his way down the Flamingo Arroyo Trail to his apartment.

He entered the apartment quietly and heard a gentle snore from the guest room. Grabbing a beer from the fridge and some pretzels, he brought them to his room, which was on the opposite side of the living room. He closed the door quietly and plopped into his chair, opening the beer as he did.

He'd been thinking through the night's events on the run home, and now that he could truly relax, all of his thoughts rushed back at once. The Marchettis were operating a cookhouse under the BBQ, and it appeared to connect to the Desert Jewel underground. What he could not understand was that if this were the case, why were they selling the casino? Was this a setup to bust Haoyun as soon as the deal closed? It made little sense. Whatever was going on, this was a major operation. Why would they risk exposure?

On the table next to his chair, his phone vibrated where he'd left it earlier in the night. He picked it up and looked at the screen, which showed two missed calls and five texts from Carolyn.

The most recent read, "Are you there, Max? WTF! I need to talk to you.”

With two thumb strokes, her phone was ringing, and he tapped the speaker button so that he could open his hummus.

“Where the hell have you been?” Carolyn asked as soon as she picked up. “I've been pinging you for hours.”

“Good morning, C,” he answered, happy to hear her voice even if it was a bit agitated. “I had to take care of something.”

“Well, I hope you're not getting deeper into this Genoa Imports thing. I did a bit of research, and I've got a pretty good idea about those canisters you found.”

“Drug production?” Max questioned, feeling like he knew.

“Yes. Molybdenum—Molly. Ecstasy. I'm sure of it.” She paused. “How did you know?”

“I found the lab.”

“Fuck, Max. At the Desert Jewel?”

“Close. But it runs through the Jewel—or at least through their catering business.”

“You've got to go to the police.”

“I will, eventually, but my first duty is to Haoyun. They need to know about this. This will re-price the deal if they're even willing to proceed. They're scheduled to sign on Monday.”

“You should go to the police, Max.” There was tension in her voice. "This is bigger than your deal."

"I know." He calmed his voice, hoping she would settle down. "I have a friend on the force. Well, more like an acquaintance, but I'll talk to him. Any luck with dirt on Geno?"

"Are you even listening?" Carolyn yelled. "Why haven't you hung up on me and called the police?"

"I hear you, Carolyn." He maintained a steady voice. "I'm going to bring this to the police, but there are several factors here that you aren't aware of. Can you humor me for a moment? Did you have any luck with Geno?"

The phone was silent for a moment. With a calmer voice, she asked, "What's her name?"

It wasn't the question that hurt but the resignation in her voice.

"Staci," he answered with a sigh. "She's young and got herself wrapped up with the Marchettis. C, you won't believe this, but she looks just like Lulu and her mannerisms are similar too. I can help her get away, but I need some leverage."

"You're not responsible for your sister's death."

"I know, but maybe I could have been there. I know I can help Staci."

Once again, the phone was quiet, but Max didn't want to push his luck. He waited.

"The books are a mess, but there was no serious red flag," she finally answered. "I checked out Tri-Star too. Same thing. I poked around Geno's email, and you could certainly make some inferences, but generally speaking there was no dirt there."

"Damn." Max put the phone on the table. "I didn't think they'd be that careful."

"Yeah."

Carolyn was holding something back, but he didn't want to press. He opened the hummus and dipped a pretzel in, careful to close his mouth before chewing slowly to reduce the noise.

"How's the pretzel?" Carolyn finally chimed back in. She knew him too well.

"Sorry. I'm starving," he answered after finishing the bite.

"Only you can starve at four in the morning," Carolyn laughed.

Max slipped another pretzel into his mouth, this time holding it until it softened before chewing. He knew Carolyn had more to say and wanted to give her time.

"There's another server," she eventually continued. "Tri-Star runs backups nightly to off-site servers."

"Isn't that fairly common?"

"It is, but I could get into the backup drive too, and the data didn't match, and neither did the bandwidth usage, so I dug a little deeper into the logs, and the company runs two backups—one to a standard backup server and another set to an unidentified server. It took me a while, but I traced the access and IP records, and it looks like Tri-Star is sending data to a server at 1 Eagles Landing Lane."

The address sounded familiar, but Max couldn't place it.

"Is that in Vegas?"

"Yup. It's where you are supposed to be going on Tuesday."

"Geno's house?" It wasn't really a question.

"It's pretty sophisticated. I can't get in without a proximity-based encryption key, but I can tell you that only data from a few employees gets sent to this server—Geno, of course, Eddie, and two others. You said you thought they weren't being careful, but it's quite the opposite."

"What if I got you a proximity key?" Max threw out the idea without really thinking about the ask.

"I'd have to be there, Max."

She wasn't saying no.

"Let me think this through," he answered. "I don't want to put you in danger, but this is pretty big. What if I got to the server?"

"It's shielded, I think."

"Meaning?"

"Meaning I can't get access through Wi-Fi or Bluetooth." She paused, and Max assumed she was running scenarios through her head. "Well, it might work. If you can access the server and run an antenna outside the barrier, I could get access through a repeater. I'd still have to be close though."

"It's been a while since you visited."

"Oh, Max, how romantic!" The sarcasm was intentionally obvious, and Carolyn was definitely not happy.

"I'm sorry, C." Max could only offer the truth. "But I could really use your help."

The phone was silent once again, and Max leaned his head back, closing his eyes and waiting for her response. When it came, his stomach twisted.

"I'll come. But this ends it, Max. For good."

A favorite saying ran through Max's mind, "Be careful what you wish for." He hoped he could make things right. It would be great to see her.

"Thank you, Carolyn."

"One condition."

"Anything."

"You go to the police about the Molly lab. Tomorrow—actually, I guess that's today. You do that, and I'll help with the server."

It was Max's turn to think. Exposing the lab too soon might be a problem too, but he'd already planned to tell Ben, and the man could be discrete when necessary.

"OK. When can you get here?"

"Sunday night. I'll text you my flight info when I'm booked."

*  *  *

Tourists know Las Vegas for casinos, entertainment, and the Las Vegas strip. That was what the world saw, but for residents, the more common strip was the ubiquitous strip mall. Max had laughed about this coincidental play on words since moving to town in 2017. Now, as he walked across the parking lot of such a strip mall, the thought returned once again. He walked toward a small tiki bar nestled in the corner of a particularly unimpressive strip mall a little over a mile north of his apartment. It was quarter to seven on Saturday evening, and he was due to meet Ben on the hour for dinner.

When he'd called Ben earlier in the day, he'd been concerned about bothering the man on the weekend, but Ben had answered on the first ring and had been receptive to the meeting. He'd asked if anything was wrong, but Max demurred and told him he'd wanted to discuss in person. They'd agreed to meet. Max had let his friend pick the venue, and he wasn't surprised when Tiki Tom's was selected. Ben had a passion for fruity island cocktails, and Max had joined him at more than one of these bars after long poker sessions over the past few years.

Vinyl graphics displaying island images filled the windows and glass door. Inside, actual bamboo posts lined them, continuing the island theme and providing suitable darkness for the daytime bar patrons.

Max pushed open the door and was immediately welcomed by vintage island music with its high-toned percussion. It was a comforting sound, and he allowed himself to take a deep breath and enjoy it while he waited for the hostess.

The bar and restaurant had two sides. Directly ahead of him was the tiki bar, complete with palm-thatched overhang and faux tiki lights. It was standing room only, and Max could see both bartenders busy with cocktail shakers. To the left was a similarly decorated seating area, about half filled.

As the hostess returned to her station, Max saw Ben raise his hand at a back table.

"Joining that old guy," he said with a smile, pointing to the back.

The young woman followed his gaze and returned a grin.

"He's not that old," she said, taking a menu and turning to escort him to the table. She wore a loose tank top and jean shorts, apropos of the island theme.

Not for the first time, Max wondered how such talent populated every gin joint in Vegas.

At the table, the hostess put the menu in front of Max's seat and told them to enjoy.

"How are things, Max?" Ben half stood and offered his hand.

"I'm well, Ben." Max clasped his friend's hand, appreciating the firm grip. "How about you?"

"I'm above ground and enjoying a mudslide at Tiki Tom's!" Ben responded enthusiastically as they both took their seats. "Life can't be that bad."

"I appreciate you meeting on short notice."

"Not a problem, Max. Like I said, wife's out of town, so I had nothing going on."

A waitress stopped by to take Max's order, and he ordered a mudslide as well.

Ben brought up a mutual friend who had cashed high in a recent hold 'em tournament, and for the next twenty minutes, the two of them were trading stories from the tables. Max relaxed and for a moment forgot why they were together. Ben was truly a genuine human being. He had a few years left before retirement, but it seemed like he was doing well enough at the tables not to worry about his pension. He was telling Max about a big pot the previous night when he paused.

"Hey, how about you?" he said. "Has your luck turned?"

"Not so much at the tables." Max had played little but he'd lost on each of his last three outings, and he was still way down for the year. "But this current gig should turn my fortunes."

"Good to hear, my friend." Ben took a sip of his fresh drink. The server had come by earlier with a second round when she took their food order. "So what brings us together tonight?"

The question was like a glass of water thrown in his face. He'd been enjoying the company, and now he had to get serious.

"I found something I think you'll want to know."

Ben said nothing but opened his eyes as if to say, "Go on."

Max leaned in closer, lowering his voice, although nobody was within earshot, especially with the island music flowing.

"I think the Marchettis are operating a Molly lab out of the Deep Texas BBQ." Max paused. "Hell, Ben, I *know* they are operating a Molly lab. I saw it. And I'm ninety percent certain they're distributing through the Jewel's catering business."

Ben looked at him with deadpan eyes. He took another sip of his drink, and as he put it down, he slowly shook his head.

"Were you seen?"

"No," Max answered reflexively then remembered locking eyes with Johnny. "Well, maybe, but I don't think so."

"What did I tell you?" Ben spoke through gritted teeth, his voice almost a hiss. "I told you to stay clear of the Marchetti family. They are big trouble."

"Ben, forget about me. Did you hear what I said?"

Ben slammed his left hand on the table, startling Max. Then he took a deep breath and leaned in to continue.

"What part of this do you think is new to me? Jesus Christ, Raider. I'm not some greenhorn who just got to town. I've been working on this problem for two months. You think I just happened to start hanging out at the Jewel?"

He sat back upright. "Fucking no-limit tables there are usually action tables. Hard to make a steady return."

Max was uncertain of what he heard, except for the fact that the Jewel's tables were "action tables," which he knew and avoided.

"So you've known about it?" he asked.

"I haven't seen it, but we're building a larger case. I would suggest you back the fuck off." He spoke slowly, emphasizing each word. "Pronto."

It was Max's turn to shake his head.

"You know that if they sign the paperwork on Monday, Tri-Star and the Marchettis will no longer own the operation?"

"Doesn't matter. And it's bigger than you know."

The server arrived with their food, and the conversation paused. They both took a few bites before Ben continued, "Look, bud, I can't tell you exactly what's going on, but I'll keep you out of it if you can promise me you'll stay away from the operation."

Max listened, wondering why his friend was making the offer.

"Not a problem," he said before taking another bite of his teriyaki burger. "But there's a chance that this deal doesn't get signed."

"Doesn't really matter to me." Ben stared across the table. "And here I thought you were coming in here to confess that you were involved in that commotion at the hospital."

Max allowed a slight smile. "Not sure what you're talking about."

It felt like a moment of professional courtesy. He wasn't sure, but it felt like Ben was saying, "I know it was you, and I'll let it pass," and Max imagined his own response would be interpreted as, "You can't prove it, so let's move on."

Of course, Max reminded himself, this was all in his head. He had no way of knowing if Ben felt that way too, and he had no intention of asking. The exchange reminded him of another place where Ben might help.

"I've got another problem though," he started, waiting for Ben's attention. "Young girl I know got caught up with the Marchettis. Took some money. I think she's in danger."

"You got a name?"

"Staci Parker," Max offered and was a little surprised when a spark of recognition lit his friend's face.

"That's Eddie's girl."

"Not for long. You may know she works at the Jewel in

accounting? Says she helped cook the books for a while and then took some for herself. Now some details have come out during the buyout, and she's scared. Look, Ben, I'm not looking for a miracle here, but I don't want to see her killed."

"And how am I supposed to help?"

"What about some kind of witness protection?"

Ben laughed.

"First, we aren't the feds. And even if we were, what would she have to offer?"

"Not sure, but will you talk to her?"

Ben paused, putting his fork on his plate.

"Sure. No promises, Max, but I can meet her on Monday. Where is she?"

"My apartment."

Ben raised an eyebrow. "Is there another reason she fears the Marchettis?"

"No." Max hadn't even thought of the implication. "Not at all. She's a scared kid, with good reason."

"Alright. I'll come by at 9 a.m. on Monday. You playing in the mini bounty tournament at the Wynn tomorrow?"

Max was a little taken aback by the change in topic. Talking about Staci had revived thoughts of Lulu.

"No," He shook his head. "I've been off my game. Think I'm going to take Staci out to the range for a change of pace."

"OK." Ben gave him a look that suggested he still questioned the relationship. "You do that. More bounties for me, though I'm always happy to take you down."

"I know, Ben." Max raised his near-empty mudslide in a toast. "And the feeling's mutual."

CHAPTER TWENTY-ONE

The traffic on Highway 15 was light on a Sunday before noon. As planned, Max had taken Staci out to the gun range for a morning's diversion. Staci, though amicable and willing to go for the ride, had shown no interest in firing the guns, though Max had convinced her to try a small caliber pistol that he had brought along for her. The range was almost an hour from his apartment, and though they were halfway home, there had been very little conversation since they'd left. For his part, Max was thinking about Carolyn, who was due to arrive that evening. If he had to guess, he'd bet Staci was still thinking about Eddie.

"A few more days," he offered, breaking the silence. "Let things cool down, and then you can call him."

"You think he's going to break up with me, don't you?" She'd been staring out the window and did not turn when she spoke.

263

Max wasn't sure what to say.

"You think he'll be pissed I stole some money?" she continued. "That what we have is that superficial?"

He remained silent. He didn't want to share the conversation he'd had with Eddie. It wasn't his place.

"What if I told you he already knows?" She turned from the window. "Would you believe me then?"

"I don't know, Staci," he answered, surprised by the idea but dismissing it. "There's a lot of things going on right now. I told you I'd keep you safe. Can you just trust me on this?"

"Do you think he's a bad man?"

*Do I know he's a criminal?* Max thought to himself but didn't say. He did sort of like Eddie, as long as he made himself forget who and what Eddie really was.

"No." He decided that was an accurate answer. "I don't think Eddie is a bad guy. I think he's probably done some bad things, but I like him."

"I do too. More than that, I love him, and he loves me."

The arid Nevada landscape rolled past them on both sides of the highway. Land that was practically worthless, although less than an hour away, similar land was selling at record prices around Las Vegas. He'd often thought about the city's history—a byproduct of the Hoover Dam, which brought both water and electricity to an otherwise barren location. Of course, the casinos and entertainment played a huge role, but none of it would have been possible without the dam. Now, the city thrived, and people like Staci came here for their piece of success.

"You ever think about going back home?" he asked.

"Not yet," she answered slowly, thinking about the question. "I wouldn't mind it though. Louisville is a great town."

Suddenly she sat up, and her voice sharpened. "Why are you asking, Max?"

"Just a question."

"Four days," she pressed. "You said four days and things would blow over. I'm not going to Louisville. Not without Eddie. Have you talked to him?"

"I haven't seen him since Friday afternoon," he answered truthfully. "And I didn't say anything about moving."

"Can I call him?" she asked, her voice losing its edge. "I'm not your prisoner, am I? I don't even know why I agreed to this."

Max put his blinker on and eased the car down an exit ramp to nowhere. At the bottom was a little-used road and on the other side a similar ramp would take them back up to the highway. He pulled to the breakdown lane at the bottom of the ramp and put the car into park, turning to the young woman who was trying his patience.

"Staci." He looked her in the eyes. "You stole money. Usually, there are legal consequences, but in your case, the people you stole from are more likely to settle things in their own way. There's a lot going down right now. If the Haoyun deal closes, I think you probably stand a chance of walking away from all this. But given what I know right now, I'm not sure that happens. And that means Tri-Star and Geno will care about the money, and you'll probably have to return it."

When she started to protest, he held up a hand for silence and continued.

"Pause for a second and remember whom you're dealing with. Remember the girls from the Wild Horse? You may know these men socially, but that's a facade. These guys are ruthless. You've got to stop thinking that everything is OK."

His words seemed to hit home, and tears welled in her eyes.

"Not Eddie." She wiped her eyes. "I know he's a part of this, but there is much more to him. Look, I appreciate your help, and I'll stay with you for a few days, but I'm going to call Eddie. I'm not asking. You can't hold me prisoner. Either I get to call or I'm leaving as soon as we get back to town."

He closed his eyes and turned forward, putting both hands on the wheel. He inhaled through his nose and exhaled slowly through his mouth, repeating it several times, trying to calm his own mind. She was right. He would not hold her against her will. There was only so much a man could do, but he also had to protect himself. How would Eddie interpret the fact that he was helping Staci hide?

He cracked the rear windows to allow for air before turning the car off and removing the keys.

"Stay here."

He got out of the car and walked into the shade of the overpass. The late-morning air was warming but still bearable, especially once he reached the shade. There was no one and nothing around, save for scattered litter. On the other side of the freeway overpass, the road stopped at a turnabout. He turned back to where his rented Honda was parked and looked beyond it, down the dirt road that vanished at the base of a hill maybe half a mile away. Somebody must use this exit, but he doubted many did.

He pulled out his phone and tapped on his contacts. It was a call he knew he'd have to make, one way or the other, and he'd given some thought to what he'd say. This wasn't exactly when and where he'd planned to call Eddie, but it would do.

"Mr. Kline." Eddie's voice was full of enthusiasm. "How are you?"

"I'm good, Eddie. How about yourself?"

"Top of the world. What inspired you to call me on this beautiful Sunday morning? Have you decided to accept my offer?"

"I'm considering it, but I have something I need to talk to you about."

"OK, shoot."

"Are you in a place where you can have an open discussion?" Max asked.

"You're getting serious. Yes. It's you and me."

"You remember our conversation on Friday?"

"Yeeeah?" Eddie's answer was slow, stretching the word to make it a question.

"Well, I've handled it."

"What did you do?" For the first time in the conversation, Eddie sounded off guard.

"Like I said, I handled it."

"I didn't ask you to handle anything." Max couldn't tell if it was anger or fear in Eddie's voice. "She's been gone all weekend. What exactly did you do?"

"I'm hiding her, Eddie." Max tried to sound like he was looking for approval. "She's out of the picture until everything gets done."

The phone was silent for a few heartbeats.

"That's not a bad call," Eddie's voice finally returned. "Where is she?"

"She's safe, but it's best we don't talk about where she is. I'll bring her back at the end of the week."

"I'm not sure I like that, Max. You can tell me."

"No."

"Hey, buddy, you're crossing a line here. Where is she?" he demanded.

It was Max's turn to stay silent. He walked toward the car as he thought of the best way to avoid Eddie's question.

"You know a bit about me—about my past—more than most but not as much as you think. Trust me when it comes to procedure."

"Procedure, my ass." Eddie's voice rose, but Max held the phone away from him and hit the mute button as he opened the driver's side door.

"OK, Staci." He looked in, making sure he had her attention. "All I ask is that you don't tell him where you are staying. Are you good with that?"

She nodded, and her red eyes shone a little brighter.

Max stood and unmuted his phone. Eddie must have finished what he was saying too.

"Hey, Eddie?"

"Yeah?"

"Here she is."

Max tossed the phone to Staci and closed the door, walking back to the shade of the overpass so that she could have privacy.

* * *

"Eddie?" she asked gingerly as she watched Max walk away.

"Staci!" Eddie's voice was warm, and there was a heavy note of concern. "Are you OK, baby?"

"I'm fine. What about you?"

"I missed you the past couple of nights. Where are you?"

"I'm with Max. He took me to a shooting range."

"What?"

She laughed. "I guess he thought it would be fun. I didn't want to shoot anything, but he insisted I try a small pistol."

"How'd you do?"

Again she laughed, partly at herself and partly because it was so nice to hear his voice. "Horrible! I don't think I hit the target the first time. Then he gave me a couple of tips, and by the end, I could at least hit the paper."

"Where are you now? I'll come get you."

She wanted so badly to see him that she almost agreed, but her eye caught Max standing in the shade of the overpass. He wasn't even looking at her, which showed a level of trust.

"I . . . I'm not sure," she lied. "Off some highway. I haven't been paying attention."

"OK. Where are you staying, then? You haven't been home."

"I promised Max I wouldn't say."

There was a long pause before Eddie's voice returned. "It's OK, baby. I'll find you. You know I won't let anything happen to you."

Tears rose unbidden in her eyes.

"I'm sorry, Eddie," she managed to say. "I don't deserve you."

"Let me talk to Max."

She looked over, and this time Max was looking at her, so she beckoned him back, but before he got within earshot, she whispered the name of Max's apartment complex.

"Gatehouse Villas."

"Got it," Eddie growled. "You stay put, baby, and I'll handle things."

* * *

When Staci gave him the phone, he took it and walked away once again. Staci did not need to hear the conversation.

"Like I said, Eddie," he said, assuming Eddie was still on. "I'll keep her safe."

The phone was silent for so long that Max lowered the screen to see if the call had ended, but the timer was still ticking the seconds.

"Eddie?"

"I don't like this, Max," Eddie finally said, with a tone of authority that Max had only heard when he was giving orders to his men. "I call the shots."

"Things were getting hot. You told me she was a problem. I handled it. Isn't that the type of thing you talked about?" Max played the game. His actions had nothing to do with helping Eddie's agenda, but there was enough ambiguity that it could look like loyalty.

"I didn't give any orders. That's not how things work."

"Maybe it's a better way."

Eddie paused before responding.

"You've got balls, Max. I'll give you that." He let out a fake laugh. "This isn't over though. We're going to have to have a sit-down about how things work."

"Yeah, OK. I'll see you tomorrow."

Max hung up the phone without waiting for a response.

Back in the car, Max turned on the engine and turned the air conditioning up to high. It hadn't been unbearable, but the temperature had climbed after even a short stint without cool air.

He turned to Staci, who finished wiping her eyes.

"What did you tell him?"

"Nothing."

"Did you tell him where you're staying?"

"I told him it was an Airbnb, near downtown."

"OK. You didn't say anything else?"

"No, Max." She was now defensive. "I told you I wouldn't say anything."

"Fine. Like you said, you're free to do what you want, but I really wish you'd let me help you."

"I'm still here." She reached over and put her hand on his shoulder. "And thank you. I know you are doing your best. Seems like I've made a mess of a lot of things."

"Some of it's not your fault." Max put the car into drive and eased toward the on-ramp. "Of course, taking the money was probably on you. How much was it anyway?"

"A little under fourteen."

The number threw Max off. He'd assumed she'd stolen a good chunk, a few hundred thousand or more.

"Thousand? They can't be upset about fourteen thousand?"

He looked over and saw a look of glee in her eyes.

"Fourteen *million*, Max. It's still a tiny fraction of the total amount of money that goes through the Jewel."

The car had reached the top of the ramp, but Max didn't enter the highway, pulling over to the side instead. He put the car back into park and turned to look at Staci again.

"It's not really my business, Staci, but what are you still doing here if you have fourteen million stuffed away?"

Some of the spark left her face, replaced by determination.

"You're right. It isn't your business, but it's also more complicated than you say."

Max took a deep breath in and exhaled as he added the new information to his knowledge of events.

"If it means anything, I am significantly more concerned for you than I was a moment ago."

She shook her head. "You don't under—"

"Stop. Please." Max cut her off. "Trust me when I tell you that I know more about what's going on than you do. You're not safe in Vegas. Do you have somewhere to go? Somewhere that's not home."

"My best friend lives in LA."

"OK, you're going to visit her."

"But—"

"No buts," he interrupted again. "What did you do with the money? Bank account? Here in Vegas, somewhere else? Please tell me it's out of the country."

"Can I speak now?" She hadn't lost her grit.

"Yes." He nodded without apology.

"The money is in Vegas, but I don't have access to it."

"How so?"

"It's in a crypto wallet, but I don't have it."

Max closed his eyes. Why couldn't things be easy?

"Explain."

"Moving the funds inside of Tri-Star was relatively easy, but moving anything outside of Tri-Star would have immediately sent up red flags. I piggy-backed on their system of extracting funds from the Jewel's operations.

"Every week, the Jewel does a crypto exchange with Tri-Star. It's a dividend of sorts. As part of that transaction, we move funds using a pair of cold storage units."

Max held up a hand. "You're not talking about a freezer, are you?"

"No." She laughed. "A remote storage device that does not have direct Internet connection. Anyway, Geno or Eddie, usually Eddie, delivers one of these devices and takes it away after the transfer. The Jewel maintains the other."

"OK. So we can assume the one Eddie has is skimming?"

"Exactly. Anyhow, I added a hidden wallet on his device, and over the course of a few months, that's where I put the money. So technically I haven't stolen anything."

A large tandem trailer drove by very close to the breakdown lane, throwing gravel into the side of the car and interrupting the conversation.

"What the fuck?" Max snarled out of reflex.

He looked down the highway, and there was barely a car to be seen, so he put the car back into drive and gunned the vehicle onto the highway. Part of him wanted to chase down the trucker and give him a piece of his mind, but he knew nothing good would come of it. Moments later, they were in the middle lane, the cruise control set at seventy.

"So what was your plan?" he asked.

"Oh, now you want to hear *my plan*? I thought you knew more about this than I did?"

"Look, Staci." Max stared ahead as he answered. "Nothing has changed. I'm concerned for your life, but if I can help you get away and still keep the money, I'm happy to. You decide."

"For one thing, I need Eddie." She relaxed slightly. "And you're trying to take me out of town."

"For a few days. Until things settle." A thought struck him. "Does Eddie really know?"

"Sort of."

"Sort of?" He mirrored. "What does that mean?"

"It means he knows that money is in the wallet, and he knows how much, but he barely understands crypto. Plus, he says he wants to keep his distance."

"I bet." Max was unsure if this was a positive development or the reverse. "And where did you learn all this?"

"I minored in comp sci." She smiled then turned to look back out the window. "It's pretty basic stuff."

* * *

When they got back to the city, they didn't go directly home. Max had arranged a meeting with Haoyun at one, and there was no time to drop Staci at his apartment. He'd bought a floppy hat at the range in anticipation and handed it to her as they pulled into the Desert Jewel parking garage.

"Nobody will recognize you with this on," he said. "I've got a room and can stash you there. Are you OK with room service? I'm comped anywhere in the building."

"I could get used to that."

She took the hat and pulled it low over her eyes, looking at herself in the small visor mirror.

"What are you going to do?"

"I have to meet with my employers. I don't think it will take too long, so you should order as soon as we get to the room."

Of course, the garage entrance led straight into the casino, and they had to traverse the floor to get to the elevator bank, but it wasn't long before the doors opened to the twenty-second floor and they walked down the hall toward his room.

"Twenty-two. This is almost whale territory," she said, referring to the nickname for the high-spending guests every casino chased after.

He waved his wallet over the keypad, and the light turned green.

"I'll be back in a bit," he said as he pushed the door inward and held it open for her. "Order me something too, please."

"Anything in particular?"

"Hamburger, maybe? But I'll take whatever you think looks good."

He released the door and headed back to the elevator, which he rode up two floors to the penthouse suite and war room of the Haoyun Casino acquisition team.

As soon as he entered, he picked up a vibe of excitement in the room. The deal was closing the next day, and though most details were finished, everyone was still working on paperwork to ensure Haoyun's readiness to complete their part of the transaction. Max had been in similar rooms before. Regardless of the size of the deal, there was always an otherworldly feeling when things came to a head.

Except for this time.

He felt a pit growing in his stomach as he prepared to break the bad news to Ling Wu and Wei Zhang. He hadn't expected Wei to be back in town, but when Ling confirmed the meeting, she'd announced he would attend.

A few bean counters nodded in greeting as he walked through the room, and he politely acknowledged them. Since the negotiations had begun, Max had found himself in an odd place with everyone but his direct bosses. They knew he was important, but he was outside of the chain of command. Nobody reported to him, but they still offered some deference.

"Max!" Ling held the conference room door open. Beyond her, at the far end of the long mahogany table, sat Wei Zhang and Jun Chen. "We've been waiting for you."

Max smiled and offered a light head bow before taking the hand she offered.

"Ling, it is good to see you." He smiled, glancing at his watch. It was still four minutes to one. He was early, and still she had implied he had left them waiting. Not a great start.

He crossed the room and exchanged formalities with Jun and Wei. Beyond them, the towers of the Las Vegas strip sparkled in the distance through the long wall of windows. Ling joined them, and a server brought water for Max, asking if anyone wanted something else to drink, but all declined.

"Max," Wei began, "you said you have something important to tell us. We're listening. Does this impact the deal?"

"In a way, yes," Max answered, leaning forward. "But it's a much bigger issue. You're going to want to postpone the signing, and it's probably enough to scuttle the whole deal."

"We know of the skimming," Jun offered defensively. "They've practically admitted it in our talks. And we know of the smaller embezzlement, which Tri-Star will make good on."

That was bad news for Staci. If Tri-Star had agreed to repay the money, they would definitely go after her to return it. Still, it was not the issue at hand.

"I appreciate that but, with respect, that's not why I'm here." He paused before posing a question. "Would you still sign this deal if you knew the Desert Jewel was a narcotic distribution center?"

The Haoyun team was silent.

Max looked at each of them in turn, but they offered no response, so he continued.

"The catering arm is distributing Molly throughout the major casinos. Worse, they are manufacturing it across Silverado at the Deep Texas BBQ. They have a full production lab underneath the restaurant. The vents from the BBQ offer it complete cover, and I'm fairly certain it connects to the Jewel through an underground tunnel."

Again, he looked from face to face. Ling had a puzzled look, but he saw almost no reaction from the two men.

"This is crazy." Ling finally spoke, looking down at the table as if working things out in her head.

"You are buying a hornets' nest," he said, unable to process their lack of response. "The police are investigating it."

"So this is about drugs?" Ling asked, but she was looking sideways at Wei and Jun, her voice slightly raised.

Wei stiffened then made a polite head bow to Max before turning to Ling.

"May we have a word outside?" he said, then turned to walk to the conference room door. Ling followed without a word, and in less than a minute, Max and Jun were alone in the room. Jun smiled and broke into light laughter.

He shook his head. "Who do you think we are? Haoyun Casino has been in operation for over fifty years. Do you think we came here innocently? We are well aware of the Molly operation. In fact, that is one of the major attractions of this deal. Where else are we going to find a casino of this size able to absorb and launder the cash flow from such a large operation and pick up the distribution network all in one neat package?"

Max couldn't believe what the man had said. He felt a chill run up his spine, and some of his hair was standing on end.

"Did Ling put you up to this?" Jun asked.

"She asked me to investigate."

Jun shook his head again.

"She overstepped. She means well, but she has the foolish notion that Haoyun Casino will someday operate in full legitimacy. Wei allows her to try, but I often think he gives her too much leash."

"Maybe you should give her a chance."

"The deal will proceed." Jun straightened in his chair.

Max was incredulous. "You're as bad as them."

"Not so," Jun replied. "I think we are far better than them, and we'll run the business with a higher profit. This isn't about drugs or gambling, Mr. Kline. It's about making money."

Max didn't reply but looked down at the table, slowly shaking his head.

"I'm sorry you were not aware of this," Jun continued. "But we assumed with the amount of money we are paying you that you had at least an inkling of the full transaction. It doesn't matter. We will pay you, per our agreement. In full. So long as this discussion ends here."

Everything Max had believed about Haoyun had turned upside down in less than a minute. He instinctively turned toward the door, but Wei and Ling were not there. Slowly, anger replaced surprise.

"I am not a part of this," he growled, turning back to Jun. "I don't want your money."

"It's too late for that, Mr. Kline. You've taken our money, and we will honor the rest of the deal." He rose from his seat and pushed his chair back in, standing behind it. "Don't let yourself get caught up in ideals. We'll respect our end, and you respect yours—which, I will remind you, includes a confidentiality clause."

"Confidentiality, my ass." Max stood.

"Oh, there's another reason for you to continue your job."

Max lifted his head.

"And that is?"

"You have a friend who has been stealing from the Desert Jewel. We have evidence that we haven't shared with the Marchettis. They only know of a small amount, a few hundred thousand, though even that has put her life in danger. If we were to reveal to Geno the full extent of her activity, I doubt she would survive the week. If we were to do the same with the authorities, she would spend a long time behind bars."

Jun seemed to enjoy the narrative.

"So I help you, and you let her go?"

"It seems a small price to pay, does it not?"

He thought about it. There was no good answer, but he couldn't leave Staci to fend for herself.

"When the deal closes, I'm done."

"Well, we may have a need for you here in Vegas for a little while longer."

Max closed his eyes and took a deep breath. They had leverage and knew it.

"For what it's worth," Jun continued, "you are better than we thought. We were quite confident in the Deep Texas operation's secrecy. The lab itself is not a long-term investment, but it serves a purpose. The new rail terminal will replace it, but we have an alternative arrangement. It doesn't matter. The work we require of you should have nothing to do with it."

"So I ignore the fact that you are drug dealers?" Max almost laughed.

"Or you can ignore the fact that you have a very traceable line of bank transactions flowing from our bank to yours." The implication was obvious. "It's business, Max. While I would have preferred that you not see the other half of this transaction, nothing really changes. You are a part of this, and you've provided invaluable help. You can try to go to the authorities, but trust me when I tell you that I don't think you will have much luck. You'd be much better served to finish the contract than to work against us. Wei Zhang does not have the same patience that I have."

Max had learned long ago that when a firefight got out of hand, there were really only two options, depending on the scenario—either escalate the fight and end it quickly, or initiate a tactical retreat. As he stood in the conference room listening to Jun, he quickly determined that he had neither an advantage nor enough information to pursue an immediate outcome, so his mind began to calculate a retreat.

"What else do you think Geno is doing?" he asked.

Jun's shoulders relaxed slightly.

"We don't know, but he'll have his hands full building the high-speed rail. As I've said, this is a good deal for both sides. They get a clean exit. We get a substantial, if not entirely legal, revenue stream." He walked the long way around the table. "They will still have a part to play, however."

"What's that?"

"The details don't matter, but you might consider one of their offers."

How much did this man know? Max played dumb and used the mirroring technique.

"Offers?"

"I'm not playing games." Anger edged Jun's voice. "You could be an asset if you were to join them." Again, the implication was obvious, but Max knew two things. First, there was no way he'd work with Eddie or Geno. Second, he would never be a double agent for Haoyun.

"I'll pass. Thanks."

"Will you be coming to the closing party?"

The question threw Max off, but he continued his retreat.

"If you want me there, I don't see why not."

"Hmmm." Jun had rounded the table and stood with his hand on the unopened door handle. "Thought you might find it useful to be there."

As Jun left the room, Max wondered who was really in charge at Haoyun.

# CHAPTER TWENTY-TWO

Sunday night was always a busy night at the airport, but largely for departing flights. Visitors of all ages fled the town, the large majority with less money than they started with. Either they spent their money on entertainment and food, or they tried their hand at the casino tables and contributed to the eighty-five percent of gamblers who went home losers. The lucky few who won and kept their winnings typically overspent and overtipped in the happy days following their win, reducing their take. Rinse and repeat.

The one thing that always bothered Max was that they—meaning the city—didn't even try to hide it.

Almost everyone coming to Las Vegas knew that the casinos always won and that everything was more expensive than one would find elsewhere—yet still they came. They even developed a slogan that allowed visitors a certain forgiveness for anything they did: "What happens in Vegas, stays in Vegas." It sure did. Lost the month's rent? The money you had planned to save for the college fund? No need to talk about it—that stayed in Vegas. Meanwhile, on Sunday night, the planes were loaded with guests returning home with a few memories and much less money—that stayed in Vegas too.

As Max walked through the check-in area of terminal three, he saw the same story repeating itself, as it did every weekend. He'd come up to this level because he knew one store carried roses, looking to tap some of the last winner's enthusiasm that a guest might have. They weren't the best flowers one could find, but it was the thought that counted, and while Carolyn was coming in to help him with a job, part of him hoped they could rekindle what seemed to be a dying flame of romance.

After the Haoyun meeting, he'd gone back to his room only to find that Staci had just ordered their food. Almost another hour passed before they received and ate their late lunch, and then Max arranged for a complete cleaning and resetting of the room for Carolyn. By the time they returned to Max's apartment, he'd barely had time to shower before heading to the airport. Staci had promised to stay put, at least for the night. He'd told her he thought things might change in the morning, but he hadn't shared the fact that she'd be meeting with a decorated LVPD detective.

He took the elevator back down to arrivals and crossed the

massive baggage claim area to wait at the base of the escalator that carried arriving passengers down from the concourse. Not ten minutes later, he caught sight of black shoulder-length hair emerging from a weathered baseball cap. He wasn't sure why it caught his eye, but it was definitely Carolyn, even though she was still far up the escalator. As she got closer, the dark birthmark on her jawline confirmed it, but even if she had been turned the other way, Max was sure he'd have known her by the beautiful coffee tone of her skin. She was wearing jeans and a white tank top with the arms of a sweatshirt wrapped around her waist. Her right hand was resting on the extended handle of her white carry-on bag, and she held a phone in her left, probably checking for a message from him. She was almost at the bottom when she pocketed the phone and looked up, immediately catching Max's eye, and the huge smile he received almost made him forget why she had come.

At the bottom of the escalator, she quickly crossed the distance to where Max was standing and threw her arms around him. Max returned the hug, savoring her warm, supple body. He hadn't seen her in person in over four months, and that departure hadn't gone well. She didn't kiss him, but the hug was long.

"It's good to see you, Max," she said, lifting her head from his shoulder, but keeping her hands on his upper arms as they separated.

"You look great," Max replied then handed her the roses he'd bought. "Welcome to Las Vegas, Ms. Toffey."

She raised an eyebrow as she took the flowers, possibly questioning the romance, but Max ignored it.

"Do you have any bags?" he asked.

"Nope. Only this."

"OK. Let's get outta here, then."

She allowed him to take her carry-on, and he put an arm around her shoulders, leading her to the parking garage.

"How was the flight?"

"Easy."

Her arm wrapped around his waist, and Max felt as if everything was back to where it had once been. He said nothing for fear of ruining the moment.

"How was your day?" she asked as they walked down the crosswalk to the garage.

Max's mood immediately darkened.

"There's a lot I need to tell you."

He felt her arm slip off his waist.

"Well?" She stopped walking, and he was forced to stop as well, turning to face her. "Out with it. How bad is it now?"

He looked around to confirm they were alone in this section of the garage.

"Apparently my employers are no better than the Marchetti family. The deal's going to go through because they've known about the Molly lab all along."

"What the hell? And you're still working for them?"

"It's complicated."

"Oh, trust me, Max. With you, everything is complicated."

"We'll sort it out," he offered, not really certain.

"So . . . what's the plan now?"

"Depends what we find on the server, I guess."

"We're still doing that?" she asked.

"Yeah." He nodded. "We're still doing that."

* * *

In less than a half hour, they were in the hallway of the Desert Jewel as Max unlocked the door and pushed it open, holding it with his left arm to allow Carolyn to enter first. The room was a junior suite and included a sitting area with two couches by the window.

"It's totally comped," he told her, following her inside. "Order anything you want whenever you want it."

"That's kind of nice."

Carolyn walked over to the window and opened the curtains,

revealing a northward view of the Las Vegas strip. She crossed her arms over her chest as if contemplating something.

"It's pretty, despite what it represents," she said.

"And what does it represent?" He thought he knew, but it was a natural follow-up.

"Materialism, corruption of society, evil—you name it, Max." She laughed. "It's called Sin City for a reason."

"OK, I'll give you some of that, but this town isn't all bad."

"Hmm." She plopped on a couch. "Apart from the gambling, so far I've heard about illegal drug production, the mafia, murder, and embezzlement. Sounds like a veritable church gathering."

He shrugged.

"What time's the prayer meeting?" she added, throwing one hand in the air.

"Alright. I deserved that. If you don't want to go any further, you don't have to. This is my mess, and I'll sort it out."

"No, I'm in." She put a smile on her lips, but her eyes were sad. "I didn't fly down here for the dry desert air. What are the police doing about the lab?"

Her question was fair, but he knew she was really asking if he had kept his end of the bargain.

"They already knew about it," he answered. "Told me to stay

away. Seems like it is part of a larger operation they are going to bring down."

"Does that even make sense?" Carolyn had a puzzled look on her face. "Allow a drug lab to operate while you work on a bigger sting? Seriously? Lives are at stake."

Max held both hands up.

"Not my call. And I thought it wouldn't be my problem once Haoyun heard. Now it looks like the deal is still on, and my employer plans to run the Las Vegas Molly trade."

"If the police won't stop this, Max, maybe we should."

Max looked over at the woman he still loved. The sadness in her gaze was gone, replaced by fierce determination. He held her eyes, slowly nodding in recognition, torn between the absolute beauty sitting across from him and the extreme peril she was suggesting.

"I don't know that we can," he breathed, not willing to admit it.

"I guess that depends on what we find on the server."

She was right, of course, but it would not be as easy as that.

"We have to get to the server first."

"I'll leave that part to you, but you get me in, and I'll find what we need."

Carolyn had been one of the most infamous gray-hat hackers in the world—her call sign was still legend, though she was no longer active.

"I'm working on that," he said.

"I'd like to meet her." Carolyn leaned back, changing the subject. "The girl you're protecting."

"There's nothing going on between us."

"I know. Stop getting defensive!" She smiled at him, and for a second he saw the glint he'd been hoping to see again. "You're a sucker for a girl in distress."

"Are you in distress?"

"Maybe. We'll see how the next couple of days go."

"She's at my apartment. Let's grab dinner downstairs, and I can take you over there after."

She stood up and crossed to the table where Max had left her suitcase, opening a side pocket and removing a small bag.

"You're in charge," she said, moving to the bathroom. "Let me brush my teeth and freshen up. I'll be ready in five."

* * *

One reason Max preferred taxis in Las Vegas was the unbearably long traffic lights around the strip and downtown areas. He still had the rental car, and they were waiting at a light that seemed to have turned red five minutes earlier. He knew it hadn't really been that long, but it sure felt like it.

Dinner had started with drinks and developed into an epic two-hour tasting course at the Jewel's top Italian restaurant. It had felt so natural being back with Carolyn that he'd forgotten about his current troubles, and it seemed like she'd felt the same way. By the end, they had been flirting like they had back in high school, and Max had been excited to take her back to the room when she'd reminded him he'd promised to take her to meet Staci. In classic Carolyn style, she wanted to take care of business first.

On the way out, he'd pointed to the BBQ and told her the full story of what he'd seen underneath. Carolyn asked several questions about the location. Who owned it? She had more questions than he could answer, but she always did.

Now, as they sat at the light, Max feared the feelings that had revived at dinner might drift away as they made the torturous twenty-minute drive to his apartment.

"Should we ring her to let her know we're on our way?" Carolyn asked.

"That's a good call." The light finally turned, and they slowly followed the cars ahead of them down the road.

He thumbed the screen and held his finger to the sensor so it unlocked, then handed it to Carolyn.

"Look for Staci Burn. I took her actual phone and gave her a burner while we wait this thing out."

"You know it's in airplane mode?" she asked immediately.

"Oh shit. I was fiddling with the settings when I got to the airport. Must've hit it."

Carolyn went to work, and Max heard several buzzes that he knew were incoming text messages. It seemed unusually active.

"OK. What have I missed?" he asked. "It hasn't been long. Who needs me?"

Carolyn was looking at the phone as she reported.

"You've got four missed calls from a Ben Carpenter. Wait. And two texts. You want to hear them?"

"Sure." It wasn't like Ben to text him. Something must have changed about the meetup with Staci planned for the morning.

"The first one says, 'Max, pick up the damn phone.'" Carolyn laughed. "The second one says, 'Please.' Max, these are only ten minutes old. You want me to text back?"

"No. We'll be at my place in five minutes. I'll call him when we get there. Better ring Staci."

Carolyn went back to tapping the phone, and then the music cut off as his car speakers yielded to the call. On the speakers, they could hear the phone ring, but it went straight to an inactive mailbox.

"Try again," Max urged, slightly annoyed that Staci hadn't answered. He had tried not to be too bossy, but he had given her only a few rules, and one of them was that she had to answer the burner phone if it rang. On the speakers, the phone rang three more times, and then the canned message sounded again.

"I guess we'll surprise her." His eyes caught activity ahead. It was still maybe a quarter mile away, but he could see smoke rising on the left side of the road. It was close to, if not within, his apartment complex.

"What's going on here?" he said out loud.

Traffic had slowed even further, as others on the road were probably seeing the same thing. As they got closer, the unmistakable flashing blue and red lights indicated the police were on the scene. Closer still, they could see fire engines deep within the complex, and the smoke, a mixture of black and white plumes, was definitely from the apartments. The hair on Max's neck stood up—if it wasn't coming from his exact building, it was very close.

"OK. Call Ben, please," he instructed Carolyn as he waited to turn.

Gatehouse Villas stretched from one avenue to the next, and they were turning on the opposite side from all the activity, so he pulled into the nearest driveway and parked. On the car speakers, the phone rang twice before Ben picked up.

"Max?" He sounded somewhat surprised.

"Hey, Ben. What's up? I—"

"Jesus, Max." Ben interrupted him. "Where are you?"

"I just got home. What's going on?"

"Shit," Ben muttered, drowned out as a new siren wailed and flashing lights passed Max's car, heading toward the commotion.

"OK. You hear me?" Ben said.

"No. What's going on, Ben?" He turned off the car and got out, putting an earbud in as he did. He was vaguely aware of Carolyn getting out of her side of the car, but he waved, indicating she should stay as he started walking toward the action.

"Max," Carolyn called.

He turned to face her. Ben hadn't answered, and he needed to cut down the variables. He held the phone away from his face and motioned with his hand.

"Stay here," he said through gritted teeth, adding, "please."

"Where are you?" Ben's voice came back through the phone.

Max started toward his building at a jog. His radar was off the charts. Something bad had happened.

"I'm in my parking lot. Where are you?" he asked.

"Which lot?" Ben was speaking in a hushed voice. "I'll come to you. You don't want to be seen."

"What are you talking about, Ben? Why are you here?"

He picked up his pace. Ahead of him, two cruisers blocked the roadway that led to his building, blue and red lights flashing. As he rounded the corner, he saw two firetrucks at the end of the street, also with lights flashing. The entire area was a swarm of activity, and beyond it, he saw the cause of the alarm. His heart sank.

The building at the end of the street, his building, was still smoldering. The windows on the top left half were all blown out—his windows.

"I told you, you don't want to be seen." Ben's voice was no longer in his phone, and a hand clamped like a vise around his arm, urging him to turn away.

Instinct resisted the pull, but the older man's strength impressed him.

"Let go." He turned to face his friend, sliding the phone into his pocket. "What happened?"

"Come with me." Ben released his arm but guided him into a passage between two of the other buildings, continuing only when they were out of sight. "Your place got bombed. That's what happened."

Ben turned to face him. The alley was still lit with pedestrian streetlights, and Max could see what looked like frustration on his friend's face.

"Why do you think I'm been trying to reach you? I thought maybe they got you. Thank God you're alive."

"Have they found any survivors?" Max felt a hole in his chest, knowing the likely answer. It was like losing Lulu a second time.

"Was the girl inside?" Ben asked.

Max nodded, and Ben took a deep inhale.

"They've focused on containing the fire. I don't think anyone's been inside. Chief's held everyone back. Wants the bomb squad to go in first."

"How would he think it's a bomb?" Max was immediately suspicious. "Why not a gas main or something?"

"Every window in your place shattered," Ben began. "The debris traveled as far as the street."

He stopped, clearly seeing Max's expression.

"OK," he continued, slightly calmer, almost relieved to be explaining. "I told the chief someone might have targeted you. It was pretty obvious already. Anyway, I have nothing else at this point, but if you show your face, you're going to be answering a lot of questions."

"Thanks, Ben." Max's mind was reeling, but he knew his friend was helping. "She was a good kid."

He was talking about Staci, but the image in his mind was of his sister, Lulu. Neither of them deserved to die so young. But how had they known she was in his apartment? He thought back to the morning, wondering if she'd unknowingly given her killer the location.

"You're in this pretty deep, Max. Why don't you get out of town for a while?"

"Is that what you'd do?" he asked. As former Special Forces, neither of them was accustomed to running from a fight.

Ben's shoulders slumped in recognition.

"I can't help you with this. My advice is the same. Stay clear of the Marchettis, the Desert Jewel, all of this. I know you won't, but my conscience is clean."

Max put his hand on Ben's shoulder.

"I'm gonna get out of here. Will you text me with any news?"

"Yeah." He gave Max a pat on the arm. "You be safe."

Max turned to go. Carolyn would be worried. Behind him, Ben called after him, "And I never saw you. Got it?"

He did not look back but raised a fist in recognition.

Staci was gone and he was heartbroken, but he could avenge her. He could avenge Lulu at the same time. He wondered if that was enough reason to pursue the Marchettis. Or should he drop it and keep Carolyn out of danger?

The answer came immediately and unbidden, but he struggled with it. As he neared the car, he could see Carolyn leaning on the hood, and when she saw him, she rushed around to come into his arms.

"Max? What is it? What's happening?"

No longer focused on passion, he held her close, enjoying the steady warmth of a woman he had always loved. He savored the moment, but he couldn't shake the thoughts that had been running through his head. He was sure they wanted this to end things, but he could not let them win. This was an act of war, and war was something he knew well.

## CHAPTER TWENTY-THREE

As he opened his eyes, Max was still weary from a dreamless sleep. The two had returned to the Jewel, but Staci's death had shattered everything that had built up earlier. Max had insisted they stop at a bar in the casino and then promptly downed three Gibsons to Carolyn's one martini. They barely talked, and when they got to the room, he'd simply apologized and flopped on top of the bed to sleep.

Carolyn was at the desk, hammering away vigorously at her computer. He watched her for some time, thinking of his good fortune, but then Staci's bad luck clouded his mind, and guilt returned. It felt like losing Lulu a second time.

"Good morning, sunshine," Carolyn spoke softly when she saw he was awake.

"Good morning," he replied, his voice slightly raspy.

"I've got something for you," she began, but he held up a hand to stop her.

"Shower first. Then breakfast. Then you tell me. OK?"

It wasn't really negotiable, but he waited for her nod before he continued to the bathroom.

This was not the first time he'd done this. In fact, it was somewhat of a routine after losing a comrade, or someone close. He'd get hammered, sleep it off, indulge in a big breakfast, and then get back to work.

It was not yet eight on a Monday morning, so the buffet was only a little over half-full. There was no wait at the omelet station, and before long, Max was returning to the table with an omelet on top of his plate of biscuits and gravy and a full side plate of bacon. To his amusement, Carolyn had already seated herself with a yogurt parfait and orange juice. Both of their coffees had been filled by the waitress. He put his plates down and pulled out his chair.

"I'm sorry, C. I know that's not the best way to deal with it, but —"

She reached over and put her hand on his.

"Max, you have a lot of issues, but this isn't one of them." She smiled. "I'm sorry."

He nodded. "Thanks. I tried so hard. I know you'll tell me I'm crazy, but it felt like I was helping Lulu."

"You aren't crazy."

They ate in silence for a few minutes before Carolyn put her spoon down purposefully.

"So," she started, "do you want me to tell you what I found?"

Max was confused but remembered her eagerness that he'd dismissed when he'd woken up.

"Sure."

"I couldn't sleep, so I began poking around the Deep Texas BBQ. It's been around for a long time and, as you know, operated by the Jewel. But they rent it, and the actual property ownership changed hands about five years ago. The current owner is Starlight Enterprises, which is a Delaware shell company, so we don't know the true ownership, but the agent on record for Starlight is a single member LLC listed as Julius Scarpeli, LLC."

Max motioned with his fork. "What does that mean to us?"

"Hang on." Carolyn held up a finger. "I recognized the name because when you asked me to look into Tri-Star, I ran into the same thing—a Delaware company listing Scarpeli as the agent of record."

Max started to speak, but she didn't give him an opening.

"A little more investigation, and Starlight has another Las Vegas investment. They own fifty-one percent of . . . wait for it . . . Genoa Imports."

Max was confused. "I thought that was Rodriguez's business?"

"It is, at least partially. Apparently, he doesn't own it all. I kept digging, and you'll appreciate that pun—Starlight is also the majority shareholder in the American Construction Corporation."

"That's Geno's for sure."

Processing what he'd heard, Max added, "Wait a second. You're suggesting that Starlight might actually be the Marchettis? So they own the lab property but are selling the operation?"

"That's what it looks like."

"And American Construction recently won the contract to build the Las Vegas terminals for the high-speed rail project."

Max pushed back in his chair and let out a breath, thinking it through as the light bulbs turned on.

Across the table, Carolyn nodded encouragement

"And the first stop in Las Vegas, the southern terminal, is right there." He was no longer asking.

"That's the plan," she confirmed. "It's two to three years out, but the Deep Texas will go away to make room for the terminal. Starlight should make a killing on the land sale and ACC soaks up the building contract."

"And, in the process, the lab gets quietly dismantled," Max continued the thought. "Haoyun operates the lab for a few years, which probably helps pay off the Jewel's mortgage, and then—*poof*—all evidence goes away."

"And by then they have the premier casino near the southern

terminal."

"Unless the lab gets busted before the terminal construction can erase it," he added. "There's still a lot of risk."

Max shook his head again. He carved off a piece of biscuit and chewed slowly as he digested what Carolyn had found. This was the piece Jun hadn't wanted to disclose. The Marchettis cash out of the Molly trade and spin that into the construction contract. Meanwhile, Haoyun absorbs the profitable drug business to offset casino losses during construction. It was nearly perfect. When the southern terminal gets built, Geno's ACC demos the lab, and everyone is back legitimate—including Starlight, presumably owned by the Marchettis, which makes a killing selling the land to the city.

"How do we bring 'em down?" he asked quietly.

She laughed. "We don't, Max. Or rather, nothing's changed. You get your cop friend to bust up the lab, but I doubt you'll be able to touch Geno or, for that matter, your employer. This is big-time stuff. I'm sure they're deeply protected. And I doubt I'll ever actually find out who owns Tri-Star or Starlight."

Max raised an eyebrow. "What does that mean?"

"Exactly what I said."

"Yeah, but you already told me these are Delaware shell companies, so why would there be any hope of finding the owners? Why did you say it that way? So why is there any hope at all?"

It was Carolyn's turn to take a breath with a shake of her head. When she was ready, she leaned closer, even though there was nobody near them.

"I poked around Scarpeli's office computer. He's got some safeguards in place, but they're nowhere near as robust as Geno's. I think I can get in."

"What are you waiting for?" Max hadn't intended to raise his voice, and he looked up to see a server holding a pot of coffee. Her eyebrows raised as if she was unsure of interrupting.

"Yes, please," he said, holding his mug out.

When the waitress left, he turned back to Carolyn with an apologetic smile.

"Sorry. How long will it take you?"

"I don't know. Not too long."

"Let's get you upstairs. I don't know how this plays out, but the more info we have, the better."

He took the last bite of his omelet, chasing it with hot coffee that burned the back of his throat.

"Believe it or not, I'm supposed to be with Haoyun in about forty-five minutes, though I don't think they really need me at this point. Then I've got to go see Ben. He'll want to know what we've learned, and I'd like to find out what's left of my apartment."

* * *

The Clark County Government Center was only a few blocks from the Las Vegas Metropolitan Police Headquarters. The complex was an impressive and award-winning structure built in the mid-nineties, but for Max, the appeal was the circular park on the western side of the complex. It was ringed by a walking path, and nicely manicured grass flowed down to a center stage. People referred to it as the "amphitheater," though it mostly served as a park and break area for those working within. Ben had agreed to meet him here rather than at his office.

It was a little after eleven. He'd ghosted the settlement meeting by stepping out to use the bathroom and then heading immediately down to the taxi stand. With any luck, he'd return to the negotiations before the lunch break, and he doubted anyone would even notice.

When Max got out of the cab, he could see Ben sitting at a picnic table beyond the outer colonnade of Grand Canyon rock pillars that encircled the amphitheater. He'd already exchanged phone numbers with the driver, whom he'd paid to find parking for the next twenty minutes.

As he approached the table, Ben rose, and not for the first time, Max looked at his friend's body, wondering if the man was in better shape than he was. He wore a tight-fitting t-shirt that hugged a lean torso with a well-defined chest and biceps that forced the sleeves wider. His close-cropped white beard glistened in the late-morning sun as he held up his left hand to shade his eyes, offering his right in friendship.

"How are you holding up?" he asked as Max clasped his hand in a firm handshake.

"You tell me," Max replied. "What's left of my place?"

Ben lifted his eyebrows and shook his head.

"Let's walk," he finally said. They followed the sidewalk inside the colonnade. "I warned you, didn't I?"

The implication hurt. Max had been dealing with his own internal guilt. Maybe Staci would be alive if he'd chosen a different path.

"It's not about what could have been," he said, voicing the thoughts he'd been convincing himself were true all morning. "It's only what we do from here."

Ben stopped and turned to face him.

"No, Max. It's not what *we* do from here. It's what *I* do from here. You get it? We've already got one dead body."

"It's confirmed, then?"

Ben looked down then resumed walking, forcing Max to keep up.

"No ID yet, but yeah. Female. Mid-twenties."

It wasn't a surprise, but it hurt nonetheless.

"I'm not going to stand down, Ben."

"Really? And how do you think you can help?"

"What do you know about the American Construction Corporation?"

Ben stopped again, this time turning a questioning expression toward Max. "Just what I read in the papers. They're working on the high-speed rail project."

"Right. They're building the terminals here in town."

"OK."

"Do you know where the southern terminal will be?"

"Not offhand, but—"

"It will surface right through the current location of the Deep Texas BBQ," Max cut him off. "And do you know who has an ownership stake in both the Deep Texas property and ACC?"

Ben whistled. "You're going to tell me, right?"

"I'm working on proof, but I'm pretty sure it involves Geno Abruzzi."

"Where are you going with this?"

"You said you were working on busting the Molly lab, but what if there's more here? Once this deal is done, the Marchetti family doesn't operate the lab, but what if I can get you proof that they own the property and plan to use the ACC contract to destroy all evidence?"

"And where are you getting this proof?" Ben was incredulous.

"That's my problem, Ben. But if I deliver it, making it stick is your problem."

Ben stared at him for a long moment, then ran his left hand over his scalp, closing his eyes briefly.

"Wait here."

He turned and walked away down the grass slope toward the stage. There were two inner rings of cement walkways on the way down to the stage, and he stopped at the second, looking up at the main government building. Max took a seat at a nearby table while his friend thought things through. Then he watched as the detective took out his phone and held it to his ear as he looked up at the six-story building. He turned, saw Max watching him, and nodded, still engaged on the phone. Eventually, he ended the call and walked back up the modest incline to where Max waited.

"I've got some leeway on this," Ben began, a few steps before reaching the top walkway. "But I'll need to know more. To be clear, officially we have nothing to do with you. But if you can help us bring down the Marchettis, I can offer some protection. I can't help you though unless you come clean on what you know and what you are planning."

Max considered it and tried to buy time.

"Ben, you can trust me." He tapped his chest with a clenched fist, acknowledging their shared service to the country.

"Cut the bullshit." Ben took a seat opposite him at the picnic table. "We're not serving anymore—or more accurately, you're not serving anymore. You're a civilian, Max. I'm a Las Vegas police detective, and if you want my help, you need to play ball. Or I throw you in with the rest of them, and that begins with assault charges for that little foray at the Crazy Kettle the other night. The choice is yours."

A warm breeze gusted through the amphitheater, causing both men to shield their eyes, and it gave Max a moment to think. Ben was more in touch with events than he had let on. What other choice did he have? Carolyn was always telling him he took too much on by himself, that he needed to trust others.

A shadow fell over the table, and Ben extended a hand to direct Max's attention behind him.

"Max, I'd like you to meet Nita Vargas. She's the Las Vegas district attorney."

Max turned to see a striking woman in her mid-forties. She had coffee-toned skin and an angular face that indicated Native American ancestry. Her black hair was pulled into a tight ponytail to one side in front of a gray pantsuit. He swung his right leg around the bench and stood as he took her outstretched hand.

"Please. Stay seated," she said in a friendly but authoritative voice. "It's a pleasure to meet you, Mr. Kline."

"Max. Nice to meet you as well." He paused, unsure of how to use her title, and it must have been obvious.

"Call me Nita." She moved around the table. "The DA thing is a mouthful."

While they spoke, Ben had shifted to the left, allowing her to sit where he had been previously.

"Ben tells me you've got an interesting story." She smiled.

He expected her to continue, but she looked at him, her eyes tightening slightly in the sun.

"Look, I don't want to be part of anything official." He broke the silence with a shake of his head.

"You realize you're sitting at the courthouse." Nita raised an eyebrow, her expression otherwise unchanged.

"It happens to be a delightful spot to meet an old friend."

"Yeah," Ben said, "but your old friend doesn't have the teeth to do what you're asking. Nita does."

"It doesn't have to be on the record," Nita added. "It sounds like we have the same objective. I can help you, but you have to be completely honest with me."

Max said nothing, pondering.

"Let me be candid," Nita continued. "I've been going after Abruzzi since my election. I'm willing to overlook a lot to bring him down. That said, I'll repeat that if you aren't completely honest with me, there's no deal. If I find out you've left anything out, I'll come after you hard."

"Well, as long as that's clear." He smiled, liking her approach. "Why wouldn't I want to help you?"

Before she could respond, he lifted his hands off the table and opened them in a modest surrender.

"Kidding," he said. "I think I can work with that."

"Good. No bullshit. How about you tell me what's been going on?"

*Why not?* he thought to himself. He'd expected to bare all to Ben. This wasn't much different.

It started with the hospital escapade. He'd been pretty sure that Ben either suspected or knew it had been him anyway, so there was no harm in coming clean. Then he explained how he'd learned about the embezzlement and how he'd wanted to help Staci, but he left out the detail of the hidden crypto wallet. He questioned himself as he did, but he decided they didn't get everything.

From there, he described the Desert Jewel transaction and his interactions with Geno, Eddie, and the Marchetti organization. He brought up his discovery at Genoa Imports and later at the Jewel.

Finally, he went into detail, describing the lab he'd discovered under the BBQ. Through it all, they listened. Ben had both arms on the table, nodding at times as if he already knew.

Nita stopped him twice to ask for details. Her knowledge of events seemed cursory, but she got the picture.

Max reviewed the ACC and his understanding of the corporate backstory, leaving out Haoyun's complicity.

"Hang on," Nita interrupted again. "Who's the black hat?"

Max had finished explaining how his source had uncovered the Delaware companies and was attempting to hack into the agent of service for Starlight.

"Gray hat, maybe, but I can't give you that." Max shook his head, unwilling to involve Carolyn's name. "That's need-to-know only."

"That's not the deal I offered."

He shrugged. "Then I guess I'm not taking your deal."

Ben lowered his head into his hands, running them down the back of his clean-shaven head. He looked up, shaking his head.

"You really try our friendship, bud."

"I'm trusting you with almost everything, Ben." He looked from Ben to the district attorney. "But I can't give you this."

Nita seemed to accept the fact, asking, "OK, what happens next?"

"Tomorrow night is the closing party."

Earlier, Max had mentioned the shielded server at Geno's home.

"I'm invited, and I use my access to get my friend onto the server. It's a gamble, but I think with that and the Delaware agent's computer, you'll have plenty of evidence." He provided some detail about the proximity key, which he did not have, but he left out the need to circumvent the shield. Carolyn would be nearby to receive the transfer, and he did not want Ben or Nita to know anything about her.

"When the night is over, I walk out with a thumb drive full of evidence," he concluded. Again, he'd distorted the story to protect Carolyn. With her on site, she could upload everything remotely. There was no need for a thumb drive.

"It's that easy?" Ben raised an eyebrow.

"Look, you don't have to risk a thing. You use the evidence to take them down."

"Illegally obtained evidence," the detective clarified.

"Has that stopped you before?"

Ben laughed, but Nita shook her head.

"It's my job to make it legal," she said as she slid out of the bench. "You can sort the details with Detective Carpenter. It was nice to meet you, Max. You're doing the right thing."

She shook his hand, and Max appreciated the firmness of her grip.

"I hope it's enough." He rose as much as he could with his legs still under the picnic table.

Nita nodded but said nothing more and walked back to the courthouse.

"You need to understand two things," Ben started as soon as she was out of earshot. "First, this is my collar. Nita can get the publicity, but I'm in charge on the street. You give everything you find to me and me alone. Second, don't engage. These guys are cold-blooded. You do the job and leave. If you're OK with that, I'll back your play."

"Sounds fair."

"The DA will collar these guys if you bring what you say you can, but, Max—"

"Yeah?"

"We can't do anything for you if this goes south—at least not while you're inside."

"Death before dishonor," Max uttered the unofficial Marine Corps motto under his breath.

"Fuck that, Marine." Ben had heard. "If things look squirrelly, you extricate yourself. This is not a hill worth dying on."

"She was twenty-five, Ben." Max couldn't help but think of Staci's panicked face when he first met her at the hospital. Even then, she had shone with the life of youth. "Somebody has to stand up to them."

"Yeah, you don't have to do it alone." He stood up and extended his hand.

Max stood as well, and they shook hands as if to cement the agreement.

"Check in with me tonight," Ben instructed. "I'm going to see about putting a task force in the area tomorrow night. Depends a little on what the DA agrees to."

"Sounds fine." He didn't need support. His mind was already thinking of the next steps. He'd need to find a proximity key and, while he wasn't sure how he would get it, he knew Eddie would be his best chance.

## CHAPTER TWENTY-FOUR

Max entered the casino through the first in a long row of doors, enjoying the sound of bells from the slots in front of him. The meeting with Ben had taken longer than he'd expected, and he guessed that the Tri-Star and Haoyun meeting had broken for lunch. He was sure to get the stink eye from Wei for his absence, but he didn't care. He started moving through the slot machines and tables in what he considered the most efficient path to the elevator bank.

Before reaching the elevators, he approached a group of mostly empty craps tables and found Eddie leaning against one, looking at him as if he had been waiting. A pair of Marchetti soldiers flanked him on either side.

"Hello, Max." Eddie pushed away from the table and offered a hand, pulling Max into an embrace when he took it.

For a moment, with the big man's arms around him, Max

wondered if Eddie knew about Staci. Then he received his answer.

"Sorry about your apartment." Eddie kept his voice low as they parted, his head still only inches from Max. "I didn't want that to happen."

The hair on Max's neck stood up, and he balled his fists to maintain control. That simple statement was as good as an admission of guilt, but he played along.

"She was a good girl," he offered, noting that Eddie hadn't mentioned her. The man clearly didn't care and definitely was not sorry. "Please accept my condolences."

Eddie lifted a hand as if to say it wasn't a big deal.

"We can talk about that, but rules are rules. This thing upstairs," he continued as if Staci was an afterthought, "it's a done deal. You didn't miss much, but it's all done. We're headed outta here, and you should come with us."

"Thanks, Eddie, but I need to show my face."

He moved toward the elevators, but two men blocked his way. One had a black eye, and Max recognized the man from the stairwell below the BBQ, but the man showed no spark of recollection.

"No. Really." Eddie's voice remained low, but there was an edge to it now. "I think you should come for a ride with us, Max. It'll be good."

He contemplated his options, unconcerned about the men. His

odds were good, but everything in the casino was on camera, and where would that leave him? Wei Zhang wouldn't be happy. There wasn't much harm in playing along. Besides, hadn't Ling explicitly asked him to monitor the Marchettis?

He consciously relaxed his posture and turned back toward the door.

"Where're we headed?" he asked as Eddie moved beside him.

"You'll see." Eddie put a meaty hand on his shoulder and steered him out of the casino.

The group crossed the moderately busy drop-off area to the far side of the pavilion, where a pair of black vehicles waited under the watchful eye of another henchman. There was a large SUV, and in front of it was Eddie's BMW. As they neared, Max recognized Johnny, and he raised a hand in greeting.

"You seem to be everywhere these days." Johnny closed the distance, clasped hands, and offered a perfunctory side hug. "How you doin'?"

"I'm good, you?"

"Never better." He gave Max a look that seemed to evaluate him as if meeting for the first time.

Max remembered their brief eye contact below the BBQ and wondered if he had, in fact, been identified, but Johnny's expression left his face as quickly as it had arrived, and he turned to open the rear door of the black BMW.

Eddie had already walked to the other side and had opened the driver's door. Johnny tossed the keys across the top of the car, which Eddie snatched with one hand.

The man with the black eye got into the front passenger seat and, behind them, the others piled into the SUV. Max didn't like the feeling of being trapped, but he got in, and the door closed behind him. In a minute, the opposite door opened, and Johnny slipped in next to him.

"Really," he said before Eddie had even entered traffic, "where are we going?"

Eddie made eye contact with him in the rearview mirror.

"We're going to see someone I think you met at the hospital."

The statement sounded innocent, but Max knew exactly what it meant. It shouldn't have been a surprise. Eddie had already tried to put him in front of the EMT once before. Max wondered if it even made a difference. Staci was gone. Then he remembered that Eddie and his crew still hadn't identified the woman from that night. He shook his head and couldn't help a smile. These guys had already solved their problem and they didn't even know it.

"Something funny?" Johnny asked from his side, less friendly than he'd been outside the car.

"No," he answered instinctively, and it was true. There was nothing funny about Staci's death. "I'm thinking about how much has happened in the past two weeks."

"Sure has," Johnny agreed. "Seems like just last night when we were trading Tequila shots at Wildfire."

After waiting at a long light to exit the Jewel, Eddie pulled out and turned left onto Silverado Ranch Boulevard, moving quickly to the right and down the highway on-ramp. Max couldn't help but look out his window at the Deep Texas BBQ, vents billowing.

"Great spot," Johnny said from the other side of the car. "They make a mean brisket. You been there, Max? Is that a hangout of yours?"

Though the remark was casual, Max felt something was wrong. It seemed as though Johnny had forced the question into the conversation.

"I've been there." Honesty was often the best cover. "Why do you ask?"

"Says a lot about a man who can tell good cooking from bad," Johnny said, leaning against his door. "What do you know about cooking?"

Across the seat from him, Johnny made no effort to hide his evaluation as he waited for a response. Max felt certain the cooking reference implied knowledge of the lab, and he considered exchanging an equally cryptic response.

"Don't listen to him," Eddie interrupted from the front. He used the mirror to look directly at Max. "Johnny's been trying to get us to host a party there for years. Let it go, John. OK?"

Eddie's eyes moved from Max to his lieutenant, and there was no mistaking the silently emphasized command.

"Yeah," Johnny answered after a couple of heartbeats. "I get it. Someday though."

* * *

Twenty minutes later, the BMW was slowly negotiating the familiar apartment complex they had visited previously. As they took a right turn toward the destination building, Max glanced back but didn't see the SUV.

"What happened to the others?" he asked Eddie, but Johnny answered.

"They've got things to do. Lots going on this week."

Max didn't want to press the issue, but that was an understatement. The Marchettis were busy, and the sale of the Jewel was almost certainly their largest single transaction.

"I'm sure there's a lot going on," he said. "I'm happy to be wrapping my end up."

"Nice and clean, right?" Johnny yanked on the door handle.

"Take your payday and go. Must be nice." He got out and closed the door as quickly as he'd opened it.

Eddie had put the car in park and nodded to the man next to him, who also exited. When they were alone, Eddie turned around and rolled his eyes at Max.

"Managing people is the worst part of the job," he said, tilting his head toward Johnny. "He'll let it go eventually. Come on. You've got someone to get reacquainted with."

They both got out of the car. Max's mind was once again planning for evasive action. If it was only the four of them, he stood a chance, but he could not assume that Eddie didn't have others inside. He wasn't sure it would matter. The EMT could identify him, but to what end? Staci was gone. There was no longer a threat and nobody he needed to protect.

A vibration interrupted his thoughts, and when he pulled his phone out, he saw Carolyn's name. He glanced over at Eddie, who was looking at him impatiently.

"It's my girl. You OK if I take this?" he asked, trying to show deference.

"Go ahead." Eddie's face relaxed. "We don't want you to get in trouble."

Max tapped the green circle.

"I thought you were coming back to the room?" Carolyn asked

before he could even get the phone up to his ear.

"I, uh, got distracted." He lowered his voice and took a few steps away from the car and the two gangsters.

"I got in."

Max turned to confirm he was out of earshot.

"To Geno's server? I thought it was shielded?"

"No." Carolyn dismissed his comment as if it were outlandish. "I got into Scarpeli's computer."

"Shit. Of course. Anything good?"

"So far nothing super incriminating, but he barely protected his drive. I have some details about the shell companies. Are you alone?"

"No, I'm with Eddie, but we can talk. What's up?"

"Here's the thing: Tri-Star ownership is exactly what you would expect—Geno and a few other Marchetti men plus a collection of additional shell companies, not run through Scarpeli. It doesn't matter." She was rambling, as she often did when problem solving, and Max knew better than to interrupt.

"Starlight, on the other hand, has four principals. The two biggest percentages are Geno and Haoyun, with forty percent each."

"Wait a sec." Max couldn't believe his ears. He started walking farther down the street. "Did you say Haoyun? As in my employer?"

"That's what I'm saying. The Desert Jewel might be an arm's-length transaction, but it's not their only connection."

"What the fuck?"

"I'm not done. You won't be surprised to hear that the mayor's wife owns twelve percent."

"Makes sense. We already know he's a crook. And?"

"An offshore entity holds the last eight percent. I couldn't trace it, but there are emails here—mostly between Geno and Eddie."

She paused, and while he wanted to tell her to spit it out, he bit his lip, waiting and trying to be patient. He took a couple of steps farther away from the car.

"Sorry, Carolyn." Max needed to move things along. "I don't have a ton of time. What did the emails say?"

"They talk about making Staci 'go away.' They were almost fighting over who would handle it."

"Who won?"

"From what I can see, Geno told Eddie to leave it alone and handed it to the Ghost. Who's the Ghost?"

"OK. Hang on." Max ignored the question as he wrapped his mind around what she had said.

He lowered the phone and closed his eyes for a second. At least Eddie hadn't been the one to do the deed, but he was far from innocent. And Haoyun's connection seemed to go deeper. The more he learned, the more he became disgusted with his own complicity. He would end this on his own terms, and the reckoning was about to begin.

He lifted the phone back to his ear. "Hey."

"You OK?" There was concern in her voice.

"Yeah. I'm good," he answered. "I guess I was hoping Eddie wasn't involved."

"I'm sorry."

"It's fine." He turned back to see Eddie lifting his hands impatiently. "Hey, I've gotta go."

"That's not all, Max. Who's the Ghost?" she repeated her question.

"He's one of Geno's men. Nobody knows his real name. He handles things for Geno."

"Well, that's not good because he's looking for you." Her voice quavered.

"There are emails about you—about getting rid of you. Eddie said he would handle things, and Geno agreed. But then Geno has a different email thread with the Ghost, and in that thread, Geno tells the Ghost to clean it up."

"OK."

"Max, are you processing this? You need to leave whatever

you're doing. I think you're in over your head."

"I'll be OK." He tried not to worry her. "Things have sort of come to a head, and I think we'll be fine."

In truth, he wasn't worried about facing Eddie and Johnny. He could use a fight to let out some aggression. He'd deal with the Ghost when and if he met him.

"Seriously, Max. What are you trying to do?" Now there was definitely concern.

"Nothing, babe. I'm not doing anything." He started walking back to join the other two. "I'll be back in a little bit. Wait in the room."

* * *

Eddie gave his keys to the fourth man with instructions to watch the car, and the three of them walked down the sidewalk to the same apartment Eddie and Max had visited previously. For the second time in as many weeks, Max geared himself to react as soon as the door opened. Eddie was saying something about the Desert Jewel, but Max tuned him out, searching for clarity. By the time they stopped at the door, he had a plan, and he shifted slightly to put Johnny between himself and Eddie, who already had a key in the door.

The door opened inward, and Eddie entered, calling out in mockery.

"Honey, I'm home."

Max used the transition to make his move. Grabbing Johnny's right wrist from behind, he immediately flipped it up and behind his back, ignoring the man's startled exclamation. He pushed him toward the door jamb, and as it approached, he used his left hand to slam Johnny's head into the wood below the hinge, knocking him unconscious. As the body slumped, he caught the weight in his right arm, while his left removed the pistol he'd seen in the man's shoulder holster.

"What the fuck?" Eddie had turned in the doorway. Anger flared in his eyes as he reached into his jacket.

Max did not wait. He barreled into Eddie, forcing him back and crashing the two of them into and over the short pony wall inside the door. They rolled over the arm of a chair on the other side and ended up on the floor. Eddie was still in shock, but his hands were empty. Whatever he was grabbing was still in his jacket, and Max was on him before he could react, one knee on his left arm, the other on his chest, and the gun he'd pulled from Johnny inches from Eddie's face.

"Stand down, Eddie," he commanded, using the moment to check the surroundings. The room was empty, but he was exposed by the door behind him. He looked back at Eddie.

"You hear me?"

"Hey, man, we're good." The big man had dropped his anger.

Max didn't listen. He needed a better position, so he held the gun right up to Eddie's forehead.

"I'm going to get off your arm, and you're going to stay calm, alright?"

"OK." Eddie nodded. "You're wrong, pal. You don't know what you're doing."

"I'll be fine."

Max slowly eased back and guided Eddie with him as he sat on the edge of the couch, his back now to the wall with his pistol on Eddie's head as he searched the man's jacket. With one hand, he removed a Glock 19 and released the magazine, allowing it to fall to the floor. He swung the gun to point it into the sofa and fired the one round left in the chamber.

"Who else is here?" he demanded, tossing the now empty weapon onto the couch.

"Jesus, Max." Eddie laughed. "You are so fucking hardcore. Are you going to come work for me?"

"Who else is here?" Max pressed the loaded gun against Eddie's head, annoyed that the man was making light of the situation.

"Only one person."

Suddenly, a scream filled the room, and Max looked up to see a woman with a towel on her head in the far doorway.

"Max, what the fuck are you doing?" she yelled, not waiting for a response but crossing the room to hug Eddie. In her haste, she forgot the towel, and it fell to the ground, letting her wet blonde hair fall loose about her shoulders. It was Staci.

He couldn't believe his eyes, but he was too well-trained to drop his focus. He stared at her then looked back at Eddie, who hadn't moved. The man's mischievous eyes said everything. Max could feel the tension of the fight subside, and he finally lowered the gun, recognizing he might have misjudged the situation.

He sat back on the couch and rubbed his eyes with his free hand.

"Somebody want to explain what's going on?" he asked. His excitement at seeing Staci alive was tempered by his confusion.

Eddie slowly stood up and moved to the door, where Johnny was on all fours, blood dripping from his forehead.

"Johnny, you alright?" Eddie asked as he took hold of the injured man's left arm and helped steady him as he rose.

"I'll be OK." Johnny winced as he touched his own forehead and then looked down at a bloodied hand. "You got a towel or something, Staci?"

Staci turned and picked up the towel that had fallen from her head, handing it to him. "It's a little wet. I'll get something else."

She rushed out of the room.

Johnny held one end of the towel against his head while the rest of it dangled past his arm and turned to look at Max.

"Dude, was that necessary?" He sounded only half-serious.

"This is on me." Eddie moved between the two of them. "Max, I thought it would be a nice surprise."

"Fill me in, Eddie?" Frustration had quickly overtaken any happiness Max had felt at seeing Staci alive. The pieces on the battlefield were shifting, but he needed more information.

"What do you mean?" Eddie spread his arms, palms up, as if everything were obvious. "Staci is here. The Ghost missed."

"Tell me more."

"When I talked to you yesterday, Staci told me where she was."

Staci had returned with a bag of ice and a smaller towel, which she exchanged for the large one Johnny had been using. As Eddie spoke, she made eye contact with Max and shrugged as if in apology.

"OK." Max was noncommittal, wanting to hear more.

"But I already knew. Look, Max, when you refused Geno the other day—the man's got two switches, on and off—he called the Ghost immediately. You've been a marked man for longer than you know, but I was with Geno Saturday night when he got the call. The Ghost told him that Staci was staying with you, and that made Geno laugh hard. He gave the Ghost the green light, saying he could solve both problems at the same time.

"When you called Sunday morning, I was actually trying to find you—find Staci. I'm glad I got her out of there."

Max listened to Eddie describe how he'd retrieved Staci only an hour before the bomb had detonated. Eddie claimed not to know anything about the Ghost's plans. He hadn't known about the bomb, only that she was in danger. He'd been lucky.

Suddenly, Max recalled his conversation with Staci that morning, and things fell into place.

"You know about the wallet, don't you?" he said.

Eddie sat down in the chair opposite him and nodded.

"It's our ticket outta here." He pulled Staci in close. "I'm done with Geno. Done with all this shit."

"Do you think you can walk away?" Max was a little surprised. "They won't find you?"

"This isn't the movies, Max." Eddie leaned back in the chair. "We find someplace out of the way and make a new life. Geno wouldn't know where to look even if he cared, and with the shit he's got going down, I don't think he'll care."

Max shook his head then purposely looked at Johnny with a raised eyebrow.

Eddie immediately caught on and answered the unasked question.

"Johnny has his own deal. He'll get his cut, and we part ways."

"Who's in the movies now, Eddie?" he asked, knowing how seldom plans worked out.

"Look, I was done with this long before you showed up." Eddie wasn't angry, but he was making a point. "We had a good plan until the Haoyun deal popped up. But that stuff with Geno and the mayor, there is no getting away from that. It's way better if they think she's dead. And by the way, thanks for getting her out of that hospital."

"You're like a bad penny, Max," Johnny added from a seat on the other side of the room. "You kept showing up where you shouldn't be."

Staci ran a hand through Eddie's hair and then stepped over to drop onto the couch next to Max. She gave him a side hug.

"And I'm so glad he did," she told Johnny.

"We weren't sure what cards he was playing." He grinned, holding the ice bag to his temple. "We had the EMT, and from his description, we thought you must be involved, but we didn't know it was Staci!"

"Staci didn't even tell me until yesterday." Eddie added "I've been chasing the two of you without knowing it. And so has the Ghost. I doubt he knows the connection, but he's hunting for both of you."

A new thought occurred to Max. "Eddie, when you grabbed Staci from my apartment, was anyone else inside?"

The big man looked puzzled.

"No," he answered hesitantly. "Why?"

"Ben said they'd found a body." His mind was processing the alternatives even as he spoke. "So, that means somebody planted a body, or Ben's lying to me, or somebody else at the Las Vegas Police Department is putting out a false report."

He looked from Eddie to Johnny, but neither man offered a response, so he continued, "I'm pretty comfortable ruling out the first two options, which means we can't trust the police either."

"You're talking about Ben Carpenter?" Eddie asked.

"Yup."

"That guy's got a hard-on for Geno. Tried to get him a few years back, but Geno walked on a technicality. He's been harassing Geno and the rest of us ever since."

"That sounds like the man I know. Alright, this is all the more reason you two should cut and run. How can I help?"

"One problem." Eddie sat forward, putting his elbows on his knees. "With the Jewel deal closing, Geno stopped the crypto skim earlier than we thought. Last week was the last drop, so the wallets are at his house."

Max laughed.

"So you guys have stolen fourteen million and left it in someone else's vault?"

"I've got access to the server room, but I don't think I could get in and out without drawing attention. Even if I could, I can't simply take the wallet. We need to move our money out of the wallet and leave the cold storage device with Geno. There's way more money on that device than our little bit. If that wallet was missing, he'd never stop the hunt."

"Can you help us, Max?" Staci asked from the couch next to him.

He turned to look at her and saw the same pleading eyes that had gotten him involved with her escapades in the first place, and it suddenly dawned on him that perhaps Eddie wasn't in charge after all. He took a deep breath and let it out slowly.

"I've been looking for an access key. I've got other business in that server room. You let me borrow your key, and I'll get you the drive."

"We'll need to make the transfer and then return it," Eddie reminded him.

"That part, I'll leave to you. Once I get in, I'll be on a short timeline. Can you handle that?" Max looked from Eddie to Staci, and when they nodded, he added, "I'm thinking forty percent."

"Forty percent?" Staci echoed.

"I put our odds at forty percent," he said, standing up as he did. "But with your luck, Staci, our odds might be far better.

"We should head out of here. That gunshot might bring the police." He tossed the empty weapon back to Eddie.

## CHAPTER TWENTY-FIVE

Max drummed his fingers on the steering wheel. He was in the parking lot waiting for Carolyn, who'd gone into the third electronics store on their route. She'd begun with a list of six items, but up to now she'd only found half of what she needed. Glancing at his watch, he hoped she was successful because it was getting late and the next store might not even be open. Across the lot, the automatic sliding door opened for a young couple and then again for a group of teenagers. Finally, the doors opened again, and Carolyn sauntered back to the car, swinging a plastic bag in her left hand. As she crossed, the light from the store silhouetted her thin figure.

She opened the door and stepped inside in one smooth motion, turning to Max with a grin.

"Mission . . . accomplished!"

"That little bag?" Max asked. "That was all you needed?"

"Sometimes big things come in little packages. I can't send you into Geno's house with a desktop. Can I?"

"Well, no, but—"

She reached over to grab his hand.

"You do your job. I'll do mine," she said in a calm voice. "I'm pretty good at this stuff, even if I don't like it."

"Thanks, C. We've got to make one more stop before we head back."

He put the car in drive and turned right when the traffic passed. Conveniently, they were already on the east side of town, so it wasn't far to his storage unit, and not ten minutes later, he parked the car in front of his roll-up door.

Earlier that day, he'd told Carolyn about his stockpile, explaining it was really a hobby, but he was unsure if he wanted her to come inside.

"I gotta see this," Carolyn said as she left the car, resolving that issue without knowing it.

At the door, Max made quick work of the lock and pulled the roller up, allowing Carolyn to enter before he followed and slid the door closed. He reached instinctively to the power switch, and the lights sprang to life. After a brief pause, the alarm chimed, and he plugged in his key code, then held his thumb to the sensor.

"Holy shit." Carolyn wasn't looking at him. "This is more than a storage unit." She moved to the doorway and looked into the larger room. "Max, what have you got in here?"

"Mostly stuff I have no use for." He tried to downplay the collection as he followed her into the main room and identified some of the contents. "This safe has long-range rifles. This one has more tactile weapons. And this last one has some fun stuff that . . . might not be legal."

He held his thumb to the center case and pulled the door open after the lock released. There was no predicting how the next night would unfold, and he was going to bring options. Without even a second thought, he pulled out his M110A1 sniper rifle. Also known as an SDMR, or squad designated marksman rifle, the weapon had been his mainstay during his time as a Marine Raider, and though there were higher-rated sniper weapons, none gave him the same comfort, and in his opinion, none provided the versatility this rifle provided. He could shoot it accurately at 500 yards, yet its semi-automatic capability made it lethal in close-fire situations. He took it into the smaller room, removed the barrel, and tucked it into a carry case.

When he stepped back into the main room, Carolyn was staring at the right wall, where his collection of pistols hung unprotected.

"I sure hope I don't need to use one of these," he sighed, "but it could get hot."

He started looking at the options, knowing he would end up with his favorite SIG Sauer P320 compact pistol. Next to it hung the P322, the 22 caliber he'd allowed Staci to fire on the range. He picked it out first and turned to Carolyn.

"You should probably have one." He held the barrel of the gun with the grip pointed toward her. "Try it out."

Carolyn took a step back and raised her hands, her face white and a look of disgust in her eyes.

"No way." She said each word clearly. "If you think I need that, maybe I shouldn't be there."

"It's a precaution," he answered sheepishly, wishing he hadn't made the offer. "Maybe you don't even have to come in. How far will your gear transmit?"

"Not far. It's a radio frequency transmitter. It will draw power from the computer, but it will only get about five volts. I can't be sure how far it will broadcast—five meters maybe, but I'll have to be inside."

"OK." He put the smaller gun on the rack and took the 9mm P320 for himself. "Exactly how much will you be able to do from your phone in the middle of a party?"

"You'd be surprised at how much a phone can do these days, but I won't be able to hide it. If we can find an out-of-the-way place, it would be best. I've already accessed the house security, so I'll be on-line quickly. Once we tap into the server though, I'm going to need a few minutes to sort through the files if I'm going to extract something worthwhile. And the longer I'm on, the more likely we're identified."

"I thought this radio frequency thing was covert."

"It is, but we're plugging it into a shielded computer, Max. If they've gone through the effort of shielding, they most certainly will have something that detects the increased power draw from the RF transmitter."

"How long?"

"Depends on how closely it's monitored. Assuming the party is a distraction? Probably ten, fifteen minutes max before it's detected."

"Shit."

"It should take longer to pinpoint my phone, but they'll shut off the transmission. It's a burner phone, so we can leave it behind."

"OK. You sure this will work?"

"One thing about hacking, I'm never one-hundred-percent sure."

"Understood. There're a lot of things that have to go right for this to succeed. I spoke to the DA again. She's still willing to play ball, but she'll need evidence before she does her part."

"I wonder if she's any better."

"They're all dirty at some level, but I think she'll hold up her end. I want to get these guys." Max felt both his anger and a surge of pride in Carolyn's abilities. "Staci's alive, but the girls from the fire are not."

Carolyn looked at him with the faraway eyes that always made him melt. She tilted her head.

"You could walk away."

"No, I can't." He turned back to retrieve an ankle holster. "I can't walk knowing what I know. Besides, I gave Staci and Eddie my word that I would help them."

"*I* could walk away."

He turned back to look at her face, which was lit by the stark-white LED lights. There was a sadness in her eyes he'd never seen before. Her mouth was closed, and he saw a slight twitch in the muscle of her jaw, above the dark-brown patch of her birthmark. She was as beautiful as ever and seemed ethereal, as if she might fade away right then. He couldn't ask her to stay.

"Yes," he answered when he regained his composure. "You can walk, and that would be fine. I'll find another way."

He didn't want to force an answer, so he moved to the opposite wall where he grabbed two Kevlar vests, inserting a ceramic plate into the chest pad of one of them. He took these, the pistol, and the holster into the other room and laid them out on the table before returning to the main room, where he grabbed a communication kit.

"I'll do it, Max." Carolyn sat on a trunk. "But I'm doing it to keep you alive. I don't agree with this."

She grabbed his hand as he moved past her, and he turned to

look at her again. Her eyes had not changed, but her lips curled up weakly. "I told you," she said. "It has to end here."

Max took in a deep breath, relieved by her decision but still concerned about her feelings.

"We're doing the right thing." he said, knowing it was less than she needed.

CHAPTER TWENTY-SIX

The Southern Nevada Golf Club was an elite community on the southern end of town—even farther south than the Desert Jewel. Though the club was relatively new in the world of golf courses, built in the late nineties, its reputation had grown, and the membership, while not the old blood in town, comprised many of the heavy hitters in the casino industry. The community built around it was now lauded as one of the richest in the United States. It was a fully gated, heavily secured private community. Max wasn't surprised Geno owned a house on the course.

Not merely a house, it was a large mansion, complete with a backyard pool and terrace that looked out over the eighteenth hole. Of course, Max had not been inside, and with the high level of security, he had not had a chance to fully reconnoiter the location, but he'd launched a drone the previous evening to get a closer look at the house and surrounding area. He'd discovered numerous exit points on the golf course that compensated for the patrolled grounds. He had first planned to station Carolyn in a nearby van but had to scrap that plan after she revealed their signal's limited range of ten yards. The good news was that the house seemed large enough to hold the closing party and still leave room for her to find some place private to complete the download.

As the taxi waited to get through security at the club entrance, Max looked over at Carolyn. She was wearing a skintight dark-blue dress that was woven with metallic threads. It reflected the light as she moved and gave her an iridescent look. Her hair was pulled back into a bun on the backside of her head, pierced by two silver chopsticks, the ends of which glimmered in the same way. She completed the outfit with a light-pink stole that hung off one shoulder.

In a word, she looked amazing, and even in a town where glamor ruled the nightlife, he was certain she would outshine them all, though he wasn't sure that was a good thing for what they needed to do. He looked down at his own rather staid tuxedo and wondered what she saw.

"You know, I'd hate to see you mess up that tux," she said, as if reading his mind. Her dress sparkled in the guardhouse's light as they neared the gate.

"If all goes well, that shouldn't happen," he answered, trying to sound confident. "I know I've already said this, but you are absolutely stunning."

She rolled her eyes dismissively.

"Dressing the part, Max." Her voice took on an edge. "I'm here for a job, like you."

As she spoke, she tapped the faux diamond broach that cinched her dress at the throat, her motion drawing attention to the fact that behind the stone was a throat microphone that Max had installed. He had a similar device behind his bowtie, and the two of them both had earpieces to complete the connection.

Ten minutes later, the cab rolled around the cul-de-sac to the drop-off in front of Geno's mansion. Max had already exchanged numbers with the driver, and he handed her a wad of cash—more than they'd agreed to.

"Please keep your phone close," he whispered.

"Will do." The driver nodded as he exited. It wasn't common for him to use a driver more than once, but he wanted a tried relationship in case things didn't go as planned.

The walkway up to the door was lit by an assortment of lights in the shapes of various jewels. At the house, two double doors were wide open, welcoming a line of guests. Max did not recognize anyone except a pair of Haoyun bean counters several spots ahead of them. He put his arm around Carolyn's shoulders, giving her a light hug, and she responded by putting her arm around his waist.

When they got to the door, they were greeted by a collection of beautiful ladies dressed in 1950s vintage cocktail uniforms, complete with a feathered plume rising behind their coiffed hair and the "DJ" of the Desert Jewel emblazoned in sequins on their uniforms. The hostesses were giving every guest an open box containing a pin with a good-sized gemstone in the center surrounded by the phrase, "Desert Jewel—The Future Is Bright!"

Guides led them through the entrance hall to a large living room, transformed into a 1950s Las Vegas-style dance hall. Chandeliers hung from a double-high ceiling, and the room featured kiosks with Desert Jewel memorabilia and nods to the classic Vegas era.

The party was in full swing, and Max could see it also spilled out into the back courtyard he had surveilled. As he looked around the room, he caught the eye of Ling Wu, who was standing with Wei Zhang, and much to Max's surprise, the two were engaged in conversation with none other than Ben Carpenter. As Ling lifted her champagne glass in salute, Wei and Ben turned to follow her gaze, and both men raised their glasses.

Max lifted his hand in greeting but steered Carolyn to the opposite side of the room. As the others resumed their conversation, he saw Ben hold his gaze a little longer than the others with a look in his eye that might have offered an apology for the surprise. It didn't matter. In the room or not, Ben would not be much help with what he had to do.

Before they reached the bar, another costumed hostess offered a tray of champagne glasses. Carolyn immediately took one with her thanks, and Max, seeing a crowd at the bar, followed suit, thanking the server and clinking glasses with Carolyn before they both took a sip.

"Mr. Kline, it is good to see you." A voice came from his left, and Max turned to see the mayor with his hand outstretched, which he shook.

"Mr. Mayor."

"It's Joe—remember?" the mayor continued, but he wasn't looking at Max. His eyes were unashamedly taking in Carolyn—all of Carolyn—as they moved down and back up. "And who do we have here?"

Max was used to the Las Vegas boys' club, but the mayor's leer was little short of disgusting. Still, he knew enough to ignore it, and he introduced Carolyn as a friend from out of town.

"Nice to meet you." The mayor extended a hand, which she shook lightly and released.

"So," he continued, "what do we have to do to keep you in town, Carolyn?" The mayor did not hide his thoughts as he glanced down once again.

Carolyn, for her part, responded with casual deference but

ignored the question.

"It's nice to meet you, Mayor. Quite the party, isn't it?"

"It is, indeed. Not often that one of our storied casinos changes hands." He looked up at the high ceiling and swung his own champagne glass in a nod to their surroundings. "Geno managed it well, but we are excited to welcome the Haoyun Casino Company to Las Vegas."

"I understand you've done a lot to improve things here," Carolyn replied, and Max smiled internally, knowing she was fueling the fire.

"Thank you. I like to think I've played a minor role."

"You're modest." Carolyn took a small sip, her eyes flashing mischievously. "You're bringing the Los Angeles high-speed rail, are you not?"

The mayor's face lit up with excitement, and he began to tell Carolyn about the rail's timeline.

Max remained standing with them but listened only partially as he scanned the room.

The guest list was nothing less than the A-list of Las Vegas. Max saw the heads of at least three publicly traded casinos, as well as several notable financiers. He knew none of them personally, but he'd read enough to recognize their faces. A few entertainment headliners were in the room, each with a slightly larger crowd in orbit. There were also a few notorious guests—again, no one he knew personally, but while Las Vegas tried to downplay their mob connections, these men were in the news enough to be recognized, though their faces appeared in a different section of the papers.

"You voted for me, didn't you, Max?" The mayor's question brought him back to the conversation.

"Of course!" he lied, raising his glass. "Love the high-speed rail project, but what are you doing about the increased drug problem in the city? Everyone says Molly has become a big problem."

The mayor's face darkened for a second. "Yes, we know there is a problem on the streets, but the Police Department is on it. We have a plan, don't we, Detective Carpenter?" The last comment was directed beyond Max's shoulder, and he turned to find Ben at his side.

"Hello, Ben."

"Evening, Max." Ben shook Max's hand and looked to Carolyn, much more politely than the mayor had. "And whom do I have the honor of meeting?"

"Ben, this is Carolyn, an old friend who was in town last weekend, and I convinced her to stick around as my guest."

Again, Carolyn offered a dainty hand, which Ben shook lightly.

"Nice to meet you." Carolyn's smile widened, then she put a quizzical expression on her face. "Did the mayor—sorry." She caught herself, putting a hand on the mayor's forearm. "Joe. Did Joe say you are a detective?"

"Yes, ma'am," Ben replied, "but I'm not on duty tonight. And to answer your next question, no, I really don't belong here." He laughed. "The mayor was kind enough to invite me."

"Detective, can we assure Mr. Kline that the Molly problem is being addressed?" The mayor refocused the conversation.

"Yes, sir." Ben nodded to the mayor before turning to Max, giving him a knowing look. "We are real close to something big, but you'll have to wait to see."

"We have full confidence in your skills, Ben." An aide was pulling the mayor away, but he resisted. Staying in the conversation longer, he turned to Carolyn while pointing to his detective. "We've come to expect excellent results from this guy. He's a known problem solver."

Ben lowered his head slightly and lifted both hands in mock surrender.

"Please, I'm only doing my job."

The mayor turned back to him, and Max thought he saw a glint of determination in his eye.

"See that you keep succeeding, Detective. I'm counting on your efforts."

The aide won the battle, and the mayor turned away, allowing the young woman to steer him into another conversation.

Ben turned as a server offered him an hors d'oeuvre, and Carolyn used the opportunity to make eye contact with Max, nodding toward the detective. Max shook his head. He wasn't sure whether having Ben on the inside was good, but he didn't need to add more variables to the plan. More importantly, Ben did not know that Carolyn was his black hat, and there was no reason to compromise her.

"So what's the plan?" Ben asked as he turned back to the two of them, still finishing his bite.

"Ah, I'm looking to have a good time and not do something that will get me fired," Max answered with a laugh as he put an arm around Carolyn, pulling her to his side where she couldn't see his face, and he gave Ben an angry stare that implied he couldn't talk in front of her.

"Did I even tell you about my first holiday party on the force?" Ben replied, instantly understanding.

"Yes, you fell asleep under the tree." He'd heard the story many times.

"Excuse me." Carolyn slipped out of his arm. "I'm going to find the loo."

"She's a non-com, an ornament," Max hissed as the two veterans were now alone in the growing crowd.

"How was I supposed to know?" Ben shrugged, indignant. "So what's the plan?"

"Nothing immediate." Max didn't enjoy lying to his friend, but he didn't want to complicate an already tricky plan, and there were still some open questions. "And maybe nothing at all, but I'll wait until after the speeches."

Ben leaned in close.

"I've got the district attorney excited about this. It better happen."

"And if things go south?"

"We've got the mayor here and two SWAT teams on alert. If things go south, I've got your back."

* * *

He found Carolyn on the far edge of the patio, looking out over the dark eighteenth hole toward the light of the clubhouse on the opposite side and beyond to the bright Las Vegas skyline with its colorful casinos. Silently joining her, he scanned the area for signs of anything out of the ordinary. He saw nothing unusual, but the calm night before him contrasted with the loud and growing party behind him.

"You're about to tell me it's not too late to bail," Carolyn said without turning.

"Yup," he answered, looking at her and admiring her jawline. "I can get the wallet, and we leave the server alone."

"And Geno gets to keep murdering girls and selling drugs?" She turned to him with a glaring look. "No, we've gone this far. Let's finish it."

"Copy that." Max reached into his coat pocket to retrieve his earpiece and slid it effortlessly into his ear. "Comms up."

Carolyn turned, tapping her right ear, but he couldn't see the nano earpiece she must have already put in place.

"Perfect," he whispered, turning away and taking a few steps closer to the pool. "How's the reception?"

"It's like you are right here." Carolyn's voice came through his own earpiece. "How about me?"

"Good to go," he replied, crossing back to stand next to her. "They are smart enough to turn off when we are close, so we won't have any feedback."

He turned to look back across the semi-crowded patio to the fully lit mansion beyond. To either side and on the house itself were more vintage Desert Jewel neon signs, and the lights were on in every room, giving off a warm white glow. The only area of the house that was dark was on the lower-left windowless section, which would be their target. Even the patio was less adorned in that area, though there was an empty table and chairs sitting off the bushes, maybe ten feet from the building. Guards, dressed in the same black uniforms as the servers, stood at fifteen-foot intervals around the areas of the house that were not a part of the party.

"Change of plans," he said, putting his arm around her waist and guiding her toward the less populated side of the terrace. "Why don't you stay here?"

"Is that the room?" she asked, looking at the large vents in the wall but not pointing.

"I think so, yes."

"Then this is fine." She plopped into a seat with her back to the building. "I hope I don't get company."

"I'll handle that." He approached the nearest guard, who stood at the edge of the bushes, closest to the party.

"Hey, pal. Can I ask a favor?"

"What's up?" The man looked at him questioningly.

"My girl's got some bullshit work call she has to take." Max shook his head and rolled his eyes. "Can you keep people away so she can get the stupid thing done?"

"I . . ." The guard started to speak, but his eye was drawn to the pair of hundreds that Max was holding in an open palm. He shook Max's hand as he accepted the bribe. "I can do that, sir."

"Thank you." Max turned and headed back into the party. "You hear that? You're on a work call. How long do you need to kill the power?"

"Not long at all." Carolyn's voice was crystal clear in his ear. "I'll be ready in a minute. You tell me when's good for you."

Back inside, Max headed to his left, where a faux neon sign read, "Restrooms." He entered a hallway that appeared to cross this section of the house. On the other end, he could see a door open to the outside. His drone survey the previous night had revealed a long bank of high-end porta-potties that had been installed in the side yard for the event. A pair of women passed him on their way back to the crowd, laughing about something. The party's music was still pumping loudly into the narrow space.

In the middle of the hallway, another corridor crossed perpendicular to his path. To the right, a short hall led to a swing door that was opening, with a server holding a tray of appetizers. Beyond him, Max could see what looked like the kitchen. On the left was a shallow space, or alcove, with a large man dressed in black standing guard over a closed mahogany door. According to Eddie's description, the door led to Geno's private office and the shielded server room. He nodded to the man and continued out to the relatively quiet side yard, where he quickly found an unoccupied john.

He took care of business, impressed that the toilets actually had running water, and then whispered, "You ready?"

"Tell me when," Carolyn responded. She was also whispering, but her throat mic was broadcasting perfectly. "You'll have at most thirty seconds before the backups kick in."

As Max exited the toilet, he estimated his time.

"Go in ten seconds," he said.

"Ten, nine, eight . . ." He hadn't asked, but Carolyn gave him a verbal countdown as he crossed to the door. It allowed him to time his entrance perfectly, and he was almost at the guard's location when the lights went out and the music cut off.

A collective gasp emanated from the party. The guard in front of Max cursed and, to Max's surprise, bolted to the hall opposite him, leaving Max alone.

"Adapt and improvise" was a phrase that Marine Raider training had permanently drilled into him, and it returned unbidden as he strode to the door and held Eddie's key card to the pad. The small rectangle of light on the top went from red to green, and Max pulled the door open and slipped inside even as the lights sprang back to life with power restored. He had expected to take out the guard, which was one of the weakest parts of his plan, so this was a win. *Adapt and improvise*, he silently repeated to himself, enjoying the minor victory.

"I'm past the guard," he updated Carolyn. "Be ready."

Inside, the noise of the party was completely gone. Ahead of him, the hall continued for twenty feet, ending in another dark-mahogany door. That was Geno's office, but partway down the hall on the left side was a plain doorway with another keypad on the wall. He quickly took the five steps to reach it and hovered the key card over the second pad. Once again, the light turned green, and this time, without the surrounding noise of the party, he heard a soft click.

As he pushed the door open, he was reminded of the hospital server room. There were similar banks of servers, both on the wall opposite him and in two rows to his right. Also reminiscent of the hospital was a computer terminal centered on the opposite wall, its two screens alive with live camera feeds from the party. More curious was the empty office chair, which was slowly rotating.

"Don't fucking move." Something hard pressed into his back. "I will blow you away if you so much as twitch."

Max knew better than to challenge the statement. The chair had given him a split second to prepare, and he knew how he would play this.

"What the fuck?" Max squealed, doing his best panicked cry. "I'm looking for the damn bathroom."

He raised his hands high over his head and dropped to his knees then slowly turned toward his assailant with an expression of terror on his face. He curled his arms slightly, as if trying to cover his head.

"Don't shoot. It was dark. I thought this was the bathroom." He cowered like a puppy, but he left his hands high and within reach of the man's weapon, and he let out another weak cry. "Oh my God."

The man with the gun gave a look of annoyance and lifted one hand to his ear while relaxing his hold on his weapon. He tapped his earpiece as if intending to report the incident to his superiors, but he never got the chance.

Max reacted instantly, snatching the gun as he pivoted and stood up, using his momentum to land a hard right hook into the man's sternum. The man collapsed, grabbing his stomach, and a second later, Max slammed the man's face into his rising right knee. The body slumped unconscious to the floor.

"Are you OK?" Carolyn asked. She must have heard Max's end of the interchange.

"I'm fine. They had a guard inside. I don't have much time."

"The main server is going to be big, and it's likely near the vents."

Max hardly needed the guidance as the wall to the left of the terminal held what was by far the largest and busiest server, guessing by the number of cables that snaked away from it in carefully wrapped bunches. Behind it, Max could see ventilation screens protruding from the wall. If he had his bearings straight, he was on the opposite side of the vents he'd seen near the patio where Carolyn sat.

"Any port?"

"No. You should see a switch nearby, probably above or below the server. It's thin and will be the one with most of the cables."

"Got it." Once again, it was easy to find.

"You need a slot with an orange light."

Max scanned the narrow switch in front of him. Almost all of the four banks of Ethernet ports were in use, but there was a row of five open slots, and they all had both orange and green lights. He reached into his breast pocket to retrieve the transmitter.

"Roger that. They've got orange and green lights."

"Should be perfect."

He plugged his cable into the nearest port and pushed the transmitter, which was a little smaller than the size of his hand, to the far back of the server rack with its antenna still bundled next to it. The rest of his work would be at the back of the server, and looking down, he released the locks on the casters and tugged the rack into the room, relieved that it rolled with ease.

"Working on your antenna now."

Navigating to the vent was a little harder than expected because of the mass of wires he needed to move past. He also had to contend with the vents, which protruded six inches into the room, shrinking his two-foot gap, but he eventually reached the server's back and slowly unspooled the transmitter wire for use as an antenna.

Behind him, he could feel the pull of air through the vents, and when the antenna was ready, he turned awkwardly in the small space, looking to see if there were any gaps where he could slide his wire through. The first layer of the vent was a honeycombed metal screen that his wire easily slipped through, but about an inch farther in were tightly woven EMI filters that Carolyn had warned him would be part of the room's shielding. He tried several angles near the corners and even in the center, but the wire continued to get stopped.

"What's taking you so long?" Carolyn asked. "I'm pretending to be on a call, but I think the guard is getting suspicious."

"Don't worry." Max cuffed his response. "He's been paid enough to sit still. EMI filters have been blocking me. I think I'm going to use the trocar."

"Shit."

Max could almost hear Carolyn refocusing.

"I can buy us ten minutes," she said, "maybe a little more, but once you puncture the filter, it's going to trigger an alarm.

"Hang on," she continued. "Someone else is on the house system. I've got to lie low."

"Are you compromised?" Max asked even as he bent to pull up his pant leg and remove the twelve-inch trocar he'd strapped there.

"No." Carolyn sounded less than confident. "I don't think so."

"Hall still clear?"

"Yes. I've got the monitor up in the corner of my screen," she told him. "I'll let you know if you have company."

"OK. Stay ready."

Max had the trocar assembled. Besides the pointed tube, he'd brought a half-inch round disk that would allow him to hammer the device through the filter. It threaded easily onto the back of the tube, but he realized he would need more room. He put his back to the server rack and slowly added pressure, hoping that none of the cables would restrict him. It rolled another six inches before something held it back. He didn't have time to find out what it was, so the added room would have to suffice.

On the vent, he selected a spot in the lower-right corner, about hip height for him, and he slid the trocar in until it stopped against the filter.

"About to puncture the EMI," he told Carolyn.

"Got it. My delay is already in place."

He allowed the trocar to rest in the bottom of one hex of the outer shield and slid it back three inches, enough that he could get some momentum. Any farther out and he would not have the leverage to drive it home. After a deep breath, he slammed the trocar forward, but it failed to puncture the filter. Worse, it got embedded, and it took almost thirty seconds for him to un-pry it. A second effort yielded the same result. And a third, but the last drive felt different, so rather than pulling back, Max pushed as hard as he could, straining against the disk on his end until finally something gave way, and his disk slid inward up to the honeycombed grate.

He prayed there was only one filter as he unscrewed the disk to reveal the open end of the tube. Picking up the transmitter wire, he started feeding it through the hollow trocar, relieved when it continued to slide well past the length of the tube.

After about three feet had gone through, Carolyn crowed, "I'm getting a signal. Wow. Loud and clear. Let me know if you need anything, but I'm going to work."

"Copy that." Max wiped his brow, leaning on the vent for a moment's respite. The night was definitely not over, and now he had to get back into the party.

* * *

After climbing out of the mess of wires behind the server rack, Max stepped quickly to the computer terminal. On the next rack, to the right of the computer as Eddie had described, was a small black box the size of a cigar case, which he opened. Inside were two pocket-sized e-wallets. Max lifted the first up. It looked like a small phone, but there were no other marks. The second looked no different. One of them was supposed to have a piece of white tape on the backside. This identified the one Eddie used, where Staci had hid their small fortune, but neither wallet had white tape.

"Max." Carolyn's voice returned. "The guard from the hallway went inside."

With no time to identify the correct wallet, he grabbed both and slipped them into his right breast pocket, securing it with the small zipper he'd had his tailor install. Closing the box, he moved toward the door, but he stopped when he saw a flash on the screen. It was an open chat, and the most recent message was fifteen seconds old.

"What the fuck, Scott?" it read on the screen. "Check in. Someone is on the network."

"Max?" Carolyn's voice had a hint of panic. "He's at the door."

"Copy that, C," he replied, taking two large strides toward the door. "They've seen you on the network. Are you out?"

"Almost."

"Fuck it. Cut your connection. It's not worth it."

"One more thing."

He heard her reply but was already focusing on the new task ahead. In front of him, the door swung open, so he gave the door a hard yank, which threw the guard off balance, sending him stumbling into the room. It was the same guard he had seen earlier, and the man's eyes widened in recognition even as Max grabbed his shoulder and swept a leg under his feet. Fortunately, he had no weapon in his hands.

The door swung closed as Max withdrew his P320 and lowered it to rest against the man's head.

"Don't pull any bullshit," he ordered. "I don't want to kill you, and you don't want to be dead."

He flipped open the man's jacket and removed a large hand-cannon from a shoulder holster.

"You're making a mistake," the guard protested.

"Let me worry about that." Max hated talking. "On your stomach. Hands wide."

Kneeling on the man's back, he pulled one of his hands where his knee could pin it. Then he grabbed the other hand, giving it a slight twist and hearing the man grunt in pain. He needed his victim distracted, as the next move was his most vulnerable. Holstering his weapon, he slid a zip tie from inside his sleeve, quickly latching it to the left wrist before easing his knee back and securing the man's right arm. He pulled the tie tighter than he should, but he couldn't risk the man getting free. Thirty seconds later, a second zip tie was around the man's legs, and he latched a third connecting the two. His victim had gone silent through the trussing but now cursed again.

"Fucking asshole. See where this gets you. No fucking way you leave here."

Max considered replying but thought better of it. He dragged the man to the far end of the server room. As the man continued to argue, Max pulled out his pistol and, holding it by the barrel, delivered a hard blow that silenced the complaints. The man's body went limp, hands and feet still held together by the zip ties.

"Max?" Carolyn said.

"I'm good," he answered. "Are you off the network?"

"I'm off the server, but I'm still in the security feed. How else could I see the cameras?"

"Get off. They know you're there."

"I can do this, Max. I'll kill the cameras for your exit, then I'll drop off."

He shook his head, knowing he would waste time trying to change her mind.

"I need one minute."

A server fan whirred to life, causing him to look up, but nothing appeared out of sorts. In thirty seconds, he'd bound the first man and dragged his limp body to the same corner of the room.

"OK," he told Carolyn. "You ready?"

"Killing cameras in three, two, one . . . You're clear."

Max eased the door open and stepped into the empty hallway. He looked down at his clothes and straightened his shirt, wiping both sleeves of some dust he must have picked up behind the server.

"Hallway?" he asked.

"Wait one second," Carolyn instructed. "Two people passing. OK, you're clear, but hurry. Someone else is coming from the bathrooms."

He opened the door to the hallway and slipped out, pulling it closed behind him. Immediately, he pulled his phone from his left breast pocket and thumbed the screen, trying to look like he had paused in the alcove.

"Cameras are live," Carolyn spoke in his ear. "Someone's coming. I'm going to cut off comms. See you inside."

"No," he howled, almost shouting. "Stay on."

When she didn't respond, he spoke again. "Carolyn?"

"Are you talking to yourself, Max?"

He looked up to see the mayor in the alcove with him.

"Or," the mayor continued, "are you on a call with the tiniest of earbuds?"

Max lowered his phone and smiled. The man had no idea how close he was to the truth.

"Sorry, I get distracted. Never check your email at a party, right?"

"Never check your email at all!" Rodriguez laughed. "Which way you headed?"

Max nodded toward the party.

"Good!" The mayor put an arm on Max's shoulder and guided him back to the main room. "Let me buy you a drink."

CHAPTER TWENTY-SEVEN

The mayor's offer had been tongue in cheek—at a party giving out gemstones, there was no buying of drinks. Even so, he made good by grabbing a pair of wine glasses from a passing server and handing one to Max before a group of supplicants pulled him away, leaving Max free to find Carolyn and Eddie.

The room was even more crowded than before, and it took him a minute or two to navigate to one side where he could scan the crowd for Carolyn. She wasn't in sight, and he was about to move to the patio when a hand grabbed his elbow, and he turned, ready for confrontation.

"Max." He didn't recognize the small brunette woman who used his name. "It's me."

"Sorry . . ." He started to turn away, but he stopped, recognizing her eyes, which now brightened. "Staci? What's with the outfit? What are you doing here?"

She wore a long red dress that hugged her hips, a glass of champagne in one hand.

"It's Carla, tonight," Staci answered, guiding him to one side, out of traffic. "Eddie needs me to make the crypto transfer."

"He told me he could do it. Where is he?"

"He's here but got a call a minute ago." She motioned toward the kitchen. "Anyway, he wouldn't even know where to look for the hidden wallet. He probably didn't want you to know he was bringing me."

Max nodded. It made sense, and this was an excellent opportunity to make the transfer. He took a moment to look around the room. The party was in full swing, and apart from the men at the edges of the event, he didn't see anyone paying them much attention.

"Open your purse," he instructed her.

"Do you have it already?" she asked, as she opened the small bag that hung from her shoulder on a long gold chain.

"I have both," he continued. "Couldn't tell them apart."

He reached into his coat and deftly unzipped the pocket, removing the two black wallets to his palm. He then put his left hand on her shoulder as he dropped the wallets into her purse and continued the motion until his hand was on her hip, leaning in to give her the classic two-cheek Italian greeting.

"Tell Eddie to return these as quickly as possible," he whispered into her ear. "His key card is between them."

As they separated, he saw Staci casually close her purse without looking.

"Why did you take both?"

"No tape. I didn't know which was yours. Is there any other way to tell?"

"I'll sort it out. You're amazing, Max," she said, putting her free hand on his arm. "Where can I—"

"Bathrooms," he interrupted, knowing exactly what she needed and pointing to the hall where he had been. "They've got the super large rentals, and you'll have privacy. You're still going to need Eddie."

"I'll find him when I'm done." She let go of his arm, but not before she squeezed it. "Thank you."

She turned and started to make her way to the bathrooms, and he watched her for a moment, hoping she would succeed, but she and Eddie were on their own now. He needed to find Carolyn and quietly depart.

As he stepped out on the patio, he tapped a quick message to his driver, asking her to be ready, but a quick scan of the crowd outside was fruitless. Carolyn was not on the patio either. The table where he had left her was empty, but the guard was still off to the side, so he walked over to him.

"Hey, pal, did you see where my gal went?" he asked.

"Nope." The man did not look him in the eye, staring out past him at the party. "She was on her phone for a while then left."

"Thanks."

He walked past the table and noticed something in her chair, and when he walked around, he found her pink stole, abandoned. Immediately, the hair on his neck bristled. Something was not right.

Picking up the scarf, he returned to the guard.

"You sure you didn't see anything weird?"

"Nah, man. She left with that cop."

"What cop?" Things were not clicking. The only cop at this party was Ben. "Black guy? About my height?"

The guard nodded.

Max wasn't sure about Ben, but better him than one of Geno's crew. He scanned the patio one last time, then re-entered the house. They couldn't be far. He wanted to try the entry hall to see if they were there, but a new hand on his arm halted his progress. This time it was Ling Wu, accompanied, as usual, by Wei Zhang.

"Hello, Max." She gave a slight head bow, which Max returned, offering the same to Wei Zhang.

"Are you enjoying yourselves?" he asked politely as his anger simmered.

"It is rare you get to celebrate the purchase of a Las Vegas landmark," Wei said with an alligator smile.

"And a drug factory," Max added, returning the grin.

Wei's face went blank, and he stared at Max for an uncomfortable moment before turning and stepping into a conversation with some others from the Haoyun team, leaving Max alone with Ling.

"That was unwise," she said before sipping her champagne.

"I don't fucking care, Ling." Max tried to hold his anger in check, but it was slipping out. "You lied to me. Or you omitted the truth. Either way, you're as bad as the Marchettis, and I don't want any part of it."

"I was in the dark too." She was mildly annoyed. "They told me this was a clean investment."

"But you had suspicions?"

"Something wasn't right, but I didn't think it was on my team. Why do you think I had you investigate?"

"Well, now you know otherwise."

"As do you, Max. And you seem to be enjoying yourself."

"The only thing I'm enjoying is the end of our relationship." He couldn't hold back the bitterness. "Drugs are killers and that makes you a killer, but I can't sit with that."

Ling was unfazed. She raised an eyebrow. "The money helps."

"Keep your fucking money," he hissed as the music in the room died out and he heard a glass clinking.

Everyone in the room turned to the patio entrance, where a small area had been cleared and Geno stood with a microphone. Next to him was Eddie, glass in one hand and butter knife in the other, tapping away to get the crowd's attention.

"Welcome." Geno's voice boomed through the room, surprising even himself. He turned to Eddie, who shrugged.

"Welcome," he said again with the microphone farther away from his mouth. Somewhere, somebody controlling the audio had adjusted the volume.

"That's better," Geno continued with a wide smile. "Welcome, everyone, and most importantly, Haoyun Casino, the newest owner of one of our oldest casinos. Welcome to Las Vegas!"

Applause followed, and Geno continued with his praise, but Max was not interested. He moved to the side of the room where Eddie had already retreated.

"Bringing her was a risk," Max whispered as soon as he was within earshot.

"So she found you? Good." Eddie glanced nervously at his boss, who was still speaking to the crowd. "Did you get the wallet?"

"She's working on it now. Side yard bathrooms. I gave her your pass too."

"OK. Thanks." Eddie's eyes betrayed fear. "Max, they are on alert. Shit's going down. You should get out of here."

"No worries," he replied, smiling so that anyone looking at them might think it was a casual conversation.

"What else did you do?" Eddie asked incredulously.

"Don't worry about it." Max didn't want or have time to explain. "Focus on your part. I'll see that you get out. Listen, I can't find my girl. Have you seen Ben Carpenter?"

"The cop? He's here, but I haven't seen him."

Eddie turned to look directly at him for the first time.

"Wait, was your girl helping you?" As he asked, he picked up an earbud that had been hanging loosely at his collar and put it back in his ear. "There was some chatter about a breach and a woman outside. Max, you should probably leave."

"I can't go without her."

"I don't know." Eddie shook his head. "Look, Geno's almost done. I gotta go find Staci, but you need to clear out."

He didn't wait for a response and headed toward the restrooms.

Max scanned the crowd for either Carolyn or Ben, with no luck. He moved around the back of the crowd toward the entrance hall, hoping he might find them there. Behind him, another round of applause punctuated Geno's speech, and Wei Zhang took the microphone.

* * *

Max pressed through the thicker crowd near the archway that separated the two rooms then emerged into the entrance hall beyond. The area was equally crowded, though fewer people were focused on the speaker who was out of sight. The din was louder, as quite a few were engaged in side conversations. Wei's voice continued through the speakers, but it felt more like ambiance.

Still no sign of Carolyn, but he recognized Staci's red dress emerging from a side door and moving toward the exit.

"All good?" he asked as he caught up and tapped her arm.

She flinched at the touch then relaxed when she saw him.

"God, don't do that," she whispered, her eyes expanding for emphasis.

"Did you make the transaction?" he asked again and saw her smile widen.

"It's done." She nodded. "BTC moved to my account. Eddie's got the wallets now."

He knew BTC was short for Bitcoin.

"Great. Now leave here and run."

"That is not a nice way to treat a lady!" Staci put her hand on Max's arm with mock offense. "But that's what I'm doin', if you let me go."

She reached up on tiptoes and gave Max a kiss on his cheek.

"Thanks so much," she said as she turned and headed to the door.

Max let her go and continued to look for Carolyn. As he was about to return inward, the side door opened again, and a waitress entered with another tray of hors d'oeuvres and, right behind her, looking dapper in his blue blazer, button-down, and khakis, was Ben Carpenter.

Max raised a hand, which Ben acknowledged, and immediately moved to meet him at the back of the room.

"Working the kitchen now?" Max offered when he was within earshot.

Ben shook his head. "Working more than you know, Max, but I was in the bathroom. Hey, did you contact the DA directly?"

The question threw Max off guard.

"I thought you were talking to her?" he countered, not really wanting to discuss the facts.

"Yeah, I was." Ben peered at him questioningly. "But she seems to know more than I've told her."

"Have you seen Carolyn?" Max changed the topic.

"Not since we met," Ben answered without changing his expression.

Max felt a pit in his stomach, for the first time wondering if Carolyn's suspicion had been correct.

"Damn." He pretended to be confused. "Guard on the patio described somebody who must look like you."

"Must be a good-looking guy." Ben opened his hands and raised his eyebrows in jest. Then he leaned closer. "Did you get the thumb drive?"

Max looked to one side then back and nodded.

"OK, give it to me now," Ben hissed in urgency. "I don't want that in the wrong hands."

Max felt a tinge of regret in his heart as he reached into his pocket for the empty thumb drive that Carolyn had given him in the car. *Maybe she's still wrong*, he thought to himself as he handed it to the detective.

Behind him, Max heard the crowd roar with the approval of something Wei had said. He'd turned at the noise, and when he turned back, Ben stepped closer and explained.

"Wei gave everyone five grand to gamble at the Jewel. They're moving the party to the casino. There's been a security breach here, and it needs to get handled."

On the speakers, he could hear Wei explaining a special high-rollers area for the party and that there would be bonus prizes for the highest stack at midnight.

Already, people were moving past them to the front doors, where a line was forming to receive chips for the next stage of the party. The bonus prizes must have conveyed a sense of urgency because people were putting down full drinks and rushing to fill the lines at the exit.

"Security breach?" he repeated. "So are you officially on duty?"

"You could say that." Ben put a hand on his shoulder. "And I could ask the same of you."

If the alarm siren had sounded earlier in the back of his head, it was now at a full wail.

"We've got a group gathering in Geno's office," Ben continued, opening his right arm to point toward the door he had come from. "You should be there."

Ben had not released the hand on his shoulder, and Max could feel a slight bit of pressure as his friend tried to steer him. He dipped his shoulder down and back, forcing Ben to let go.

"Sorry, I've got to find Carolyn."

He turned back to resume his search, but Ben followed, putting his left hand on Max's left shoulder and stopping his motion. His face was now uncomfortably close.

"On second thought . . ." Ben growled in a tone he'd never heard from his poker buddy. "I think I can help you with that, soldier."

The detective dropped his left hand and took a step back, sweeping his right arm back out toward the inner door.

"You really need to join us if you want to help your girl."

As if that weren't clear enough, the detective put his left hand in his pocket, purposefully pushing his blazer back and revealing the black handle of a pistol tucked into his belt.

Max paused, knowing things had changed. He took in a deep breath as he looked at the man he thought had been his brother and friend. This was not how he had expected things to develop.

There was little he could do except follow Ben's direction. Carolyn's safety was paramount, so if she was in Geno's office, that was where he had to go. There would still be cards to play, but he'd have to wait for an opportunity.

# CHAPTER TWENTY-EIGHT

Ben took him through the side door that led past the kitchen and into the hall where Max had been earlier. Two guards now stood at the mahogany door, and they held the door open when Ben approached. Inside, they headed down the hall to the second wood door, passing the now open door to the server room, which was abuzz with activity. Max caught a brief glimpse of someone kneeling where he'd left the guards and saw another small crowd by the computer terminal.

Ben had only to rap quietly on the door, and it opened inward, revealing an opulent office filled with faces Max knew all too well. A Marchetti man stepped past Ben and patted down Max, removing his phone and the pistol from the ankle holster. He retrieved the earbud case from Max's jacket pocket and held his hand out for the missing bud, which Max dutifully removed from his ear and dropped into the waiting palm. When the search was done, the man stepped to one side and allowed them to enter.

Geno sat at a large desk that dominated the room. Behind him stood Eddie and a few other Marchetti henchmen. At a chair in front of the desk, Wei Zhang sat rigidly, turned halfway to the door. Both men nodded to them as they entered, but no words were spoken until Max heard the door close behind them.

"Hello, Max." Geno's voice was calm, but there was an edge to it. "It seems like you've been busy this evening, and not in a good way. Wei assures me this was not something he ordered. So why have you attacked us?"

Max met Geno's glare and held it. Out of the corner of his eye, he saw Wei nod when his name was mentioned.

"I don't know what you're talking about," he answered coolly, knowing at least for now there would be little hard evidence.

Geno stared back at him then glanced to the right, which was Max's only warning.

He swung his arm backward and only just deflected a blow meant for his kidney. Instinct took over, and he grabbed the man's hand, pulling it with him as he spun, dropping the man to the floor. Seconds later, his left foot was on the man's throat, and he held the man's arm vertical in a twisted position. Any additional torque and the man's shoulder would separate.

As fast as the motion had been, it was soon followed by the noise of several guns drawn and now pointing at him. His moment of victory instantly returned to submission. He looked from his would-be assailant back to Geno and then released the arm, lifting his foot from the man's throat.

"I'm good," he said, raising empty hands above his waist.

"This doesn't have to get violent," Geno offered.

Max didn't think it was worth pointing out that he was the one who had been attacked.

Abruptly, Wei stood up, looking from Max to Geno.

"If you'll excuse me," he said slowly and politely, addressing Geno, "I have to attend the party at the Jewel. Somebody needs to award the prizes. Congratulations on the transaction, and we look forward to partnering with the ACC."

"The pleasure was mine, Wei." Geno stood and quickly rounded the desk. Wei had offered a bow, but Geno grabbed his hand in a solid handshake and then pulled him in for the two-cheek hug. Max could see the tension in Wei's back as he acquiesced.

When the two separated, Wei walked past Max without acknowledging him, and Geno resumed his seat.

As soon as the door closed again, Max felt the hard nozzle of a gun at the side of his head as another man drew his arms behind his back and handcuffed him tightly.

"Take a knee, soldier," the man with the gun commanded, and

only when Max was on his knees did he withdraw the weapon.

"I'm still a bit confused about what you are doing here tonight," Geno said matter-of-factly.

"Where's Carolyn?" Max asked.

"That your hacker friend?" The mob boss motioned for the men to lower their weapons. "She's safe. We need to talk to her a bit more—you know, find out what she took."

"She didn't take anything." Max knew it wouldn't work, but his only option was to maintain the specter of innocence, at least until he formulated a plan. "She's here as my guest. Where is she?"

"Easy, Max." Geno pushed back in his chair. "You know, my offer was sincere. You could have found a good home here."

"Thanks." Max tried to keep the disgust out of his tone. "I've got a good home, or I had one before you blew it up."

"Now, now," Geno feigned offense. "Let's not throw out unfounded accusations. I'm sorry about your apartment, but it seems like you've been snooping around things in town that aren't really your business. More importantly, where have you been this evening?"

"You're kidding, right?" Max kept the story going. "I've been here."

"Yes, but we had a security breach this evening, and your girl is involved."

Max started to reply, but Geno cut him off.

"Cut the shit, Max. I don't need to hear another lie. What did you do with the wallets?"

Someone behind Max kicked him in the upper back, sending him crashing forward with no hands to break his fall. He twisted his shoulder to take the brunt of the impact, but his face still hit the floor, cracking a lip. It wasn't painful, but Max tasted his own blood. The man pulled on the link of the handcuffs to lift him back to his knees.

"You think I'm a pickpocket?" Max allowed a smile to come to his face. He knew what the man had asked, and his own answer was so dumb that the smile was genuine.

Geno leaned forward.

"Someone removed two crypto wallets from our server room. They are effectively worthless to anyone but me—I don't care how good your hacker is. It's a twenty-four-word recovery seed phrase."

Before Max could respond, Eddie stepped forward from the wall behind Geno.

"I'm sorry, boss." He pulled the two wallets out of his blazer pocket and put them on the desk. "I didn't realize you were looking for these. I was in the server room after the attack, and with everyone in there, I thought it best that I remove any temptation."

As Eddie stepped back, his expression was unflinching. The entire act was so casual that all Geno could do was look at the wallets as he took in a deep breath.

"Well, we solved that problem." He turned to a man standing off to Max's right. "Go on, Mike. Let's check 'em out. Make sure everything's still there."

"No offense to you." Geno turned to look at Eddie. "But if they were in the server room during the breach, we still need to be sure."

"Understood," Eddie answered and nodded with pursed lips.

"I don't know what games you're playing, Max." Geno turned back, putting his elbows on his desk and closing his fingers together with his index fingers pointing skyward. Max couldn't help but think of the children's rhyme about a church and steeple.

"So," Geno continued, "we're going to have a bit of a chat, which may not be super comfortable for you. And then we'll see about your girl."

Two of the men stepped in and lifted Max to his feet as a third man opened a door on the right-hand wall. Max could see a courtyard beyond, but before they moved, the door behind him opened, and a new man walked over to Geno, leaning to whisper something in his ear.

"Now?" the boss questioned.

The man stepped back and shrugged, answering openly. "That's what he said. You want me to tell him you're not here?"

"No." Geno was already on his feet and moving to the door. "I'll talk to him."

When he reached Max, he stopped, his face inches from Max's own.

"You could have had a home here," he repeated, disgust in his voice, then turned to the door, calling over his shoulder to his men. "Take him to the garage. People are still at the party. I won't be long, but be careful he doesn't get too banged up while I'm away."

* * *

In the courtyard, an ivied wall on his right ran from the house about twenty yards to another building, which Max assumed was the garage. Light and music spilled over the wall from the other side, where the luxury porta-potties had served the guests. He wondered if anyone was still using them but thought better of shouting. Even if anyone heard him above the soundtrack, they were unlikely to come to his aid. He tested his bond, but they were real handcuffs and did not budge.

The first blow was unexpected. They had not yet reached the garage when the man behind him hooked his back foot and shoved his shoulders forward. For the second time, Max was only barely able to roll his shoulder under himself to absorb the impact. Before he could react, someone's shoe drove hard into his solar plexus, and he instinctively curled his body to protect the core. With his arms bound behind him, the action did little to protect him, but his options were limited.

He was on the ground and exposed to the group of men above him. Another blow smacked his face below his right eye, and the pain flared even as his eye shut. He had the bizarre thought about the effectiveness of dress shoes for the beating as several more kicks landed on his torso.

"Enough, fellas." Eddie's voice interrupted the onslaught. "What the fuck? Nobody told you to beat him up. There are still guests here. Pick him up and get him inside."

Max was gasping for breath and thankful that the torrent had ended. There was little he could do except try to prepare himself for whatever came next.

Hands grabbed him roughly and pulled him back to his feet. They guided him toward the door, and as he stepped in, his captor yanked him to the left, slamming his forehead against the doorjamb. The sound was worse than the pain—it was a meat slap if he'd ever heard one, and he felt a trickle of blood dripping down the side of his face.

"I said enough, Mickey." Eddie's voice again. This time, he sounded angry. "We need more information from this guy, and until Geno gives the order, he needs to stay alive."

"No problem," the man grunted.

Max thought there might be some mob politics at play. It didn't matter. Staying alive mattered. Finding Carolyn mattered.

The door closed behind them, and lights sprang to life, illuminating a large garage. Directly ahead of them was the black Mercedes Max had ridden in the week before, and beyond it he could see more sports cars in various colors. To their left was an area with a couch and several leather chairs. On the wall, a large-screen TV was showing highlights of the PGA tour, the volume on but very low. To the right was an open kitchen complete with ovens, a fridge, and a sink. Separating the two areas, a long wood bar extended into the room to the right of the door.

"We taking him to the warehouse too?" someone asked as they pushed him into an armchair.

Max spun as he fell, but he landed awkwardly and twisted the pinkie on his left hand, causing almost as much pain as the assaults outside. Still, the well-padded chair provided a temporary oasis after the beating. Around him, the conversation continued.

"Not sure," Eddie replied to the question. "Give me a rag or something, will ya? This guy's bleeding on the cushions."

There were five men in the room, and even if Eddie helped, Max didn't think he could take them all, not with his arms bound. His right eye was already swelling, but it wasn't the worst he'd had. He could still use it.

"Hang on, Max." Eddie stepped closer after one man handed him a rag. "I'm going to clean your face."

As he spoke, he dabbed the left side of Max's face with a rag that was cool and wet.

"Shit, Mickey." The motion paused. "Get me a dry one."

Max saw the other man move away, and Eddie's face came in close.

"Sorry about that, pal. These guys can get carried away." He continued to dab Max's face then bent close to Max's right ear, whispering, "I don't know what your fucking plan is, but it doesn't seem to be going well. Your girl is at the Henderson warehouse. Give me some kinda signal, and I'll help."

Eddie pulled back slightly, and for a second they locked eyes. Max could see the sincerity and a touch of sadness as the man looked at him.

"It's just a flesh wound," he joked.

"Here you go." Mickey was back, extending a dry rag to Eddie, and their brief conversation ended.

Eddie took the towel and dried Max's face. When he was done, he put the towel on the back of the chair and turned Max's head to rest against it.

"Apply a little pressure, and it should stop makin' a mess," he said as he stepped back.

"You're taking good care of him," Mickey commented.

"The guy helped me out at the Kettle. You remember the night you bailed?"

Mickey threw his hands up, palms forward.

"Hey, you know I woulda been there."

"Forget it." Eddie walked away, and Max saw him toss the bloodied rag into the sink.

"You seemed tougher." Mickey was now standing next to the chair.

Max continued to lean his head against the chair. Whatever happened next, it would be better if the bleeding stopped.

"Take off the cuffs," he suggested.

"What's that?" Mickey bent closer, and Max was tempted to take him down with his legs, but that was vanity talking, and he pushed the thought aside. Shaming Mickey would be a momentary win, but it would only put them all more on guard.

"Take off the cuffs," he repeated. "And then let's see who's tough."

Mickey let out a short laugh and shook his head.

"It doesn't work like that." He opened his blazer to reveal a shoulder-holstered pistol. "You know that expression 'Don't bring a knife to a gun fight'? You might beat me in a fair fight, but that's the illusion. Who promised you a fair fight in life?

"Nah, man." He straightened, looking down at Max with clear derision. "Like my mom says, you get what you get, and you don't get upset."

Max didn't like the messenger, but the man spoke the truth. Even so, he couldn't resist the chance to get under his skin.

"Yes. That's what she said when she gave me crabs."

"What the . . ." Mickey had been walking away, but he spun around, and in an instant, his hand was inside his blazer.

"What did you say?" he demanded.

The door flew open, and Geno entered, slamming it immediately shut behind him. For a moment, he looked around the room. Everyone turned to look at him as he put his hands on his hips and took several deep breaths. It was so quiet that for the first time, Max could hear the announcers on the TV.

"What happened to him?" When Geno finally spoke, he was looking at Eddie, one arm extended to point at Max.

"The boys got a little overzealous on the way here." Eddie stepped away from the sink, still on the other side of the bar. "He'll be fine, a little banged up."

"You learn anything?"

"Not yet, but we've got time. Thought we were leaving here?"

"We are, but he isn't." The big man looked beyond Eddie to the kitchen. "Johnny, get me a scotch, will ya?"

"Are you sayin' we're going to whack him?" Eddie asked, clearly surprised. "Here?"

Geno stepped farther into the room and leaned against the bar.

"Are you that fucking stupid, Eddie?" He didn't look at Eddie. He'd turned to look at Max but continued to talk to his lieutenant. "No, we're leaving, and Mr. Kline will leave with someone else."

Johnny delivered a crystal glass filled with scotch over ice, which Geno accepted and drank deeply, mumbling his thanks.

A moment later, the mafia boss was standing in front of Max's chair.

"You look like shit, but you are one lucky motherfucker," he spoke slowly. "I don't like it when people refuse me. And I take personal offense when people steal from me. I don't know that we're done—you and I—but it doesn't end tonight."

He finished the scotch and held the empty glass to Johnny, who quickly stepped over with the still-open bottle of scotch and refilled it.

"As much as I want to teach you a lesson, I've got to be smart here. We've got too much riding on this deal, so I've got to do something I really hate. I'm going to let you leave as a gesture of good faith to your Chinese employers."

Max said nothing. This was good, but it was far from over.

"We're going to talk to the girl though. If you didn't take the wallets, we still gotta find out what you did take."

"She doesn't know shit." Max lifted his head and sat up. "She's here visiting."

"OK, so why don't you tell me what you were doing, then?"

The plan had been to blame everything on orders from Haoyun, but now that they'd intervened on his behalf, Max's mind raced for a new story.

"I'm looking for the Ghost," he muttered. "Need to talk about my apartment."

"Bullshit." Geno turned and stepped back to the bar, putting his glass down. "You won't find the Ghost on my server, but maybe he'll find you." He paused then waved a dismissive hand. "I don't have time for this. Uncuff him, Mickey."

* * *

As they escorted him back through the house, Max was impressed by how rapidly the place had emptied. No guests remained, someone had dismantled the bars, and crews were already removing the decorations. Mickey stepped ahead and opened the right side of the double front doors. His expression was one of disappointment, but he didn't say a word. For a brief second, Max considered lashing out with a quick blow to the throat, but he remained calm and allowed the thought to pass through him.

The outside was as empty as the house. The area was well lit thanks to floodlights, but it was void of activity. As the door closed behind him, Max looked down the stone walkway lined on both sides with knee-high light to see a black sedan idling at the end. Jun was standing in the shadows at the back of the car. The red glow of his cigarette flared to life, followed by a plume of smoke.

Max finally allowed himself to relax, and he rolled his neck as he walked down the path. His right eye was mostly closed but still functional. Apart from that, the rest of the damage was more superficial. He'd have bruises on his torso, for sure, but nothing that would hold him back. Jun made no effort to move, so when Max reached the street, he joined him behind the car.

"I received a call about two hours ago." Jun took a quick puff of his cigarette and then flicked the butt into the street, smoke still leaving his mouth as he spoke. "Nita Vargas, Las Vegas district attorney.

"She told me quite the story. Wanted me to know that the property we had purchased was under investigation. She informed me that a drug lab was operating out of the Deep Texas BBQ and using our catering operation for distribution."

Jun reached into his breast pocket and pulled out a cigarette case. He put one in his mouth and held the open case toward Max as his other hand adroitly flared a light to life.

"No, thank you," Max declined, wanting the conversation to

move faster.

"She made it quite clear that she 'knew' Haoyun Casino had been unaware of the activity and assured me that the Jewel's casino operation would continue unabated." He paused to take another puff, and for the first time he looked straight at Max. His piercing eyes were almost black in the low light, and there was no mistaking the flare of anger. "She even implied that so long as she got her collar at the Deep Texas, she wouldn't need to look deeply at the distribution."

He inhaled his cigarette and blew a plume of smoke into the air before continuing. "It was almost like she was confirming a deal, Max —a deal I did not authorize."

Max knew Jun was not looking for a response, and anything he said would prolong the conversation, so he remained silent.

"This is not what I wanted." Jun switched to Chinese and continued in a softer voice. "But the lab was always a short-term solution. It won't affect us, but whatever you've done, Haoyun Casino is in the clear, so this . . ." He motioned with his cigarette toward the house. "This is professional courtesy, but it also ends our relationship."

"That's fair," Max responded, pulling his phone out of his back pocket. He didn't really care what Jun said, as long as he was free. Geno's men had returned the phone as they walked through the house, and if this was over, he needed to find Carolyn.

His driver had left nine messages that were increasingly concerned. Both the first and the last simply read, "What's up?"

"I'm ready now," he typed quickly. "You still here?"

"Be right there." Her response was almost instantaneous.

"You know," Jun continued, still speaking Chinese. "This deal is bigger than the Jewel. The Marchettis are technically our partners, so it would not be appropriate for anyone in our organization to cause them harm."

The cab had just rolled into the roundabout, and Max stepped toward it then turned to reply in polite Mandarin.

"As you said, Jun, I no longer work for you."

His former boss pursed his lips, and his head slowly bobbed in recognition.

"I see we continue to understand one another." The Haoyun boss offered a slight smile then ducked into the back seat of his car.

# CHAPTER TWENTY-NINE

Carolyn was waking up, but it was hard. She could hear noises around her but couldn't understand what they were or where she was. This continued for what seemed like hours, but she knew it hadn't been that long. Finally, as if struck by cold water, she snapped back to consciousness. Forcing her eyes open, she took in a bizarre scene.

She was in a chair in a large room, a warehouse. Her hands were bound behind her back. People were shouting, but not to her. A cool wind blew on her face, and she turned to see a wide opening spilling light out onto open ground with a plane sitting at the end of the light—an airport hangar.

"Look who's awake," someone spoke from her right side, and she turned to see a large man in a dark suit. Things started to come back to her. The party. She had been on the patio, and then the officer had told her to come with him. It began politely, but then others grabbed her. She had struggled, then nothing.

"That shit can knock you out, right?" the man continued. "The good news is it leaves fast. You'll be right as rain in a minute—which is good, because we have some questions."

He put a hand on her shoulder, and she tried to move away, only to be reminded that her hands were tied behind her back and to the chair.

"Geno, she's awake," the man called toward a group that was crossing the floor.

The man in the lead stopped and turned toward them, forcing the others to fan out as he changed course. Carolyn recognized him immediately from the many news stories—Geno Abruzzi. He was bigger in real life.

Her captor had been right—the sense of distortion had basically evaporated, leaving her feeling completely normal except for the gap in time from the party to now, whenever now was.

In a few seconds, Geno was standing before her in the same outfit she'd seen at the party. He wore a deep-blue blazer that tilted toward purple. She guessed it was some kind of silk-cashmere blend, well tailored and perfectly draped over his colossal frame. His red-and-gold-striped tie, neatly knotted at his throat, accented a white shirt with light-blue checks.

"Well, good morning, sunshine." He seemed polite, but there was no hiding the derision in his voice. "You want to tell me what you were doing stealing from my server?"

"I didn't steal anything," she answered.

"OK, let's pretend I believe that." He gave her a menacing stare. "What were you doing on my server, then?"

"Hey, boss." Another man came into view. She'd seen him in her research too but couldn't remember his name. "Are we sure she's involved?"

"You turning soft on me, Eddie?" Geno turned away from her. "Your boy definitely had something going down tonight. Whoever got into the server room installed a transmitter, but it triggered an alert, and the Ghost tracked the signal to her location. She's dirty, but I don't know what she was after."

He turned and stepped closer to her. "What were you doing on my server?" he repeated.

"You should really be more concerned about other servers," she muttered, hoping to distract him.

"Meaning?"

"Meaning your agent of record in Delaware, Julius Scarpeli. Sound familiar?" She watched as a hint of recognition flared on the big man's face. It felt like she had scored. "If I were you, I'd be more concerned about his computers."

A sudden, sharp pain exploded on the left side of her face, and something knocked her head violently to one side. Tears filled her eyes as she tried to understand what had happened. She tasted blood in her mouth as she turned back to face Geno, realizing as she did that he had delivered the backhand blow.

"Who are you working with?" he demanded. "And what is it you want?"

The initial shock was over, but the pain in her face throbbed. She knew she couldn't tell the truth, but she didn't want to get hit again, so her mind raced for an answer. She looked past Geno. Two men were walking with a luggage cart across the floor. When she turned her head, she could see a plane outside the hangar entrance.

"Where are you headed?" she asked, hoping it wouldn't bring another blow.

Geno turned to look at the plane. When he looked back, he had a mischievous look on his face.

"That depends on what I hear from you, sweetie. Right now, it might be a long flight over the desert."

He lifted his hand high with fingers and thumb together then dramatically opened them as if dropping something. The message was obvious.

The mob boss continued to stare at her for a long moment before looking up and past her.

"Mickey, see what she knows—and take care of things."

"On it." The terse response was immediate, and Carolyn saw the first man return to her line of sight. He had appeared kind before, but his expression showed no compassion now.

"Eddie, you come with me for a sec." Geno called over his shoulder as he moved toward the edge of the hangar.

Eddie followed, giving her an almost apologetic look as he passed.

"You heard the man," Mickey said, bending his face closer to hers. "Time to talk."

Carolyn tried to think of something to say, but before she could speak, a new pain erupted in her right eye, and she toppled backward in her chair, landing awkwardly on her pinned arms.

"How'd that feel?" Mickey's smiling face hovered over hers, and he reached down to lift the back of her chair and set her upright once again. "Geno can be a nice guy. He sometimes forgets to remind folks about who is in charge. That was your reminder."

Tears dripped unbidden down her face. She tried to keep herself calm, but a sense of panic swelled. *What would Max do?* The thought popped into her head, but she quickly dismissed it—she was not Max. What would he want her to do? That was easy. He'd tell her not to resist. To let them have whatever they wanted. She took a big inhale through her mouth and closed her eyes, trying to center herself but unable to do so.

"I told him already. I didn't take anything." She allowed her fear to come to the surface, and it was genuine. "Please don't hit me again."

She hoped he would pity her. A line of pain now ran diagonally through her face, from her right eye to her left jaw. Would she get out of this alive? The thought hadn't occurred to her before now, but she'd seen who they were. Would they let her live?

"Let's start with who you are working for."

"This is crazy." She let the panic flow, screaming. "I didn't take anything."

Mickey half turned away then swung a backhand blow hard into the left side of her face.

This one, she saw coming and could turn her head so the blow struck her ear, but the action threw her off balance in the small chair, and she crashed again, unable to break the fall. The right side of her face slammed against the floor, reviving the pain from Geno's blow.

"Up you go." Mickey was almost talking to himself as he pulled her chair upright and stepped back in front of her. "Do we need to keep doing this?"

Something gave way inside her. If she was going to get through this, the most important part would be to stay alive. She gave in to the inner voice that told her Max wouldn't want her to resist.

"No," she answered with a gasping breath. All attempts to center herself were out the window. "I . . . left . . . behind . . . a little . . . code." Each word was spat out on its own as she struggled to calm herself, sucking in air after each.

"There you go." There was no mistaking the derision in Mickey's voice. "Was that so hard? And what is this code going to do?"

"I connected it to the house Wi-Fi. It's going to send out data to the DA." Her breathing was calming, but she knew she had to offer more to stay alive. "I can stop it."

Another shudder ran through her core, and she waited for it to stop, half expecting another punishing blow that didn't come.

"I can remove the code," she continued, looking back up at her tormentor with pleading eyes. "I'm sorry."

Mickey's face did not show any sign of forgiveness.

"I don't think so." He reached into his jacket and pulled out a large black pistol, which he used to point toward Geno and Eddie. "You think they'll trust you? You've done enough harm for one night. Tell me one reason I shouldn't use this."

"Anything. I don't want to die," she pleaded. "I have money."

Mickey chuckled. "I bet you do, sweetheart, but I was just asking for fun. I've got orders."

She watched as he glanced toward the plane then back to her, raising the gun to within inches of her forehead. A sense of shock ran through her body and she lost control of her bladder. Closing her eyes, she waited for the end.

She expected loud noise but only heard a soft pop, and someone spat warm water on the side of her face. Then something heavy fell on top of her, and once again, she was tumbling to the floor. Somewhere she heard a shout of alarm, then her head hit the hard surface below her.

## CHAPTER THIRTY

Unlike Harry Reid International, Henderson Airfield was a private airstrip that carried with it a much lower security profile. Max had expected a potential return to the Genoa warehouse and a few days earlier had scouted the surrounding area, where modest fences were the principal deterrent to unwanted guests at the airstrip. The warehouse itself had two entrances for the public—at the front, and the side entrance that he had used on his first visit. Inside the airport perimeter though, the warehouse doubled as a hangar with huge open doors, and given the relatively lax airport security, that would be his best avenue of approach.

The Genoa facility was on the southern end of the airstrip, and as his cab rolled past, he saw a couple of cars but the entrance was dark. His driver continued to the end of the road and turned left, heading past the runway and toward a large planned community. He wouldn't be going that far, but this area of town had sprung up with the Las Vegas boom at the turn of the century and was now one of the more coveted areas to live.

"This will be great." He spoke for the first time since he'd given her the address and instructions.

He watched as she checked her mirrors and pulled over to the side of the road. They were maybe one hundred yards past the end of the runway. To the right, a tall concrete wall ran down the side of the road, set back fifteen feet but imposing nonetheless. Over the top, Max could see the roofs of houses that made up the lower end of the neighborhoods in this community. Opposite them, the east side of the airstrip was largely a wasteland of scrub brush stretching from the airfield for about a half mile before the houses of the master planned community spread to the north.

"Can you pop the trunk?"

He'd changed into his night camo during the fifteen-minute drive, and as he stepped out of the back seat, he carried his dress clothes wrapped in a ball inside his blazer. The trunk popped open as he rounded the back of the cab, and he glanced around to make sure they were alone before opening the hatch fully and tucking his clothes to one side. He unzipped the large black bag he had loaded earlier in the night and removed the M110A1, immediately assembling it before pulling out his tactical armor and putting it on.

"I really don't want to know anything about this." The driver was standing near the end of the car—far enough that she could see into his still-open bag.

"I totally get it," he answered as he loaded his vest with ammunition, tucking his pistol into a shoulder holster.

The girl said something else, but he ignored her as he ran through a quick checklist in his head.

"The deal remains," he told her as he zipped up the mostly empty bag. "I'll see you in two days to pick up the rest of this gear."

He retrieved the SDMR before closing the trunk.

"You're free to do as you wish with that bag, but I'll pay you far more than it's worth to get it back."

"Do you work for the government?" she asked, clearly taken aback by the outfit he wore and gear he now held. "Some kind of assassin?"

"No." He shook his head. "But you shouldn't ask questions, and you need to get far away from here. I'll see you in two days. Same place we met today."

He started to move but stopped without looking back, scanning the area for activity as he waited for confirmation.

"OK," she finally responded, releasing him into the night.

In front of him, the airstrip was well lit but relatively quiet, and he ran across the road into the waste. On his previous visit, he'd found easy access through the two fence lines that protected the airfield. His major point of weakness on this approach would be crossing the runway. Even though he had no intention of stepping on the tarmac, the route was lit for several hundred yards past the end of the strip, even though, at this hour, they were only flashing yellow beacons. He had to hope nobody was looking.

He moved as quickly as he could, trying to stay in depressions and away from the light. He doubted there was any perimeter security, but if spotted, he might lose any chance of retrieving Carolyn. It took maybe fifteen minutes to cross the south end of the strip and get into position at the edge of the taxiway. Two hundred yards away, the back of the Genoa warehouse was the only activity in the area. Half of the tall hangar doors were open, allowing a shaft of light to spill out onto the tarmac, illuminating the area in front and stretching out to the taxiway where a small jet waited, lights on and boarding stairs lowered.

There was activity within the building, but he couldn't make out details. Rolling on his back, he pulled out the muzzle suppressor, twisted it into place on the end of the rifle, then extended the bipod near the end of the barrel. He flipped back over, and in one motion, the weapon was in position. The fingers of his right hand had already removed the scope covers by the time he leaned in for a closer look at his target.

He saw nothing but a blur. His swollen right eye forced him to adjust his position several times before he could use the scope. Once he had a view, he calibrated the focus to accommodate his eye. This was something he'd done many times before, both in practice and on the battlefield.

The jet idled, ready for takeoff. He could see a pilot in the cockpit, and the thermal waves were visible at the engine. Someone was carrying a bag toward the plane, but Max could not identify him. He used the mil-dots in his scope to get his size and confirm the distance at 325 yards. Then he swung his attention to the building, and the scene inside was exactly what he had feared.

* * *

Carolyn was tied to a chair close to the far wall of the hangar, the metallic threads in her fancy dress still shimmering. It looked like she had blood on her lip. Geno and Eddie were in front of her, and the thug, Mickey, stood behind the chair. Max's finger itched toward the trigger, but he still needed to get his bearings. He moved the gun slowly to scan the rest of the hangar. Geno's Mercedes was on the left side, trunk open, and two men were loading some kind of cart. Seven men total, including the pilot.

The two at the car closed the trunk and rolled the cart toward the plane. Max pointed his weapon at Geno and zoomed in, but the big man walked to the edge of the hangar, and Eddie followed him. They stopped at the edge of the light when Max's attention returned to Carolyn as Mickey moved in front of her then punched her in the right eye. Her chair tumbled backward, and it was all Max could do to hold himself in check. Rage could be good in battle, but for what he needed to do, he had to stay calm. He magnified his zoom as Mickey lifted her chair. She was conscious, but looked scared. The eye was half closed and her left cheek was red. He zoomed out slightly to see the other two. Eddie stood with just his right side as a target. Not what he wanted.

Carolyn was saying something, but Max didn't like the position of Mickey's body. Another blow was coming, but he didn't have the shot set up. He watched helplessly as Mickey backhanded the woman he loved, and she tumbled to the floor for a second time, still bound to the chair.

"Motherfucker," he said out loud.

As he watched Mickey pick her up, he adjusted the scope for the distance. The night air was relatively calm, but a light breeze pushed in from the southwest so he made another slight tweak. Carolyn was talking again. Her eye was swelling, and the look of fear on her face broke his heart. He would not let her get hit again.

While he was setting up, he had instinctively allowed his breathing to calm. Now he slowed it even further as the first shot neared. He left the zoom a little wide so that he could see both targets and considered a shot at Eddie, but he still didn't have the angle.

Back inside, Mickey had pulled out a gun, holding it out to his side, pointing toward Eddie, but he was still facing Carolyn. Then he swung the gun to point at her.

Game time.

Max didn't need to think anymore as held the crosshairs on the back of Mickey's head and slowly squeezed the trigger, watching long enough to see the puff of red mist as the bullet shattered the man's skull before moving his aim to his second target. There had been a muffled thud as the suppressor quelled the sound, but he doubted they heard anything.

Tightening his zoom, he honed in on the two men at the edge of the light. This was a harder shot. Both men now looked inward, but fortunately, Eddie turned and looked down the runway. He couldn't know it, but he was practically staring at Max's position. His expression was relatively calm, as if he was piecing together something in his head.

*Brave man*, he thought to himself as he lined up the shot.

Eddie was still wearing a blazer with a white pocket square. Max allowed himself a breath as he took aim three inches below the white marker. He pulled the trigger, and Eddie's body flew backward on impact. Geno, who had been yelling to someone inside, jumped back with his hands up at his shoulders as if he didn't want them to touch anything. He looked from Eddie's crumpled form to Mickey's then turned as Eddie had to look in Max's direction. He pointed and yelled something before ducking and running in a low crouch toward the plane.

Max could easily have taken him out, but this wasn't the night for that. Geno's survival was part of his plan, and even if it weren't, the unstated understanding with Jun probably had limits. He pulled back his zoom to see the hangar was largely empty. The two with the luggage were with Geno at the plane. Mickey's body had fallen on Carolyn, but he didn't see any movement. There should have been one more—the man who had been walking from the plane. Max scanned the scene but couldn't find him.

Several gunshots erupted from the area of the plane, but Max had little concern. Even if they knew his position, they had little chance of hitting him at this distance. He scanned the area one last time, unable to find the missing man, then pushed himself up to his knees, deftly removing the suppressor with one hand. There was no longer any need for stealth. He slipped it into a strap on his leg, followed by the scope.

On the airfield, the whine of the jet's engines grew louder. Geno and his boys were not planning to stick around, and that was fine with him. The plane started to roll toward the runway. Maybe the missing man was on board as well, but something in his gut told him it would not be so easy.

In moments, he was on the tarmac, jogging at a good clip with his weapon still in hand. Although exposed, he didn't have time to sneak around the outskirts. Carolyn was still there but not moving. If she was hurt, he had to help her.

As he neared, he continued his visual search of the area, and as if out of nowhere, he saw someone moving in the hangar. It looked like he was pulling Mickey's body away from Carolyn. Then he knelt by her side, his back to the airstrip.

Max was still maybe one hundred yards out and couldn't see what the man was doing, so he slowed and fired three rounds into the wall high above the scene. Without the suppressor, the sound roared into the night, clearly announcing his presence, but the huddled man did not move.

"Hey!" Max shouted. "Back away or you're next."

He was bluffing. He couldn't fire anywhere near the man with Carolyn there. While the SDMR was a precision weapon, there were too many risks in standard combat. He resumed his jog and watched as the figure slowly rose and lifted his arms over his head, opening and closing them as if hailing a ship. As Max approached the hangar door, recognition dawned as the figure turned and he saw the grim face of Ben Carpenter. His hands continued to open and close above his head, but Max now saw that he had a pistol in one hand.

* * *

"She's fine," Ben called across the remaining twenty yards that separated them. "That was some good shooting, Marine."

Unlike the others, Ben had changed since the party. He wore dark multi-cam fatigues with a black plate-carrier vest. Even without knowing his history, the uniform spoke volumes.

"Step aside and let me see her," Max demanded.

"I told you she's fine. A little banged up, but she only hit her head in the fall. Pulse is good and breathing fine."

Max's own head was spinning. Carolyn had suspected that Ben was dirty, which was why they had bypassed him when they followed-up with the district attorney, but even after the incident earlier, Max had a hard time connecting the man he knew with the Marchetti family.

Then the last piece clicked into place.

"You're the Ghost."

It wasn't a question. It wasn't even really meant for Ben to hear. Max blurted out his realization, and as he did, he lowered the barrel of his weapon to point it at his onetime friend.

"Hang on, soldier." Ben raised an empty right hand, palm forward, while his left hand moved to point his pistol at Carolyn's still-unconscious head. "I don't want to die, and you want the girl to live. We can handle this a better way."

Behind him, Max heard the whir of the jet's engines roar to life as it began down the runway for takeoff. He waited for the noise to end before answering, taking a few steps closer.

"Is it true?" Max asked, still unsure if he believed. "Were you the one who torched the Wild Horse?"

"They were a bunch of misfits who got caught in the crossfire." Ben shrugged. "Occupational hazard."

"They were kids, Ben." Max shook his head. "I can't believe I once called you a friend. I'm not sure why I haven't already fragged your ass."

"I'll give you two reasons. Your beautiful friend here." He motioned with his pistol as if accenting the threat. "And you've got too much honor, Marine."

"So, what's the better way?"

"We're still friends, Max. And I don't want you dead. So you put your weapon down, and then I'll put my weapon down." A light seemed to flare in his eyes as he nodded to the open area behind Max. "Then we'll have our little talk—mano a mano. You've been wondering for a long time which one of us comes out ahead in a fight."

Max thought about it. Ben was older than he was but in good shape, and he had a height and weight advantage. He was right too. Max had often wondered who would win if they went at it. If he were in the field, he'd prefer a straight takeout. With his weapon already on target, there was only a slight chance Ben could get a shot off if Max fired first. The odds and his training told him it was the right move. But there was still a chance that Ben could pull it off, and the odds were only numbers built without knowing the identity of the potential victim. Max would not take that risk with Carolyn.

"I'm not really asking, Max." Ben lowered his gun to hover inches from Carolyn's face.

"Relax, Ben. I'm disarming."

He eased his hand off the trigger and used his left hand to lower the gun to the floor, never breaking eye contact with his opponent. With his right hand, he slowly unholstered his pistol and placed it next to the SDMR. He hoped Ben still held on to the core of honor among Special Forces vets.

Ben stood up, switching the pistol to his right hand.

"I had a feeling you were in a little too deep." Ben moved to his left, toward the runway. "Didn't think you'd go behind my back to the DA though. That's going to take me some time to clean up."

"We thought you might be on the take." Max backed up so they had a clear space. "Didn't realize you were the fucking Ghost."

Ben smiled. "Geno loves that name. He thinks it gives him some kind of aura of invincibility."

His hand twitched, but Max had nowhere to go.

Pain flared in his left chest as he flew backward and crashed to the ground, barely able to break his fall as his body spun with the impact. He struggled for breath, and as he did, the burning intensified in his chest. It took him a few seconds to recover his bearings. Ben had intentionally shot him in his tactical vest. The shot wasn't meant to kill, but it definitely broke a rib or two.

"What the fuck?" he said, but each breath felt like a knife was stabbing him. He instinctively held his hand to his chest to try to ease the pain.

"That's what I'll call an equalizer." Ben was smiling as he put his pistol on the floor and then stepped closer. "You've got over ten years on me, Raider."

Max regained his feet but leaned to the left, cradling his arm to limit the pain in his chest. He still struggled to breathe, and it took all his concentration to focus on his opponent and not the pain of his broken ribs.

"You know I could have taken you out over that hospital thing," Ben offered. "I was hoping you might stand down. Could have removed you from the field, but then we wouldn't be having so much fun."

"You didn't have evidence." It hurt even to speak.

"As a detective? You're absolutely right. But as the Ghost, my intuition was enough." He grinned, shaking his head. "I thought that team at the strip club might make you rethink your loyalties."

The two men were now only eight feet apart and circled one another. Max allowed his opponent to set the pace and moved opposite him, watching for signs of an attack. He wanted to say something—to tell the man what he thought—but speaking would be painful, and it wouldn't accomplish anything.

Ben didn't waste time, moving in quickly with a feint to Max's head before dropping low and sweeping his leg.

Max anticipated the feint and thought he could avoid the attack, but as he reacted, fire flared again up his torso, and he couldn't finish the motion. The impact knocked his left leg into his right, sending him down on his hands and knees. He sucked in air, trying to ignore the pain that came with each inhale.

Before he could stabilize, Ben returned with a kick to his left ribs that nearly knocked him out, flipping him onto his back as the agony in his ribs took on the intensity of a supernova.

For a moment, everything seemed to slow down. The intense suffering brought Max out of himself, and he felt like he could leave it behind. The familiar sense of battlefield focus took over. He could still feel the torture in his side, but it was someone else's torture. There, but not there.

"Maybe I didn't need the equalizer," Ben said from a few feet away. "Or maybe you Raiders aren't as tough as you think. We should have known something was up after Task Force Violent."

The slur hurt, but he'd heard it before. *Let him talk*, he told himself as he regained his footing. The pain was distant. He had moved into a zone and could trust in his training. His opponent circled him once again, and he pivoted with him, his motions more fluid, the pain no longer restricting him.

Ben came in with another feint similar to the last, but he followed it with an actual attack using the same hand. Max saw everything as it unfolded. He saw Ben's hips turn for the blow, and when it came, he jerked his head back while he grabbed Ben's shoulder with his right hand and pulled the man's weight forward over his outstretched leg. Ben cursed in surprise as he tumbled to the floor.

Max could not press his advantage. He used the few seconds' reprieve to take a couple of deep breaths, still ignoring the constant pain on his left side.

"Well, wakey-wakey." Ben picked himself up, smiling and making a show of dusting off his pants. "I guess there's a little fight left in you."

He immediately charged at Max, making no attempt at subtlety. Somewhere in the back of his head, Max acknowledged it was a smart move. If Ben could get him to the floor, he'd have the upper hand.

It was all Max could do to slip to the side, avoiding the clasp of his opponent and using the man's own momentum to throw him against a crate along the wall.

Again, he drew breath while Ben collected himself. He wouldn't be that lucky on the next attack.

"You want to end this, Max?" Ben asked, raising an eyebrow. "Leave now? With the girl? Tell me what you took from the server and we'll forget this whole thing happened."

It was Max's turn to laugh. He glanced at his watch.

"No, Ben, that ship has sailed." It hurt to talk, but better to pause the fight. "We didn't take anything ourselves, but we left behind some code, and a connection. By now Nita has already received her first batch of files."

Ben's eyes widened slightly, and for the first time he looked slightly off his game.

After a few seconds, he straightened, and the look in his eyes turned to anger. "Tell me you did not do that."

"You'll find out one way or the other." Max wanted him angry. Anger led to mistakes.

Ben closed the distance, and the two men circled once again, each testing the other's defenses. Max could hold him off with a few jabs, but he had no follow-through—his left side was still a wall of hurt.

Gradually, Ben's attack intensified, and Max knew he had to do something, so he allowed an opening in his defense, and Ben took the bait.

The detective tried for a leg sweep, again targeting Max's left side, but Max was ready, and he leapt up and over the attack. He was aware of torment flaring in his side, but it was a muted sensation. He was in the zone, and as he landed, he delivered a right to Ben's face, followed by a smashing left hand using all the torque he could muster.

Ben dropped to the floor, and Max leapt on top of him, but he was running out of time. Even with the rush of adrenaline, Max could feel his left side on fire and could no longer use his left arm. Ben was hurt but not out of it, and he must have sensed Max's condition because he surged up with renewed strength and a blow against Max's inoperable left side.

In a quick moment, the tides had turned, and Ben was now on top of Max with his elbow pressed against his throat.

"That was the last fucking move for you, Raider," he growled through a bloody mouth.

Max could not respond if he wanted to. Ben's elbow had cut off his air. His left side was still on fire, but he stretched his right hand down his pant leg, trying to retrieve the ceramic blade in his pocket flap.

Suddenly, a boot slammed into Ben's head, knocking him upright and away from Max, who immediately sucked in air. Ben turned with a puzzled look in his eye, and the room exploded with the sound of gunshots, each one answered by a new hole in Ben's chest. Five shots hit the detective in quick succession, knocking him off Max. A final shot hit him in the forehead, sending a spray of blood behind him and leaving no life in his body.

Max took another deep breath, unable to lift his head, but he could turn enough to find out where the shots had come from.

Standing not three paces away, still dressed in his party attire but with an ugly hole in his breast pocket, was Eddie Difusco, a pistol hanging from his right hand. His eyes had followed Ben's body, but he slowly turned to look at Max.

"He deserved that." He winced as he spoke. "Now, let's talk about the fact that you shot me."

# CHAPTER THIRTY-ONE

Eddie tossed his weapon onto the lifeless corpse that had once been, and now truly was, the Ghost. He stepped over to Max, knelt down, and clasped his hand in a warrior grip, forearms connecting.

"That hurt like a motherfucker." He winced again.

"Tell me about it." Max used his friend's grip to lever himself while Eddie helped him to stand, both men heavily favoring their left sides. "Ben did the same thing to me, but I hadn't agreed to it."

He moved gingerly to Carolyn, using his right hand to pull Mickey's body farther away from hers. She was still unconscious, but he could see her breathing looked normal.

In a few seconds, he had her hands freed and away from the chair, but everything was taking longer than it should, and they needed to leave soon.

"Staci is a few blocks away," Eddie said from behind him then knelt closer. "She gonna be OK?"

"I think so," Max answered. "You got the bag?"

"One sec." Eddie walked toward one of the rear storage racks.

Max stood and surveyed the area. His SDMR and pistol were on the floor where he'd placed them, but otherwise the area was relatively clear. While he'd looked after Carolyn, Eddie had pulled the two corpses together at the base of the long row of racks that held crates and pallets of goods.

He retrieved his weapons, holstering the pistol and laying the rifle near Carolyn as Eddie returned with the black knapsack that Max had given him earlier in the day.

"Perfect," he said as he opened it and pulled out the first of three carefully wrapped bundles, moving over to the bodies as he did.

"What is that shit?" Eddie asked.

"This is your resurrection," Max answered without looking back. He placed the first package by Ben's head and retrieved the second, setting it on his chest.

"Where's the fuel?" he asked without looking up.

"That's over here." Eddie crossed the hangar to the other side.

"And what about the doors?" Max asked. "You know how to close them?"

Eddie did not respond, but as Max finished placing his parcels, he heard a large clunk followed by a mechanical whine, and he looked up to see the large doors beginning to slide together.

Eddie was already halfway across the floor with a gas can in his right hand.

"Seriously, what are those?" Eddie handed Max the gas.

"Thermite charges."

"Like bombs?"

"Sort of." Max reviewed his placement, knowing he only had one chance. "Except they don't explode. They burn super hot. They won't even light with a normal flame, but the gas will ignite the magnesium fuses. Anyway, they burn so hot that Ben's body will not be identifiable—at least not without serious DNA shit."

He twisted off the cap and splashed gasoline on Ben's body and on the floor nearby.

"What about him?" Eddie motioned to Mickey's body as Max reached him with the ever-widening pool of gas.

"He'll burn, but I think we want them to ID him." He set the half-empty gas can on the floor, allowing it to spill its contents under the storage racks.

"So why the special treatment for the cop?"

"It's not for Ben. It's for you." Max stood back and surveyed his work. Everything seemed in place.

"We didn't have time to make a complete deal with the district attorney. She wouldn't give me immunity, but she agreed to report you as deceased. I'm making her promise easier." He pointed at the two bodies. "They won't be able to identify Ben, but they'll find Mickey, and this will go down as a mob-related incident. After a few days, the DA will identify the second corpse as Eddie Difusco. Geno saw you get shot, so it will make sense to him. He's going to wonder what happened to his Ghost, and he may never know."

Eddie stared back at him, astonished.

"I'm out." A smile grew on face. "Holy shit, Max. I'm fucking out!"

"Not yet, Eddie." Max enjoyed seeing the man happy, but they were not in the clear. "Help me move Carolyn to the door."

The two men gently carried Carolyn's limp body to the side entrance, but as they put her down, she started to come to.

Max bent close, whispering her name. Her eyes fluttered open, and as they did, she grasped his arm in a panicked grip, a look of horror in her eyes.

"Max!" It would have been a scream, but her strength was low. "Max!" she repeated before closing her eyes, and her grip relaxed. He eased her head back to the floor, wishing he could hold her longer.

"Call Staci." He stood and pushed open the door. In the distance, he could hear the wail of sirens and knew their time was limited. The parking lot was empty except for a silver Toyota pulling into the entrance. He raised his right arm and waved before moving back inside.

"She's here," he told Eddie, knowing they needed to hurry. "Have her park here. Leave the engine running, and she gets in the passenger seat."

Eddie started to reply, but Max cut him off.

"No time to talk. Do exactly what I say, and be ready to help me put Carolyn in the car. I'll be back in a second."

Inside, the area was now eerily quiet, and even his steps seemed to echo as he trotted back to the scene. It was a large space, but fortunately, the bodies were near the storage racks, and with any luck, at least this side of the warehouse would burn for a little while.

He risked stepping into the spreading pool of gas to ensure that the magnesium fuses were still well placed. Outside on the airstrip, he could hear another siren and knew they had no time left. He backed toward the door, digging through the mostly empty pack to grab the road flare and tossing the sack back into the pool of gas.

Knowing he still had gas on his shoes, he stepped several paces away from the bodies, removing the cap from the flare and sparking it to life.

*Thanks for your help, Ben,* he thought to himself as the burning stick arced toward the bodies.

When it landed, the gas ignited with a whoosh, and he watched until he saw the white glow of burning magnesium. He was happy to see that some of the crates had already caught fire in addition to the pool of flames that surrounded the bodies.

At the door, Eddie knelt at Carolyn's side, and as soon as Max arrived, the two men gently eased her outside and into the waiting car. Eddie slid inside ahead of her, moving remarkably well given his large size, and pulled her into the back seat as Max closed the door behind her. The driver's side door was open, and Max was inside almost instantly, pausing for a second to look back at the warehouse. Inside, another whoosh reverberated, and the light from the inferno intensified —at least one of the thermite packets had lit.

Someone shouted from the other side of the chain-link fence that separated them from the airstrip, but Max ignored them as he pulled his door shut and put the car into gear.

"There's an alley almost directly across from the exit," Eddie called from the back. "It will take us away from the action."

Max looked to his right as they neared the street. In the distance, the towers of the strip continued to light up the sky, but closer to them —much closer—the familiar blue and red lights of police cruisers were visible headed toward the airstrip. They were just about to turn down the street toward them when he slammed his foot on the gas, and they shot across the street and into the alley that Eddie had identified.

# CHAPTER THIRTY-TWO

After a while, the somewhat muffled sound of gunfire became part of the ambiance. In a way, it was almost soothing. Max had been working on his laptop at the Down Range Cafe for over an hour. He'd arrived early to survey the range and the customers to be safe, but he and his friends were unlikely to be recognized. He wore combat fatigues, a black ball cap pulled tightly over his head, and wraparound sunglasses.

The bells jingled as the door opened, and Max looked over his laptop to see Eddie and Staci enter the restaurant, immediately moving to join him. He stood and shook Eddie's hand. He could tell that Eddie's instinct was to go in for a hug, but both men were nursing bruises on their left side, and there was an unspoken acknowledgement that the handshake was enough.

Max turned to Staci, who looked up at him with a smile and a glint in her eye that spoke of happiness. It almost made it worth it.

"Max!" She grabbed him in a hug before he could stop her, and pain flared in his left ribs.

He couldn't avoid a grimace, but her head was against his chest, and she didn't see.

Eddie gently pulled her away.

"Easy, baby," he said. "He's hurt, same as me."

"Oh my God!" Staci put a hand to her mouth. "I'm so sorry."

"Don't be. It felt good," Max half-lied. He enjoyed her gratitude. "No problems finding the place?"

"You took me here last weekend!" Staci looked surprised. "I may be blonde, but I'm not that blonde!"

"Yeah, well, there was a lot going on."

The three of them sat down at the small table. Max could see Eddie was moving as gingerly as he was.

"Sorry about that," he offered, pointing toward Eddie's chest. It was, after all, his shot that had injured his friend.

"It doesn't hurt as much as being dead." Eddie smiled back at him. "I assume you saw they've listed my name."

"Yep."

As expected, the story had been all over the news the day before, and by the end of the day, Mickey's name had been released as a victim along with an "unidentified male." But early in the morning, now the second day after the incident, the Las Vegas police had announced the second body as Eddie Difusco.

A waitress stopped to bring coffee and take their orders.

When she left, Eddie continued, "It's surreal. How did you get them to agree to that?"

"You don't want to know," Max answered honestly. "You don't exist. Be happy with that."

"We're out, baby." Staci patted Eddie's hand, turning her smile on Max. "And we owe it all to this man."

"So what's your plan?" Max asked, brushing off the effusive praise.

"Mexico," Eddie answered with no need to think. "At least for a while. We've got a small villa booked already. Use the time to decide where to go. Do some research on new identities. Figure out where we want to settle."

"Sounds good."

"What about you?" Eddie asked. "Geno will look for you."

"Yeah, I've had a good run here, but I've overstayed my welcome in this town," Max answered as honestly as he could. "Cards haven't been coming my way, so I think I'll hit the road for a while too."

"Come with us," Eddie suggested. "We've got room."

"Yes!" Staci jumped in. "It's the least we could do. You won't take money—though the offer is still there—so come with us!"

Max allowed himself a moment to enjoy the youth and enthusiasm of his friends, allowing a grin to fill his face before replying.

"It sounds great, honestly, and I'm happy for you. But it wouldn't be safe. I'm going to lie low, but I'm not changing my identity. This is a great opportunity for you, but I'm already on a path. I don't think Geno will pursue me if I duck out."

"He's got bigger problems," Eddie agreed. "I bet he stays outta jail, but the district attorney has not held back."

That was the other story that pervaded the Las Vegas news flow. DA Vargas had announced the results of her investigation into the Marchetti crime family with accusations of illegal drug activity, money laundering, and political corruption. Charges were not yet filed, but she'd launched an all-out media assault, implicating Geno in particular with claims that she had firsthand evidence of his participation, and Max knew she did. Eddie and Staci probably suspected Max's involvement, but they were not privy to that part of his activity, and it was better that way.

"Is your company going down?" Eddie asked.

"Haoyun Casino? They'll be fine." Max disliked the association. "But they're not my company. I worked for them, but that's over too. They're actually more than fine. The Desert Jewel is caught up in this

Marchetti thing, but with the deal signed, they should keep the property, and all the heat will fall on Geno."

The waitress returned with their food, and Max was relieved by the distraction. A lot had transpired over the previous two weeks. They'd gone from strangers to friends in a short time, and now it felt like a separation that might be permanent. He enjoyed the meal and small talk that ensued, but he also had to keep moving.

"I've gotta roll," he said when they were all mostly finished. "Remember to check in through the Gmail account every few months."

He had opened a Gmail account and given them the credentials. It was a low-tech solution, but if they needed to communicate, all they had to do was write a draft email. Max would check the account and could see what they wrote. He would do the same. At least until things settled down. No email would actually be sent, so it would be relatively secure.

"Hey, Max." Staci reached across the table and grasped his hand. "You remember asking me if I was a Southern belle?"

"Of course."

"Well, you don't think I'm going to let you get out of here without a proper thank you, do you?"

She pushed a small box across the table.

He opened it to reveal a silver St. Christopher pedant.

"To keep you safe." Staci offered.

Several thoughts ran through his mind. He didn't want to tell her he was Jewish. The gift still had meaning and it was Staci's intention that mattered.

"Thank you."

"No, Max." She spoke softly. "Thank's to you, we're alive."

Max said nothing further but shook his head slightly, looking down as he stood up, pocketing the necklace.

The others rose with him, and Staci moved closer, blocking his path.

"You men might want to push things like this under the rug, but we owe you everything. Max, thank you so much."

He looked down to see Staci's watery eyes gleaming with her appreciation. It felt good. She wrapped an arm around his right side, clearly conscious of his wounds, and he returned it awkwardly. He was happy for her, and it was no longer associated with his sister. He was happy for Staci.

"She's right, Max." Eddie clasped his hand, and the two bumped right shoulder to right shoulder. "We're in your debt."

"It's all good, man," he responded, trying to end the conversation. "Pay it forward. I'm sure there's someone in Mexico who will need your help."

Max pushed his hand into his pocket and pulled out a few

twenties, tossing them on the table.

"Let's see you do that with crypto," he laughed, waving at the waitress as he pushed out the door.

He didn't look back or say goodbye.

* * *

There was some irony in the fact that Carolyn's room was on the second floor, not five doors down from the server room. She had been admitted immediately when they brought her in, and the surgery had followed quickly. Geno's blow had apparently broken her jaw. They'd reported it as a mugging, but Max had been subject to several questions before they allowed him to leave, and he was sure they suspected domestic violence. Nobody connected it to the other big story involving the fire at Henderson Airfield.

Carolyn had come out of surgery sore and definitely unhappy, but Max had been with her all day. The trauma had taken a lot out of her, and aided by the pain medication, she had slept most of the time. With her jaw wired shut, she could only communicate with handwritten notes or text messages when she was conscious, but even those were short.

Max hoped she would be better today. He wanted to make things right—see if maybe they could restart. He was so focused on his thoughts that he almost walked into the woman standing in the hall.

"Sorry!" he said, pulling short at the last minute and edging around, his hands up in defense. "Wasn't looking—"

Recognition flared.

"I thought you'd be here earlier." Nita raised an eyebrow. She wore a dark-blue pantsuit, her hair pulled back in a ponytail. "Got a moment?"

It wasn't a question.

"Sure." He looked past her for the first time and saw a pair of police officers a few steps down the hall.

"Step over here." The district attorney crossed the hall to the small empty seating area. She stopped by a pair of chairs but did not sit down, turning to Max. "Somebody destroyed the lab last night."

Max looked directly into her eyes, knowing what she was saying, and he thought he saw a flicker of approval. He took a breath before responding.

"Is that a good thing or a bad thing?" he asked.

"It's good that it stops the trade, but it's bad for my investigation." She seemed more frustrated than upset. "No, I'm not going to say it's bad. But we don't condone vigilantism in Clark County."

This time, her eyes left no doubt as to what she suspected, but the undertone was one of acceptance.

"I can only imagine," he said without confirming. "That's another reason I'm leaving town. I'll come back when somebody's cleaned things up."

Nita smiled. "That's exactly what we're doing."

"I saw the news. Seems like you're laying the groundwork for a run at the mayor's office?"

"One thing at a time, Max." Her smile lingered briefly then left her face entirely. "The data you've provided is incomplete. I need more from you if I'm going to hold up my end of the bargain."

"You're kidding, right?" He wasn't.

"Can you get back on to the server?" she continued, ignoring his statement. "I've only got third-party references on Rodriguez. Nothing will stick. There's clearly more there, but the files are truncated."

"I thought you were after Geno?"

"There's that too. Everything we've got is on the Jewel and the lab—the now defunct lab." Her tone hardened. "It's past history, Max. We're missing details on the American Construction Corporation. I thought you'd hacked into the ownership structure. We need more."

He'd heard enough. He purposefully glanced past her to look at the officers before turning to meet her eyes again.

"With respect, what are you going to do? What part of the

bargain are you even holding up?"

"Maybe we misidentified Eddie," she said, meeting his glare. "Mistakes happen."

"Yes, they do," Max answered slowly. "Maybe that body isn't Eddie. Maybe that body is a missing police detective—a dirty detective who was an assassin for the Marchetti mob family. Maybe that's the same detective who had been working hand in hand with you for the past year, Nita. I think you're right. Mistakes happen."

He had no interest in hearing any more and turned to leave, but she took a step to the side, blocking him slightly.

"We had a deal, Max."

"Good phrase." He sighed. "We *had* a deal, Nita. Past tense. I offered you the whole thing, but you refused to back us. Your end of the bargain? What's that? Hiding the death of a corrupt employee? That helped you as much as it helped me. You want more, you're going to have to work for it."

She worked her tongue inside her mouth before responding.

"I hope you're clean, Max, because if you're not on my team, I'll take you down as quickly as the rest."

"I'll take my chances." He pushed past her, twisting to avoid contact with his left side.

In three paces, he was walking past the police, whose eyes were flickering between him and the DA, who must have waved them off because they did not try to stop him. Carolyn's room was about halfway down the hall, and he paused before it, taking a deep breath to clear his head of the bullshit he had just heard. He prayed she was in a better mood and hopefully off the heavy meds.

As soon as he opened the door, he knew the answer. The TV was on, turned to one of the cable news stations, and Carolyn was sitting up in her bed with her laptop in front of her.

"Good morning, sunshine!" he said, and despite the setting and her injury, he meant it. The spark in her eyes was enough to light his world. "You look a lot better."

She rolled her eyes and picked up her phone to answer via text. Max was silently thankful that he could still chat verbally.

"Better, yes. Normal—far from it," her text read.

"Sorry." He bent over and gave her a kiss on the forehead then backed up and sat on the end of the bed.

"Painful too, but . . . I'm alive," the text continued.

"Sorry," he said, hating the tubes that still ran out of her arm.

Her thumbs immediately typed her reply.

"How are you?"

"I'm good. DA accosted me in the hallway, but I'm good."

"She was in here too. Wanted me to work for her."

"I don't doubt it. What did you say?"

"What do you think? How about no? Even if I wanted to, I've got a life in San Francisco."

"I said the same, except the bit about San Francisco."

He paused. It was as good of a segue as he was going to get, and he was about to ask when Carolyn broke the silence.

"Tell me," she said through a clenched jaw, but he heard her. She closed her eyes. "What happened?"

For a second, Max didn't understand, but then he realized they hadn't talked about the airstrip.

"I arrived too late, for one."

She gently shook her head and typed a response.

"No. I don't want an apology or your own self-pity. Tell me what happened after they hit me."

That stung a little. He hadn't intended self-pity, if that was what it was.

"OK," he began. "I got there in time to stop Ben. Geno fled, but I was able to take down Eddie first. Or at least it looked that way. It was a clean shot. Dead center of the armor plate I'd given him. He's still sore, but he'll be fine."

He described the rest of the night, crediting Eddie for saving the day and leaving out his own broken ribs. He explained how Nita had already launched a major investigation and had helped misidentify the dead body. Then he described his meeting with Staci and Eddie and their plans to go off the grid.

"Your man, Jun, stopped by this morning," Carolyn typed.

"What?"

"He was very polite. He introduced himself and explained the work you'd done for him. Then he said he wanted to thank me in person for the help I'd provided."

"I didn't tell them about you," Max growled, suddenly more alert.

Carolyn's eyes widened in acknowledgment, and her thumbs worked a quick response.

"Yeah, that's when it got creepy. He started talking about working too hard and knowing when to stop. Then he said, 'Take Mr. Abruzzi, for example. It's helpful that he's under some heat, but his ACC is doing more than building tunnels. We knew the current lab was forfeit —and thanks to someone's action is now out of commission—but the ACC is building us another.'"

It was all Max could do to remain seated. Jun was sending a message.

"Did you tell this to Nita?" he asked, trying to keep his voice calm.

"Fuck no," Carolyn typed. "He didn't stop there. He sat where you are sitting and told me that the district attorney and others would be extremely interested in that information . . . but if I shared it, he feared for your life."

"My life?"

"His exact words were, 'In fact, if this goes any further, I would fear for Mr. Kline's life.'"

Jun did not want any further reprisal. Max moved to the bedside chair to collect his thoughts. It was better that she didn't pick up on it, but by delivering the message through Carolyn, Jun was also using her as a leverage point. He may not have made it explicit, but he was threatening her life as well.

"Max?" Carolyn spoke aloud to catch his attention, and when he looked at her, she raised her phone.

He glanced at the text he had missed.

"Are you in danger?" she'd asked.

"No." The word slipped out defensively, but he knew it wasn't enough. "Maybe a little, but I think Haoyun Casino wants things to settle down as much as we do. That was clearly a message for me— one he didn't want to deliver directly."

He rubbed his face with his hand, building the courage to continue.

"Look, Carolyn. I'm going to go on the road for a bit. I can't stick around here. Not sure where, but I'm going to do some traveling, and I'm wondering if you'll join me."

He looked across the bed at her and saw tears welling in her eyes. For a few seconds, hope dawned in his chest, but then she began to shake her head slowly. She dropped her hands to her side and turned her head away as he waited. Her eyes closed.

After a long time, she moved again, pushing herself more upright as she began typing again, noticeably not making eye contact.

"We are done, Max." The first message was brief and painful, but she continued to type, so Max held his response. The next several messages came through without pause.

"I was pretty sure of it before I even boarded the plane, but I wanted to see you again."

"I love you, Max."

"I always have."

"But this isn't the life for me."

"And you're not going to change."

"I can change," Max blurted out, but even as he did, he knew he couldn't dissuade her.

Carolyn had stopped typing and put her phone in her lap. Tears still filled her eyes as she looked at him and raised her hand toward him, bidding him to take it.

He rose and moved closer, clasping her hand in both of his, feeling tears gather in his own eyes.

"Carolyn," he whispered as the emptiness grew within him.

He wanted to fight—to tell her he could make things right—but deep inside he knew she was doing the right thing. Worse, he respected her for it.

Looking at her face, he saw she'd closed her eyes once more. He leaned farther and placed a slow kiss on her forehead, lingering for as long as he dared, and he felt her grip let go of his hand.

He put her hand down and stepped back, gazing once more at her beautiful face, but she remained still with her eyes closed. The only movement was the slow rise and fall of her chest.

"I love you," he whispered, more for his own benefit than for hers.

In the hallway, he paused, wondering if he should go back inside, but he knew it was over.

Thank you for reading Odds of Destruction

Creating this story has been a special pleasure and I hope you've enjoyed it as much as I have!

Please share your thoughts with other readers by returning to Amazon and leaving a review.

Questions or comments? E-mail me at:

Thomas.Puck@TomSchnurr.com

If you'd like to receive free updates and bonus material, please sign up for my mailing list here:

Https://tomschnurr.com/thomas-puck/

## About the author:

I grew up in Sheffield, a small town nestled in the Berkshire mountains of western Massachusetts. I was fortunate to attend Berkshire School (also in Sheffield) and later graduated from the College of the Holy Cross with a B.A. in Economics.

For most of my adult life, I pursued a career in finance but throughout that time, I maintained a passion for  books. Then I encountered a break in my career, and I found the time to pursue writing.

I now live in Moraga, CA with my wife, Megan, and our children; Lillian, Cooper & Kipling (though they are largely out of the house.) When I'm not writing, I enjoy golf, fishing and playing board games.

www.ingramcontent.com/pod-product-compliance
Lightning Source LLC
Chambersburg PA
CBHW022255310726
48973CB00001B/76